RAVENMARKED

Amy Rose Davis

amy rose davis

Ravenmarked

Copyright © 2011 by Amy Rose Davis

Excerpt from *Silver Thaw* copyright © 2011 by Amy Rose Davis

Cover design by Robin Ludwig, Robin Ludwig Design, Inc.

Interior design and formatting by Lisa Nowak

The text of this book is set in 11-point Georgia.

Print Edition, License Notes

ALL RIGHTS RESERVED. This book contains material protected under International and Federal Copyright Laws and Treaties. Any unauthorized reprint or use of this material is prohibited. No part of this book may be reproduced or transmitted in any form or by any means, electronic or mechanical, including photocopying, recording, or by any information storage and retrieval system without express written permission from the author / publisher.

This book is a work of fiction. Names, characters, places, and incidents are products of the author's imagination or are used fictitiously. Any resemblance to actual events, locales, or persons, living or dead, is entirely coincidental.

ISBN: 978-1-945557-90-3

First Edition

ACKNOWLEDGMENTS

Many heartfelt thanks to the following wonderful people:

To Linda Kincaid, who shall henceforth be known as Map Maker Extraordinaire. You took my generic scribbles and turned them into a world that looked even better than what I had in my head, and you did it for nothing but my gratitude. I am in your debt.

To Robin Ludwig, cover artist extraordinaire. Thank you for sharing your amazing talent with the world and for giving Connor Mac Niall a face.

To Lisa Nowak, fellow indie author, who formatted this book for print. You're a godsend.

To Leanne Stewart, Aleta Sanstrum, Bethany Learn, and all of the many other folks who served as beta readers and editors for me. You've been far more gracious with your time than I ever had any right to expect, and I am grateful for all of your input.

And above all, always, to the love of my life, Bryce. Thank you for making me laugh, keeping me honest, pushing me to succeed, and giving me some of Connor Mac Niall's best lines. And, thank you for putting up with all the crazy that comes with being married to a writer. You're a saint. I love you.

The Three Lands of the West
Eirya
Galoch Sea
Maghara
Ragged Isles
Port of Sorrow
Galbragh
Hanan's Road
Culidar
Starling's Cross
Firth of Chullen
Leiden
Wilds
Wilds
Brae Sidh Village
Kiern
Cahall's Channel
Stone Coast
Tribal Territory
Taura
Torlach
To Espara
Nar Sidhe Territory
N

PROLOGUE

For one with the ravenmark, there is no balance.
— Tribal lore

Water is no substitute for a good steak. Connor's stomach clenched, contracting in hunger, and the water of the fast-running stream at his feet didn't satisfy it. *Four days.* He poked at a log with his makeshift walking stick, knocking off a layer of bark. A dozen or more grubs scurried for cover. *Food.* He shook his head. *I promised. But it's been four days. When will this vision show up?*

He stepped carefully over the rocks at the edge of the stream to the mossy forest floor. The scents of the forest swirled around him. Though he'd agreed not to use his Sidh air talent during this tribal initiation, he couldn't help his strong sense of smell. His Sidh magic quickened late—he was thirteen the first time he wove the air braids—but it quickened strong. It had been a year since he'd first learned to weave the braids, and odors still sometimes overwhelmed him to the point of nausea. *Seems like I should be able to weave the braids better for all the trouble I have controlling the odors,* he thought.

In the distance, a faint scent of wood smoke beckoned, and his stomach grumbled again. He twisted his mouth and walked in a different direction. It was part of the agreement—stay away from the tribes until the earth revealed herself. It was why he was here in the forest, naked, hungry, and sleep-deprived. *I could just give up. I'm not a tribal boy. I'm Taurin. There are plenty of forests to hunt in Taura.*

He sighed. No, he wasn't tribal, and yet he'd promised himself he'd do this. Edgar, his father's best friend and chieftain of the wolf tribe, had promised him a place in the tribe if he passed the initiation. And most importantly, he'd promised his father he would finish the initiation. "Manhood isn't about bedding a woman or running a duchy or beating other men in battle," Culain Mac Niall always said. "Manhood is about keeping promises. A real man keeps his promises."

Connor gritted his teeth. *I wish the earth would keep her promise.*

He finally crouched near a fir tree in the deepest part of the forest and wiped sweat from his forehead. He took a deep breath. A new scent tickled his nose, and he frowned. *Carrion.*

Above him, a raven sat on a branch, head cocked to one side, staring at him.

Connor shivered. *If there's carrion nearby, why is the raven here?* He recalled a line from tribal lore: *When Alshada left, the ravens came. Their cries keened for the dead and dying; their wings blackened the sun.*

The raven spread its wings and croaked at him. It flapped into the air and circled, landed on the branch again, and fixed one dark eye on Connor.

Connor stood. One foot moved, and then the other, and when the raven flew to another branch, Connor followed.

The raven led him to a small clearing under a thick fir canopy. Connor stopped at the edge of the clearing, a cold ache settling in the pit of his belly. *Not a fir canopy—a canopy of ravens. Raven sky.*

Dozens, hundreds, more—the ravens fluttered and flapped and cawed and croaked all around the clearing, a swirling black mass of feathers. A stench of rotting flesh rose from the carrion on the ground. The birds landed, pecked, flew again. One carried a thick chunk of skin in its mouth.

Bile rose in Connor's throat, but he had nothing to vomit. The scent of rot threatened to overwhelm his senses. *Damn Sidh blood.* In the clearing lay a dead man, his features destroyed by the birds as they had pecked out eyes and torn flesh away from bone and muscle. Connor held his arm up to his nose to keep from retching.

One of the ravens dropped down to land in front of Connor. With frightening precision, the others joined it. They faced him, their beaks and feet wet and their feathers matted. He clutched his stick in both hands and prepared to defend himself. "I'm still alive," he said. "You wouldn't want me."

It was only a twitch of a blur at first, but Connor blinked. *I can't have seen that.* The ravens coalesced, roiling and joining and churning into a form that stood the same height as Connor. Dozens of wet eyes and talons and blue-black feathers undulated into the legs, hips, waist, breasts, head of a woman. *But not a woman—a raven.* The female shape was covered in raven feathers, and two dark eyes stared from a smooth, black face.

Connor dropped his walking stick. "What—"

The woman took a gliding step forward and lifted one arm. A rasping, genderless voice spoke from the void where a mouth should be. "You will be my first. The others will come, and you will lead them."

His feet rooted to the floor of the forest, Connor couldn't step back. He swallowed. *The Morrag.* He knew her from myth and legend—the earth's avenging spirit, the creature who stalked criminals and evildoers to mete out punishment. *What did I do to earn her wrath?* "Your first what?"

"My first warrior. My angel of death. My avenger."

Cold fear shivered down his spine. "What do you want from me?" he whispered.

"Heed my call." She took another step forward and touched the inside of his left thigh.

Connor cried out at the sudden piercing agony in his leg. Ravens swarmed the clearing in a black curtain, croaking and diving and beating the air into submission. Fear seized Connor's chest, and he threw his arms over his head and fell to the ground to protect his face from the birds.

The Morrag's fingers—no, *talons*—sank into his arms and pulled them away from his face. "Watch," she said. "You will avenge a great evil."

A scene of torment unfolded before Connor. Men and women and children, dead and dying, bleeding, moaning, desperate for relief writhed in agony on the forest floor. Among them, a creature walked—something evil, the scent of his soul befouling the air even above the rotten flesh.

His father's words rang in Connor's head: *You are a Mac Niall. It's your duty to defend those weaker than you. Never let evil triumph without a fight.*

The Morrag pointed at the creature. "Behold your enemy. You will avenge the evil he has done."

Connor struggled to stand. "No—I won't—" he said, but it came out only in desperate gasps. His chest constricted, and he struggled to draw a full breath.

"You will be bound to me all of your days, Connor Mac Niall."

The battlefield vision faded, and the Morrag lifted her talons from his arms. He curled up on the floor of the forest clutching his leg. "I'm not a killer," he whispered. "I'm not a murderer."

"You are ravenmarked. You are my first warrior."

"I can't be the first—there were others in the legends—"

"You are first in stature."

He shook his head. "No. I won't do it. I don't want it. Give me another calling—anything—I'm not a killer." He sat up and looked at his leg. Inside his thigh, the skin red and raw around it, was a brand of a raven's feather. He swallowed hard again. *Ravenmarked.* "I'm not a murderer. I'm not an assassin or an avenger. I'm a hunter and a warrior, but I won't seek out people to kill, not for the earth or Alshada or anyone else."

"You are marked," the woman said. "But you are not forsaken. Alshada has his hand on you. You will be a warrior, a mighty king, and your descendants will rule many lands."

He struggled to stand, determined to meet her gaze as a man, not a boy. He winced when he put weight on his leg. "I'll be nothing. I'm bastard born. I have no title."

"I care not for titles of men. You are my raven."

"I've heard stories in the tribes. The ravenmarked are doomed to fall into madness or destruction. There is no balance when one is bound to the earth." Blood trickled down his arms from where her claws had pierced his skin. "I won't do it."

"It is as it will be."

His chest constricted. He clenched his fists at his sides. "I am slave to no one," he said. "If you want me, you will have to take me, and I will not go without a fight." His heart thumped in a frantic combination of fear and rage, and sweat rolled down his temples and cheeks. "Do you hear me? You will force me. I won't marry—I won't have children or lead anyone. If you want me, you take me, and I'll suffer your touch alone."

The woman burst in an eruption of cawing and flapping. As the birds flew skyward, the voice of the Morrag echoed in the clearing: *You will be my first raven.*

When the forest returned to normal, Connor sank to the ground. He looked at both arms, but there was no trace of blood or claw marks. The brand on his leg was real, however—raw, red, and real. He ran two fingers over it and winced. *Ravenmarked. I'm ravenmarked.*

Connor put his head in his hands. There were stories and legends of the ravenmarked throughout tribal lore. Called by the Morrag, the ravenmarked were men destined to exact vengeance against evil whenever the Morrag called. But madness came with the mark, for when evil was banished, the men still needed to kill. Some men took their own lives for fear of harming others. Worse, some killed their own lords, friends, even families because of the drive of the Morrag. The tribes had even been forced to kill their own ravenmarked brethren for the good of the people. *For the one with the ravenmark, there can be no balance,* the tribes said.

When he finally stood, the sun had lowered over the forest, cloaking the world in muted orange hues. He turned south. His father waited with the tribe. The earth guardians would feed him, clothe him, and brand his palm with the warriormark. Edgar would tattoo him with the wolf's head.

He looked at his palm. They would put the warriormark there—the swirl that would channel the earth magic and give him the power to banish the dark warrior spirits of Namha, the great enemy. He closed his palm. *No. I won't take it. Not if it gives the earth another way to hold onto me.*

Near midnight, he stumbled into the village and found his father and Edgar sitting before the fire, waiting. Culain Mac Niall stood. "Connor—gods, son, what is it?"

They see it. He swallowed hard and tried to turn so they couldn't see the brand. "What do you mean?"

Culain started to say something, but stopped himself. "Nothing. For a moment—" He straightened his shoulders. "You completed the trial."

Edgar stood, too. His green eyes narrowed. "You've been marked," he said.

Connor returned the chieftain's stare. "My quest is over. I've sought the visions. I've returned to the tribe. I humbly ask, traitha—accept me as your son, warrior, brother in the web of life."

Edgar picked up the white kaltan and approached Connor to wrap it around his waist. "I name you Ulfrich Wolfbrother and accept you as my tribal son." Edgar picked up Connor's right hand. "Are you ready to receive the warriormark?"

"No."

Edgar blinked.

"I choose not to receive it."

"Connor, this is all you've talked about for months," Culain said.

"I choose not to receive it," Connor repeated, looking at his father.

"I can't force him to take the mark, Culain," Edgar said. "It is his choice." He examined Connor's face with a critical eye. "If the earth has given him a reason not to take it, we must respect Connor's wishes."

Culain nodded. "What about the tribal mark?"

"He will receive the mark of the wolf tribe and the honor of the braids at first morning's light."

"Why do I have to wait?" Connor asked.

Edgar grinned. "You don't want my hand slipping and giving you a wolf's head with a crooked nose, do you?" He put a hand on Connor's shoulder. "Go rest in the vision hut. Take the ceremonial bread and water. It will be enough until after the tattooing."

Connor nodded and walked away to the vision hut.

His father followed. "Connor."

He turned back. "I can't tell you what I saw."

"I know." Culain sighed. "I can't tell you everything—I promised your mother—but there are more things about you than you know. Your magic, your destiny—it's all more complicated than you think. Don't let this vision rob you of your future."

"What do you mean?"

In the faint glow of the moon and the distant fire, Connor saw Culain close his eyes for a moment. "A vision is just that—a vision," he said when he opened his eyes. "It's not fate or destiny in itself. It can be a piece of one of those things. It can give us a glimpse into the future or perhaps even a prophecy. But it's just a piece, and usually a small piece." He paused. "Whatever you saw, it doesn't have to be the final word on your future."

Connor inclined his head. "Yes, sir. I understand."

"I don't think you do." Culain put both hands on his son's shoulders. They stood nearly eye to eye since Connor's last growth spurt. "This is just one thing, Connor. Our lives are thousands and thousands of things. We are all our own webs, and one little choice made because of this vision could ripple through the rest of your web and make it stronger or destroy it. Don't let this one vision write your future. You write your future."

Connor nodded. "I will." *I've already started.*

Culain put one rough hand on his son's head. "You're a man now, Connor. You can take the tattoo and wear the braids, but there's more to being a man than marks. Find a just cause to fight for and a woman to love, and then spend your life building a legacy. And always keep your word."

A lump formed in Connor's throat. *Men don't cry.* He swallowed hard. "Yes, sir."

Culain let him go. "I'll see you in the morning." He returned to the fire, and Connor continued into the vision hut.

A dozen mats were scattered around the perimeter of the large hut, and a basket of flatbread sat in the center of the mats next to a large trough of water. Connor drank and took two pieces of flatbread to a mat. His thigh burned and his head reeled. *What legacy can a man doomed to madness build? And what kind of woman would love a man who could turn on her any moment?* He discarded the bread and lay down on his side. *A bastard-born half-breed with weak magic. And now a spirit of death to bear, too. Alshada has a cruel humor.*

A rasping cackle echoed around him. Connor bolted upright, hand searching for a weapon. *I'm alone. But—*

The Morrag's rasping croak came back in his head as clearly as when she'd stood before him in the clearing.

You will be my first. My raven.

CHAPTER ONE

> *Be it henceforth known:*
> *By acts of treason against the Raven Throne, House Mac Niall hereby forfeits all lands, holdings, titles, and money to House Mac Rian.*
> — *Royal Taurin Proclamation, issued in the ninth month of Year of Creation 5987*

Razor-sharp scales glinted in the Esparan sun. Connor gripped his harpoon, ready to strike the massive fish. He adjusted his footing on the sandy sea bottom, dropped chum, and waited. The bloodhunter's mouth cut through the water toward his leg. Connor held the harpoon ready.

Another shimmer distracted him. "Damn it!" He missed his chance to strike and leapt away to avoid losing a thigh to the razorfish's teeth. Coral stabbed between his toes. He gritted his teeth as the razorfish circled.

"Connor." Violet braids of air carried her voice over crashing surf and crying gulls.

"Not now!" The fish charged. Connor thrust his harpoon into its neck. The creature thrashed, and salt water stung Connor's eyes. He drew a knife and stabbed the fish between the eyes. When it stopped moving, he lifted the harpoon out of the bloody water and grinned. *Not bad for a quick morning swim.*

When he turned toward the shore, the grin faded. "Mother. You nearly cost me a leg."

Queen Maeve stood on the white sand, hands on hips and mouth in a grim frown. "How in the name of Bachi's teeth did you end up in Espara?"

He waded toward her. "I'm on holiday. Helene invited me."

"Who?"

"The countess who owns this island." He gestured to the sprawling villa behind her. "Did you come to release me?"

She folded her arms. "No."

"Then we have nothing to discuss." He hefted the harpoon over his shoulder and walked toward Helene's villa.

"Your foot is bleeding."

"I stepped on a piece of coral. Goodbye, Mother."

Within a few paces, the air braids gathered in his path again. They faded to reveal his mother. "I need to talk to you."

"Not until you release me."

"Connor—"

"No, Mother. Release me or go."

She crossed her arms.

He shrugged. "As you will." He walked around her.

He made it to the steps of the villa before she blocked him again. "Connor, please. I need your help."

"You have the nerve to ask for help after what you did to me?"

"Please, just listen."

He stared down into dark brown eyes that matched his own. "Tell me."

"There's a woman who needs an escort from Taura to Sveklant. I need you to take her."

"Why me?"

Her mouth twisted as if she'd swallowed unripe fernberries. "Because you're the best. Because when people mention freelancers, your name is always at the top of the list."

"Flattery won't work. I'm busy."

She raised an eyebrow.

"I am. I have to lead a merchant train through Nar Sidhe territory and then I'm going to Taura for the tribal hunt and then I'm wintering in Dal'Imur."

"With torturers and savages?"

"With rich silk merchants who pay well. It's warm there, and the women think I'm intriguing." He started walking again. "Find someone else."

She took two steps for every one of his. "I don't have time to find someone else. Things are changing in Taura. Regent Fergus is ailing. He and his Table have chosen a new successor, but we think Prince Braedan is mounting a coup. He's built an army in Culidar. Duke Kerry pretends neutrality, but he's building up his own forces and sending money to help Braedan."

"Kerry—Braedan's uncle?"

"Yes."

"How do you know all of this?"

"I have one loyal to me among Braedan's men. He's sent a few messages."

The sand merged with rare translucent marble paving stones cut from the mountains of the Eastern Ridge in Tal'Amun. A servant wearing ochre-hued silks and a silver collar awaited Connor on the marble patio. Connor set down the fish and harpoon. "Deliver that to the kitchen. Prepare it however the lady wishes."

The man bowed. "Yes, my lord. And wine?"

"Veidara. The lady prefers it."

The man held out a kerchief to Connor. "For your foot, my lord. Do you need a repha?"

"It's a scratch. No healer is necessary."

"Of course, my lord." He tried to lift the fish, but settled for dragging it away. Within moments, another servant arrived with a pail of water to clean the bloody drops Connor had trailed up the steps and patio area. Rarely did even an olive leaf linger on a courtyard stone more than a few moments at Helene's villa.

Connor tied the kerchief around his bleeding foot and walked up to the balcony outside Helene's bedchamber with Maeve close behind him. "Why bring this to me? I don't care if Fergus' son becomes regent."

"He doesn't want the regency. He wants to set himself up as king." When her revelation didn't garner the response she wanted, she spoke as if to a small child. "To call himself king, he must get rid of the rightful Taurin heir."

He stopped and turned to her. "This woman I'm supposed to escort—she's the heir?"

"Yes."

Now—after a thousand years? Prophets and scholars and religious fanatics had spoken of the eventual upset of the regency and return of the rightful Taurin line to the Raven Throne, and every now and then, a pretender would emerge to claim his birthright. Maeve never gave them a moment's thought. *She must believe it or she wouldn't have brought this to me.* "How do you know she's real?"

"She fulfills the prophecies."

"According to who?"

"According to a very trustworthy woman on Taura."

Connor pulled his braids over one shoulder and squeezed water onto the balcony. "A religious woman?"

Maeve's mouth tightened. "This isn't the time to discuss your issues with the kirok."

"But it's time to discuss forgotten royal lines and legendary heirs?" He shook his head. "I don't believe it."

"I've seen her. I've watched her for years. She's the one, Connor. Her line will reunite the Western Lands."

He walked through the gauzy drapes that separated Helene's bedchamber from the outside world. "It's not my concern."

Maeve followed him into the room. "This is your country. Your people. How can you—"

"I'm only half Taurin—the attainted half. I told you six years ago. I want nothing to do with any of it."

She eyed his tattooed arm and frowned. "You've visited the tribes."

He crossed his arms, accentuating the blue dye. "The tribes aren't Taurin."

"So you've visited the tribes, but you've not seen fit to visit me."

"If you wanted me to visit, you could have forced it."

She flinched. "Have you seen Edgar?"

"No. I've stayed in the south."

"You won't even return to your own tribe?"

"Did you forget? Edgar agreed with you binding me. I won't be subject to a chieftain who would see my will bound to my mother's." He stepped closer to her again. "Release me from the magic, and we can talk."

Her voice dropped. "Connor, I can't. Please believe me. I'm trying to protect you."

He turned away. "Go, Mother. We're done." He picked up Helene's sarana, the long piece of fabric he'd wrapped around her when she emerged from her bath. It had only stayed on her long enough for them to share a meal. The bed was still unmade, and the scent of their night together hung in the air, honey and jasmine and veidara and passion woven with salt air and silk. *Why would I leave any sooner than I have to?*

Maeve's eyes followed him as he moved around the room. Six years before, she had taken advantage of their shared Sidh blood by binding his will to hers through the *codagha*, the binding web that connected her to the Brae Sidh. "I've not used the bond on you in all this time, and you're still angry?"

He whirled to face her. "Wouldn't you be angry? To be bound to your mother's will knowing that if you make a wrong move she'll snap the bond back and force you to do her bidding? To wonder, 'Is this the day she'll make me come back? Is this the day I'll stop making my own decisions and be subject to my mother's whims?' I'm a grown man. I've never asked you for a thing—for money, for a home, for a title—and yet you bind me like an infant at the tit."

Her eyes watered, but her voice remained steady. "I don't want to lose you. You're all I have left."

"And you think binding my will to yours will keep me safe? Tame?"

She closed her eyes. "What if the Morrag calls you?"

A faint tremor in her voice was her only concession to the fear, but he knew what she thought—that the Morrag would call him to avenge the murder of his father and sisters. *Or worse, go on a murderous rampage.* The only thing worse than the threat of her control over his will was the constant ache of the Morrag in his chest.

The rasping voice of the vengeful spirit resounded in his head—an eerie echo with more substance than dream, less than reality. *You'll be my first. My raven.*

You'll never have what you want from me. He crossed his arms. "I can control the Morrag."

"Other men thought the same once."

Do you think I don't know that? "Do you think it hasn't flared in all this time? I can control it."

Conflict hovered on her ageless, fine-boned face. The Sidh Queen still had the beauty of a young woman, despite her indeterminate age. Her ebony curls still tumbled heavy and full to her waist, and her face was unlined. Connor had his mother's Sidh coloring but his father's stature. "I worry for you," she said.

"I can take care of myself."

"I feel it every time you kill. When you're escorting someone, when you fight, when you're wounded, I feel it. I sense your rage. I tell myself that when it comes for you—when the Morrag calls—I can stop it. I can use the binding to keep you free of it."

He scoffed, tossed his handful of clothes back on the floor, and threw up his hands. "So this is my fate—to be bound to you or to her?" He bit off a curse, took a deep breath, and stepped closer to her. "Give me my will, Mother. Let me be a free man as long as I can. I'll worry about the Morrag later."

She didn't speak for some time. The salt air hung about them, heavy with the promise of warm, brief rains and the tension of unspoken emotions and griefs. "Will you do this for me? Take this girl to Sveklant?"

He sighed. "You really believe she's the rightful heir?"

"Yes."

"And you can't find anyone else? Can't you go to the tribes? Edgar—"

"If you want to dance in the heather with painted beasts, so be it." Her voice rose in indignation. "I'm not going anywhere near the tribes." She paused. "I'll pay you if I must."

"There's not enough gold in all the Sidh vaults to make me do this for you." He picked up a thin blanket from the bed. "Couldn't she go somewhere else? Somewhere closer? What about Eirya? I could get through tribal territory—"

"There's a town in Sveklant—Albard. There are people there who will teach her and help her build an army. Besides, the prophecy says the heir will return from the place where fire meets ice."

He snorted a laugh. "There's always a prophecy. Some underfed kiron takes a few extra sips of wine and sees fire and ice, and we all assume it means Sveklant. Why can't it mean Eirya? I'll take a torch to a glacier myself if it saves me a trip to Sveklant."

Her mouth was tight again. "This doesn't come from me, Connor. There are other forces at work here."

Don't drag me into this. "I don't want to have anything to do with Taurin royalty." He walked behind a partition and removed the short linen breeches he wore for swimming, brushed sand onto the floor, and tied the blanket around his hips.

When he stepped out from behind the partition again, Maeve's eyes were hard, and a muscle twitched in her jaw. The queen had a towering fury. Her dedication to her people and her powerful Sidh magic gave her a steely edge that far outweighed his skill as a warrior. "I could compel you to do this," she said.

"Try it. See how easy it is for you to run roughshod over my will. I will fight you every step. You may succeed, but not without great pain to you and the Sidh."

She took a deep breath. "I'm asking you, Connor. Please. For me. Would you just put your life—" her voice held an edge that said she didn't think his life was worth going back to "—aside for a short time and take this woman to Sveklant?"

"Escort her. Nothing more? She's not expecting me to help build this army, is she?"

"She's expecting nothing more than an escort. Get her to Albard, and then you'll be free to leave her."

"And then you'll leave me alone? Let me get back to my own life?"

"Such as it is, yes, I will. If that's what you want."

"It's not the life of a pauper, Mother." He gestured at the room. The low bed was large, comfortable, and covered in woven blankets and soft pillows. A cedar table near the opening to the balcony held a tray of fresh fruit next to a carafe of wine and two goblets. Every morning, he swam in the warm Aldorean Seas and lay in the sun, and at night, he slept ensconced in the breezy waves of warm Esparan air with a beautiful woman who smelled of jasmine and cinnamon.

Being with Helene was easy. They didn't discuss certain subjects, neither of them expected commitment or obligation, and she paid him only for protection—nothing more. When he wanted to leave, he would find another noble or merchant to escort or a battle to fight where his skill with a sword would earn him a good wage. The freelance life eased his restlessness and brought all the money, adventure, and women he wanted.

Maeve twisted her mouth and gestured around the room. "Connor, does this fulfill you? Are you happy?"

"You're not one to lecture on happiness." His tone was more irritable than he intended, and he regretted the words.

A shadow of old pain crossed Maeve's face. Maeve and his father had loved each other deeply, but her magic, his nobility, her duties, the law—all had conspired to keep them from being wed. They were always torn between their two worlds. "Are you going to help me or not?"

"It means I'll miss the hunt. And I'll have to spend the winter in Sveklant. I was looking forward to Dal'Imur."

"For the money?"

"And the sun."

The jaw muscle twitched again. "Please."

He considered it. "Will you release me from the bond?"

"Now?"

"Yes."

"Connor—"

"That's my price. Release me from the bond, and I'll take this woman to Sveklant."

"After you deliver her." She held up a hand when he started to protest. "I want to know exactly what you are doing any time I wish it."

He laughed. "You want to spy on me?"

"Yes. This girl was raised in the Order of Sai Atena. She's only known the life of the sayada. She's young and chaste and innocent, and I don't want you defiling her."

"She must be pretty or you wouldn't warn me."

"Connor!"

"I swear, Mother, you think I'm a ten-year-old boy."

She folded her arms. "Only when you act like one."

"Gods." He sighed. "I promise to keep my hands and everything else to myself. But I won't be something I'm not. You ask me to do this, you get me—not some soft Brae Sidh water talent who's never eaten meat and can't swing a sword. I can keep my breeches on, but I can't promise that she won't be a little shocked by everything else that I am."

Maeve rolled her eyes. "So we're agreed? If I release you when you're done, you will do this?"

He hesitated just enough to make her squirm. "Yes." Maeve blew out a long breath. "But I don't want anyone associating my name with this. I don't want anyone thinking I'm involved in Taurin politics when I go back to my work."

"Use your Sidh name."

"All right. You'll warn the sayas about who you're sending?"

"Yes. When can you be here?"

"I have to take this merchant train first. I'll leave tomorrow and see if I can talk them into leaving a few days early, but I can't back out. I don't know anyone close who can take them through Nar Sidhe country."

"Is that the best you can do?"

"I made a promise."

"Very well. I'll meet you on Macha Tor when you get to Taura."

He sat down on the bed. "One more thing—when I'm done with this, I'm done. This is the last obligation I have to the Sidh. Don't ask me to do anything for duty or prophecy or magic again. Release me from the bond and that's it. I'm done with the Sidh, with Taura, with everything. Agreed?"

The tight frown returned, and she crossed her arms. "You can't run from your magic. It's in your blood."

"I'll deal with the magic, but I want your assurance that I'll be free of obligation to you."

"Very well. Just hurry, will you? And Connor—" She reached out and grabbed a handful of his braids.

"Ow! What was that for?"

"Cut your hair. The tattoos I can't do anything about, but this girl—she doesn't need to be escorted by some savage beast. Can you do that much?"

Even the braids? He'd earned the right to wear them. They were a sign of his high tribal rank. *They'll grow back.* He gave her a grudging nod. "Mother." He took her hand. "I think of my father every day."

"So do I." She turned her head, but not before he saw one tear fall. Her voice was tight when she spoke. "Six years—it's too long. I miss you. I've tried to respect your privacy, but you're the only tie I have to him."

"You have Edgar."

She shook her head. "I haven't seen Edgar since—" A soft sob escaped her throat.

He knew how much that sob cost her. "Since the day we buried my father."

She nodded.

"I chose the tribes. Edgar didn't talk me into it."

She kept her eyes averted, her shoulders tense as she took several calming breaths. When she turned back, her tears were gone. "Edgar didn't agree with me," she finally said. "He was afraid for me. When you walked away, he took me to task for binding you. He wanted me to release you."

Connor didn't expect that admission. He only remembered Edgar's fist connecting with his jaw when he fought the binding magic. Edgar had promised that if Connor hurt Maeve again, he would call down the wrath of the entire wolf tribe on Connor's head.

The words in Connor's mind slipped out without warning. "I could have slit Mac Rian's throat in his sleep before anyone knew what happened."

Maeve's hand jerked at the mention of the duke who killed Connor's father, but she kept her face a mask of queenly composure. "Don't say—"

"Why not?"

"Because of his daughter." Her voice quivered when she spoke, but this time, it shook with fear rather than grief. "Olwyn Mac Rian is not a woman to challenge," she whispered. "Please believe me. There is evil there."

His hand tightened on hers. "When I'm released from this bond, I'll consider visiting again."

She nodded and kissed his head. "I'll see you on Macha Tor." She lifted her arms, and magic pricked his skin as she commanded the air to carry her back to Taura. Violet air braids wrapped her body from head to toe, concealing her inside the air, and she disappeared over the Aldorean Seas.

Connor let out a long breath and flopped back on the bed, covering his face with one arm. He hadn't been to Taura in a year, and it had been more than six years since he'd been to the Sidh village, the wolf tribe, his father's old holdings, or even the capitol city of Torlach. He only returned to participate in the ritual hunt each year. Hunting with the earth magic around him helped sate the Morrag.

The constant ache of her presence flared in his chest like the greeting of an unwelcome relative. He pressed it back. He had tasted the Morrag's kiss and killed in her name once, and he would not submit to her willingly. *How long? How much more time will you give me before you make me yours?*

Only the rasping cackle of the raven replied.

The sweet scent of jasmine and the soft rustle of silk teased him from his thoughts. Helene's thick Esparan accent tickled his ears as she wrapped her tongue around Taurin words. "I heard a woman's voice."

He propped himself up on his elbows. Even nearing her fortieth year, Helene had a beauty that stole his breath. She wore a white sleeveless gown that draped over her body in loose folds. Her light brown arms gave a stunning contrast to the gold filigree trim, and she had belted the simple dress with a beaded belt. Thick black hair hung straight and heavy to her waist, and kohl accented her dark, exotic eyes. "It's one of those things," Connor said.

Her mouth tilted into a seductive smile. "Oh. One of those things." She bent and put her hands on either side of his legs. The curtain of hair fell to one side as she leaned in to kiss his neck, revealing an ear pierced from lobe to crest with the small gold rings of her rank. "You leave sand on the bed."

He shivered at the sensation of her warm breath on his skin. "That's the price of your supper. Did you see the fish I caught?"

"Men and fish. You all think yours is the biggest." Her lips drifted up his neck to his mouth. "You will make amends, yes?"

"If you insist." Warm lips against his erased the salty taste of the sea. "I have to go," he said when she drew away from him. "Tomorrow."

She frowned. "So soon? After but two days?"

"It is regrettable, but duty calls."

Helene straightened. "I did as you asked. I paid for freedom for my slaves."

"I know. Your servants told me."

"Then why—"

"I can't tell you."

The crash of waves echoed in the room. "I can pay you more."

"You know that's not how this works."

"Then I have you until tomorrow, yes?"

She untied the blanket around his hips and slid one hand up his thigh to tighten over the blue raven feather on his leg. In Helene's bedroom, the ravenmark was a curiosity, not a destiny. Connor grinned and pulled her down to the bed. "Till tomorrow, yes."

CHAPTER TWO

> *Kings and queens will pass away.*
> *The age of regents will come.*
> *When the Unbeliever takes the throne,*
> *the Forbidden will rise again.*
> *— The Scrolls of Prophecy in the Syrafi Keep,*
> *Year of Creation 743*

Mairead jumped into a run. A battering ram pounded the front gate of the sayada, and the walls rattled around her. *Now is not the time to walk. Proper sayada behavior will get me killed.*

The smoke of a dozen torches hovered above her head as she ran down

Sayana Muriel's private corridor. The sayana had never summoned Mairead to her private quarters before. Now, even as her heart hammered her chest, Mairead's footsteps slowed when she noticed the runes and drawings on the corridor walls. She stopped to read one, but another crash from above drove her into a run again, fear and necessity replacing curiosity.

At the end of the corridor, she stopped at the sayana's door. Thin torchlight shone through a crack, and Mairead paused at the sound of anxious voices.

"She's no child," one woman said. Mairead recognized Saya Hana's voice. "She's of age. She's been anointed. Bring her forward and let her challenge the usurper." A long pause. "This is why she was brought to us—why Alshada led her father here. This is what you've always believed, Muriel. You trained her, prepared her to take her throne, to bring her line back to Taura."

"I didn't count on Braedan," Sayana Muriel said. "He's too strong."

"Stronger than our god?"

Muriel gave a weak laugh. "Our god rarely stops axes from severing heads, Hana. No, she has to go. It's the only way to keep her safe."

Mairead started to push open the door, but stopped when Hana spoke again. "Then pursue the other course."

Muriel's voice could have shattered glaciers. "Forcing her to marry that unbeliever would be as good as turning the reliquary over to our enemies. I will not do it."

A knot formed in Mairead's belly. *Marry me to Braedan? That's what they've wanted to do?*

"It would give him what he wants—a rightful claim to the throne. And he is her age, and—"

"I said no, Hana. You don't remember Braedan's mother and the way his father drove her to the unthinkable. I won't let that happen to Mairead, and I won't risk the relics falling into the wrong hands."

Mairead cleared her throat and pushed open the thick oak door. "Sayana? I'm not afraid. I'll stay, if you wish it."

Sayana Muriel turned to Mairead and folded her hands before her. "And would you live with a man who would forever challenge your faith? Or even try to kill you?"

Mairead lifted her chin. "I would do what I must for Taura."

A bittersweet smile creased Muriel's grizzled features. Years of the harsh Taurin weather had battered her once-smooth face, but where beauty had reigned, wisdom now held sway. She laid one wrinkled hand on Mairead's arm. "Your courage is not in question, Mairead. But at the moment, what's best for Taura is to ensure that you live to return and claim your throne."

Mairead's stomach lurched. "But, sayana, I . . ." Words failed her. No amount of education or prayer had readied her heart for this late-night escape. *Fifteen years—it's not enough.* "I need more time. I have so much more to learn—" Her voice caught. She whispered around the lump in her throat. "This is my home."

"And if you wish to return to it someday, you must leave it now." Muriel took her hands. "I've taught you all I can teach you. It's time for you to seek your path with Alshada's guidance." Another crash sounded from above. Muriel gestured to a bundle on the floor. "There is no more time. Braedan will kill you if he finds you here. You need to leave your sayada robes behind. Change into those."

Mairead shed her white wool robes. "Why is Saya Hana here?"

"Saya Hana will serve as your guardian. A guard will accompany you, but it wouldn't be proper for you to travel alone with a man. Hana will attend you."

Hana inclined her head, and Mairead winced. *Saya Hana? Well, if it must be.* She liked Saya Hana, but the woman had a sense of propriety that Mairead thought would have interfered with the creation of the world if Alshada had asked her opinion. "I am thankful for your company, Saya Hana." She slipped a gray wool dress over her shift and pulled on thick, sturdy shoes that matched Hana's. When she straightened, she noticed Muriel's eyes glistening. "Sayana, what is it?"

"I see a vision of the girl I raised now become a woman. No small thing." She pulled Mairead into an embrace. The frailty of age belied the strength of the sayana's heart and her devotion to duty. "Build an army. Strengthen the rightful royal line, and return when you can claim your throne."

"Will we ever see each other again?"

"Alshada alone knows."

Mairead put her arms around Muriel. She struggled to find words. "You've been more to me than my own mother could have been," she finally said.

Muriel's arms tightened. "Our order is a demanding one, but it is not without its rewards. I grieve the loss of future years watching you grow, but I cherish the years we've had together. I could not be prouder of you, Mairead."

Three heavy knocks shook the door. Hana opened it. A cloaked figure stepped into the room. He pushed the cloak off his shoulders and lowered his hood, and Mairead noticed the sword on his hip and daggers in his belt and boots. He had broad shoulders and a lethal demeanor that tempted Mairead to shrink back, but when he met her eyes, she saw a hint of mischief. A flicker of a grin crossed his mouth as his eyes passed over her. Behind the urgency and fear of the moment, her stomach fluttered, and she felt heat creep up her face.

"This is Connor SilverAir," Muriel said. "He comes from the Brae Sidh. He'll escort you to safety."

Brae Sidh? But he's so tall. I thought the hidden folk were tiny. "But the stories—" She stopped. *Now's not the time to confess to stealing books from the library.* "You told me the Sidh were a myth."

Connor glared at Muriel. "I'm hardly a myth, sayana."

"It has been necessary to keep certain things from you," Muriel told Mairead. "There are some difficult truths in the world. I wanted to keep you from them as long as I could." She returned Connor's angry glare with one of her own. "I trust, Connor, that you can fill in some of the gaps in Mairead's education about the magic on Taura?"

Mairead forced herself to swallow. "Magic on Taura? But—"

"Sayana," Hana said. "I must protest again. To teach heresy—"

Mairead clenched her fists behind her skirts. "If there is magic on Taura or even if the populace just *believes* there's magic here, I have a duty to know."

"Sayana, this is not what I agreed to," Connor said. "I was only asked to escort her."

Muriel held up her hands, and everyone fell silent. "Hana, Mairead is right. As heir to the Raven Throne, it's her duty to know as much of Taurin history as possible, whether the history is kirok-sanctioned or not." Hana frowned, but she gave Muriel a terse nod. Muriel turned to Connor. "Much may yet be expected of you. You were asked to do this for a reason. I trust our faith in you was not misplaced."

The battering ram shook the walls again. "Too late for second thoughts now," Connor said. "Sounds like faith is all you have." He surveyed Mairead and Hana with tight lips. "Dresses, sayana? We're not going dancing."

"If you don't want this job, you can leave," Muriel said.

Mairead could see that the thought tempted him, but when he spoke, there was grudging acquiescence. "You could have had them dress more appropriately."

"Traveling dresses are appropriate. We are doing Alshada's work," Hana said.

Connor scoffed. He muttered something that sounded like cursing to Mairead, but she couldn't make out the words. "A boat is waiting outside the city to take us across the channel and into Culidar before morning."

Mairead pulled on a dark cloak that Muriel passed her. "How will we get out of Torlach?"

"There are old Sidh passages under the sayada. One comes out north of the castle, beyond the north gate."

"Can't we take some of the other sisters with us? If I can get out, we can help more escape," Mairead said.

Connor shook his head. "It's too risky. You may not care about your own skin, saya, but I won't die in Braedan's dungeon."

"We've sent many away already," Muriel said. "Minerva and I started sending them away one at a time when we saw that Fergus was on his deathbed. If any of them are captured, they'll distract the soldiers from you." She turned to Hana. "You will make sure this young man behaves appropriately around our charge?"

"You don't trust me, sayana?" Connor asked in an amused tone.

Muriel turned a cool gaze toward him. "You have a reputation that requires prudence on my part."

"I promised Queen Maeve that I would behave. I keep my promises."

Hana gave him a doubtful look. "On my honor, sayana."

A final crash jolted the sayada, and any more questions Mairead had were lost to the sounds of panic above. Muriel ushered everyone into the corridor. "Go—quickly."

Connor guided Mairead and Hana away from the chaos, further into the most ancient parts of the sayada. He held his torch near the walls to read the runes and drawings.

"What are you doing?" Mairead asked.

"Reading the map."

"Don't you already know the way?"

He kept his eyes on the runes. "No."

"Then how—"

"The Brae Sidh stone talents who built these tunnels put instructions in the drawings. Hush."

Hana drew in a sharp breath. "Do not speak to the heir that way. She is your liege. Remember your place."

He turned to the saya, eyes dark and mouth grim in the flickering light. "I bow to no one save the Sidh queen, and that is grudging. I like my head on my shoulders. I'll speak to your little girl however I wish if it means I can keep it there."

Hana started to say something, but Mairead shook her head and fell in step behind Connor. He kicked rats aside and cleared cobwebs. The scent of musty earth grew stronger, and the stone walls merged with firmly packed soil.

At last Connor stopped. He held out his hand, touched the earth wall before him, and whispered foreign words. The wall shimmered and faded into nothing. Fresh night air rushed into the passageway. "Is this the way out?" Mairead whispered.

"Yes."

"Are you a stone talent?"

He put out the torch. "No. I just know the right words and have the right blood." He motioned for silence and listened. "We're well beyond the wall, but they'll be patrolling it. We'll have to run for the trees."

"How will we—"

He cast her a look of irritation. "Do you ever stop asking questions? Let me figure out their patrol pattern." The hair on Mairead's arms stood up, and she saw thin, faint lines pass through the air before them. The lines twined together in violet braided patterns and snaked out of the opening into the night air. When they returned, Connor grunted and turned to the women again. "I think I have their rhythm down. When I tell you, both of you run for the trees."

He waited, still and silent as a hunting cat. Mairead closed her eyes and tried to will her heart to stop pounding. *Alshada, keep us safe.*

Connor motioned. "Run."

Mairead ran. Her skirts tangled around her legs, and her shoes tried to slip on the dew-moistened ground. She heard a yelp and a thump and shouts from a distance. She slowed. *I should go back—I should help.* But arrows fell to either side of her, and she quickened her pace again.

Connor caught up. "This way." He steered her into the trees, stopping near a small rill that ran toward the channel. Distant shouts and the sound of great hounds baying replaced the whir of arrows. "Damn it. Dogs," he said. "Your escort, Hana—she's dead."

Mairead gasped. "No—dead?" Her stomach lurched, and she swallowed over a lump in her throat. "How?"

"An arrow to the back. There's nothing you can do." He motioned her to step into the water of the rill. "You'll just have to be alone with me."

"But Muriel said—"

He returned to her side. "You want to go back? Fine. I have better things to do than pamper a weak girl."

She straightened. "I'm not weak."

He pointed to the rill. "Prove it."

She stepped into the water. It flooded her shoes, and her toes ached and cramped with the cold. "Which way?"

"Toward the channel." Connor guided her forward in the faint glow of an eclipsed moon.

The baying of the hounds grew louder, closer. Connor cursed again. "They picked up our scent—hurry."

Mairead's shoe slipped, but she balanced herself. "I'm going as fast as I can."

"Then go faster."

She struggled to match his pace with grim determination. Connor led her out of the water and down a rocky trail to the channel. Never had Mairead been so grateful for the scent of sea air. A small, unmanned boat waited in a little cove. "That's it?"

"Did you picture a royal pleasure barge?"

"I don't know. I just—" She bit off the words. Connor helped her step into the boat, and she settled her feet next to two bundles at the stern as he untied it. He pushed it out toward the strong current of the channel and jumped in.

Waves lifted the tiny boat. It picked up speed, and the air rushed past her face and brought the scent of gulls and fish. In the water, vibrant blue and green lines wound around the bottom of the boat in snaking braids similar to the ones she'd seen in the passageway. *Sidh water talents.* She'd read of them in stories stolen from the sayada library and devoured by candlelight when the sayas were asleep. *Elemental magic—the creatures who helped Alshada build the world with their stone, water, and air talent. Not a myth after all. And the reliquary is real, too. What else did they keep from me?* The salt spray stung her eyes, and she blinked back tears. *The magic is real, or seems to be. They wanted me to take the throne, but how? And now, Hana is dead and I'm left with this man I don't even know to teach me things he doesn't seem to want to talk about. Alshada, how will I do this?*

Within moments, the boat slowed, and the rocky coast of Culidar came into view. Connor jumped onto the rocks. He helped Mairead out, picked up the two bundles, and then kicked the boat back into the channel. The braids took hold of it and steered it north into darkness.

On the far shore, dogs bayed near the water. Connor pulled Mairead down to the rocks and put his arm and cloak around her. "Don't move."

"They can't swim the channel, can they?"

"They're dogs, not dolphins. Still, I'd rather they didn't see us. If they see the boat, they might think we went north."

They sat very still for some time, huddled against the spray of the sea. Mairead's legs grew stiff and numb, and her hands ached. One foot started to cramp and tingle. At last, Connor let out a long breath and took his arm away from her. "I think they've given up. Come on." He stood.

She straightened from her crouch and shook feeling back into her leg. "This is Culidar?"

"Yes. There's a cave nearby where we can spend the night."

"A cave? They say the Nar Sidhe use the caves of Culidar for their fertility rites." She grimaced at the high pitch of her voice. *You squeak like a frightened mouse*, she scolded herself. *But if the Brae Sidh aren't myth, what else is real?*

"The Nar Sidhe don't venture to this part of Culidar," Connor said. He swung the bundles over his shoulder and pointed. "That's where we're going."

Connor began to climb, and she followed. The slick, stiff soles of her shoes made it difficult to get traction on the wet rocks, and she tripped on her dress several times. Once, she caught herself on a sharp rock and hissed.

He turned back. "Are you all right?"

Tears stung her eyes at the pain, but she fought them back. *He already thinks I'm weak.* She regained her balance and lifted her hand. "I cut myself." Blood glinted off her palm and the rock in the faint light.

He pulled a kerchief from the pocket of his jerkin and tied it around her hand. "This will have to do until we get to the cave. It's going to hurt to climb. Can you do it?"

I don't know. "Yes."

It was slow going without the full use of one hand. By the time she reached the large opening in the cliff face, her other hand and both knees were bloodied, and her teeth chattered with damp cold.

Connor unrolled two blankets and gestured to one. "Sit. Let me see your hand."

She held it out. He opened his hand next to hers, and a small blue flame appeared on his palm. "How do you do that?"

"Magic."

"But what—"

"It's a useful trick. The Sidh use palmlight instead of torches or lanterns. They don't like fire." He examined her hand in the blue light. "It's not bad—long, but not deep. I'll dress it."

"Thank you."

He gave her a terse nod and dressed the cut with some ointment from his pack. "I'll check it again in the morning. You should rest. We have a long walk come daylight. I'll keep watch."

Her teeth chattered and she pulled her cloak tighter. "A-all r-right."

"Are you that cold?"

She nodded.

"I don't want to build a fire. The wood here is wet, and your enemies might see the fire or smoke from the docks."

"It's all right. I'll w-warm up in a f-few m-minutes." But her teeth chattered still, and she ached with the cold.

He sighed and lowered his head in resignation. When he lifted it, he motioned to her to move, picked up the blankets, and crawled further into the cave. He lay one blanket down across the rocks, sat down, and beckoned her over. "You'll be warmer if you sleep next to me."

She hesitated. "Sleep next to you?"

"Until you're warm. I'll give you my blanket."

"I don't have a guardian now."

"I have nothing improper in mind. I'm not cold and you are, and I'll not be saddled with a sickly woman at the beginning of a long journey."

The promise of warmth tempted her, but she shook her head and crawled to a dry place near the cave wall. "I'll warm up."

"As you wish. But I won't slow down for you if you get sick." He tossed her his blanket. "At least use both blankets."

She yawned, succumbing to exhaustion as she pulled the second blanket over herself. "Why aren't you cold?"

He crawled to the cave entrance and sat down with his back to her. "I don't get cold."

She leaned her head against the rock wall and closed her eyes. Her hand throbbed. *Alshada, keep us safe. Keep Muriel safe. I trust you, but I'm afraid. I don't know if I'm strong enough for this. Make me strong.*

CHAPTER THREE

Carved in ebony, the raven rises.
From justice born, the king returns.
— Scrolls of Prophecy in the Syrafi Keep,
Year of Creation 656

It's smaller than I remember, Braedan thought. When Fergus sat in the ancient ebony seat, bestowing favors on his trusted councilors and dispensing justice in the name of kings and queens long dead, the Raven Throne had seemed massive. It frightened Braedan as a child. The great crest of the seat formed a raven in full wing, its beak lifted in a cry to the heavens. The wings seemed to emerge from Fergus' back, and the open mouth looked like horns on his head. Braedan remembered clutching his mother's hand and hiding behind her skirts until his father called him forward and showed him the throne was just wood.

The Raven Throne sat empty now. Fergus the Grand, legendary for his magnanimity, had died cursing his son. Repha Felix wouldn't tell Braedan his father's dying words. Braedan stared at the carved throne before him and tried to conjure some emotion. None came.

He stepped up the dais and traced the carvings of braided vines that wound up the throne. He sat down and closed his eyes. *It's just a chair. It's just wood. I have as much right as anyone.*

The rhythmic sound of steel on stone announced Ronan Kerry's arrival. Braedan's uncle tipped his boots with steel on the toes and heel. He said it gave him an edge in a fight and on horseback. Braedan thought it simple vanity. "Come to see what kind of a chair your money buys?" he asked.

The clicking stopped. "It suits you, your majesty."

Braedan opened his eyes. Ronan had the same bright blue eyes as Braedan, but there the similarities ended. Ronan was a big man, muscular, with the red-blond hair of the people on the northeastern coast of Taura, while Braedan was shorter, lither, and had his father's coal-black hair. The rising sun of House Kerry was embroidered in gold on Ronan's indigo longcoat. His uncle's close-trimmed beard hid a prominent chin, and his ruddy face had the weather-beaten look of a man who lived subject to the harsh elements of the northern coast.

Braedan saw his mother's face under Ronan's wrinkles. "You were here when he died. Did he know? Did he see you?"

Ronan shifted his feet. "I was here as was my right as councilor, but he refused to see me. He insisted to the end that your cousin Daron would take the regency."

"And Daron?"

"His head decorates the Noble Gate, majesty. As you ordered."

As I ordered. "What of my father's forces in the city?"

"Taken. There have been few casualties. My men control the streets, and yours took the castle easily."

"And the Table?"

Twelve ducal houses sat on the Table of Councilors. There had once been thirteen, but House Mac Niall fell from favor before Braedan's exile. Duke Mac Niall was killed and named a traitor to the crown. "Those who were in Torlach are now imprisoned in the west tower in separate rooms, as you ordered," Ronan said. "I've dispatched forces to the other dukes with messages demanding their allegiance under threat of forfeiture of their holdings. I don't think it will be difficult to convince them. Most of my peers tired of your father's extravagance and piety years ago." He paused. "The Mac Corin holdings are yours to dispense. You have many loyal nobles who would love to have some rich southern soil since Daron no longer has a need for it."

"Including you, uncle?"

"If it pleases your majesty."

"Daron had no heir?"

"Daron left a young wife and no children. The lady is from House Seannan. If you want Duke Seannan's loyalty, return the lady to him."

Braedan leaned back on the throne. "You speak of holding the lady hostage."

"Call her a ward of the crown."

"While her father lives?"

"Her father lives at your pleasure."

Braedan rubbed his chin. "I never wanted to rule by fear."

"Have you ever caught a bird in your hand?"

Braedan snickered. "A bird? No."

"The trick is getting a firm grip on it, even if it's just by a wing or a leg. You can control the whole bird if your grip is firm enough. But if you don't get that first hold, you'll lose your chance. A firm grip is called for now. You can loosen it later."

"And if I accidentally snap its neck?"

Ronan tipped his head. "Regrets, nephew?"

"No. But I want to rule by vision. Men will follow a vision if they believe in it."

"Your mother had a vision, too. She wanted to restore the old ways. She believed in the earth magic. Her marriage to your father was one of expedience and hope. She thought she could temper his righteousness enough to find a way for the old ways to live with the new, that the Great Kirok in Aliom could find a path alongside what it called witchcraft." He took one step closer to Braedan, pain and anger and grief in his eyes. None of it was for Fergus. "What did she get for her vision, Braedan? A broken heart, an empty bed, an empty womb, and a husband who shunned her in favor of his divine mission."

Braedan remembered. He had seen the Lady Alison weep more times than he could count, her hair hiding her face and her thin shoulders shaking with quiet sobs, as his father pushed the earth magic and the tribes further and further from peaceful relations with Taura. After she'd given him a son,

Fergus had even forsaken her bed. She had given up hope in the end and taken her own life when Braedan was ten. "Without vision—"

"—people waste and die. You sound just like her when you say it." Ronan's voice cracked. "Keep religion out of the affairs of state and govern wisely, and you can build your vision. But securing thrones is a messy business. For now, you must tighten your grip."

Braedan rested his hands on the arms of the throne. "Bring Daron's wife to Torlach, but ensure that she is treated with the highest honor. Send word to her father that he can come retrieve her here. I will meet with him when he arrives."

Ronan inclined his head. "As you wish, sire. As for who will hold the lands?"

"I suppose I will."

"You?"

"Why not? It's my family. The crown needs the money and the men." He saw hesitation on Ronan's face. "Who would you see hold the lands?"

"Perhaps you could place them in care of a steward and give them to your sons, when you have them. But I would not wish to see your attention divided between ruling a country and running your holdings. And I won't live forever. Eventually, you'll have to run Stone Coast as well."

Ronan's wife, the Lady Ilyssa, had never been able to carry a child. Ronan refused to set his Esparan lady aside. He named Braedan his heir instead. Braedan knew Ronan's allegiance to Ilyssa went only as far as his public persona and her wealth. His uncle had no qualms about bedding any woman who appealed to him, and there were rumors that he'd fathered at least two bastards, though none had ever come forward.

"What of an alliance with Lady Seannan?" Braedan asked.

"Wed her? Perhaps. An allegiance with an old house would be valuable. Her family could run your holdings in your stead. If you rid yourself of her brother, all the better."

Braedan shook his head. "No. I'll not murder nobles who can be turned. He will have a chance to swear fealty." He straightened. "I need you to work with my seneschal to begin arranging audiences with the foreign ambassadors who are still in the city. Close the docks. I don't want anyone else leaving."

"As you wish. The Eiryan ambassador—Duncan Guinness—left two weeks ago. His wife was expecting a child. She wanted to be near her family, I believe." Ronan paused. "This was more successful than we had dared hope. History will say this was a bloodless coup. Braedan the Merciful? Braedan the Bloodless."

Braedan shifted his weight, hoping his uncle didn't notice the flinch of discomfort. *Daron and his men would disagree. I've become a kinslayer.* "Not bloodless."

Ronan nodded toward the Raven Throne. "Did you know your father tried to have that removed?"

"The throne? Why?"

"He believed it possessed by dark magic. He thought it a pagan abomination. He hired the best carpenters and masons in the country and no one—not one of them—could budge the throne. They took axes and picks and chisels to it, hoping to carve it into a new image, and they couldn't even dent it."

Braedan lifted an eyebrow. "Magic?"

Ronan shrugged. "Who can say?"

"I remember he had another chair for a time. He put it in front of the Raven Throne."

"The Council finally convinced him to return to the Raven Throne. Dispensing justice from another chair is an insult to Taura itself."

The door to the hall opened, and two guards entered. "You're dismissed," Braedan said.

Ronan bowed. "Of course, your majesty." He nodded once at the senior guard. "Mac Kendrick."

"My lord." Logan returned the nod.

As Ronan's footsteps faded, Braedan turned to Logan. "What did you find at the sayada?"

Logan Mac Kendrick bowed to Braedan. The mail under his green and gold surcoat creaked when he straightened. His face and clothes were streaked with charcoal and dirt, but he had no visible wounds. His mail coif lay against his shoulders, and his hair was matted against his head. The surcoat boasted a raven in flight against the dark green wool; gold thread edged the surcoat, and Logan wore a gold cord to signify his place as High Commander. The other man was similarly garbed, but held a lesser rank. "Only one hundred four of the sayas remained," Logan said.

Braedan cursed. *One hundred four. There were fifty more a week ago.* "She's gone?"

"If she was ever there. I could never confirm that anyone of royal blood was there except the Eiryan princess."

Braedan looked at the other guard. "How did they get out of the sayada, guardsman?"

"Sire, I swear we have monitored every entrance and exit for the last week while the regular castle guards were distracted with the regent's illness. We saw no one leave until—" The man licked his lips. "The men patrolling the north wall of the castle and the sayada saw three figures running for the trees earlier tonight. They killed one—a sister—but the other two got away. When they looked for the exit beyond the north wall, they couldn't find anything."

What if they killed her? "I said I didn't want them killed until I could question them. Why were you firing at them?"

"My lord—"

"Lord?" Braedan crossed his arms. "Do you forget why we did this?"

"His majesty reminds you that addressing him as 'lord' is not appropriate," Logan said. "As king, he is entitled to the address of 'sire' or 'majesty.'"

The man hesitated. "Sire. Forgive me. We wanted to stop them. We fired hoping to wound them."

"And you want me to believe they just appeared out of nowhere and ran for the trees."

"It looks that way, majesty."

Damn it. "You found no sign of them?"

"We sent the hounds, but they lost the scent at the edge of the channel. The men saw a boat heading north." The guard shifted his feet in a nervous shuffle.

"North. When the current flows south, a boat was heading north. Was it sailing?"

"No, majesty."

Braedan frowned. "How is that possible, guardsman? How do two people row against a current as strong as that?"

"Sire, I can only report what we saw."

Braedan turned to Logan. "The sayas must have sent decoys from the sayada—women who will pretend to be the Taurin heir. Take your men and search every kirok on the island, one at a time, and find these women. Bring them back alive. I need the one they believe is the rightful Taurin heir. Then burn the kiroks to the ground, destroy the Holy Scriptures, and bring any kirons you find to me. We'll put them on a ship back to Aliom. That will be the kirok's punishment for hiding her from me."

Logan bowed. "Yes, sire."

Braedan looked at the cowering guard. "Select a small contingent of men to sail out of the channel and look for this boat. They need to leave immediately. If they can't find the boat, send them to Culidar and have them try to pick up the trail of these two you lost."

"At low tide in the middle of the night? Sire—"

"Do you believe it's wise to question me?" The man fell silent. Braedan turned to Logan. "Are you breeding insolence, commander?"

"No, sire. I will see to discipline."

"Good. Perhaps you can use this one as an example. Have him whipped and returned to duty."

Logan inclined his head. "Yes, sire."

"Have someone see to the ship tonight," Braedan said. "Cormac will prepare formal orders for the seizure of the kiroks. You'll have them in the morning. If the men meet resistance, they'll have my authority to deal with it as they see fit."

"Yes, sire."

"This guard—I won't find more like him, will I?"

Logan stood stoic. "No, sire. The man was green. I gave him too much authority too soon. That was my mistake. If you wish, I'll take his lashes."

"I won't punish you for a mistake of leadership if you rectify it quickly."

Logan inclined his head. "Yes, sire."

Braedan folded his hands and considered the news of the sayada. "The sayas—you say I shouldn't kill them."

"Majesty, the sayas are well-loved. Killing a few nobles who stand in the way of you taking the crown—the people can forgive that. But these women care for the unfortunate and downtrodden." Logan paused. "If you kill them all, you will incite the people."

"Incite them? Put fear into them, perhaps."

"Do you wish to rule by fear or by vision, sire?"

Vision. But my uncle says it takes fear. "Perhaps it will take both."

"As you wish, majesty. Did your meeting with Sayana Muriel today yield any results?"

Braedan's jaw tightened. "No. She refuses to do more than proselytize." *Rule by fear. If I kill them, the people will fear me. Is that what I want?* He turned back to the throne. "There's nothing to be learned from the sayas. Prepare the gallows."

"Majesty."

Braedan turned back.

"You may be able to get Muriel's cooperation if you keep the other women prisoner. She would do anything to save her charges."

"Other counselors told me to kill them all—that as long as the kirok was alive and well on Taura, I would never be secure on my throne."

A muscle twitched in Logan's jaw. "I'm sure your lord uncle means well, your majesty."

Not my uncle. Braedan crossed his arms. "And the Eiryan princess—what do you recommend I do with her?"

"Send her home. Don't risk war with Eirya," Logan said.

"You don't think she's a spy?"

A hint of a grin flickered across Logan's mouth. "Forgive me, majesty, but no. That's not King Cedric's way. He dotes on his daughter. He would not send her to do such work."

Braedan grunted an acknowledgement. "You offer wise counsel, Logan. What have you done with the sayas?"

"The sayas have been taken to the dungeons. I await your orders on what to do with them."

Braedan nodded. "I will consider what to do with the sayas overnight. Tell the Dal'Imuri to guard them, but they aren't to touch them unless I give orders." *That should terrify them into submission. Grown men have soiled themselves under the glare of one of the Dal'Imuri.*

"As you wish, majesty. And the princess?"

"Show her to my study. I would speak with her where we can have more privacy." He paused. "I've heard she's a rare beauty. Is it true?"

Logan's face remained implacable. "The lady is very pleasing to the eye. Her voice leaves something to be desired, however."

Braedan grinned. "Shrill?"

"It's not for me to gossip about a highborn lady, majesty." He took a wineskin from around his neck and handed it to Braedan. "From our own stores, sire. If I may be excused?"

Braedan took the wineskin. "See to your duties." He sat down and leaned his head back against the cool ebony of the throne as Logan's footsteps retreated. The sayada of the Order of Sai Atena posed no threat to the regency, but to a man who would establish a monarchy, they were a stumbling block. They believed the rightful heir to the Raven Throne would return one day, and they would not quietly accept any king or queen who did not have the blood of ancient King Aiden and Queen Brenna. *But that bloodline is gone— disappeared into myth or lost in history or battle.* He rubbed his chin. *Aiden* and Brenna died a thousand years ago, and no one ever found their son. There's no reason to believe this woman they say is the heir was really of a royal bloodline. But still, if they believe it, they can rally people around her. I have to deal with this woman.

Braedan picked up the wineskin Logan had left behind. He removed the stopper and inhaled. The rich aroma of a dark red wine tempted him. *Securing thrones is a messy business. I'll do it with a clear head.* He took one drink, went to the privy, and emptied the rest of the skin down the shaft.

CHAPTER FOUR

*It's easier to treat with a bear in spring
than with an Eiryan noblewoman.
— King Cedric Mac Roy, r. 5965-6007*

Locks rattled on the cell doors, and the sayas around Igraine sobbed and wailed in fear. "Alshada help us," one woman whispered.

Igraine straightened from her resting pose against the stone wall of the dungeon. "We left him in the sayada," she said.

The woman wrung her hands, her face pale and her breath shallow. "They'll take us and—"

Igraine resisted the urge to slap the woman. "Never fear, lass. You have me."

The door opened, and a tall, dark figure wearing a royal hauberk and gold cord stepped into the room. His eyes fell on her right away. "Your highness. The king—"

She gave him a derisive snort. "King? He thinks himself a king, does he?"

His expression didn't even twitch. "The king requests your presence." He held out an arm.

She gestured to the women behind her. "And these? What will be done with them?"

"You can ask his majesty."

She tightened her mouth and walked out the door, refusing the guard's arm. He took her elbow and guided her through the winding underground passageways. Somewhere, a man wept, and the stench of waste and blood threatened to choke Igraine. They walked past a lithe, masked man clad completely in black and carrying a long iron prod with a barbed end. She raised her chin. *This boy-king will find himself with an armada of Eiryan pirates at his door if he doesn't stop this immediately.*

The guard guided her through the palace with an occasional hand on her elbow to redirect her until they reached the upper floors. He nodded to two guards in front of a wide oak door. "His majesty is expecting us." The guards stepped aside, and the man leading Igraine opened the door for her.

Igraine entered the well-appointed room and strode to the desk. The man behind it started to stand and speak, but she didn't let him. "You'd be the boy who thinks himself a king, then?"

He inclined his head. "Your highness," he started. "I—"

Igraine held up a hand. "I've no interest in your niceties. I don't know what you're about, lad, but this treatment of the Order of Sai Atena is a violation of Aliom's treaty with Taura. The Great Kirok has been guaranteed freedom to preach, guide, and comfort in the name of Alshada since the breaking of the world. I demand to see the Eiryan ambassador. Now."

His mouth twitched at one corner. "A lot of demands for a woman in your position," he said. He picked up a carafe and a goblet. "Wine, my lady?"

"I've no desire for prison food."

He laughed. "Prison food? I assure you, no one in the dungeons is receiving wine tonight." He poured and held out the goblet. "Take it," he said when she hesitated. "I promise you it isn't poisoned."

She lifted the goblet to her nose and swirled the wine, inhaling the heady, distinct aroma of the rich soils around the Aldorean Seas. "Esparan?"

He inclined his head again. "I have connections." He sat behind his desk once more.

Igraine sipped the wine. *Alshada's breath, he's easy to look at.* There was humor in Braedan's eyes and an easy manner about him that reminded her of her own brothers. "How considerate of you to prepare for my visit."

He swirled his own wine. "Would you like to tell me why an Eiryan princess hides in a sayada filled with misguided fools who still believe in creation myths and an ancient god-man? Or shall I just guess?"

"Myths, is it? And how would you be knowing a thing like that?"

"Few thinking men believe in Alshada. The kirok belongs to another era. The stories do little more than comfort the uneducated."

"And women? Is that what you're thinking, then? That only a foolish woman would take the vows of Sai Atena?"

Blue eyes twinkled over the rim of his goblet. "I've been thinking about it for some time. I can't see any reason for a woman of your rank to waste her time in a sayada. If you need an education, there are other places for that. I wonder if your father sent you to watch the Taurin throne."

Igraine gave him a cool smile. "No. He would not burden me with such trifling concerns." She gathered her sayada robes around her and sat down.

The tilted grin widened. "You have a rare cheek for a noblewoman."

"Perhaps you've not met enough Eiryan noblewomen."

He pulled a dagger out of his belt and toyed with it. "How long have you been at the sayada, highness?"

Is that supposed to intimidate me? "Not long."

"Have you taken the oaths?"

"No."

"Why not? Do you harbor doubts?"

I have nothing but doubts. She sipped her wine. "Have I done something to offend you?"

"Not yet."

"Then I fail to see why my religious convictions are any business of yours."

He stood, put the knife in his belt, and went around the desk. "What was it? The vow of chastity? Or the one of poverty? What kept you from vowing to serve the sayada? I have to say that I cannot see why the Order of Sai Atena would appeal to a woman like you. I can see you are not accustomed to deprivation." He leaned forward and lifted her hair in one hand.

She eyed the dagger in his belt. "I'm also not accustomed to men showing a woman of my rank such disrespect."

"Disrespect? No, my lady, you misunderstand."

She pulled her hair away from his hand and put it behind her back. "Do I? Even the boldest of suitors would not have dared touch my hair without my leave. You presume much for a thief."

He smirked. "Your father made no secret of his support for my cousin. Did your father send you to the sayada to watch the regency and report back to him?"

She laughed. "No. My father has far better means of gathering information about foreign governments than sending his own daughter to spy."

"Do you know of any Eiryan spies here in the city?"

"No, but if I did, I'd not tell you." She set her wine on the desk. "I have no intention of discussing Eiryan policy with you. If that's what you wish, you can return me to the prison."

"And risk war with Eirya when King Cedric finds out I have his only daughter locked up in a dungeon? I'm not stupid." He swirled the wine in his goblet, but didn't drink. "Is it true what they say about the Eiryan army? That your father brings in swordmasters from Tal'Amun to train them?"

She smiled. "Do you see your entrails hanging from a ha'kari sword, Braedan?"

"I would be a fool if the rumors about the Eiryan army didn't give me pause."

"Then what do you have planned for me?"

"I merely wish to offer you the hospitality of the Taurin crown until you can return home."

This is too easy. "And when will that be?"

"You may write to your father as soon as you wish. Send a message with a merchant ship when I reopen the harbor."

"And that's it? That's all you want? Just to send me home?"

Braedan set down his goblet and spread his hands. "Eirya has given no offense as far as I can see. You may leave when you wish."

My father will have me married off before my trunks are unpacked. "What will you do with the sayas?"

"I'm afraid the sayas will remain my guests for now."

"Why?"

He gave her a tilted smile. "Ah, my lady, I fear I can't share that information."

She crossed her arms. "You need something from them. Otherwise, you'd kill them or exile them." She leaned forward. "Perhaps I can help you, if you tell me what it is."

"Perhaps another time." He straightened and held out an arm. "I'll see you to quarters where you'll be comfortable until your father sends someone for you. You'll have every comfort due your rank, your highness."

Damn it. "You're making a mistake," she said.

"A mistake?"

"Persecuting the kirok will only bring you trouble, I promise you."

He folded his arms and tipped his head to one side. "All right," he said finally. "I'm listening."

Igraine's stomach fluttered when her eyes met Braedan's steely blue gaze. His lithe build and strong, steady posture spoke of an accomplished athlete, and she had a sudden, unwelcome picture of what he might look like without his tunic. *Well, not entirely unwelcome.* She wet her lips. *Don't be a fool. Pull yourself together, lass. He's just a man like any other.* "As you point out, it is your country and you can do as you wish. But the kirok is more powerful than you seem to realize. It may be wiser to cultivate that alliance than to sever it. You threaten to take away a source of comfort and guidance for the common people. Peasants may not be well-armed or organized, but they can still cause problems if they don't support you. If you wish to head off the revolt that may be coming by your coup, it might be better to get the kirok to support you rather than to condemn you."

"And how do you propose I get the kirok to support me?"

"The kirok in Aliom has powerful connections to merchant money. You want to see money flow into Taura? Ask Aliom to build and repair kiroks here. When they brought their kiroks to Eirya, my father's treasury overflowed without raising a single tax."

"How so?"

"The kirok brings plans and money and little else. If they build kiroks on Taura, they'll need timber and stone and all manner of other materials, as well as craftsmen and builders. Elders and kirons will come to Taura as well, bringing families and money with them. When they draw people away from the countryside and into the holdings of your nobles, the nobles will become wealthier, resulting in more for your treasury without raising taxes."

He tilted his head. "You have a sharp mind."

She bristled at the condescension in his voice. "Does that surprise you?"

He offered a crooked grin. "It's rare to find such a sharp mind in such a beautiful woman."

He's baiting me! "Would you be surprised to find thorns on a rose?"

"Thorns. I don't see how that's possible."

"I am an Eiryan princess with three older brothers. I can assure you, Braedan—I have thorns."

"I can't just let the sayas go. They and the kirok have hidden someone they believe can challenge my authority. I can't allow them to influence the people against me, nor can I allow such dissidence to remain unpunished."

"Keep the sayas imprisoned until you establish a treaty with Aliom. Send them somewhere else as part of the treaty." She paused. "You should know that if you have the sayas tortured, you will call down the wrath of the kirok on yourself."

He laughed at that. "Should that concern me?"

"I would be concerned if I were you. The kirok employs its own Dal'Imuri."

A single eyebrow rose. "Igraine, you push the truth too far."

She lifted one shoulder and sipped her wine. "They're your entrails. I can only tell you what I've heard."

"And what is that?"

"That nobles who challenge the kirok have a way of disappearing." She thought his face paled. "I have no reason to lie to you. You have told me I'm free to go. You fear war with Eirya. I don't have to tell you any of this. I could just let you anger the kirok and find out for yourself. But, if you intend to rule Taura, you should do it with your eyes open."

He frowned. "And who would arrange this new treaty?"

Keep yourself together, she thought. *You have him. And if you play this well, you won't ever have to go home.* "Have you ever been to Aliom?"

"I have not had the desire or the need to visit the kirok's headquarters."

"I have. And my father has hosted kirok elders many times. He is close to Prelate Johanan, and the kirok has a strong presence on Eirya." She kept her hands folded so he wouldn't see the tremor in them. "You need someone to treat with the kirok. I know the kirok. Let me treat with them for you."

"I have nobles loyal to me. Why would I need an Eiryan noblewoman to do the work of an ambassador?"

"It gives the appearance of neutrality. Use your own nobles who have been bought or threatened, and the kirok elders will not take you seriously. Use me, and they will see a foreign princess with a long history of service and loyalty to the kirok who has no reason to support your ascension but does anyway."

"How do I know you will not betray me?"

"You don't. But if I am here in your presence every day you can ensure that I am working in your favor, can't you?"

Silence hovered. "Why would you do this, Igraine?"

"Why do you seize the throne this way?"

"For the good of Taura. To build something great."

"I can help you do that. You were right, Braedan. I was not raised for the life of the sayas. I was raised to be a noblewoman. But a life of playing court does not appeal to me. I wish to do greater things than marry and bear children."

He turned away, folded his arms, and walked to the window. "A woman ambassador. Such things are unheard of."

I have him. "It would set you apart—make your court appear to be more than just an angry son's revenge against his father. You seek to create a new era? Do something unheard of. Give a woman a position of authority in your court."

"What do you want in return?"

"Give the sayas humane treatment. If you would have me as an ambassador to the kirok, you will need to expect that kirok elders will want to see the women when they arrive."

He nodded and turned back. "What else?"

"I want the same considerations as any other ambassador you hire—payment for the services I give in addition to whatever I need to accomplish my duties. You will treat me as an honored guest in the castle and give me the freedom to roam and visit the sayas whenever I wish."

"And what kind of payment will you expect?"

"Offices and rooms of my own, and three maids, at a minimum. And I will need clothing that befits my station, as well as gold to maintain a standard befitting a noblewoman and ambassador. I fear my belongings from Eirya were left in the sayada, and I assume they were burned with everything else."

"All right. What will your father say when he hears of this? The Eiryan ambassador left shortly before I took Torlach, but he will be back. Will I be facing your father's wrath when Lord Guinness returns?"

"I can handle my father."

"What makes you so certain?"

She smiled. "Lord Guinness owes me a favor. He can intercede for me."

He tipped his head. "A favor."

"Aye."

A long silence fell. "I don't suppose I can find out what that favor might be."

"It's between me and Lord Guinness."

He crossed the room, nearly closing the gap between them. "I don't trust you, Igraine."

"I don't trust you, Braedan."

He nodded. "I want you to work with my seneschal. He will oversee everything you do until I know that you are acting in my best interests. And I want you here in the castle—not in the Eiryan ambassador's house."

"I work for you, not for the Eiryan crown." She held out her hand to clasp his as a man would. "Do we have a bargain?"

His mouth twitched with a suppressed smile. "I may yet regret my decision to keep you alive."

"Then I will have to ensure that you don't."

He clasped her arm. A slow smile crossed his mouth. "A woman ambassador. You have much to prove, your highness."

"Do you doubt me, Braedan?"

"No." Vague surprise hovered in his voice. "I don't." He offered her his arm again. "For now, you may stay in my mother's old chambers. My father—" He stopped and cleared his throat. It was a crack in his armor that Igraine did not miss. "Her things are still there," he said, his voice steady again.

He led her through the corridor to another oak door and a room very much like the study they had just left. Lush tapestries that told the old Taurin legends decorated one wall. A fire crackled in the hearth, and silver sconces flickered around the room. In the corner, a large oak door stood ajar. A carpet woven in the warm hues of Tal'Amun covered the stone floor, and the carved teak chairs near the desk were lined with soft silk cushions. The door to the side of the desk stood ajar; he led her through it to a bedchamber. "I trust this will meet your needs?" he asked.

She walked into the room and ran a hand over the carved cherry dressing table. "The tapestries—they tell the stories of old Taura."

He joined her next to one. "My mother loved the old stories."

"Your father must have loved her to leave her things in here all these years."

He stared at the tapestry with his arms crossed. When he spoke, his voice was low and rough. He pointed at a man on horseback holding a woman at sword point. Above them hovered the Ferimin, huge black-winged raven-like creatures of myth. "The story goes that Ohmin discovered his wife had betrayed him. He killed her and let the Ferimin feed on her flesh and the flesh of her men."

Igraine turned to him. "A warning?"

Haunted blue eyes met hers. "For my father or my mother? I was never certain."

Igraine gestured to the picture. "The stories are mine, too. My ancestors came from these shores centuries ago. When Ohmin's wife died, her blood drew the wrath of the earth on Ohmin's head. The Morrag called Cuhail and his warriors, and they destroyed Ohmin and his men. If I recall, the Ferimin feasted with equal vigor on Ohmin's entrails as they had on his wife's." She shrugged one shoulder. "I would say there was warning for both your father and mother."

Braedan's eyes locked on hers. "Perhaps." He turned away. "I hope you'll make use of my mother's belongings. It would please me to see you dressed in something other than sayada robes." He opened the wardrobe doors, revealing silk dresses trimmed in lace or filament, fur robes, palace slippers, riding clothes, boots, and other finery.

She pulled out one of the gowns, a dark blue silk with an impossibly small waistline. *Did his mother never eat?* "Your mother must have had similar coloring to mine."

"Her hair was more blond than red, and she had blue eyes, not green, but her skin was fair as yours." He fixed his eyes on her face. "You are a beauty, my lady. Forgive my insolence, but you shine as a single poppy in a field of dull grass."

Does he think he can charm me? She tilted her head and toyed with a chain around her neck. "Do you know there are no snakes in Eirya?"

He laughed. "Truly?"

"Aye. 'Tis said they grew tired of their charms being ignored and left to find more gullible ears."

He grinned. "And you think you can ignore my charms?"

"I think you will grow tired of using them on me."

He pointed at her neck. "I thought the sayas didn't wear jewels."

She pulled the chain free of her robes and lifted the murky gray stone. "Being a royal lady has some advantages. My mother gave it to me. I wear it to remind me of home." *And I promised I'd never take it off.*

A long silence fell. Braedan shifted his feet. "I am not the monster you believe I am. I am just doing what must be done for the good of my country."

She gave him a cool smile. "Of course you are."

He inclined his head. "I look forward to seeing you tomorrow, your highness."

She returned the gesture. "Good night, sire."

When he shut the outer door, she sat down on the bed and let out a long breath. Eirya waited across the rough Galoch Sea—Eirya, a suitor from the west, and a father who insisted she wed or find a path in the kirok. Igraine chose the kirok. Religious devotion didn't enter into it. Serving in the sayada was less awful than staying on Eirya to marry the man her father had chosen for her.

She rang for a servant and requested ink and parchment. When it arrived, she sat down at the writing desk, twisting the stone on its chain, the quill poised in her hand as her thoughts tumbled. *Write my father—he makes it sound so simple. What do I say? How do I tell him I can't come home, that I can't live the life he's chosen for me?* With a deep breath, she dipped the quill in the inkwell and began to write.

A king's bedchamber. Emrys picked up a goblet on the night table near Braedan's bed and sniffed. *Water. When he could have wine. And an empty bed when he could have any harlot waiting for him.* He snuffed out torches on the wall, sat in a corner, and waited.

He'd listened to Braedan and Igraine's entire conversation, but the Taurin wards still prevented him from acting directly on this world. That sacrifices made two thousand years ago still protected this island and the relics hidden somewhere on it gave Emrys no end of grief. To find an ambitious, charismatic man of noble blood—one with a grudge, at that—who could be convinced to do Emrys' bidding was no small thing. Emrys had thought to have some influence over the state of Taurin affairs through this princeling. But now, if he was already making his own choices . . . .

Emrys lifted his hand into the light from the fires of the sayada below. He clenched a fist. His body was still weak, despite his frequent feedings. The wards took a toll. Just being on Taura was painful. *But a few weeks ago, I couldn't even be here for an hour. Months ago, I couldn't be here at all. The wards weaken.*

The door creaked open, and a thin shaft of light pierced the room. "I told you to kill them," Emrys said.

Braedan's hand flew to the hilt of his sword. He stood very still, eyes fixed on the corner of the room. "I was convinced that it might not be prudent. Many of their number were missing, anyway. I assume the heir was among them."

Emrys stood. "She is no longer on Taura. Send your men into Culidar to find her."

"I already did. Boats are preparing to sail tonight." Braedan folded his arms. "You didn't tell me an Eiryan princess lived in the sayada."

"You were supposed to kill them. You didn't need to know."

"You almost sent me to war with Eirya. I can't risk that. The throne is too precarious to go to war with anyone right now, and Eirya has powerful allies."

"If you had killed them all, you could have told the Eiryan king you didn't know she was there and apologized after she was dead. Now, you risk your throne. You led her to believe that you might give the kirok some power, but I tell you that as long as those faithful to Alshada remain on this island, you will never be secure on your throne."

Braedan stepped closer. "I think the throne can be stronger than the faith these people have, and I think Igraine will prove useful."

Emrys clenched his fists and buried the anger rising in his chest. *Oh, you foolish boy—you don't know what you tempt. I could feed on you for days.* "This course will cost you the throne."

"I disagree. I can't go to war, and perhaps, if I treat her well, I can use her to gain leverage with Cedric. I can treat with Cedric. He's not a fool, and he sees the advantage of maintaining ties with Taura. Without Taura, Eirya's merchants have to sail to Espara to find a good harbor." He grinned. "Besides, the princess amuses me. She has a sharp mind."

You are an idiotic whelp who thinks only of what's between her legs. "There are other women of noble blood. I can give you one. But this one is not for you."

Braedan frowned. "What do you mean?"

She is a powerful, dangerous creature. "She has powerful protection. Pursue her, and you will lose your position. Kill her, take another noblewoman to wife, and your descendants will reign in Taura for generations."

Braedan scoffed. "What kind of protection is so powerful that it could harm me now? I have a force of loyal men that you helped me gather. Are you saying the men you sent me aren't as talented as you claimed they were?"

"If you wish to lose your throne, I cannot stop you. I ask one more thing of you."

"You want me to find the Sidh village."

As if it will be so easy. "The village is still hidden from the eyes of men. You will have to go through the tribes to find it."

The single remaining torch flickered as a cold breeze passed through the room. Braedan rubbed his arms and shivered. He latched the window, never taking his eyes from Emrys' face. "The tribes are best left on their own. Going into the great forest will awaken their anger. How do you propose I contact them without angering them?"

"You claim to be a king. If you can't even perform such a simple task, how can you rule a whole kingdom?"

Braedan flinched. "If I find this village, are we done? Is this the last thing?"

"Yes. Find the Sidh for me, and you will never see me again."

"Very well," Braedan said.

Emrys held Braedan's eyes. *I could feed on you for days—but not yet.* He nodded once and slipped into the space between the elements to return to Culidar.

CHAPTER FIVE

Trust a tribesman, trust a thief.
— Brae Sidh saying

The first fingers of dawn and the sound of waves against rocks awakened Mairead after a few hours of edgy sleep. She rubbed gritty eyes. Her hand throbbed with a dull rhythm and her knees protested as she straightened fresh scabs.

Connor lay on his back at the cave entrance. When she sat up, he turned his head. "How long have you been awake?" she asked.

"Since just before dawn." He sat up. "Let me see your hand."

She stepped into the light. "It still aches, but it's not too bad."

He untied the cloth around her hand. "It's raw. Try to keep from using it too much. You don't want it to split open."

"I'll try." As he retied the kerchief, she studied his dark skin, bold nose, and strong chin. A faded silver scar above his left eye and another smaller one on his chin hinted at past skirmishes. Short, spiky black hair rose in a haphazard muss on his head. He wore brown doeskin breeches and a leather jerkin over a green linen tunic. "I don't suppose you have some more suitable travel clothes for me?" she asked.

He chuckled. "You don't think a serviceable woolen dress will suffice?"

"No. I don't."

"You're smarter than I thought." He gestured to one of the two packs in the cave. "There's a change of clothes in there." He brushed her hair off her shoulders. "Put your hair up, too. It'll get in the way like that."

She touched her hair. "It's a sin—"

"Putting your hair up is a sin?"

Her face grew warm. "We were taught it makes us look like the women of the city—the ones who seek a man for—" She stopped. "Can't I just braid it?"

"Braided hair isn't a sin?"

"Not in service to Alshada. I think this counts."

"If you can manage with that hand." He stood. "I'll wait over there."

Mairead changed into the woolen breeches, linen tunic, and leather boots she found in the pack. She folded the wool dress, wrapping the stiff shoes into it. A pang of loss passed through her as she thought of Saya Hana, Sayana Muriel, and the women who left the sayada to distract Braedan. "Alshada, help me be strong," she whispered. She tried to braid her hair, but the cut made the exercise cumbersome and difficult. She brushed her hair out with her fingers.

As she stepped out of the cave, she took a deep breath of the fresh salt air and blinked to adjust her vision. Smoke hovered above Torlach.

"Braedan burned the sayada sometime last night," Connor said.

Mairead swallowed the lump in her throat and nodded. *You are royalty. Tears are for others. You must be strong.* "I need a few minutes. I need to say morning prayers."

He blinked. "You're joking, right?"

"No—why?"

The sea spray wet her face as she waited for him to answer. "I'll wait over there," he said, pointing to a nearby rock.

Mairead knelt, lowered her head, and folded her hands. She recited memorized words: "Alshada, give me wisdom. Open my ears to hear your voice. Open my eyes to see your ways. Open my heart to understand and obey you. I pray for safety and wisdom, and I pray that we would show your love to those we encounter. Please guard our steps today. So be it." Her voice broke near the end, and she realized it was the first morning prayer she could remember without Sayana Muriel's voice leading and a chorus of female voices, young and old, speaking together. She squeezed her eyes and shook her head. *The sayada—burned. What about the women? Muriel?* She put her folded hands to her forehead and lowered her face to the ground. *Alshada, please protect them.* In a few moments, she stood and turned back to Connor.

He gave her a small piece of jerky. "Breakfast. I have some hard tack, too. Why didn't you braid your hair?"

"I couldn't—my hand—"

"Do you want me to do it?"

"You?"

"I'm a tribesman. Braids are easy."

"I thought you were Sidh."

"Can't I be both?"

She touched her hair. "I shouldn't let a man—"

"As you wish." He dug through his pack and pulled out a leather strip. "Tie it back with this."

She pulled her hair into a mass with the strip, fighting the ache in her hand, while he turned back to the cave and busied himself with packing her blanket. When he finished, he lifted his pack onto his shoulders and helped her put on the smaller one. As he tested the straps and the weight, she caught his eye. "Something amiss, saya?" he asked.

She shook her head. *I can't tell him he puts me off-balance. He'll think I'm an idiot.* "Which way are we going?"

He pointed at a narrow animal trail. "That path leads to level ground."

Mairead kept a short distance between them and watched Connor's feet, stepping where he stepped. His lithe stride surprised her. He made less noise than she did as he walked, and he had no trouble balancing himself while she had to steady herself several times. "How did you know about that cave and the trail?" she asked.

"My work."

"What kind of work is that?"

"I'm a freelance." He didn't slow or look back.

"Do you often need to hide fleeing royalty in caves?"

He chuckled. "No. You're my first. I do my research. I knew I'd be sneaking you out at night, and I knew you had to get off Taura as quickly as possible, so I found a cave and arranged for a boat."

She panted with the effort of climbing. "The boat—those were water talents?"

"Yes. No more talking—just climb."

When they reached the top of the cliff, Connor hoisted himself up over the last hurdle in one fluid movement. He reached down to offer Mairead a hand up. As he pulled her up to level ground, she slipped. He steadied her with a hand on her arm. "You all right?"

"Yes." Her hands tightened on his forearms as she regained her balance. "The ground is slick."

He grunted an acknowledgement. "Keep moving. We have a long way to go before dusk."

The first hints of early autumn had descended along the shore. Mairead followed Connor's lead, trying to avoid trampling the dry leaves that littered the ground. A brisk breeze wafted through the few tendrils of hair that had escaped the leather strip, and once, she shivered and drew her cloak tighter about her. "The wind smells like autumn," she said.

"What does autumn smell like?"

"Apples and squash. Dry leaves. Rain."

He laughed.

"What's funny?"

"I think you'll be tired of smelling rain by the time this journey is done."

They walked in silence for some time. "Can I call you Connor?"

"Most people do."

"How did you come by this task?"

"Sayana Muriel asked the Brae Sidh queen to find someone who could escort you to a safe place. Queen Maeve chose me."

Then Muriel believed in the Sidh all along. Why would she lie to me? "Did she choose you for your magic?"

He scoffed. "No. I'm only half Sidh. I don't have much magic."

"But there was that palmlight."

"All Sidh can do that. It's just a trick."

"What about in the tunnel? I saw something."

He turned to her. "What did you see?"

"It looked like a braid of violet threads. And then I saw blue and green ones when we were in the boat."

He frowned. "You shouldn't be able to see the braids unless you have Sidh blood."

"There are stories that say Queen Brenna was part Sidh. Perhaps they are true."

"It would have to be very thin by now."

Mairead shifted her feet, nervous under his piercing stare. *Does he think he can see the Sidh blood if he looks hard enough?* "Why ask you to do this if you aren't strong in the Sidh magic?"

He started walking again. "I was trained by tribesmen and I'm good with a sword, and I know how to get through the Wilds of Culidar." He paused. "Muriel said certain things were kept from you."

Heat crept up her neck. *A naughty child caught in a lie—that's all I am.* "She tried, but I read a lot of books."

He snickered. "So my charge isn't as innocent as everyone thinks she is."

She focused on the trail ahead and adjusted the straps of the pack on her shoulders. "I'm descended from the line of Queen Brenna. I have a responsibility to be educated about my ancestry."

"But you thought the Brae Sidh were a myth."

"I know the stories, but I don't know what's true and what's not. I asked the sayana about the Sidh after I read the First Book of the Wisdomkeepers. She said they were a myth." She paused. "The kirok would have us believe that there is no magic in the world."

"It has always confused me how the kirok could refute the magic when Alshada is the one responsible for it."

"Do you believe in Alshada?"

He hesitated. "I believe he exists, but we parted ways several years ago.

And I don't believe in the kirok."

His tone suggested she should leave that line of questions aside. "Do you know why Sayana Muriel waited so long to send me away from Taura?"

"Two reasons. The first was Braedan. He was wilier than anyone thought. When Fergus banished him six years ago, everyone said it was because he was a drunken whoreson. It turns out he was slowly infiltrating his own father's ranks all this time with men loyal to him. It was only recently that someone loyal to the Sidh queen was able to get a message to her."

"And the second reason?"

"Me. I was delayed in reaching Taura. I was escorting a merchant train and didn't arrive until yesterday morning."

Mairead frowned. "Do you think Fergus knew I was there?"

Connor walked for several paces before he responded. "I don't know. Did the sayas ever talk to you about taking the throne?"

"Only in vague terms. They said I was the first person in a thousand years who met the requirements."

"Why keep you in Taura? Why not send you away years ago? You'd have been safer."

Mairead bit her lip. "I asked Sayana Muriel once. She said she wanted me to know the country I would lead. She wanted me to be Taurin in more than just blood." She shrugged. "Everyone believes the rightful line died out when Brenna and Aiden died. No one ever found their son. There was no reason to think I'd be in danger as long as the sayas kept the secret."

"But somehow, Braedan found out you were there."

Her stomach twisted. *All those women—dead or hurt or scattered because of me.* "Somehow," she whispered. *Did a saya betray me?*

The breeze picked up. Though the morning had dawned clear, dark clouds now obscured the channel and encroached along the coastline. Connor raised his face to the sky. "This is going to be an ugly storm. I guess you'll be walking in the rain."

"I don't mind." But when the torrent began, she pulled her cloak around her and wished for a warm cup of tea. The mud crept up their boots and the bottoms of their cloaks. Connor's stride was long and quick. The ground in the meadow quickly grew soft and muddy, and when she tried to keep up with him, she slipped and fell.

He held out his hand and helped her up. "Are you all right?"

Her hips hurt from the shock of the fall, and water seeped into her boots. Her toes and fingers ached with the damp cold. Her nose dripped, and she wiped it on her sleeve. "Fine. I'm fine."

His gaze softened. He pointed toward a copse of trees. "My feet are soaked. Let's dry off and wait for it to pass."

He slowed his stride so that she could keep up. The canopy of firs brought instant relief from the storm. Connor sat on a bed of dry needles under a fir tree. He pulled his boots and stockings off and wrung them out.

Mairead forced her boots off. "Not the best time of year to travel, is it?"

He spread his stockings out on the fir needles. "I don't mind it. I like being out of doors."

"Where are you taking me, anyway?"

"Sveklant."

She shuddered. "Sveklant? Why?"

"Apparently there are people waiting for you in a town called Albard."

"Do you know anything about them?"

"No."

So I'm to be shuffled off to some pagan land to live with people I don't know who could be enemies just as easily as friends. How will I know who to trust? She rubbed the feeling back into her feet. "Have you ever been to Sveklant?"

"A couple of times. It's not my favorite place."

"Because it's so pagan?"

He laughed. "No, because of all the snow. I'd rather be somewhere warm."

"But you said you don't get cold."

"I still prefer the sun." He leaned back against the tree. "How do you know Sveklant is so pagan if you've never been there?"

"Sayana Muriel always told us to pray for the kirok in Sveklant, that the kirons might build kiroks and win followers to Alshada. She said kirons have died for defying the old pagan gods."

"Perhaps you filled your reading with too much kirok history. Sveklant was one of the Western Lands once—Taura, Culidar, and Sveklant were one united kingdom before the breaking. When the Svek went to war with Taura centuries later, they sought only to reunite the kingdom."

"The Svek destroyed northern Taura," she answered. "The displaced northerners drained the south of food and resources. It took decades for the northern territories to recover and rebuild. Are you saying there is some kind of justification for that kind of destruction?"

"You sound like a kirok tutor," he said. "The Svek had a prophecy that a man would arise to reunite the Western Lands. They had a king who thought he had a divine right to conquer Taura and Culidar. The kirok supported him. Didn't your books cover that bit?"

She bristled. "The kirok can't be responsible for one man's prideful actions."

"No, but it is responsible for its own response to those actions. Don't worry, though—the Svek suffered, too. Their monarchy dissolved. There aren't even any nobles left in Sveklant—just farmers, traders, and hunters."

"Are there any who follow Alshada?"

"There are pockets—small kiroks, family groups, towns that worship him in ways similar to the kirok in Aliom. Some follow the old earth gods. Some say they are waiting for a champion to unite their land under a single standard once again."

She sighed.

"Afraid you're a little less prepared than you thought you'd be?"

Yes. "No. It's just a lot to think about."

"I won't leave you with anyone who will expect you to drink pig's blood." She laughed when she saw his grin. "You have a wicked side."

"I'll not deny that." He reached for his pack.

"Why take me so far away? Couldn't you take me somewhere closer?"

He laughed. "I asked the Sidh queen that same question. I tried to convince her to let me take you to Eirya, but she wouldn't. It seems you have to be at the edge of civilization to satisfy some obscure prophecy." He opened his pack and offered her some hard tack and jerky. "How much do you know about the magic and the prophecies about the rightful royal line?"

She nibbled on the hard tack. "I read the First Book of the Wisdomkeepers. I know the stories about how the Syraf Namha rebelled against Alshada and caused the rending of the Western Lands. I've read how the Sidh were split into two groups and how the Syrafi who followed Namha were cursed to be Ferimin. And I know about the Forbidden." She shuddered. Half Syrafi, half human, the Forbidden fed on human transgressions and devoured souls to strengthen themselves. The darker a person's soul, the more it strengthened the Forbidden. She took the skin of water he offered and drank. "The sayana said the stories were myths and legends of a pagan people."

Connor snorted a laugh and pointed at the scar on his chin. "I got this from one of those myths when I was escorting a train of livestock through Nar Sidhe territory. Nar Sidhe bastard attacked at night when he thought we were asleep."

Mairead shivered. "Then it's all true?"

"All of it."

"Even the Forbidden?"

A haunted look passed over Connor's face. "I don't know."

"But you believe the rest of it."

His mouth tightened. "I do." He took the waterskin from her and drank. "Do you know about the reliquary?"

"Yes. Some."

"Some? That could mean a lot of different things."

"I've read about the relics, and I overheard the sayas talk about it once." Mairead swallowed. "Is it as powerful as legends say?"

"In the wrong hands, it can channel powerful earth magic that would trigger earthquakes, volcanoes, tidal waves, and floods. In the hands of a benevolent god, it could heal the earth and wipe evil away for eternity." He paused. "Or at least, that's what legends say. Queen Brenna was the last rightful queen of Taura. You are, presumably, the only living person with her blood. You are a threat to the safety of the reliquary by your existence. Unless you are the one meant to carry it. Are you?"

"I don't think so." She remembered what she'd read years before. During the war, the Brae Sidh, Syrafi, and tribes fought the Nar Sidhe, Ferimin, and Forbidden. When the Sidh queen died, her people saved the stone from her crown, and when the Syrafi chieftain died, his people saved his tears in a jar. Cuhail, the tribal chieftain, died during the final battle. His own blood mingled with the earth of Taura on his sword. When the sword was recovered, it was placed in a box with the queen's stone and the Syrafi tears. The relics were rumored to be stored somewhere on Taura and protected by the Sidh. Only a human with the blood of the rightful ruling line could touch them. *Or so the stories say. This is so much to believe.* Mairead put her food aside. "You say it's safe?"

"For now. The Sidh queen keeps it hidden, and she would rather be flayed alive than give it to anyone but the one in the prophecies. But the Sidh village is only hidden as long as there is peace—or at least political stability—on Taura. With Braedan bringing chaos to the Taurin government and the Sidh and the tribes still at odds, the protections around the Sidh village weaken every day. If the village is visible and the Sidh are unprotected, anyone can find them and try to force Queen Maeve to reveal the reliquary."

"But someone would need me to carry it, you said. I would never do that."

"Are you sure?"

She couldn't answer.

"Be careful, saya. Namha is beguiling."

She drew her knees close to her chin. "I don't like this conversation."

"Too real?"

"Perhaps. Tell me about you. Did you grow up with the Brae Sidh?"

"I spent much of my childhood with the Sidh, but my father lived in the town of Kiern."

Mairead's stomach lurched. "Did you have family there when . . . when they came?"

Connor nodded. "My sisters and my father died that day."

"What have you done since then?"

He shrugged. "Hunted. Wandered. I've traveled through Culidar, through Sveklant, to Tal'Amun and the Aldorean Seas. I've escorted nobles or merchants who need a ready man-at-arms, and I've fought in a few battles."

"Your mother is Brae Sidh?"

"Yes. My parents knew each other for many years before my father's wife died. When my father was widowed, my parents confessed their affection for each other. I was the result." He paused and drank from his waterskin. "What about your parents? I know one of them must have been the Taurin heir."

She nodded. "I don't know which one, though. My father worked as a butcher in the town of Endar. My mother worked as a seamstress, but she died of a fever when I was four. My father left me at the sayada. He never visited me. I think he must have died."

"How do you know you're the Taurin heir?"

"I was anointed. Sayana Muriel took me to Macha Tor when I first came to the sayada. I have this vague memory of a man in white robes walking up the other side of the tor. He took some kind of oil from a bottle and rubbed it on my forehead." She smiled. "I remember it smelled sweet—like a flower."

Connor leaned back against the tree. "And the sayas taught you everything about the kirok, but nothing about magic? Did it ever occur to them to ask the Sidh or the tribes or someone else for help? Or to have the kirok give you an army and help you take back your throne?"

Mairead's spine stiffened. "The Order of Sai Atena is devoted to caring for the poor, not to building armies. Those women would never—"

He held up his hands. "Calm yourself, saya. I'm only asking. I don't care what happens to Taura—I don't live there, and I have no allegiance to the throne. It just seems to me that they raised a saya, not a queen. I'm curious what they thought you would do."

She bit her lip. "I think they only wanted me to marry and have children. I doubt they expected all of this to happen."

"And who would you have wed? Some farmer or merchant or shepherd?" He snickered. "What a fine royal bloodline that would be."

She turned away so he wouldn't see the heat rising in her face. "I think they had hoped to wed me to Braedan, at one point. I do remember being introduced to several noble sons. I think Muriel hoped one of them would take an interest in me and she could arrange a marriage and then tell him who I was."

"So your whole life revolves around having the right blood and passing it on," he said. "There was never any intention of putting you on the throne—no real intention, anyway."

She picked at a loose thread on her breeches. "No," she whispered. "I suppose not."

"You have no family left on Taura?"

"The sayas were my family." The pang of loss hit her again. Her eyes watered. "I suppose if the sayada is gone, I have no other family." Tears spilled over accompanied by hesitant sobs. "I'm sorry. I know I should be strong—it's my duty to be strong—but they were all I had."

Connor's voice softened. "You're not betraying your duty to grieve a great loss, saya. I know what it is to lose family." He pulled another kerchief from his pack and handed it to her.

She held the kerchief over her face. *I'm alone. I don't know what I'm doing. Everything I knew could be wrong, and all I'm prepared to do is care for the poor and become a wife and mother.* She curled into a ball against the tree and sobbed as the storm raged overhead.

CHAPTER SIX

In the days before the rending, human and Syrafi mated.
But their children had too much power,
so Alshada banished them from the world of men.
They are the Forbidden.
When they rise again, they will deliver us to our glory.
— Nar Sidhe legend

When the sun broke through the clouds, Connor reached for his boots. "We should keep going." *The sooner I get you to Sveklant, the sooner I can be rid of this binding.*

Mairead wiped puffy eyes and gave him a wan smile. She choked out a rueful laugh. "I fear I'm using all of your clean kerchiefs."

He put the kerchief in a pocket. "They can all be washed. Feel better?"

She nodded. "It's just hard."

His heart softened as he realized how much he'd expected of her. *She can't be more than twenty. Raised in a sayada, eating easy foods, only the exercise of caring for her sayas and the poor, and now, everything she had taken from her, sent with a stranger on a journey across foreign lands. It's amazing she hasn't been sobbing this entire time.* He looked toward the northeast. *Damn it. I wanted to go around.* But when he saw the saya's rain-soaked clothing and pale, tear-streaked face, his resolve melted. "There's a village up ahead where I used to know some people. If they're still there, we can spend the night with them and get some supplies."

She sniffed. "Are you sure? We don't have to stop. I can keep going."

The weariness in her voice suggested otherwise. "We need horses, anyway. May as well get them now."

They put on their boots and packs and started walking. Other than an occasional sniffle, Mairead made little noise as they walked. He tried to slow his gait to allow her to keep up. *She's not prepared for this journey at all.*

Mairead's pace started to slow in the afternoon, and he turned to her. "Hungry?" he asked.

"Yes. How did you know?"

"You're slowing down." He sniffed the air. "There's an apple tree just over there."

The tree's branches sagged with ripening fruit. Connor picked an apple and gave it to her. "It's not much, but it will help you get to the village."

"Thank you." She bit into it. "Mmm . . . So crisp and sweet."

He grinned. "Didn't you have apples at the sayada?"

"Not this kind, and not from our own tree."

"I'll pick a few more for you. For later."

Her eyes brightened. "Would you?"

He picked several apples and put them in his pack. "They'll weigh my pack down."

"I'll carry them." She held out her hand.

"No. They'll just slow you down."

"You picked them for me. I'll carry them."

He gave her his pack.

She moved the apples and smiled when she put the pack over her shoulders. "Which way?"

They approached a small village as shadows started to deepen with the setting sun. Connor stopped and stared at the rundown buildings along the main street. His chest tightened. In a tree to the side of the road, a raven croaked.

"A bad omen?" Mairead pointed at the raven.

Connor flinched. The raven cocked its head and stared at him. Three more landed to share the gnarled branch with the first. "I don't believe in omens." He turned to Mairead. Her hair had begun to fall out of its hasty tie, her boots and the bottom of her cloak were wet and muddy, and her eyes were still rimmed with red. "Stay close to me. I'm not sure what this place is like these days."

"How long has it been since—"

"Eight years." He grimaced at the tension in his voice and hoped she didn't hear it.

They entered the village, and Connor put a hand on the small of Mairead's back to keep her close. She tensed, but she didn't pull away. Raucous laughter floated out of a tavern, and the streets were sodden, muddy, and strewn with garbage. Connor leaned closer to Mairead. "Keep your hood up." She pulled her hood further over her head, hiding her face in the shadow.

The tavern door burst open ahead of them, and two men tumbled into the street. Connor put his hand on his sword, and Mairead gasped. "It's just a bar fight. We'll go around," he said.

"Just a minute." She walked to an alley at the side of the tavern and crouched in front of a sick, thin woman huddled in the shadows. The woman wore a threadbare dress, and her unclad feet were covered in the street filth.

Connor stepped after her. "Saya—"

"I said just a minute." She opened her pack and removed the wool dress she'd worn from the sayada. She gave it to the woman. "There are shoes wrapped inside the dress. I hope they fit you."

The woman lifted weary eyes to Mairead's face. "Ye'd do that?"

"I have no need of these. Please take them." She held out the dress and shoes and gave the woman the apples Connor had picked.

"Alshada bless ye, lady."

"And you, lady." Mairead stood and hoisted her pack on her back again. She avoided Connor's eyes. "What were you saying?"

He put his hand on her elbow and pulled her away from the woman. She flinched, and he loosened his grip. He directed her around the fighting men and down the main street. "What was that?" he asked.

"What?"

"You gave away a dress and shoes you might need and apples I just picked for you."

"You made it quite clear that a woolen dress and sturdy shoes weren't appropriate travel attire. And I'm sure Alshada has planted more than one apple tree in Culidar."

He clenched his jaw to hold back a curse. "Could you at least ask me before you do that sort of thing? What if there had been a man with her who wanted to rob us?"

She twisted her mouth in a thoughtful expression. "I'll consider that next time."

At the far end of the main street, a well-kept cottage surrounded by a sturdy fence stood out from the rundown village. A path of rough-hewn stones paved the way to a heavy oak door. Candles burned in the windows, and Connor smelled roasting pig. *Nice to know some things never change.* They walked to the gate, and he stopped. He put his hand on the latch and hesitated. *Will they even let me in?*

Mairead waited. "What is it?"

"Nothing." He opened the latch, walked to the front door, and knocked.

Memories tumbled out of the house as a plump woman with upswept gray hair answered the door. Her face broke into a wide grin. "Connor Reid. I dinna think I'd ever see ye back this way again." She threw her arms around his neck and kissed his cheek.

She's exactly the same. "Hello, Aileen." He returned the embrace and kissed her cheek. "We were wondering if you could put us up for the night."

"O' course, lad." She put an arm around Mairead and led her into the house. "'Tis a fair long season since we've seen ye this way, Connor. Do ye tell me ye've finally married?"

He shifted his feet and cleared his throat. "No. This is Mairead. I'm just escorting her north."

"Ach, 'tis a shame." She took Mairead's cloak and pack. "Ne'er mind. There's room enough for both o' ye. Call me Aileen, lady. My husband, Donal, will be here for supper soon."

Mairead offered a quick curtsy. "It's a pleasure, Aileen. Please, call me Mairead."

Connor pointed at the door. "I'm going out to find some supplies and horses. I'll be back soon."

Aileen took his pack with gentle force. "Nonsense. Ye'll sit and eat with us first. There'll be time for all o' that later."

Months of living under Aileen Mac Rae's roof had taught Connor not to cross her, and the warmth of her welcome brought a hesitant smile. "You haven't changed."

She slapped him on the shoulder. "Telling me ye'll be going out in the village. Foolish. 'Tis nearly supper. I'd not be a Mac Rae if I turned away a traveler in need."

"I'd understand if you—"

"Ye foolish boy," she said, her voice tinged with a soft laugh. She put a hand on his forearm. "Ye've always been welcome here, Connor. Always." She squeezed his arm and let out a deep breath. "Come, dear," she said, turning to Mairead. "Ye need a good freshening up. Let me show ye to a room. The great ogre can carry your pack."

Mairead stood with arms folded and head tipped to one side, her eyes narrowed in confusion at the brief exchange. Connor shifted his feet. "Thank you," Mairead said, turning to Aileen. "I am a bit wet and cold."

"O' course ye are. Traveling at this time of year? It must be a great need."

She led Mairead and Connor to a quiet room appointed with a large feather mattress and a ewer and bowl on a small stand. Scented water was in the ewer, and linen towels lay in a tidy pile next to the bowl. Fresh rushes were scattered on the floor. Rough-knit woolen blankets in bright dyes covered the feather mattress, and tapestries warmed the room with rich color.

Aileen bustled around the room lighting candles. "'Tisn't much, but 'tis warm and safe. I keep it ready for travelers. Ye never know when some poor soul will need a room." She pointed to the door. "Connor, ye can take the room down the hall."

"No, I'll stay here. I'll sleep on the floor," he said when Mairead's face turned red and Aileen gave him a stern look. "I'm charged with her protection, Aileen. I can't leave."

"She's safe here, lad. Ye'll sleep in the other room."

"Aileen—"

"No, there's naught for it. Ye'll do as I say or ye'll sleep in the barn."

You're not exactly in a position to argue about something like this with Aileen, he reminded himself. He nodded. "I suppose the room down the hall is closer than the barn. Very well."

Aileen nodded and turned to Mairead, who was studying one of the tapestries. "My daughter made it," Aileen said. "She's a weaver in the north. All o' my children have grown and gone. 'Tis a blessing to have raised them, but they've all moved away. I miss them and my grandchildren."

"I would think you would move to be closer to them, Aileen," Mairead said.

Aileen laughed. "Nae. This is my home. 'Tis enough that they visit their old ma and da every now and then." She wiped her hands on her skirts. "Freshen yourselves up, now. Supper's almost ready. I'll call ye when 'tis time."

Connor found the room he'd shared with Aileen's sons and washed his hands and face. When he was done, he wandered back through the small house, running his hand along familiar walls and doors as memories filled his head. He stopped at the door to her room. *Aine's room.* He closed his eyes. *What kind of mercy is this that these people would welcome me again?* He put his hand on the latch, tempted to open the door, but he couldn't. The memory of the anger, pain, fear, and still—*still*—love in her eyes the last time he'd seen her hovered in that corridor. *I didn't mean to hurt you.* He leaned his forehead against the door.

The Morrag tightened his chest. *Remember.*

You don't let me forget. When will I stop hearing the screams of dying men? Or Aine's sobs?

She didn't answer.

He found Aileen putting the finishing touches on her lavish meal. Fresh bread sat on the long table, and a large haunch of pig rested on a platter, waiting to be carved. A separate platter held roasted red beets, and somewhere, Connor smelled something with pears. Fresh carrots, sliced cheese, preserved meats and jellies—Aileen had left nothing out.

She handed him a knife. "Ye look much more presentable. Carve the pig, will ye?"

He reached for a piece of bread. "Even when I'm a guest you expect me to work for my supper?"

She slapped his hand away from the bread and pointed at the roast. "Ye'll work and be glad o' the meal."

He took the knife and laughed. "I can't argue with that."

A door closed in the back of the house. "Aileen! It's not Faltian, woman—why're ye cooking such a feast?"

Donal's voice rang through the house with the same booming echo Connor remembered. Connor's hand faltered, and he cut a much smaller slice of roast than he intended. *A girl's mother is one thing, but her father?* He straightened and turned, preparing to run back to his room, gather his things, and leave in the dark if he had to.

Aileen called back. "We've company, ye great ogre. Alshada must have known they were coming when he prompted me to prepare a feast."

Donal entered the room, ducking to avoid hitting his head. His eyes widened, but his mouth broke into a wide grin inside his full gray beard. "Connor."

Connor swallowed the nervous lump in his throat and inclined his head. "Donal. It's good to—"

But Donal cut off his words with a massive bear hug. "'Tis been too long, lad."

Connor tolerated the hug, but when Donal let go of him, he clasped Donal's arm in greeting. "It has. Thank you for taking us in tonight."

"Seems a right fair season since we've seen ye. Where ye been, lad?"

"Freelancing. Spent some time in Espara. I haven't been this way in a few years." He scrubbed a hand through his hair, the carving forgotten. *Ask before the saya shows up.* "How are you both? How is Aine?"

Donal put one hand on Connor's shoulder. "Aine is well. Just had her third bairn, and living on a pretty farm north of the Wilds. We took her and the babe north after ye left. She married a good man. Took in the first bairn as if she were his own. Loves them all the same."

"She had a girl?"

"Aye. A lovely lass who looks just like her ma. And now she has two boys, too."

A girl. "I'm happy for her."

Donal leaned to kiss his wife on the cheek. "I'll wash up, love."

Connor turned toward hesitant footsteps in the corridor, and Mairead stepped into the doorway. Her freshly brushed hair shimmered in the candlelight, heavy, honey-colored waves that cascaded almost to her waist. Her green eyes sparkled, and even the rough woolen breeches and linen tunic Connor had given her could not diminish her fair-skinned beauty. *This job would be a lot easier if she weren't so damn pretty.* For a moment, he forgot he stood where he'd thought the same thing of Aine once.

Aileen bustled over to put an arm around Mairead's shoulders and guide her into the room. "Ye look to be feeling better, lass. Come—sit."

Mairead smiled. "I'd be happy to help with something."

"Nonsense." She pushed Mairead into a seat at the table.

Connor leaned down to Mairead's ear. "You won't win against her," he said.

She laughed, a soft, breathy sound. "They're lovely people," she whispered.

"They are." He returned to carving the roast.

By the time he'd finished, Donal had returned. He carried a small cask and put it down in the center of the table. "Oiska. Can I tempt ye, lad?"

Connor held out his cup. "I've never turned down oiska, especially yours."

Donal poured for himself, Connor, and Aileen. "And lady? Care for a bit?" he asked Mairead. "Although I must say, ye don't look like ye've had more than a sip or two in your life."

She held up her cup. "I'd love some." Donal poured, and Mairead sniffed it. "What is it?"

"Ah, 'tis the water of life, lass!" Donal lifted his cup. "A tribal toast—may the earth's wings shield you on your journey!"

Connor hesitated. *I'd rather not have anything to do with the earth's wings.* "What about an Eiryan sailing toast? To fair winds and calm seas."

Donal's eyes twinkled. "'Tis all one as long as we drink."

Connor laughed. "Indeed." They all lifted their cups and drank. Connor, Donal, and Aileen watched with mild amusement as Mairead coughed and sputtered through her shot.

Aileen poured Mairead some water. "Here. Drink. Don't let these great ogres talk ye into more. 'Tis not for everyone. Oiska bites back."

Mairead, her face red and her eyes watering, caught her breath and drank her water. "Strong. Water of life, you say?"

Connor smirked. "You've never tried it?"

She shook her head and drank more water. Her voice rasped when she spoke. "I was never allowed. It was a sin." She bit her lip.

Donal chuckled. "Aye, some say 'tis a sin. But 'tis also said Alshada serves it at his own table."

"Perhaps in the great golden city, I will be made of stouter stuff," Mairead said.

Donal laughed and offered another round. Mairead declined with a polite shake of her head, but Connor held out his cup for more. "That's a good batch—one of the finest I've ever had. You haven't lost your knack for it."

Donal grinned and pointed to the cask. "Been aging for more'n three years."

As the evening passed, Aileen's good food, Donal's oiska, and the pleasant conversation conjured memories of evenings Connor spent with the Mac Rae family. *Has it been eight years? How did I let so much time go by? How can they still welcome me?*

When he'd eaten his fill, Connor downed a final cup of oiska and stood. "Aileen, thank you for this feast, but I must go into the town and find some horses and supplies."

Donal motioned him to his seat as he tamped down a pipe. He fished around in the pockets of his jerkin and pulled out a second pipe, offering it to Connor. "Sit, lad, sit. What's an evening feast without a pipe to finish it off?"

"You'll have me here all night with a pipe and oiska. I need to get supplies. We'll leave at dawn."

"In that case, let us provide what ye need," Aileen said. "We have much, and we're happy to share it."

Connor hesitated. "I need horses. Do you have some you can sell me?"

Donal took a long draw off his pipe. He blew out the smoke. "'Tis funny—just today, not a league away, I noticed two sturdy beasts grazing in the old Kinnon pasture," he said to Aileen.

"The one up on the north fork of the stream?"

"That's the one. Let me walk right up to them, they did. Looked all over them for a brand, but they have nothing to say where they came from. Seems to me they may be Alshada's gift to ye, Connor. They're tied up outside right now, if ye care to look 'em over."

Strange. "How much would you want for them?"

Donal rose, pipe still in his mouth, and waved off the question. "Ach, lad, they're found blessings. Ye can have 'em. 'Twill save me the trouble of feeding them. Come, I'll show ye."

Connor followed Donal out the back of the house. The moon and the light from the house illuminated Donal's well-kept animal pens and outbuildings. Several sheep bleated in surprise. "Hush—'tis only me." They quieted. Donal led Connor around the back of the pen and pointed to two horses eating from a small feedbox. "There. One stallion, one mare. They have the look o' being cared for, but no markings. I'd return them to their owner, but I don't recognize them. In perfect health, both of 'em—ye could do no better."

Connor ran his hands over both horses' necks. The proud sorrel stallion tossed his head and whickered, but the palomino mare nudged him for more attention. "What about tack? Do you have saddles, bits, bridles? I can buy them from you."

"Ye're welcome to any tack. We'll have no need of it."

"I'd love to take them, but I must leave you some money for them." Connor held up a hand to Donal's protest. "I'll leave you a generous price. Just hold onto it. If the owner comes for them, you can give it to him."

Donal thought it over and nodded. "'Tis fair."

A commotion rose from the distant streets, and in the midst of the shouting, Connor heard a quickly muffled scream. He put his hand on his sword, but Donal gestured and sighed. "Nae, lad, 'twill do no good. Ye'll only get yourself killed."

Connor kept his hand on his sword. "This place has changed. Where did all the farmers go? The elders?"

"The families ye remember moved on. There was an attack after ye left. Slavers." He paused. "I was glad our kin had moved on. They took the young ones, the strong ones, and left us old folk alone." He brushed his eyes. "'Tis ugly, this slave trade. Now the town is just a stop for venom runners and slavers."

Connor put his hand on the older man's arm. "You need to move on, Donal."

Donal shook off his melancholy. "Nae, lad. We can serve Alshada better here." He pulled the spare pipe from his pocket. "Will ye enjoy a pipe with me? 'Tis been a long time since we shared a pipe."

"I will. And a cup or two more of that fine drink?"

Donal laughed. "What would a pipe be without it?"

Donal retrieved the oiska and their cups from the house while Connor waited on the back steps. When Donal emerged from the house again, he was chuckling. "My sweet wife. She's got your lady sitting by the fire with a cup o' tea, chattering on about children and grandchildren and what have ye." He handed Connor a cup and poured them each a generous shot of oiska.

They sat down on the steps, and Donal lit Connor's pipe. "She's not my lady," Connor said. "I'm just taking her north."

Donal took a long drag off his pipe and gave a slight grunt as he blew the smoke out. "Ye still canna settle down, eh?"

"I don't think settling down is for me." He stared into the distance, unable to look at the older man. "Donal, I regret . . . I wish things had ended better with Aine."

Donal was quiet for a long time. "Aine loved ye, but 'twas a childish love. She is well. Settled. Happy. She holds ye no ill will, Connor."

Connor scoffed. "She should."

"Nae, lad. She made her own choices." He gestured back toward the house. "'Tis none of my business, but the lass, Mairead—she has a spark. And ye could do worse. She's a beauty."

"It's just a job, Donal."

"Are they all just jobs to ye, then?"

Connor couldn't answer.

"'Tis a lonely way, lad. Ye canna tell me ye're happy."

Connor stared out past the pens to the distant fields. He drew on his pipe. The sweet flavor of the tabak lingered in his mouth when he exhaled. He drank another shot of oiska and considered what to say. "I'm happy as I can expect. I'm well-paid. Beautiful women pursue me. What more could I want?"

"'Tis a lonely way. Ye're not meant to be a farmer, that's certain. But lad, do ye not want a woman to love ye? A home?" Donal sighed. "Course, hard for me to judge, I suppose. Aileen and me, we grew up together in this village, married, ne'er left. Raised five children. Ne'er needed to go anywhere else."

"How long have you been married?"

"Near to forty years. It seems but a moment ago that I asked her." He smiled at Connor and poured him another shot. "I loved her from the moment I saw her. Took me a while to figure it out, though. She was a beauty, but 'twas more than that. She had something else—a spark, a fire, life, call it what ye will. She's kept me honest. I ne'er wanted another woman since I first saw her."

Connor finished his pipe and stood. "I must get to bed. We need to leave at dawn. I thank you for your kindness, Donal. You've been a great blessing to us."

Donal stood and clapped him on the back. "We still owe ye much, lad. If it weren't for ye—well, we wouldn't have our Aine, would we?"

"You give me too much credit. If it weren't for me, Aine—"

Donal's hand tightened on Connor's shoulder. "Aine made her choices. She ran after ye because she loved ye, but ye dinna force her to do it. Ye saved her, lad."

Connor couldn't speak. He clapped Donal on the shoulder and walked away before his emotions betrayed him.

Connor lay awake for some time that night, hands behind his head, eyes toward the ceiling. He heard Aileen tidying her house as Donal spoke in his low, easy voice. The sweet odors of pear pudding and pipe hung in the air. *This place—if I believed in spirits, I would believe they were here in these walls.* He closed his eyes and remembered days of hard work and nights of ease at Aileen's hearth with Aine and her brothers and sisters. If he concentrated, he could almost hear Aine laughing.

Emrys stood in the shadows of the brothel and stared at the empty field in front of him. A flash of light behind him alerted him to her presence. He didn't turn. "Mistress."

Her low voice tickled his ear. "Have you found the heir?"

"I've tracked her from Taura. I feel her presence, but I cannot reach her." He turned.

Her dark eyes glittered like cold onyx in the moonlight. "The Syrafi protect them here. The raven has a strong connection to this village." She stared at the field with him. "Wait until they leave the Syrafi. When they are on their own, you must separate them. Then you can capture the woman."

"How do you suggest I separate them? He is fanatical about finishing the jobs he takes."

She turned to him and put one hand on his cheek. "You have ever been beguiling, Emrys. You will think of something."

He folded his arms. "What are you doing while I'm here?"

"I am repairing your mistake in Taura. The princess is still in the castle. I will see that she dies and create the chaos I need to reveal the Brae Sidh village."

"How?"

The cold eyes narrowed. "You need only worry about the heir. I will be ready to use her when you bring her to me." She nodded toward the brothel. "Go feed yourself. You will need your strength."

Emrys snatched her wrist. "How do you do it? How do you stay on Taura, inside the wards?"

A twisted smile crossed the elegant, noble features of her dark face. "I do not share your qualms about using our power." The elements around them separated to reveal dark spaces, and she slipped into one of the gaps. Another flash lit the darkness when the elements joined again.

Emrys stood alone, staring out at the field, until a woman wearing little but thin undergarments approached him. She slid one arm around his shoulders. He pushed her away. She gestured toward the field. "Nothin' out there, love."

He turned to her. "Has there ever been a house there?"

She shuddered when her eyes met his. "Once. Folks moved on years ago. Took a daughter and left. Rest of the family followed."

"What happened to the house?"

"Burned. Faltian fires got outta hand a few years ago." She tugged on his cloak. "Come, love. Ye canna be out here all night."

His mistress was right. He needed strength. Panic flickered across the woman's face when he grasped her wrist. He forced her to the dark corner of the alley and pushed her against the wall. One hand held her still as he pressed the other over her heart. Terror rose in her eyes. By the time he had drawn the sweetness of her soul into himself, her limp body hung in his hand. He let her go and walked away, strengthened by the darkness of her many transgressions.

CHAPTER SEVEN

Beside the great waters will my people find peace.
By the sea will they find sanctuary.
— *Songs of King Aiden, Book 8, Verse 10, Year of Creation 4993*

Minerva reined in at the edge of the great forest. Night still blanketed the road, and she was grateful for the faint moonlight shining through the fog. *Their eyes are already on me.* Her palm burned with the proximity to so many warriors. She pulled her hood up further over her head. *Alshada, forgive me. I must warn them. I promised Muriel.*

She'd passed a tense and cold three nights since leaving the sayada in Torlach. Shelter was hard to find for a woman with meager coin, and she feared revealing her identity, so she slept in farmers' fields and sheltered groves between the city and the great forest. She traveled far away from the main roads. *If it weren't for Braedan, I could go to a village with a kirok. They'd feed and shelter me.* But the days of kirok sanctuary were waning. Braedan had plans for Taura, and Minerva suspected they didn't include the work of kirons and sayas.

She stared at the trees, her heart racing with fear. *Stay calm. The mark buys you passage.* She opened her hand and stared down at the faint glow under the brand on her palm. Memories returned in a rush—a husband's smile, a father's anger, a sister's tears. She squeezed her hand and her eyes shut. *This isn't about returning to the tribes. This is about warning them. I'm just warning them.* She clenched her jaw. *And if he kills me, I'll die in service to Alshada.* She spurred her horse forward.

Warriors dressed in woolen kaltans or leather breeches met her at the boundary. To a man, they displayed multiple hunting tattoos on bare, muscular arms. Two great wolfhounds sat nearby, unconcerned, tongues lolling in long pink curls against shaggy gray coats. *Hound tribe.* She held up her hand, revealing the circled cross to the warriors. "I have business with the hound tribe."

They looked at her palm, and one clenched and unclenched his fist. He thumped the butt end of a spear into the ground. "You are a guardian?"

The words wanted to catch in her throat, but she forced them free. "I am. I bring news from Torlach."

The man snorted. His hand twitched on his spear. Another man took a bow from his shoulder. "News from Torlach does not concern the people."

"This news does. Your chieftain will want to hear."

He narrowed his eyes. "What tribe are you, guardian?"

A lump formed in her throat. She swallowed and coughed. "Salmon," she said. "Or I was, many years ago."

He frowned, surveying her silently for several moments. Finally, he nodded once and stepped aside. "The village is straight ahead."

She inclined her head once and rode forward.

Autumn gray clung to the tops of pines and firs in the thick southern forest. Minerva smiled. *So much like the day I first came here.* That first winter with the people, eating and sleeping and training with the other guardian initiates, returned in a rush. *They're all guardians by now, perhaps mothers and wives, doing their rituals and raising babes.* The pain of grief struck again, but this time, it wasn't just for her husband. That time with the other initiates was the first time Minerva felt like she belonged somewhere—that she had something to offer, that people wanted her to be part of their lives.

She thought of the first time she danced the rites after a hunt and remembered her warrior's brown eyes on her. She drew him into the circle with her, emboldened by the heat of the fires and the swirling magic of the lifespirit around them. "I'm only an initiate," she whispered when he spun her close.

His breath warmed her neck, and she shivered. "You are strong in the wisdom. I sense it."

She closed her eyes and let her body flow in time to the music. "They call me Esma."

"Esma," he whispered. He put his mouth on her neck and nipped at her. "Esma. I could whisper that for hours."

Minerva shook away the memories. *Forgive me, One—Alshada. Being here—I want to fall into the tribal ways. Forgive me. You are Alshada, not the One Hand.*

She came to the edge of the village as the sun crested the horizon in the distance. Village sounds drifted to her—women stirring cook fires and soothing babes in the huts, goats bleating for food and milking, warriors returning home after night watches. Most wore leather breeches or dark woolen kaltans over their legs and wool tunics and furs over their arms and torsos.

A hound bayed, and Minerva startled. A burly, graying tribesman wearing only breeches stepped out of the fog to meet Minerva at the edge of the village. He hushed his gray wolfhound, patted the dog's massive head, and pointed at his foot. The dog wagged his tail and lowered his head, and the rest of the village dogs quieted.

She lifted her chin and took a deep breath. *Hrogarth.* The snaking brand across his face gave him away, but if it hadn't, she would have remembered the fierce, chiseled features and intense stare. *Careful. Don't let him know who you are.* "Traitha Hrogarth. I am Saya Minerva. I bring news from Torlach."

He crossed his arms over his chest. "News from Torlach doesn't concern the tribes."

"Grant me a moment, I beg you."

"A moment."

"Fergus has died. Braedan has claimed the throne for himself. He has stormed the sayada and taken most of the sayas prisoner, including Sayana Muriel. He will come after the tribes next."

Hrogarth grunted. "I saw the dark moon. I knew Fergus' time had come. But the unbeliever will not come after the tribes. He is bound by ancient treaty to stay out of the great forest."

"Braedan isn't afraid to break faith, and he will drive his men to seek you." She paused. "He seeks the Sidh."

His eyebrows raised a fraction, the only concession to surprise. "He shouldn't know about them. No regent has ever known unless the Sidh queen allows it. How do you know this?"

"The Sidh queen told Sayana Muriel. She believes he is seeking Cuhail's reliquary."

"Can one spoiled brat destroy enchantments two thousand years old?"

"The enchantments are fading—they've been fading for decades. Queen Maeve told Sayana Muriel that the protections around the Sidh village have been weakening ever since the tribes and the Sidh rejected each other. Braedan has been asking questions about the Sidh since he returned. He will come to the tribes seeking them."

"It's a fool's quest. The unbeliever is human. He cannot use the reliquary. And since he does not carry Brenna's blood, he cannot be the rightful deliverer, either."

Stubborn man! "It doesn't matter what is true." Her voice rose. "Whether he believes he can use it or not, he still seeks it. He still threatens the safety of the Sidh and the tribes. Traitha, please—you must go to Queen Maeve. You must offer your protection once more."

Hrogarth spat. "I'll not crawl to offer my protection when they rejected it. Let them have their magic and their gold."

Despair twisted Minerva's stomach. "But they have nothing. They have no way to defend themselves should Braedan reveal their village. They need tribal swords and spears. You cannot reject—"

"I reject nothing. The Sidh reject it. They told us their magic could protect the artifacts. Let them depend on the elements."

"Hrogarth, the time of chaos is coming. Braedan listens to evil counselors. They push him to find the relics. If he unleashes the full power of the earth, this feud will be nothing but a petty spat that will destroy you. Namha will be loosed, and the Forbidden will rule all."

Hrogarth's mouth flickered into a frown. His eyes narrowed, and he took three steps toward her. Minerva flinched. "No," he said. "I swore when I was a child—I will not bend my knee. I will not return what they rejected."

Her voice wavered. "Please, traitha."

"You bought passage with the wisdommark. I will be merciful now, but if you ever return, Esma, you will die. I will not abide an oathbreaker in my village."

She lifted her chin and straightened in the saddle. "The blood of the Brae Sidh will be on your head."

"That may be. But I will face the gods or the earth for that, not some oathbreaker playing at being prophetess."

Tears stung her eyes, but she blinked them back and swallowed. *Salt and vinegar—my sister was right. I'm only salt and vinegar.* She drew up the reins of her horse and started to turn, but her eyes fell on a woman in the distance.

Alfrig.

Alfrig approached wrapped in furs, her thick, dark hair awry, and stopped a dozen paces behind Hrogarth. Her eyes narrowed, then widened in recognition. Her mouth trembled. Her foot started toward Minerva and stopped.

A swell of emotion rose in Minerva's chest, and she struggled to keep her composure. Alfrig, chief priestess over the nine tribes, wife to Hrogarth, heir apparent to the wisdomkeeper in the far north. *And once my friend, and the only mother I knew, for a time.* Her palm burned. The words formed on her tongue. *Great Mother, hear our laughter. Great Mother, hear our sorrow. Great Mother, hear our pleas.* She opened her mouth, but her eyes fell on Hrogarth's face again, and she snapped her lips shut.

Alfrig gave a small shake of her head. She turned her hand out just enough for Minerva to see the faint glow of her own wisdommark. *We are still sisters,* the gesture told Minerva. *We are still joined by ritual and blood, and I will not betray you. But he is my husband, and you broke your vows. Go, now, while he is merciful.*

Minerva wheeled her horse around before she could change her mind. Alfrig's eyes stayed on her back, and as she rode away, the traitha and the guardian spoke in low, heated tones.

She rode out of the hound tribe's territory, away from most tribal eyes except the few sentries who lined the road. When she was as alone as she could be, she dismounted, knelt at the foot of a massive fir tree, and started to shake and sob in relief, despair, and sorrow all at once.

Great Mother, hear our sorrow.

She wiped her nose on her sleeve and shook her head. "No," she said. "No. I don't pray to the earthspirit anymore. I don't speak to the wisdomkeeper. I am a servant of the One—of Alshada."

She opened her hand. The crossed circle still glowed, even some distance away from the warriors. Minerva scrambled to her horse and rummaged through her pack in desperation until she found her gloves. She pulled them on and let out a long breath. *I can't keep it from flaring, but I can keep anyone from seeing it.*

A snap behind her startled her, and she whirled. The hound warrior who had first greeted her stepped out of the trees. "I meant for you to hear me," he said. He tipped his spear at her. "I gave you time to draw."

Minerva backed up against the horse. "Hrogarth let me go."

"He did not give you permission to remain in the forest."

"Please," Minerva whispered. "I need to stay. I need to find the Sidh."

"The Sidh?" Amber eyes narrowed. He worked his mouth as if chewing words. The lines of his face softened. "Find the wolf tribe. North—near Kiern. Their traitha is sympathetic to the Sidh. You may get help from them."

She inclined her head. "I thank you."

He grunted. "Not all of us believe as Hrogarth does," he said, and he disappeared into the trees.

Minerva let out a long breath and leaned against her horse. The mare whickered and twisted her head to nudge Minerva. When Minerva could trust her legs again, she mounted. "We ride north," she said.

CHAPTER EIGHT

The earth itself marked Brenna as its own.
It gave her the ravenmark and called her to its service.
— Second Book of the Wisdomkeepers,
Year of Creation 5037 (approximate)

There was a comforting continuity to the farm life Donal and Aileen had carved for themselves, Connor thought. *Slavers may threaten, but goats still need milking, pigs need slopping, and fences need mending.* Connor watched the quiet bustle around him in the predawn light as he packed the horses and waited for Mairead. It soothed him to think that the Mac Raes still woke before dawn to repeat their routines.

Aileen joined him. She held out a warm, wrapped package. "Some pasties for your journey. The lady is up and dressing."

Connor took the pasties. "I don't know how I can thank you for your many kindnesses." He opened his purse and pulled out several coins. "These are for the owner of the horses if he comes for them. What can I give you and Donal?"

Aileen smiled. "Well, it wouldn't be hospitality if we expected payment, would it?" She put the coins in her apron pocket and pushed his hand away when he offered more. "Put it away, lad. We're blessed to help ye. We still owe ye for what ye did for us."

"It was my fault she ran away. It was my responsibility to bring her back."

"Well, we're grateful."

He thought he should send some message to Aine. "Tell Aine I'm glad she's happy. I wish her the best. She deserves it."

Aileen put a hand on his arm. "I will."

Memories tugged at his composure. "We were so young. She deserved—deserves—better than I could have given her."

"Still singing that song, are ye? We'd have had ye for a son and been glad of it." Aileen lowered her voice. "Ye might want to reconsider your views of marriage, Connor. 'Tis a good journey. 'Tis good to have a friend to journey with. My Donal, I wouldn't trade the great ogre for anything."

"You know I'm too wild for marriage."

"Ye just haven't found the right woman."

Mairead came out of the house dressed in breeches, tunic, and cloak, her hair braided and drawn over one shoulder. She gave Aileen a warm embrace. "Dear lady, thank you so much for your great hospitality. I hope we meet again one day."

Aileen laughed and returned the embrace. "Ach, o' course we will—in the great golden city if nowhere else."

Donal joined them just as Mairead met her horse for the first time. He chuckled. "You're a bit pale, lass."

Mairead stared at the palomino with wide eyes. "She's so big."

"Have ye never ridden a horse afore?"

Mairead shook her head. "I lived in the city. We walked everywhere. I've ridden in a wagon a few times, but I've never ridden a horse."

He patted the horse's withers. "'Tis easy. This is a gentle lass. She'll be easy to ride."

The mare whickered and nosed Mairead's hand. Mairead patted her nose, and the horse begged for more.

Connor grabbed a handful of grass and handed it to Mairead. "Here. Hold it out to her."

Mairead took the grass. "How do I—"

"Just hold it under her nose."

Mairead's hand moved slowly toward the mare's nose. The palomino sniffed and nibbled up the grass with her lips. Mairead startled, but she didn't step back. The horse chewed the grass while Mairead patted her nose, neck, and withers.

Donal put an arm around Mairead and squeezed her shoulders. "Lass, ye remind me of my own daughters. Take care o' the mare, and she'll take care o' you."

Mairead turned and stretched up to kiss Donal's cheek. "Thank you for everything."

Donal patted her back and then turned to Connor. He clasped Connor's arm. "And ye—take care o' the lady." His voice dropped. "I've put a special skin in your pack. Use it wisely, lad—'tis some of my best."

Connor grinned. "I will."

Mairead stared at the saddle, her forehead drawn into lines.

"Left foot in the stirrup, lift up, swing over," Connor said.

She didn't move. He stepped toward her to help, but she pushed him away. "I can do it." She put her hands on the saddle and left foot in the stirrup, but only managed to hop halfway up to the saddle. She tried again, managing to straighten her leg before she stumbled back to the ground.

Connor steadied her with one hand on her back. He laughed. "Careful."

"Don't laugh at me."

"I'm not—I swear. I've been doing this so long I forgot how hard it was at first."

"You're lying."

"A little." Behind him, Donal chuckled. "Let me help—just this once," Connor said.

She sighed. "All right." She put her hands on the saddle again and her foot in the stirrup, and he held her waist as she lifted up and swung her leg over.

"There. Not so bad, is it?"

"Not so bad," she said, but her eyes were wide, and her voice quivered.

Aileen stepped closer to Donal and let him put one arm around her. "Safe journey. Alshada's blessings on ye both," she said.

Connor mounted the sorrel and turned toward the hills in the northeast. Mairead fell in next to him. He glanced at her. "You were able to braid your hair today."

"My hand is much better." Her hands gripped the reins and her legs were tense around the horse's back, but the palomino walked with demure patience next to Connor's sorrel. She sighed. "That felt like going home."

"Don't get used to it. I don't know many people as hospitable or safe as

Donal and Aileen between here and Sveklant."

Fog dampened the colors of the burgeoning dawn, and Connor was grateful for Mairead's silence as they rode. The between times of dawn and twilight were sacred to the Brae Sidh. Though he avoided the village and his magic, there was a draw in those moments that he couldn't deny.

When the sun began to peek over the distant horizon, Connor turned back. He frowned. "Saya, do you see the farm?"

She turned, blinked, and frowned. "Where is it?"

He wheeled his horse around. The fog had lifted from ground level, and Connor saw the ragged line of village rooftops, but nothing more. "I see the village, but the farm—" He stopped. "What the—"

From the location of Aileen and Donal's house, two enormous white birds lifted into the air. *Syrafi. They were Syrafi. Gods. If the Syrafi are protecting this woman, she must be who they said she is.* A chill ran down his spine. *Unless they were here to send me a message. But what message would they have needed to give me? And what happened to Donal and Aileen? The Syrafi don't murder people—do they?* He shook his head and blinked, but the birds were still there.

Mairead gasped. "Oh, they're beautiful."

The two beasts hovered in mid-air. As the sun banished the purple of the night sky, they flapped their massive wings and raced into the darkness in the distance. In the span of a breath, they were out of sight.

"What are they?" Mairead's voice was reverent in the misty dawn. "Are they Syr—"

"I don't know." *I can't be involved in this. The last thing I need in my life is more magic.* Connor whirled his sorrel around before she could say more.

Connor kept an easy pace as Mairead learned how to control her horse. The palomino had a gentle spirit and fell in next to the stallion on her own most of the time. Mairead grew more comfortable as the day wore on, and by evening, she had even spurred her horse into an easy canter a few times at Connor's urging.

As sunset approached, he directed her to an open field and dismounted near a patch of scrubby grass. "It's clear tonight. It'll be cold, but we won't be rained on. I'll build a fire."

She dismounted. "Can I help?"

"No. It'll just take a few minutes." He knelt to start making the fire pit.

"Is there something else I can do? I don't like just standing around."

"Can you cook?"

"Not really."

"Hunt or fish? Gather roots or plants for eating?"

"No."

"Then just sit and be quiet and let me work."

She sighed. "I suppose I can say my evening prayers."

"Fine. Go over there, will you? I'd prefer silence."

"Of course." She walked some distance away and knelt.

This is going to be a long trip if she insists on that every morning and evening, Connor thought.

She rejoined him just as the fire started to crackle. "You prayed for some time," he said.

"You didn't seem to want my help."

He unpacked some of the salted meat and bread Aileen had given them. "This might be the last fresh bread you see for a while, saya."

She took the bread he offered. "You know, you don't have to call me 'saya.' I never took the oaths. You can call me Mairead."

"If you wish."

"Have I done something to offend you?"

He shook his head. "No. Why?"

"You seem upset. Bothered by me."

"I'm just doing my job. I'm here to escort you, not entertain you." She opened her mouth to say something, but he gestured toward the food. "Eat. We should get to sleep early. We need to keep riding while the weather is good." They ate in silence.

When night fell, Connor spread out his blanket, took off his boots and jerkin, and lay down. "You can spread your blanket on the other side of the fire. If you get cold, I'll build it back up."

She pulled her blanket out of her pack and lay down on her side facing him. "Can I ask you something?"

"You can ask."

"What were those creatures we saw this morning?"

He closed his eyes. "I don't know."

"The legends of the Syrafi say—"

"I don't want to talk about it. Good night."

She sighed. "Good night." She rolled away from him.

The morning and the next day and night passed with few words between them. It wasn't for lack of trying on her part. She initiated multiple conversations that he cut off with terse replies and contrived distractions. *If I start talking to her, she'll start asking about the Mac Raes and what we saw at the farm. She doesn't need to know my past, and I don't have any answers for her about the Syrafi.* But as she continued to offer her help with camp chores, his resolve weakened. There was an easy grace and kindness about her manner that chipped at the demeanor he'd affected since Donal and Aileen's house.

In typical fashion, autumn gave them two cold, misty mornings followed by dry, warm afternoons that made Connor think of the harvest festivals within the tribes. The equinox was only two weeks away. He'd miss the hunt. *This girl had better be the real Taurin heir.*

He caught the scent of deer nearby and motioned Mairead to a stop. The herd emerged from the trees, and Connor picked up his bow and nocked an arrow. He aimed at the smallest deer and fired. The youngling staggered a few steps and fell as the others scattered.

Connor dismounted, and Mairead followed him. "Why did you shoot it?" she asked, her voice shaking.

"For your supper."

"We have food."

"The salt pork will keep. We eat fresh when we can. Deer are plentiful." He pulled the deer aside and started to butcher it.

"Where did you learn this?"

"All boys learn this in the real world. You're not in the kirok anymore." He started to skin the animal.

"You said you're a tribesman."

"I am."

"I met a tribesman once when I was a little girl."

He grunted. "Did you? Where?"

"In a village where my father and I lived. A few tribesmen came through one day. I ran away from my teacher and went to ask one of them about the marks on his face."

"If he had marks on his face, he was a chieftain."

"I know. He told me. He said his name was Hrogarth."

Connor chuckled.

"What's funny?"

"Just that you met our king, if tribesmen have a king, and you didn't even know it. Hrogarth is the chief of the nine tribes and the hound tribe."

"Well, he was just a nice man to me." She knelt next to him. "Why don't you wear the braids?"

"I did until this job. The Sidh queen said they might offend you."

"Do you have tattoos?"

"Several."

"Where?"

He stopped cutting and pointed to his right arm. "I have thirteen circles on my arm for the thirteen hunts I've been on. Each one combines the animal symbol of the tribe I hunted with and a knotwork design that goes all the way around the arm."

"What do they do when you run out of room on your arm?"

"Go to the other side. Some of the old men have the tattoos of the hunt even down their legs." He pointed to his left shoulder blade. "I have a wolf's head on my shoulder. I was initiated into the wolf tribe when I was fourteen. I have knotwork on my chest—one endless knot that's a symbol for the web of life." He pointed at his right shoulder with the bloody knife. "I have one here that says I'm old enough to marry but haven't taken a wife. If I ever were to marry, I would have the knotwork finished." He grasped the deer's windpipe and pulled organs and viscera free of the carcass. He left them at one side for wolves and ravens, drained the body, and hung it from a limb.

"Doesn't it hurt? Being tattooed, I mean?" Mairead asked.

"It's not as bad as you would think."

"Do the tribal women get the tattoos also?"

"Yes. It's not for no reason. All of the tattoos mean something."

She shuddered. "I don't think I could do that—be tattooed like that."

"You could if you were a tribal woman. It would just be a way of life."

"Perhaps. How do you do that so quickly?"

He peeled the skin away from the deer's back. "Practice. I've butchered hundreds of deer and elk. It's not hard once you know how. A sharp knife helps." He started to slice meat free of the body. "You seem to have put some of your grief behind you the last few days."

She sat on the mossy bank near the road. "I am trying. I knew I would have to leave the sayada someday, so I had already prepared myself for that. I just didn't think it would happen so brutally." She paused. "Do you ever wonder what you might have had if Kiern had not been attacked?"

A large steak came off in his hand, and he set it on a cloth. "Not really. I miss my father, but I didn't have any other reason to stay."

"You never wanted to marry?"

His knife faltered. Memories of Aine filled his head. *I did the right thing—she needed someone faithful. Tame.* "No. I'm not interested in marrying."

"What about children?"

"That's too much responsibility."

"How did you know Donal and Aileen?"

"They let me work on their farm when I left Taura."

"Is that all?"

What did Aileen tell her? "No, but the rest is a story for another time."

"Those creatures—what were they?"

He turned to her, his hands sticky with blood and the scent of the animal hovering around him. "I don't suppose you'll let this go, will you?"

"Why would I? Aren't you curious?"

"Don't you have prayers or something holy to do?"

"Connor."

He lowered his knife at the regal insistence in her voice.

"What was that place?"

His conscience nagged at him. "It was a farm once. I don't know what it was when we were there, but I think you're right. The creatures we saw fly away were probably Syrafi."

Her eyes softened. "Why didn't you want to talk about it?"

Because you don't need to know about all of that. "Because it worries me. The whole village has changed. Donal—or the creature I thought was Donal—said slavers came and took the young and strong and left the old ones alone. What happened to the real Donal and Aileen?"

She sat quiet for a moment. "Their family meant a lot to you."

"Donal and Aileen took me in and gave me work. When I was there, they were real people. They were good to me."

"Why did you leave?"

Ravens gathered in the trees around them, drawn by the scent of the dead animal. Connor went back to work, pressing back the memories of other scents, other bodies. His chest tightened. "One of their daughters thought she loved me. I hurt her."

You will be my first—my raven. The Morrag's voice whispered in his head.

"Aileen told me that you're the reason they still had Aine."

A spate of Brae Sidh curses ran through his head. "Yes, but what she didn't say was that their daughter wouldn't have been in trouble if it weren't for me."

He waved his hand; a smattering of blood flew onto the road, and a raven dove down to investigate. "Enough. I don't want to talk about this anymore. It's in the past. Aine is fine. He said she's married and has children and a home and all of the things I couldn't give her. I don't know why the Syrafi were there, but I'll assume they told us the truth about Aine and that Donal and Aileen are all right. In any case, they helped us, so for that I am grateful."

She was silent for a long time. "Aileen called you Connor Reid. I thought your surname was SilverAir."

He held back a curse. "It is. I made up a human surname when I worked for the Mac Raes. It was just the first thing that came to mind." He went back to the deer.

The sounds of the horses and the croaking ravens hovered for a moment. "Do you have any other tattoos?"

"Just one."

"What is it?"

"It's a raven feather—right here." He pointed at the inside of his left thigh with the hilt of his knife.

"The ravenmark?"

He fumbled the knife in surprise. "You know about it?"

"Only a bit—what I've read from the ancient stories of the great battle." She folded her arms. "It's not a myth either, then?"

He barked a laugh. "No. It's definitely not a myth."

"How were you marked?"

"I had a vision when I went through the tribal initiation. I saw a flock of ravens feeding on carrion. The ravens turned into a woman, and she put her hand on my leg. When she took it away, the mark was there."

"What does it mean?"

"The raven is a sign of vengeance. The tribes believe that when an injustice has been committed, the earth demands the blood of the one who committed it. They believe the ravenmarked wield the power of the avenging earth." He waited while she studied him, her arms folded, her head tipped to one side. *She looks at me without judgment. Even my own mother can't do that.* "Doesn't it frighten you—traveling with a raven?"

"No. I feel safe with you. I know you wouldn't harm me." She smiled. "I trust you, Connor."

"You've known me for three days and already you trust me?"

"You've had a dozen or more chances to harm me and you haven't. You take your work seriously. I know I'm safe with you."

She's so innocent. "Mairead—" He stopped as the breeze brought an odor of decay. *Rot—not the deer.* The hair stood up on his neck. He drew his sword. "There is an evil thing here. Get into the trees."

The horses tossed their heads and stomped anxious hooves. He snatched their reins and pushed them and Mairead into the trees. He held a finger to his lips. A screech split the late afternoon skies, and a vast pair of black wings cast a chilling shadow down to the ground. "Don't move."

The massive raven-beast dove without warning. Connor shut out Mairead's cries and channeled his focus toward the creature. He swung at the creature's talons, catching a toe before the creature rose again. It screeched with the sting of the injury, circled, and dove again. Connor swung. He caught its wing with his sword and ducked. Dark blood sprayed and a mass of black feathers hit the ground.

The beast fell, one wing limp and useless at its side. Connor charged, avoiding talons and the other wing as he swung for the neck. It jumped backward, and he scratched it. The creature's good wing struck out and knocked him down onto his back. Breath rushed out of his lungs; his vision blurred. Mairead screamed. Connor shook his head, struggling to sit up. Warm air passed over him, and his nose filled with the stench. He gagged, forced his sword up for defense—

The creature's shriek sent a cold chill through Connor's bones. A massive white owl hovered over the black bird, its talons secure in the flesh of the raven beast's back. The Syrafi's hooked beak struck at the beast's face. Bloody sockets remained where eyes had been. The owl struck again and again, shredding the black bird's flesh and cratering its neck until the creature's screams stopped. It collapsed in a heap, and a dark, inky cloud rose from its body.

The bloodied white bird lifted on massive wings and circled Connor and Mairead. It cried out once and then flew north, disappearing over the trees.

Connor shook his head, trying to clear his vision and his hearing. He took a deep breath and stood. His sword dripped with foul black blood. "You all right?" he asked Mairead.

She stood with her back flat against a tree, her face pale. "I—I thought you would die—I thought it was going to kill you. What was that thing?"

"Ferimin. They serve Namha and the Forbidden."

"You've seen them before?"

"No. But it's not hard to figure out they're not friendly."

She let out a breath. "How did it know where to find us?"

"I don't know. Someone must be tracking you—or me." He wiped his sword clean with moss and put on his cloak. "I'm not going to rely on divine help. We need to find water and a more secure place to spend the night." He picked up the steaks he'd carved, and they mounted the horses and picked their way into the trees. By the time the sun set, they'd found a sheltered grove near a small stream.

They both dismounted. Mairead startled when they heard another screech in the distance. "How many are there?"

"I don't know." It screeched again. "We can't build a fire tonight. I don't want it to see us," Connor said.

She stepped closer to him. "It's angry."

"Don't worry. I haven't lost anyone I've escorted yet. We'll be all right."

"Promise?"

"I promise."

Emrys slipped off the back of the Ferimin when it landed near the bloody carcass of its mate. "Feed yourself," he told it. The beast lifted its face to the sky and gave one long, keening screech before it sank its beak into the body and tore away a strip of bloody flesh. While it ate, Emrys walked to the edge of the trees and crouched near the deer carcass.

The Syrafi had killed the Ferimin, but Emrys had no doubt that the man would have finished the job given enough time. He needed only to draw on his power, and the Ferimin had no chance against him. *Why didn't he draw his power?*

Emrys twisted his mouth. *If I attack him now, I'll ensure my own defeat. Even if he's not using his power, he's still stronger than I am. I need strength.* But the raven had to be separated from the girl. Every moment they were together strengthened the protection around her, and as long as she was protected, Emrys couldn't touch her. She had to be betrayed. He needed someone else to turn her over to him.

He turned to the Ferimin behind him. It lifted its head and cawed. Its blood-matted feathers shimmered with a dull sheen in the rising moon. "Go back to your mistress. I have no more need of you."

The thing screeched again, lifted its wings, and rose into the sky. Emrys pulled his hood over his head. He lifted his nose and smelled a fire in the distance. Thieves, slavers—it didn't matter. They could deliver the girl. He fixed his mind on the fire and carved a space between the elements.

The Taurin soldiers jumped to their feet when he slipped out of the elements and the light closed the gap. He held up a hand. The seven men stood still and wary. He lowered his hood. They quailed when they saw his eyes. "Your king sent you after the girl—the Taurin heir."

One—the leader, he assumed—snorted. "A fool's quest."

Emrys picked out a man with a craggy face and a medium build, and in two steps, he had his hand around the man's throat. Life faded from the man before he could cry out, and Emrys drew the Taurin soldier's soul into himself. The man's transgressions were dark and vile; they filled Emrys with strength. He turned back to the others as the limp body fell. They all took a step back. "I know where she is."

CHAPTER NINE

I cannot be what he is.
I am death. He is music and light.
— Queen Brenna's diary, on Aiden, Year of Creation 4989

Connor splashed water onto his face and chest. He crouched near the stream, resting his forearms on his knees, and rubbed a hand across his jaw. *It's too easy to find us—too much blood and animal scent. I don't like this.* The forest sounded normal, but a scent hovered around the clearing he'd shared with Mairead, and he couldn't place the source. *Not another Ferimin—there's not enough rot. Bear? Wolf? It's not animal. Men?* He refilled his waterskin and straightened. *I don't like it.*

Sleep had consisted of a few snatches of dozing against a tree. Mairead had slept next to him, torn between staying close for safety and warmth and moving away for propriety. When her head had bobbed so much that she couldn't stay upright, he helped her lie down and covered her with a blanket. While she slept, he alternately paced the clearing, checked the horses, toyed with a dagger, and sat down to doze for a few minutes. *It's just being in the Wilds again,* he told himself. *You've gotten soft. Being with Helene and taking easy jobs has ruined you.*

He turned away from the stream to see Mairead kneeling nearby in her morning prayer pose. He grimaced and pulled a leather jerkin, spiked bracers, and a bronze torc from his pack. By the time she stood and approached, he was lacing up the bracers. "Morning."

She gestured. "Is there a point to the new attire?"

"Intimidation. Sometimes you can avoid a fight just by looking like a jackass." He picked up two extra daggers and slipped them into his boots. "Let's get back to the road. We can eat while we ride." He tucked his flail into a loop on his saddle.

She mounted her horse. "Did you see any more of those creatures?"

"No. I think the trees sheltered us. Now we have to watch for thieves." He mounted. "Something doesn't smell right."

They started to ride out of the trees. "What do you mean?"

He shook his head and lifted his face. "I can't explain it. The Sidh talent helps me sense things in the air that others can't. Something just doesn't smell right about this place."

"Is that how you first sensed the creature yesterday? An odor?"

"Decay. Death. The wind carried it to me. It didn't smell like an animal decaying. It smelled like evil. Like the death of a soul." Connor's skin prickled with the weight of the forest. *Something is watching us.* He resisted the urge to rub the back of his neck. Birds still fluttered through the high branches around them, but he heard nothing in the underbrush. *As if there's a predator nearby.*

Mairead rode silent beside him, her knuckles white on the reins and her face pale.

"Pull up your hood," he said.

She startled at his voice. "What? Oh, yes." She pulled her hood up and frowned. They emerged where Haman's Road cut a wide swath under the thick canopy of trees, and her voice dropped to a whisper. "Someone is watching us."

He nodded and put a hand on a dagger in his belt. He reined in. "Show yourselves."

Six armed men stepped out of the trees, fanning out to block the road. All of them wore some sloppy version of royal Taurin livery. One man wore brown woolen breeches instead of the normal black. Three wore padded armor under green hauberks, two wore leather jerkins, and none of them had shaved or donned a helmet. Connor grimaced. "You are the most motley group of soldiers I've ever seen," he said. "If you were my men, I'd whip you all and make you mend clothes with the camp women."

Mairead's voice quivered. "C-Connor?"

One of the men drew a sword. "By order of His Majesty Braedan Mac

Corin of Taura, this woman is commanded to accompany us back to stand trial for crimes against the crown."

Connor snorted. "Crimes against the crown? What do you think a girl like this could possibly do to threaten a king?"

"She conspired to overthrow his majesty and take the throne for herself. She claims to be descended from ancient kings and queens."

Connor laughed and gestured to Mairead. "*This* girl? Look at her. She's pretty, but noble? Hardly. And she doesn't have two coppers to rub together. How do you think she's formed this massive rebellion?"

The man's eyes darted between Connor and Mairead, and the point of his sword dipped. "I'm under orders—"

"Do you think I give a damn what your orders are? I'm not turning this girl over to a group of thugs with nothing but an outrageous claim." He drew a dagger. "I suggest you move on."

Inside his chest, the familiar ache returned. *Yes, raven,* the Morrag whispered. *Destroy. Rake them open. Kill.*

I won't kill them if they don't attack. I won't be yours.

Three men put hands on swords, and one drew a flail and started to twirl it. The leader pointed at Mairead with his sword. "We're not moving on without her."

This is just a job. This isn't the Morrag—it's just your job. Connor put his hand on another dagger. "Last warning: leave now, or die."

"I have orders."

In a quick, practiced move, Connor flipped the daggers and spun them toward two of the soldiers. The blades landed in a chest and a belly, killing one and driving the other to his knees. *I warned them.*

Connor dismounted and drew his sword to meet the onslaught of the four remaining soldiers. In his head, the Morrag cackled, exulting in the fight. *Yes, raven. Claw them open. Tear them. They deserve death.*

The four men bore down on him, but they were as unpracticed and sloppy as their uniforms. The first who drove toward him with a blade out met a foot of Connor's sword through the midsection. Connor pushed him off the sword and onto the ground. Behind him, a whisper of air ruffled his hair, and he ducked, spun, and met another man's leg with a dagger. The man roared and dropped to his knees. Connor cut off his scream with a strike through the neck.

The last two soldiers were too close to him to swing his sword. He dropped his sword, drew a dagger from his boot, and waited. "You can still leave," he said. "I won't pursue you."

Why do you wait, raven? Her voice grew frustrated. *Rake them open.*

The soldiers drove at him from either side, and he spun again, striking one man through the head with both his dagger and the spiked bracer. Bone crunched and blood sprayed; the man fell, unconscious. The last man wore nothing but a hauberk and undertunic, and Connor's final dagger thrust drove easily under the ribs and into the man's heart. A gush of warmth covered Connor's hand as life faded from the man's eyes.

Connor drew long, deep breaths. The Morrag's satisfaction eased the ache in Connor's chest. *Yes, my raven.*

I didn't kill them for you, bitch. Behind her exultant laugh, he heard the screams of dying men and the sobs of a terrified girl.

He shook his head. *Focus. This is just a job. Just your job.* He checked the bodies. Four dead, two still alive. If the unconscious man ever woke, he wouldn't be able to eat, and he'd likely be a simpleton from the damage to his head. Connor knelt and drove his knife into the back of the man's skull; he twitched and went limp.

The first soldier had pulled Connor's dagger from his belly, and blood soaked the ground beneath him. Connor knelt and examined the wound, dimly aware that Mairead had dismounted and joined him. ""You're dying," he said. "Your choice now is whether you want a quick end or a slow one. I need answers."

The man shivered. "End it—"

"I will as soon as you give me answers. How did you find her?"

"Dark man. Campfire. He led us—" He coughed, moaning with the pain. "Mercy. Give me death, please."

"Who was this man?"

"Don't know—swear I don't. Comes and goes at will—in flashes of light. Please, kill me." Another coughing fit overtook him. "My sons—gods, my sons."

Connor nodded. He picked up his dagger. "This will be quick." He turned the man to position the tip of the blade at the base of his skull.

"No, wait!"

Connor's hand faltered. Mairead knelt on the other side of the man and took his hand. "What's your name?"

"Merwyn."

She put one hand on his forehead and closed her eyes. "Alshada, forgive Merwyn his crimes. Bring him to your rest. Bring him peace in his final moments. Care for his family, and give them peace to know he died doing his duty, that he was brave to the end."

The soldier's face filled with gratitude, and Mairead opened her eyes and gave the man a sad smile. Merwyn's eyes watered. "I'm sorry," he said. The color drained from his face.

"I forgive you." She brushed the hair from his forehead. "You were doing your duty to your king. I hold you no ill will."

Her hand on his forehead seemed to calm him. He closed his eyes. "Let him do it. Please, lady."

"I'll hold your hand." She nodded to Connor.

His hand found the hilt of the blade, but he hesitated, staring at Mairead. He searched for words, but could only gape at her. Merwyn gave a choking sob. *Focus. Just a job.* He drove the dagger into Merwyn's skull, severing nerves and ending pain. Merwyn tensed, twitched, and went limp.

Connor stood. "What was that?"

"It was me giving a dying man some measure of peace. Why?"

"He tried to take you back to Braedan."

"I'm aware of that."

"And you *prayed* for him. With him. You forgave him—or said you did. What was that?"

She stood and met his eyes. "Mercy."

Mercy? He stepped closer to her. She stiffened, but she didn't step back or lower her gaze. "Do you think what I did wasn't merciful?"

"You can practice mercy your way. I'll do it mine." She pointed at the dead men. "What will we do with these?"

His eyes lingered on her for a moment before he knelt again to wipe his dagger clean on a corner of Merwyn's clothes. "I'll drag them off the road."

"I'll help you." She picked up Merwyn's hands and started to drag him away, struggling with the weight.

He's not a small man, and he's dead weight. What's the heaviest thing she's ever lifted? A small child? He dropped his head for a moment. *This woman will be my undoing.* He put a hand on her arm. "Get his feet."

She nodded and picked up the man's feet as Connor picked him up under the arms, and together, they moved him to the side of the road.

When they had moved all of the men he'd killed, he stopped her from mounting her horse. "Why did you do that?"

"Because I won't be useless." She put both feet on the ground.

"Useless. Is that what you think you are?"

"Don't you?"

"No. I just think of you as a woman I'm supposed to protect and take to Sveklant. Whether you're useless or not doesn't really enter into it. I'm just doing my job." He nodded toward the dead men. "Their story of the strange dark man who appears in flashes of light bothers me."

Mairead shivered. "I read that the Forbidden can appear and disappear in flashes of light. The stories say when a king returns to Taura, the Forbidden will rise to power again." She paused. "Do you think it's true? Have they returned?"

Connor grunted and folded his arms. *They never left. They just hid for a very long time.* "Do you know much about the earth magic?"

Her face paled again. "N-no. I only know the pag—the tribes believe the earth has power."

He nodded. "In the beginning of the world, Alshada created the earth with a spirit of her own, perfectly balanced. But during the war between the magical races, when Alshada created the chasm and cast Namha into it, the earthspirit was divided—split into a lifespirit and a spirit of vengeance and death. To keep the spirit of death away, the tribes perform blood sacrifices."

"Human sacrifice?" Her voice rose to a squeak.

He laughed. "No. Gods, no. Animals. The annual hunt is part of it. The spirit of vengeance—the Morrag—demands blood to pay for the transgressions. For now, she takes animal blood. But when the tribes can no longer satisfy her with sacrifices, it will be the sign that the Forbidden have returned to power. She'll need more than animal blood to sate her."

She folded her arms and bit her lip. "The Morrag. And you are ravenmarked."

He nodded.

"And the stories say only the ravenmarked can defeat the Forbidden."

"They do say that."

She let out a long breath. "This is a lot to believe."

"Believe it or not. It's the truth." He paused. "If the Forbidden are chasing you, this journey will be a lot more dangerous than I thought. I can fight Braedan's men every day if I must, but the Forbidden? I don't know."

"If you taught me how to fight, I could help you."

He laughed. "Teach you to fight?"

"Yes. What's funny about that?"

"I don't see you wielding a sword. You could barely mount a horse three days ago."

She squared her shoulders. "I'm descended from the kings and queens of old Taura and the Western Lands."

"You're a silly girl who was raised in a sayada and puts far too much faith in a god whose greatest gift to the earth was leaving it alone."

Anger flashed in her eyes, and her face flushed pink. "How dare you—"

"How dare I? I'm the best freelance in the known world. Merchants and nobles pay me very well to make sure they get where they're going. I've made a career of evaluating clients and threats. I look at you and I know—you're prey."

"*Prey?*"

"Yes, prey." He gestured toward the dead men. "What if those had been thieves? Slavers? Do you know what they would have done to you? They would have stripped you, beaten you, raped you, and left you dying in the forest. If you were really unlucky, they might have beaten you, raped you, and sold you to a brothel." He stepped closer to her. "You may not like it, but I'm the best protection you have."

"Then teach me to fight so I can defend myself if the next attackers are thieves or slavers."

"You have me to protect you. You don't need to fight."

She clenched her jaw. He saw what she intended the moment her hand flicked out. *She wouldn't—* But she did. She grabbed the hilt of a dagger in his belt, and his hand snatched her wrist and twisted her arm up. "Drop it," he said.

"No. Teach me to fight."

"No." He tightened his hand on her wrist. His fingers overlapped around the fine, slender bones, and he knew he could break them if he wanted to. She gave one faint grunt, and a flicker of pain passed over her brow, but she didn't drop the blade. *This is one determined woman.* She swung her other arm up in a broad, clumsy arc toward his head. He grabbed her other wrist. "I don't like to hurt women. I don't want to hurt you, but I will if I have to. Drop the blade."

"Teach me to fight."

He sighed. "If you want it this way—"

He brought one leg forward, kicked her legs out from under her with a lazy swipe, and let go of her arms. She slammed into the ground. The blade fell in the dirt. She gulped for air, choking and gasping.

He knelt next to her, picked up the blade, and stuck it in his belt. "Just lie still and breathe. You'll be all right. You just got the air knocked out of you." He paused. "I did warn you. I don't like to hurt women, but no one steals my knives."

She closed her eyes, drawing slow, even breaths. "I don't like this. I don't like being weak."

"You're not weak."

"I am. I've never been the weak one before. At the sayada, I was the strong one. I was the one who worked later, the one who served more. I was the one Sayana Muriel turned to when she needed help. For the first time in my life, I don't know how to take care of myself. You've had to do everything for me since we started this, and I don't like it. I don't know how to find food or start a fire or treat a wound or fight or anything."

When have I ever escorted a woman who would ask this of me? It's not her fault she's defenseless. She was raised to marry and have children. He stared out into the forest, thinking. *How many men can say they serve their country by training its queen to fight? I suppose if it's all I do for Taura, it will be enough.* When she opened her eyes, he offered a hand. "You look better. Do you think you can sit up?"

"Yes."

He helped her sit up, let go, and crouched next to her. "If I teach you what you want to know, will you bring justice to Kiern?"

"Justice?"

He nodded. "For Duke Mac Niall and his family and the townspeople who died when Mac Rian attacked. I want the duke's name cleared and his holdings given to someone worthy of them—someone who will live in peace with the tribes and the Sidh, and who will maintain the lands the way Duke Mac Niall would have. Will you promise me that much?"

"Did you know Duke Mac Niall?"

Old grief reared its head. *She doesn't need to know who I am. Not yet.* "Only in passing."

"He had a son, didn't he? I heard stories."

He grinned. "Really? Stories about a son? What did you hear?"

"That he's illegitimate and lives wild. They say his mother is a witch or a sorceress. Duke Mac Niall would never say who she was. I heard he was bewitched into siring his son and that his son has some kind of dark magic."

Dark. You could say that. He snickered. "Do you think it's true?"

"I don't know what's true anymore." She paused. "Do you know him?"

"It's accurate to say I know him fairly well."

"And you don't think those stories are true?"

"He is illegitimate, and the wild part is probably true. The rest?" He shrugged. "People make up stories when they can't verify the truth. His mother is not a sorceress." *Though she is a harpy.*

She frowned. "How do you know him?"

"He's a freelance, like me. I'm better, though."

She stared. "What are you not telling me?"

"What makes you think I'm not telling you something?"

"I don't know." She narrowed her eyes. "Would the younger Mac Niall want the estate?"

"No. I can promise you he would not want the Mac Niall holdings." He held out his hand. "Do we have a bargain? Do you promise to bring justice to Mac Niall's family and town when you ascend your throne if I teach you what you want to know?"

"I promise. If you teach me to fight, I swear I will bring justice to the Mac Niall name. But if I discover something you haven't told me—if I discover that Mac Rian was right and Mac Niall conspired against the crown—"

"You won't."

She gave him a slow nod. "All right. I swear it." She paused. "You'll promise to teach me to fight?"

"My word is my promise. I say what I mean." *I sound like my father.*

She clasped his arm. "Thank you."

He put one hand on top of hers. "Don't think I'll give you quarter because you're a woman or a noble. I'll train you the way I was trained."

"I expect nothing less."

I'm sure you don't. He stood and held out his hand to her. "Can you stand?"

She nodded and took his hand. He helped her to her feet and held her arm until her balance returned. When she was steady, he took the sheathed dagger from his belt. "Take this."

"Why?"

"You risked your safety to reach for it. You must know that I could have killed you, but you did it anyway. You're the only woman I've ever met who had the fire to reach for a blade of mine. You are either very brave or very stupid, and I don't think you're stupid. I do think you're stubborn, but at least you know what you want. I like that." He offered it again. "Take it. You'll need a blade for practice."

She took the blade and ran a light touch over it. "Thank you."

He turned to the horses. "We should get moving. We've already wasted too much of the morning."

Mairead tucked the dagger into the top of her breeches and mounted her horse. As Connor set his stallion at a walk, she fell in next to him. He fixed his eyes ahead. *This woman may be my undoing, but at least it will be an entertaining trip.*

CHAPTER TEN

My servant's voice fades into the sky.
It returns through the strength of stone.
– Second Book of the Wisdomkeepers

The edge of autumn teased Minerva with frosty fingers as she traveled north through tribal territory. Each night, she slept in the earth shrines and sacred groves that dotted the forest. The brand in her palm itched and burned when she entered the shrines. She chewed willow bark for the pain and prayed to Alshada for forgiveness. *The shrines bring warmth and safety,* she said in her prayers. *Forgive me for entering them.*

Behind her prayers, she knew the truth—if she would make the blood sacrifice, the mark would cease to bother her. But to perform the rites would forsake her vows to Alshada. *I will not forsake my vows. I will not be an oathbreaker again.*

She ate from her meager provisions and the late berries and nuts she found, and on the second morning away from the hound tribe, she woke to find a freshly killed rabbit next to her. She stood, scanning the brush for signs of the warrior who left it, but saw only a wisdommark scratched in the ground near the rabbit. "Thank you," she said, then shook her head. *You are in their world, now.* "The earth bless you as you have blessed her guardian."

A faint rustle of branches nearby was the only response.

She took the time to build a fire and cook the rabbit, but she ate while she rode, skirting the edge of the stag tribe. Her breath formed white puffs in front of her, and she pulled her cloak close around her, wishing for the fur sashes and pelts she used to wear as a guardian. The days were cold and the nights colder, but the rain held off. *Better cold than soaked to the bone.*

The third morning, she found another rabbit outside the earth shrine, and the fourth morning brought a quail. Each time, she spoke the words of thanks and heard the rustle in the bushes that indicated a retreating warrior. She never saw them, and she didn't know if they knew her identity or merely helped her out of obligation to her mark, but she was grateful for the food. Despite being an oathbreaker, she felt safer traveling in tribal territory than she had traveling from Torlach. Few places in the world were as safe for a woman as the tribes. Wives, lovers, guardians were held in high esteem, and men who abused any woman were usually taken deep into the forest and disciplined in brutal ways by tribal elders.

The fifth morning, she smelled fires and heard the distant, familiar sounds of a tribal village. She took a deep breath and approached the sentries again, tugging the glove off her right hand. "I come from Torlach," she said when the men in leathers dropped out of the trees. She opened her palm. "I seek your traitha, Edgar Wolfbrother."

A muscular man of medium height stepped forward. The twisted, snaking brand of a traitha wound over his face, and the hunting tattoos circled his arms almost all the way to both wrists. A mass of dark auburn, gray-streaked braids fell to his shoulder blades. "Your quest is rewarded. I am Edgar."

She frowned. "You serve as sentry?"

"It was my turn." His eyes passed over her in appraisal. "You have the wisdommark, but you dress as a Taurin woman."

Minerva's stomach twisted. "A hound warrior told me you could help me find the Sidh."

Edgar's hand twitched toward his sword. His eyes narrowed. "What do you want with the Sidh?"

Two wolf warriors closed in toward Minerva's horse. "I mean no harm," she said. "I—I am Sidh."

One of the warriors snorted. Edgar silenced him with a sharp gesture. "If you were Sidh, you would not need my help."

Minerva's heart rose in her throat. "I'm only p-part Sidh. My b-blood is thin. I come with a warning for the Sidh queen. Please, traitha—if you can't help me find them, would you at least take a message to her?"

A jumble of emotions crossed Edgar's face, ending in a stony frown. "Come," he said. "The warriors will care for your horse."

"But—"

"We have things to discuss."

A warrior took her horse's reins. She dismounted. The traitha turned and walked into the village, and Minerva stepped quickly to catch up. He led her to a hut just inside the edge of the village and opened the door.

Minerva hesitated. "Your hut?"

He inclined his head.

She peeked inside. Weapons, a sleeping mat, a small fire pit, a few provisions—and no sign of a woman or children. She turned back to Edgar. "I am a saya. It wouldn't be proper for me to enter your hut without an escort."

"You're free to leave. But I can help you, and without my information, you could wander around this forest for months or years before you find the Sidh—if you ever do."

She lifted her chin. "My blood will lead me."

"Are you certain?"

It hasn't yet. She stepped into the hut, and Edgar entered and let the door fall shut. "Can you leave that open?"

"Don't worry. No woman leaves my hut weeping."

Minerva's face heated. "I just meant—"

He held up a hand. "Enough. Tell me what you want with the Sidh."

The hound warrior's words rang in Minerva's memory. *Not all of us believe as Hrogarth does.* She straightened her shoulders. "Braedan Mac Corin has claimed the Raven Throne and installed himself as king. He listens to evil counsel, and they tell him to seek the Sidh. He wants Queen Maeve to reveal the reliquary."

Edgar folded his arms. "And how does he expect to accomplish this?"

I don't know. "Sayana Muriel believes he will come through the tribes. He needs a guardian to reveal the village."

He chewed the inside of his cheek and tilted his head. "What makes your sayana think a guardian can reveal the Sidh village?"

"B-because—because I told her." His eyes widened, and Minerva continued in a tumble of words. "Forgive me, traitha. The sayana asked if there was any way Braedan could find the village, and I remembered my lessons. I told her. She fears for the Sidh."

"And why do you not simply reveal the village yourself, guardian?" His voice held an edge, but there was also curiosity in it.

"I never finished my training in the earth wisdom," she said, ducking her eyes away from his. "I never came into the full power of a guardian. I don't have the strength to thin the veil."

He took a step closer to her. "Why do you bring this to me? Hrogarth represents the tribes with Torlach."

"I've seen Hrogarth. He refuses to set aside his pride and fulfill his obligations."

"Then I don't know what you expect me to do. Hrogarth is my traitha. To defy him would split the tribes. I will not be an oathbreaker."

Does he know who I am? She wet her lips and met his eyes again. "I thought if I could warn the Sidh—if I could just tell Queen Maeve what Braedan intends to do—perhaps she could move the Sidh."

Edgar snorted a laugh and gave her a tilted grin. "You'd have better luck asking a mountain to throw itself into the sea." He held up his hand when she started to speak. "You say you have Sidh blood? You can find the village. Go to the shrine on the northern edge of the village. Wait for sunset. If you have enough blood, you'll see the veil thin and you'll be able to walk through."

She nodded. "And if I don't see it? Will you promise me you will protect the Sidh if I can't warn Queen Maeve?"

His green eyes bored holes into her own. "I am bound by my oath to Hrogarth," he said. "I can lift no weapon in defense of the Sidh unless he gives leave." His grin turned feral. "But I do promise you, guardian: I defend my own tribe and all of its environs with every breath in my body. Any Taurin who finds himself near my territory without my leave will find ravens feeding on his entrails."

He protects the Sidh without their knowledge or Hrogarth's leave. Shame flooded her face. *I have misjudged this man.* She nodded. "I thank you for your help."

He opened the door to his hut. "Will you stay with us today? Eat and drink?"

She thought of the guardians she might see and shook her head. "I—I thank you, traitha, but no. I will spend the day in the forest in meditation and prayer."

"As you will."

Minerva stepped outside, Edgar close behind. She took the reins of her horse from a warrior outside Edgar's hut and turned back to Edgar. "Alshada bless you and keep you, traitha."

His eyes twinkled in amusement, but he gave her a respectful bow. "The earthspirit guide your steps, guardian."

Minerva tensed, prepared to remind him that she no longer served the earthspirit, but she stopped herself and forced a smile and a nod. She took the reins of her horse and walked away. Edgar's eyes followed her out of the village.

She found the shrine just outside the northern edge of the village and spent most of the day wandering the forest around it, but she saw no signs of the Sidh village. *I feel them, though.* She'd known the sensation since she was a small girl. "The watchers," her sister always said when they'd both rub their arms and look around their rooms with wary eyes. Pretty Aurel's face always shone more brightly when she felt them near, and she'd look up in eager anticipation. "They watch over us."

Minerva leaned against the tree and let a smile touch her lips. *Where are you now, Aurel? So many years—gone. Do you have babes?* Her forehead tightened. If Aurel had wed and given birth, any child would be at least five or six, perhaps older. *A decade. More. The world can change in a decade.*

Their father called Minerva and Aurel his moon and sun. Though they both had his dark eyes and skin, Aurel had the beauty and spirit of a summer day, where Minerva shone quiet like a winter half-moon, he always said. "I can tell your moods by the moon," he always told Minerva, lifting her chin and smiling down at her. "Aurel is always the same—bright and constant. She brings warmth everywhere. You are different every day, and yet always the same."

Not the same, Father, she thought. Her palm itched. She clenched her fist tight and burrowed deeper into her cloak to ward off the chill of the afternoon. *Never the same. My heart is inconstant.*

By the time the sun hovered at the edge of the horizon, her palm itched so much she feared she would break the skin from digging her fingernails into the brand. She clenched her fist. *I will not forsake my vows.*

The thick canopy of trees overhead shielded her from all but the thinnest streams of waning sunlight. Shadows deepened around her. She stood, motionless and silent, and stared into the forest away from the tribal village. The horse stood next to her, nibbling at low plants on the forest floor, unconcerned. The sun continued to lower . . . lower . . . .

A quick shimmer darted in front of her. *Was that one of them?* She focused on the trees. Another shimmer. Another. As the sun lowered, more and more of them. The shimmers turned to sparks and spots of light that flashed in and out of the trees. She heard laughter, music, snatches of conversation. She shivered and rubbed her arms. *The watchers.* The sun fell below the horizon, and the sparks and flickers transformed into the flesh and blood forms of the Brae Sidh.

For one moment, the veil between the world of human and Sidh disappeared, and Minerva might have been standing at the entrance to any village in Taura. Women called children in for supper, men tended to business in the open square, and animals roamed free.

Except that it was entirely unlike any village Minerva had ever seen. And in the moment she waited, gaping, the veil shimmered again. Startled, she jumped forward, crossing the boundary, and realized that her blood was strong enough. Another human would have seen the shimmers and reduced them to tricks of the light or heard the voices and thought them the wind in the trees. She rubbed her arms again. *The watchers. And Alshada help me, I am one of them.*

Her father had told her of the Sidh village, but none of his stories had prepared her for the first vision of it. The small huts of the hidden folk merged with hillocks, trees, and small pools of water in seamless, graceful lines. She couldn't tell where homes ended and the forest began. All around, moonbugs flitted above the ancient paths, lighting the village with a golden aura. Scattered stones gave off light of varying hues—mauve, ochre, violet, azure—the colors of sky and earth and water. The Sidh burned no candles or lamps. The entire village emitted an eerie glow of its own, part magic and part nature.

The people were dressed in a wispy, thin fabric that shimmered in the light—*sidhsilk*, they called it. Woven from particles in the air that the Sidh weavers gathered and spun into threads as strong as spidersilk, the fabric helped shield the Sidh from sight. Sidhsilk held the temperature of the season it was woven in. A gown of spun summer brought warmth in winter, but a pair of breeches woven in winter would cool during the heat of summer.

All around her, children and forest animals scampered together. The Sidh queens protected all animals on their lands. More than one tribal hunter who wandered into Sidh territory after a prize stag came away muttering inanely and refusing to hunt again. Some humans had wandered into Sidh territory and never returned, living out their days with the Sidh queens and her ladies.

Minerva stopped walking as a Sidh man approached her. He wore breeches and tunic the color of fresh straw, but no shoes or weapons. He had the hale look of youth and the dark hair and eyes typical of the Sidh. Minerva reminded herself that he could be centuries old. "Blessings upon you," he said, bowing. "I am Llew. We are honored by your presence."

He is beautiful. The magic shines in his eyes. "I am Saya Minerva. I need to see Queen Maeve."

"The majesty is not accustomed to seeing outlanders."

"It's very important. I have news for her from Torlach."

He bowed again. "I will take you to her." He took her arm. Though he was small for a man, Minerva was only a finger taller. "You are saya, but you have the blood of the people."

"My father's side. I'm not sure who it was. Some say one of my grandmothers fell in love with a Sidh man and went to live with him. Others say it was a grandfather of mine who captured a Sidh girl as a pet and then became utterly devoted to her." She stopped. "Forgive me. I prattle on. I've never seen your village. It's a feast for the senses."

He laughed. "Yes, outlanders say so. To us, it is just home."

A pang of sadness hit her. *They have no idea what awaits them.* "Your people—do you hear much of what is happening in Torlach?"

"The majesty tells us what we need through the *codagha*. You know of this?"

She nodded. "The binding web that connects you to her."

He inclined his head. "There is little from the world of outlanders that concerns the Sidh."

The world of the outlanders may concern you soon. "What is your talent, Llew?"

"I am stone. You?"

She laughed. "I have no elemental talent. My blood is too weak."

"But you have magic. I sense it." He stopped and turned to her.

Minerva clenched her fist. "I was tribal, once. I have the earth magic." *Why tell him that? Why tempt him to fear you?*

But Llew only smiled. "Ah. The earth magic. I know of this." He lifted her hand and turned it over to examine the brand. "Minerva of the tribes and the sayada and the Sidh. How is this so?"

"It's a long tale. Too long."

"Perhaps you might stay and tell me after you speak with the majesty?" His eyes were earnest and curious.

"No, I can't—"

"You fear the stories."

She couldn't answer.

He laughed. "Servant of Alshada, we do not take prisoners. We are Sidh. But many who come are beguiled by our ways and wish to stay. It is easy to lose track of time when there is nothing but ease." He brushed her hair from her shoulders.

Minerva's cheeks flamed. "Perhaps you should take me to Queen Maeve now."

"As you wish it, saya."

They walked in silence. The simplicity of Sidh life awed Minerva. *I could have lived here,* she thought. But no, her father wanted to be in the outland. He'd always wanted that—to live close to power, to marry his daughters to wealth and importance. *A Sidh life would have bored him. It did bore him when he came here. He acknowledged his blood only for the power it brought him as a healer.*

She shook her head. *Alshada, forgive me. I should not think ill of him.* Still, her father remained close to wealth and power. *Should he remember how to find the Sidh village—should Braedan discover his blood—* She blinked back tears. *These people have no defense. They still believe their magic will protect them. What will they do when enchantments fade and Braedan finds them? What if my father leads him here?*

The dirt trail Minerva walked turned into a stone path. Llew led her to the door of a hut at the end of one of the wending streets. He knocked. "Majesty, a saya of Alshada is here to see you." Maeve's door opened, and Minerva walked into the queen's hut.

Queen Maeve sat in a soft chair near a large warming stone that glowed a muted orange. She was smaller than Minerva expected, small even compared to the other women in the village. Her thin silver circlet sparkled in the muted light, and the stone in the crown's center glowed with a faint golden aura. She wore a sidhsilk gown dyed the deep indigo of early morning.

Maeve smiled at Minerva. "Saya. Your presence here tells me the unbeliever has succeeded."

Minerva knelt before Maeve and bowed her head. She felt ungainly and clumsy next to the tiny royal. "Your majesty. I wish we could have met under different circumstances."

Maeve touched Minerva's head, and Minerva straightened. "As do I." She gestured to another chair. "Sit, saya. Would you like oiska?"

Minerva shook her head. "It has been many years since I tasted oiska. Or mead or ale, for that matter. Service to Alshada required me to put away such things."

"Something warm, then. And to eat?"

"As you wish, majesty."

A flicker of a smile crossed Maeve's face. "I make decisions every day, saya. There are days I wish someone would take this mantle and make decisions for me. No matter. My lady will bring us some savories and sweets."

She made no move to call anyone. "Tell me your news."

Minerva removed her cloak and sat in the chair next to Maeve. "The unbeliever has made his stand and taken the throne. Sayana Muriel and most of the sayas were taken to the castle prison. Some of us got out before the siege, but I fear the rest are lost."

"Have you found any of the others yet?"

"No. I needed to find the tribes and you first."

A Sidh woman interrupted them with a tray of stuffed mushrooms, sweet cakes, dates, and almonds. The infusion in a small ceramic pot on the tray filled the hut with a sweet, heady scent. The woman's sidhsilk gown shimmered in the colors of sunset as she moved. She gave Minerva a cup of the steaming infusion, and Minerva sipped, enjoying the sharp sweetness of the unfamiliar taste.

"Black currant," Maeve said. "My favorite. Thank you, Evie." The woman curtsied and left.

Minerva twisted her cup in her hands. "I've been to see Hrogarth."

Maeve sipped again. "Please, saya—eat. I'm sure your journey must have been difficult."

"Your majesty, you cannot ignore this. You need the tribes."

Maeve's face turned to regal ice. "You have no authority here, guardian."

How does she know I'm a guardian? Minerva clenched her fist again and thought of Llew. *Did he tell her through the* codagha? *Or can she sense it?* "Forgive me, your majesty, but chaos is coming. The earth is preparing to fight." She held up her hand to show Maeve the faint glow of her wisdommark. "The earthspirit is calling those with her marks—the ravens, the guardians, the traithas. Those she has branded will do her bidding or die."

"The earthspirit's brands do not concern the Sidh."

"They do if you cannot make peace with the tribes." Minerva caught the rising panic in her voice and lowered it. "Majesty, please. There are those in the tribes who would rather die or destroy you than ally with you once more. I beg you—put your anger aside and make peace. Strengthen your enchantments and alliances before Braedan finds you. Give the earthspirit time to raise her army."

Maeve set down her cup and tilted her head. "I'm curious. Did you use your mark to reveal the village? Or was it your Sidh blood?"

Minerva closed her hand. "It was my Sidh blood. But the fact that someone with such a small amount of blood as I have could see the village shows how weak the enchantments already are."

"Your father—Felix, the king's repha. I knew him. He came here to learn his magic many years ago. It's the Sidh magic that makes him a good healer. He has a fine sense for air and water. He discerns symptoms that some other human healers would miss, and he's a very talented apothecary. Does your father still live, or has Braedan taken out his wrath against his father on all of the old castle workers?"

"When I left, my father was alive. He knows how to play Braedan's games." She hoped Maeve didn't hear bitterness in her voice.

Queen Maeve took a deep breath. "I will not go to the tribes. I will not grovel before them. They want Sidh gold. I will not beg before greedy savages."

Minerva opened her hand again. "I am one of those greedy savages."

Silence fell around them. "It was not always this way between the Sidh and the tribes," Maeve finally said. "Once we both served Alshada. They have lost much. They allowed greed and arrogance to replace the truth of Alshada's ways."

"As you have allowed faith in your magic and the enchantments around you to replace the relationship Alshada gave you with the tribes?"

Maeve's spine stiffened. "I know what you say is true," she said. Her voice was quiet, but it held a proud, unyielding edge. "I know that the enchantments are fading and the unbeliever is on the throne. I see these truths as well. I feel the magic fade every day, all around me." She leaned forward and fixed a fierce gaze on Minerva's eyes. "Hear me, saya: I will not go to the tribes."

Minerva's stomach twisted. "Then you will sit and wait until Braedan hunts you down, destroys you, and takes the relics?"

Maeve leaned back in her seat and straightened her robes with regal self-assurance. "He will never find the reliquary. It is well-hidden. I am the only one who can reveal it, and I am bound by the magic to protect it until the rightful deliverer comes." She sipped her tea. "How much do you know about the reliquary, saya?"

Not enough, and too much. "I know Braedan and the Forbidden want it."

The queen gave her a thin smile. "They cannot use it, saya. Only one without any human blood can use it. Even if they find it—"

"No human blood. As a Ferimin, perhaps? Or Syrafi? Like Namha?"

The queen raised an eyebrow. "Perhaps," she conceded. "But not even they would have the power to control it."

"No, only to destroy mountains, shift rivers, and flood plains. They want chaos, your majesty. In chaos, humans commit the greatest evil. The greatest transgressions give Namha the greatest strength." She put down her cup and knelt before Maeve. "Your majesty, I do not doubt that you would never give up the reliquary, but Braedan listens to evil counselors. Do you not believe he would strip you down to the bone if it meant finding the reliquary? If Alshada removes his hand from Taura and your Sidh magic fades, all that will be left is the earth magic. You and the reliquary will be laid bare if you do not have the tribes to protect you."

"You wish me to choose between two enemies. Must it be either the unbeliever or the tribes? Is there no other way?"

"Make peace with the tribes before it is too late. Use me. I am part Sidh. I can go to the tribes—I can go between you and Hrogarth." *If he doesn't kill me.* "Or move your people. Take them somewhere safe. Go to Eirya—to the mountains. Please, your majesty."

Maeve's mouth was tight and her face pale. "You can leave in the morning. Go find your sayas, Minerva. Rebuild your sayada somewhere away from this place. Go to Eirya or Culidar or the far north. Braedan's arm is not long enough to reach everywhere."

Minerva bowed her head. *This is futile.* "No, your majesty. I will go now."

"You cannot leave. The veil is not thin enough until morning." Maeve stood. "Llew will shelter you."

Minerva's heart raced. "Llew? Forgive me, but it wouldn't be proper—"

"Here, you are Sidh. Let go of your false sense of propriety." Maeve's voice carried an edge. "He led you to my door. It is his privilege to host you. Should you refuse, you will shame him."

Minerva's mouth went dry. She forced herself to swallow and respond to the queen. "Forgive me. I have your blood, but I know little of Sidh ways."

"Llew can take you to the boundary in the morning."

The dismissal was final. Before Minerva could say anything else, the door opened. Llew stood there. She tried to smile at him, but she couldn't manage it. *Alshada, forgive me.* "Llew. I will be glad of your company tonight."

When the saya left, Maeve took off her circlet and buried her head in her hands. *This is so hard.* She knew Minerva's words were true. She knew the Brae Sidh needed the alliance with the tribes. She knew all of this, but she could not bring herself to go to Hrogarth or Edgar.

An owl's screech beckoned her to the rear window of her hut. The massive bird landed and shimmered into the form of an ageless woman with flaming red hair and green eyes. She clothed herself in robes the color of the forest and pulled a hood over her hair, giving some measure of disguise should any of the Sidh look in her direction. "Minerva has been to see you," she said, tucking her hair inside the hood.

"I sent her away."

The Syrafi woman's mouth tightened. "Maeve, you need the tribes. You need to let this hatred go."

"They expect too much. Pay them? For the task Alshada gave them? I won't."

"You hold on to more than that."

"They took my son, Bronwyn. I cannot forgive them for that," Maeve said.

"They did not take him. He chose that path. And it was chosen for him."

"My son was not yours to take. He was not Alshada's to take, or the tribe's. He was mine and Culain's, and we never had the chance—"

"You had him for seventeen years. More, if you consider that he visited you still after he left. He would visit you now if you would—"

"Did you just come to vex me? I can go to Edgar for that."

Bronwyn paused. "Maeve. Why do you spew your anger on me?"

Maeve closed her eyes and folded her arms. "I've sensed him fight. I know he's been in danger. I delivered him as you asked, and I was told he would be protected."

"He is protected, but the journey is not without peril. Your son will fight many things on this path. I can tell you what was told me: your son is the only person who can perform this duty. Protections or no, it is something he is meant to do." She paused. "Have you told him about his power yet?"

The question stabbed another painful reminder through Maeve. "You don't know what you ask."

"I know more than you think. He needs to know what he is."

"I can't. Not now. I can't travel by air when the Ferimin haunt the skies. I can't risk that they might find me."

"Travel through the water, then, or stone."

Maeve shook her head. "This isn't just fear for him. There has never been one like him. A man with all three talents, who hunts and has human blood and tribal training—a man like that is dangerous, Bronwyn. To all of us. He could destroy mountains, rivers, oceans on a whim." *He's as dangerous as the reliquary.*

"You cannot stop it from quickening. His power will come when the need becomes too great. It doesn't matter how strong your blocks are. If he needs the water or the stone talent, they will come." She paused. "You need to release him from the bond. When the Morrag calls him, your hold on him will do no good and will only wound you."

Maeve sighed again, rubbing her temples. *I'm so tired.* "What are the tribes doing now? Minerva said she went to Hrogarth."

Bronwyn hesitated. "I cannot say for sure, but I can tell you that Braedan's men are traveling toward the forest. If the tribes keep the king's men away from their own homes, they will protect yours as well." Another screech echoed over the forest, and Bronwyn tensed. "I must go. I cannot risk exposing you. I will contact you again when I can." She shimmered into her owl form and rose into the sky.

Maeve sat on her bed and brushed a hand over her eyes. *I should go to Edgar. I should ask for his protection. Would an alliance between the Sidh and the wolf tribe be enough to strengthen the enchantments?* She shook her head. Only Hrogarth could treat with the Sidh, and Maeve would not go to Hrogarth. *My mother would return from the great golden city herself if I went to Hrogarth.*

She let out a long breath. Magic could only go so far, and even if she strengthened the enchantments around the village and allied herself with the tribes again, it would still come to naught if Alshada removed his hand from Taura. She pulled a blanket around her shoulders. *Culain, these are the times I miss you the most. I never felt alone when you were alive.*

Minerva passed a peaceful night in Llew's hut. He allayed her fears by promising her only a restful night's sleep, and then he gave her wine, fruit, and bread. He washed her feet and wrapped them in sidhsilk and then rubbed the weariness out of her arms and back with Sidh warming stones. When he finally pulled the sidhsilk blankets over her and wished her a restful sleep, Minerva was only awake enough to realize that he left the hut and allowed her to sleep alone.

In the morning, he woke her with quiet tapping on the door and waited outside while she washed up and put on her boots. When they reached the boundary just before sunrise, Minerva saw her horse on the other side, still waiting patiently. She turned to Llew. "Thank you for your hospitality. You have shown me much honor."

He took her hands. "May I tell you one thing?"

She nodded.

"You hide too many things. You run when you should share and speak."

Few respect the words of an oathbreaker. She pulled her hands away. "Goodbye, Llew." She stepped to her horse, turned back, and the village was gone.

Minerva mounted and rode for the day. Tribal eyes followed her. When night fell, she found a quiet place in the trees and wrapped her cloak around her, longing for the warmth of Llew's hut. She curled into a ball under the trees, her eyes closed, the sounds of the forest soothing her and the watchful eyes of tribesmen guarding her. *They wouldn't let anything happen to me. The mark buys passage.* The thought was a sleepy one, and it quickly dissipated with a final yawn.

In the morning, she woke to see Edgar crouching across from her. She sat up and rubbed a hand over her eyes. "Traitha."

"I take it your meeting with Maeve didn't go as you hoped."

She stood and started to fold up her blanket. The magic flared inside her palm. "I am a servant of Alshada. I sought to warn Queen Maeve of unrest in Taura. I accomplished my goal. She will do as she wishes."

Edgar chuckled. "Queen Maeve has always done as she wishes, guardian."

"You honor me with a title that's no longer mine."

"You were never shed of the magic. You still own the title." He stood and put a hand on her arm, turning her to face him. "Where will you go?"

She folded the blanket against her body and lowered her eyes. "I will seek the other sayas. I cannot stay in the forest. Hrogarth—"

"—Hrogarth holds grudges," Edgar said. "I do not. The wolf tribe would welcome you."

To stay with the wolf tribe? To know my sisters, my tribal brothers again? "You cannot protect me from Hrogarth."

"He is my traitha, but I control my tribe. Stay with us. I will put you under my protection."

She flinched away from him. "Under your protection. You would expect me to share your bed?"

He held up a hand. "Protection only, I promise you." He paused. "You have no obligation to me, guardian, but I have one to you." He picked up her hand and put a small bag in her palm. Coins clinked together. "I have heard that Duke Dylan is loyal to the kirok and the heir. He may know where some of your sayas are. His holdings are in the northeast—near Starling's Cross."

The small purse shifted in her hands. "Traitha—"

"It isn't much, but it will help." He gestured toward a horse nearby. "We've brought you a fresh horse, and our women have given furs and clothing and food for your journey."

Overcome, Minerva didn't know how to respond. "How could you do this for me? For one who—"

"You are in need. That is yours whether you stay with us or go. But winter pads closer each day, and a woman traveling alone in northern Taura puts herself at great risk." He shrugged. "Stay or go. I will not force you either way."

She closed her eyes. *If I stay, I tempt the earthspirit. But if I go . . . . He's right about traveling alone this time of year. And if I stay, perhaps I can have another chance to speak with Maeve. There will be no kiroks left in another moon or so. I could wait out the winter here and then look for the sayas.* She let out a long breath. *Alshada, forgive me.* "I will stay."

CHAPTER ELEVEN

In that place, with her wounds, there was little else to identify her.
But when I touched her mind, there was no mistaking it:
The girl—this wounded thing barely more than a child—
she had the talent of a hundred of my Emperor's best men.
— Journal of Chief Eunuch to the Emperor of the Nine Seas of Tal'Amun, Year of Creation 5993

Connor watched Mairead nock an arrow. "No, you're drawing the string wrong." He put his hand over hers and adjusted her fingers around the fletching. "Try that."

She gave a terse nod. "Like this?"

"Yes." She nocked the arrow and drew the string a few more times. "You need to draw back further, all the way to your ear. And adjust your stance." He put his hands on her shoulders and turned her upper body. "Your legs, too—turn so your body is in line." She tried to follow his instructions, but her stance was still off. "Like this." He put his hands on her hips.

She jumped away from him. "What are you doing?"

"Teaching you to shoot."

"You don't need to touch my hips for that."

"I'm just trying to adjust your stance."

She didn't move. "Can't you just show me?"

"I tried that. You still didn't have it right." He stepped closer to her. "Mairead, if you want me to teach you to fight, we're going to have to touch each other. You have to decide right now if it's worth it. If it's not, we can stop. Your choice."

She bit her lip, returned to her position, and focused on the stump. "Show me."

He stood behind her and turned her shoulders. "Everything should be in line to the target." He put his hands on her hips again and turned her lower body to line it up with her shoulders. "Nock the arrow again."

"So, to that rotten stump?"

"If you can. Mastering a bow can take years. Don't be discouraged if you can't hit it."

She drew the string. The bow creaked, and she released the arrow too soon. It flipped into the air over them.

Connor caught it in one hand and laughed. "Try again."

She snatched the arrow away from him. "Don't laugh."

"I'm sorry. It'll take some practice."

She lowered the bow, nocked the arrow, and drew. Her eyes narrowed, and her fingers loosed the string. The arrow fired straight ahead, but fell far short of the target.

He gave her another arrow. "Don't squint this time. You've got the form down. Keep trying."

When she drew back the third arrow, Connor tensed. *She's going to hit it.* She loosed the arrow, and it landed squarely in the stump with a solid *thunk*.

Mairead gasped and lowered the bow, her face alight. "I did it."

"You did. How did you do that on your third arrow?"

"I don't know." She drew another arrow from the quiver. "Let me try again."

He watched with his arms folded as she fired the entire quiver. Though not all of them hit the target, they all covered the distance to it. *She has a talent for it. Her aim will be better than mine if she practices.*

When the quiver was empty, she lowered the bow. "How was that?"

"Have you done this before?"

"No, never."

He shook his head. "I have never seen anyone learn a bow so quickly."

Her face colored, but she smiled. He reached out to take the bow and pulled her arm toward him. She winced when he ran light fingers over the raw, red skin. *The bowstring struck her every time, and she never said a word.* "Why didn't you say something?"

"I didn't want you to think I was complaining. I'll get used to it, won't I?"

Complaining? "We need to adjust your pose, but I can give you my bracers for practice. There's no reason to shred your skin for the sake of learning the bow. I'll buy you some of your own as soon as I can."

"I don't want you to buy me anything more than necessary. It's too much to expect."

"I have money. It's not a concern."

"But—"

"Don't worry, Mairead. I have enough. I'll buy you bracers and some better clothes when we come to a bigger city."

They gathered the arrows as mist began to fall, and Mairead lifted her face to the sky. *She's smiling. When have I ever met a woman who could smile when the clouds were pissing on her?*

In the few days of travel since the ambush by the Taurin guards, Connor had discovered that Mairead's stubbornness was exceeded only by her eagerness to learn. She asked him questions about everything he did, and though he answered at first with grudging patience, her wit and intelligence soon erased all his doubts about her abilities. He assigned her a series of strengthening exercises each day and made her walk while he rode. He pushed her to the limits of her endurance by having her hold positions until her muscles ached and she sweated and tears welled in her eyes. She never complained, and his respect for her grew each day.

The forest ebbed and flowed as they traveled along Haman's Road. Where the forest was darkest, they camped under the trees at the side of the road, and when the trees opened to reveal a small farm or village, they took rest and shelter in some farmer's barn or ate a meal in a tavern. The peasants were always willing to sell fresh bread, a meal, or a night under a roof.

Connor tried to keep his distance from Mairead, but it wasn't easy. When they bedded down each night, the scent of her hair would tickle his nose, and he'd roll away from her and curse the Sidh talent that made odors so strong. She asked him to teach her to fish and cook over the fire, and whenever his hands touched hers, the ache of the Morrag faded. Her humor was easy and quick. If he occasionally teased her with a bawdy joke, she laughed and gave him a mild scolding with a twinkle in her eye.

The morning after he taught her to use the bow, he began teaching her to fight with her hands. She held her body tense at first, but the more they fought, the more she relaxed and learned to trust him. They sparred with their fists and feet every morning, and though she yelped at the occasional punch or kick, he never heard another sound from her about any of the mild injuries he inflicted. Once when they stopped at a stream, she went to the water while he adjusted the saddles. He turned to see that she had turned down the edge of her breeches to examine a large purple welt on the top of her hip. "You all right?" he asked.

She pulled the breeches up quickly, her face red. "Fine. It's fine."

"You can admit pain. I won't respect you less."

She shook her head. "It doesn't hurt. I just wondered how bad it was." She turned back to the stream and didn't mention the bruise again.

The rain continued for days, falling at one moment as a fine misty spray and the next as a heavy pounding stream that drowned out all other sound. One night after they'd eaten, Mairead pulled her cloak around her and leaned against a tree. "It's damp, but it is a pleasant sound, isn't it?"

"The rain on the trees? I like it. I find it soothing."

She closed her eyes. "You know those warm, humid nights Taura gets in the summer when the air is heavy with rain that won't start?"

"Yes."

"I used to go up on the roof of the sayada. I'd sleep under the clouds and wait for the rain. When it came, it always washed the air clean. It made me think of—" She stopped. "Never mind. It's silly."

"I want to hear."

She smiled. "It made me think of the stories of the creation of the world—how the Sidh worked with Alshada, and how the stirring of the elements caused storms and earthquakes and floods until everything calmed and settled. And then Alshada sent a rain that lasted for months, and it washed the air and the earth clean and prepared it for mankind. I thought perhaps those nights were his way of reminding us of his power to cleanse the earth and everything on it."

Connor grinned. "It's a poetic idea, but do you know what I heard?"

"What?"

"That the innocent heir to the throne used to sneak out at night in disobedience."

"Yes, well . . . I learned a lot that way."

"Like what?"

She hesitated. "I know Prince Braedan was intimately acquainted with more than a few sayas. I ran into him in a passageway once in the middle of the night and he suggested . . . Well . . . ." He saw her face redden even in the dim light of the campfire. "I don't think he knew who I was. He was drunk and thought I was pretty. I convinced him to sleep off his drink, and he told me if he ever found me in a passageway again he'd . . . ." She trailed off.

Connor let silence hover for a few moments. "Mairead, Braedan is not good to women. I don't know if he ever truly forced a woman, but he suggested many of them might pay a price if they turned him down."

"Do you know him?"

He cursed himself. *You forget—she doesn't know your name.* "I've heard stories."

She met his eyes. "Is that the kind of reputation you have?"

"I hope not. Threats and suggestions of consequences are the same as a knife or a rope." He paused. "I've been in a few battles. I've seen what men do."

The fire crackled. "Have you ever—"

"The world is ugly. Men are ugly. Men after a battle are inhuman, sometimes. They see a woman, old or young, fair or ugly, and they think only to spread their seed, expend some energy, or humiliate the conquered. I've kicked more than a few off some woman, and I've—" *You can't tell her that. Not now.*

She waited, but he didn't continue. "You've seen a lot."

"Not as much as some."

She was quiet. "I think you're a more honorable man than you like to admit."

Honor. A tainted name and tainted blood. That's all I have. "You didn't say—why were you in the passageway in the middle of the night?"

She sighed and smiled. "I was sneaking back to my room from the library. I was up reading and didn't want to have my privileges revoked."

"What were you reading?"

"Military journals and treatises. Battle plans. Stories about famous battles."

He laughed.

"Why do you laugh?"

He stared at the fire. "I don't know. You surprise me. I should know by now that you are no ordinary noblewoman."

After another night and day in the rain, they came to a fair-sized village and found a tavern where he thought they could order a hot meal and ale. Mairead huddled next to his shoulder as they entered. "I don't like this place," she whispered.

He escorted her to a table in the corner. "It's rough, but you'll be fine if you stay close to me."

She watched one table where two men sat drinking and casting occasional leers in her direction. "Those men—they're watching us."

Connor sat up straighter. "Something you need, friend?" he asked.

A thin man with greasy blond hair stood. The odors of ale and sweat approached with him, and he nodded toward Mairead. She shrank back. "The lass—how much?"

Connor put a hand on his dagger. "What do you want her for?"

"My master, Allyn, buys pretty 'uns like her. Puts 'em in his brothels. He'd burst his pockets with the gold she'd turn." He leaned toward Connor. "I'd pay ye well, lad."

The Morrag croaked. *Kill him, raven. He's evil.*

Connor's hand tightened around the dagger. Unbidden, the thought of steel sliding under the man's ribs swam in his head.

The Morrag cackled. *So easy for you. So easy to part flesh from spirit. Rake him open, raven.*

Connor shook his head. *I won't kill him for you.* He stood, towering over the man. "She's not for sale." He guided Mairead behind him and backed out of the tavern, one hand on his sword until the door closed and they were both on their horses again.

Mairead was quiet the rest of the day. When they stopped to eat, she picked at her food. "I can't stop thinking about it," she whispered.

"Don't worry about it. That's why you have me."

Tears glistened in her eyes. "I heard them when we walked in. They talked about buying children and women from their own families, capturing girls and putting them in brothels, taking men to sell into piracy." She shook her head. "I'm going to bed." She picked up her blanket and lay down near the fire.

Connor listened to her cry herself to sleep. He considered offering her a sympathetic shoulder, but didn't want her to think he expected more.

The next village came into sight late the next day. Mairead was hesitant to pass through it, but Connor insisted. "You could use a hot meal and a good night's sleep. And if you're not comfortable with the place, we'll leave. Fair?"

She let out a long breath and nodded. "Fair."

As they rode into the village, they passed an alley where an old man sat begging for alms. Mairead stopped, and Connor reined in. "I'm not giving him money."

"I didn't ask you to." She held out her hand. "Give me your pack."

"What? Why?"

"Because we have plenty of flatbread and leftover quail, and he could use them."

Connor hesitated. "Mairead—"

"Were you planning to eat it tonight?"

"No, but—"

"Then let's give it away before it spoils."

He sighed, fished out the food that would spoil, and gave it to her. "You can't save him, Mairead. He's a beggar. He'll probably be dead in a few days. You only prolong his pain by helping him."

She wrapped the meat in the flatbread, dismounted, and knelt in the alley before the old man while other townsfolk passed. His eyes were clouded over with age, and he had few teeth left. She squeezed his hands together over the bread. "Be at peace, sir. Alshada is with you." She took his empty begging cup and poured water into it from her skin.

The man's mouth broke into a wide smile. "Lady, 'tis you—the one—he told me ye'd come."

Connor startled. *Who told him she'd come? Has the Forbidden been here?* "Mairead, this may not be safe."

"Hush." She lifted the cup to the man's lips and helped him drink. "I will pray for you, sir."

Tears streamed down the man's face. "Ye've given me peace. Ye'll bring peace to this land. Thank him—I got to see ye." He rasped a sigh. "You're as beautiful as I imagined. I'm at peace now. I can go to him in peace."

Connor gaped as Mairead helped the man finish the food and water. There was no grudging obedience or superiority on her face. She grasped the man's hands and closed her eyes, speaking quiet words of prayer that Connor couldn't make out. When she lifted her eyes to the man's face, she touched his cheek with one slim hand. "Alshada keep you," she said, and leaned forward to place a soft kiss on the wispy white hairs on his head.

She straightened and returned to Connor's side. "What was all that about?" Connor asked.

She mounted her horse. "The ravings of an old man, perhaps."

More than ravings. "He said he'd been waiting for you. How did he know you'd be here?"

"A vision."

Visions? "Mairead, you have to understand—the people chasing you are very, very dangerous. You can't keep helping every poor soul you come across."

She fixed him with a fierce gaze, and her mouth tightened into a stubborn line. "I'm a servant of the Order of Sai Atena. It's my duty to look after those less fortunate. Would you like it if I told you who to kill and who to spare?"

Gods, this woman! "That's different."

"How? You do your job. Let me do mine."

He tried to think of some response, but nothing came. "He called you beautiful, but his eyes were clouded. He couldn't see you."

"Are you saying I'm not beautiful?"

"No, that's—I mean, you are, but . . . ." His face grew hot.

She grinned as he stumbled over his words. "Leave it, Connor. He was just an old beggar."

He let it go, but the image haunted him.

They found a small inn and stabled the horses nearby. Connor asked for one room. Mairead inhaled a sharp breath. "One room? But—"

"Mairead." She bit off the words at the tone in his voice. When he'd paid for the room, he took her by the arm and led her to it. "Never act like I don't have the right to share your room again. Do you want them thinking we don't belong together?"

Her eyes flickered with anger. "We don't belong together. You are escorting me, not sharing my bed."

Connor pointed to the common room. "He doesn't know that. We deflect suspicion by having one room. I'll sleep on the floor, but I won't leave you alone in a place where I can't trust the people."

She started to say something, but stopped and nodded. "You're right. I'm sorry."

He put down his pack. "Let's go eat."

They returned to the common room and sat down at the long trestle table. A pretty maid with dark blond curls came to the table. "Oiska, lad?"

Connor looked up at her green eyes and freckled face. "For me. The lady will have mead, and we'll both have a meal."

She turned to Mairead. "Sorry, love—dinna see ye." She curtsied and walked away.

Mairead raised one eyebrow at Connor. "She didn't see me?"

"Jealous?"

"No." She leaned back in her chair. "This is a better place than the last one."

"This is a better village. These places that are a little larger have elders and constables and people in position to defend the town."

"Imagine."

"What?"

"Living in fear. Wondering if you would wake up to someone stealing your home and family, or someone selling you as a piece of bread or a goat." She shuddered.

"I ignore it. It's just the way of things."

"That doesn't mean it has to stay that way."

The girl came back within a few moments with a tray of roasted meat, vegetables, bread, oiska, and mead. She set it down in front of Connor and brushed against him as she stood. She winked at him. *What's the harm? It's been weeks.* He tossed back a shot of oiska. *It might be worth it.*

When they finished eating, the maid hovered close to them. Mairead sighed. "Do you need to go?"

He caught the girl's eye again. She smiled. She didn't seem put off by Mairead's presence. "I wouldn't mind. You could have the room to yourself for a while."

"What about not leaving me alone with people you can't trust?"

He glanced back at the maid. "I'll be right back."

The maid was bent over a table, clearing empty cups and bits of food. She cast him a smile. "Ye need more oiska?"

He stood next to her. "I wanted something less demanding."

She grinned, her eyes flitting over him in appraisal. "We have that sort of thing. But I figured ye for the type who likes a bit o' something that bites back."

"It has its place." He put one hand in her hair. "I was hoping for something sweeter."

She pressed herself up against him. "Your lady's not the jealous kind?"

"She doesn't care what I do. But here's the problem—I have to guard her."

"There's an empty room next to yours."

"I'll meet you there in a few minutes."

Connor escorted Mairead to their room and made sure she locked the door when he left. The maid walked up behind him. She slipped a hand into his and led him into the next room, candle in her other hand. She closed the door, set down the candle, and turned to Connor. "Tell me what ye like, lad," she said, sliding her arms around his neck.

Connor grinned. "And you'll take care of me?"

"Aye. If ye promise ye'll not be too rough."

"I've never had any complaints."

She let him unlace her dress. He ran his hands along her exposed skin. She pushed his jerkin to the floor, but he was too tall for her to pull his tunic off. He pulled it off for her. *Mairead is taller.* The maid ran her fingers over his tattoos. She kissed his chest, the sensation of her lips and fingers teasing his skin into gooseflesh. He cupped her face and turned it to his. *Mairead's eyes are lighter.* He shook the thought away. He bent and buried his face in the girl's hair. "What's your name?"

"Keely. Yours?"

"Connor." He inhaled, but her scent was wrong—not what he expected. He pulled her close. *This would be easy. I don't have to think about this.* He pushed her dress off her shoulders, pulled it down to her waist, put his hands on her breasts—

He straightened. *This isn't right. Something isn't right.* He took his hands away and stepped back. "I think . . . I'd rather not, Keely. I'm tired. I need to sleep. Thank you for the offer, but I think I'm road-weary. Good night."

He picked up his tunic and jerkin and left the room before she could say anything. He knocked on the door to his room.

"Who is it?" Mairead called in a nervous voice.

"It's me."

She opened the door. She had a blanket wrapped around her shoulders. The linen shift she wore stopped just above her knees. "I thought you'd be busy for a while."

"I changed my mind. I decided I was too tired." He stepped into the room. "Is everything all right?"

"Fine." She pulled her blanket tighter around her shoulders. "You can take the bed. I don't mind. I'll sleep on the floor."

Where does she get it—this unselfish nature? She has every right to demand the bed. He rubbed a thumb across a smudge of dirt on her cheek. "You look like you could use a bath."

She took a step back. "I'm fine. Do you want the bed?"

"No. I'm used to sleeping rough. Take the bed."

"Connor—"

"Mairead, I'm not such an ass that I'd let the woman I'm working for sleep on the floor while I'm using a bed."

She gave him a weak laugh. "All right. If you're sure."

"I am."

She lay down in the bed and turned away from him as he spread a blanket on the floor. When he blew out the candles and lay down, he thought of Keely. *It was just the weariness of travel and the rough surroundings. There's always a willing woman.* He closed his eyes.

Sleep was just beginning to take over when a voice jerked him back to consciousness. Different than the rough cackle of the Morrag, it had a slightly lyric quality under its sharp, insistent edge, and he knew it at once. *Connor.*

He sighed. *Mother. Now you can invade my thoughts? Damn it, leave me alone.*

There was a pause. *You tried to bed her, didn't you?*

What if I did?

He sensed her irritation. *Keep your hands off the heir, Connor.*

He considered something. *Did you use the bond to stop me?* There was silence. *Mother, tell me the truth—did you use the bond to stop me?*

No. If I had used the bond, you would know it. I'd make sure you knew it.

He knew she wouldn't pass up an opportunity to punish him if she thought he was disobeying her. That meant he had turned down Keely on his own. He didn't know what to make of that. *It wasn't the heir. It was a tavern girl.*

And she turned you down?

He hesitated. *No. I turned her down.*

There was a long pause. *Why do you tell me this?*

I don't know. It's important that you know.

She paused again. *Are you safe?*

For the moment.

Get some sleep. Her presence disappeared.

Connor rolled to his side and closed his eyes, and then something occurred to him. *If she knew I tried to bed the tavern girl, then she's sensed everything I've done for the past six years. So many women . . . And she didn't just spy on me—she saw everything they did, too.* He groaned. *By the gods, Mother. Just a little peace—a chance to be a grown man—that's all I'm asking.* But if she heard, she didn't answer. He rolled to his back and listened to Mairead's slow, even breathing. *Damn it. She steals my privacy and my sleep. Between my mother, the Morrag, and Mairead, I'll never have any peace. Alshada has a wicked humor to curse me with these women.*

Behind the inn, Emrys hovered in the spaces between the elements, a mere shadow that no one would notice, out of sight of thieves and prostitutes who occasionally ducked into the alley. He waited at the back door for the pretty maid he'd spoken with earlier. The raven and the heir had been inside long enough for a meal. If the maid had done her duty properly, the raven would be in her bed now.

The back door opened, and Emrys slipped out of the shadows to meet the maid. She startled, but she recovered quickly and held out the coins he'd given her. "He wouldn't bed me. I canna take your coins. I dinna do as ye asked."

He folded his arms. *The heir has bonded him, even before she knows her power. Her blood is strong. The earth protects her. He won't take another woman now. I need to find something too tempting to turn down, something that will separate him from her.*

In the meantime, there were other things he needed. "Do you want to keep the coins?"

She closed her hand around the money. "'Tis a lot."

"Enough to take you home."

"What would I have to do?"

He stepped closer to her and lowered his hood. She drew in a breath and backed away, but he snatched her wrist and held her. "Something wrong?"

"Ye look so much like the other lad," she said.

"He's my brother. But I need your silence. He doesn't know."

She hesitated. He tightened his grip on her arm. He didn't need her soul, but he wouldn't give her a chance to scream.

She finally nodded. "I'll not say a word."

"Take me to your room."

Her face paled. He relished the pain of his touch on her fresh skin. "You're hurting me."

"If you don't want it to hurt more, you'll do exactly what I tell you."

Kill them, raven. Rake them open.

Connor threw off his blanket and sat up, his breath coming in gasps. He clutched at his chest with one hand. *Not now—don't call me now. I can't—*

You must bring justice.

He squeezed his eyes shut and shook his head, trying to clear the vision of blood and death the Morrag planted in his mind. It only grew more vivid. He stood and pulled his boots on.

Mairead stirred and propped herself on one elbow. "Connor?"

He picked up his sword. "I'm going out."

Her hair shimmered in the faint moonlight that lit the oiled skins covering the windows. "Going to see your maid?"

"I don't know. I need air." He tucked his daggers in his boots. "Do you have your dagger?"

She sat up all the way. "Yes. Why? Am I in danger?"

"I've got to check something. Keep it with you just in case."

He left the room and crept down the stairs, following where the ache led. He stopped in the empty common room. Keely's soft cry drifted to him. He drew a dagger and walked through the inn to a small room. "Keely?" He pushed on the partially open door.

She sat in a linen shift on a little cot, her face in her hands. She wiped her tears in a frantic swipe and stood when he entered. "Don't—" she started, tense, and then relaxed. "'Tis you. I—I thought ye were—" Her wrists were bruised, and the skin exposed by her shift was red and raw.

Kill them, raven.

The screams of dying men and the sobs of a frightened girl . . . He shook his head. "Are you well?"

"Some men aren't so gentle as others."

The ache flared again. Blood stained the thin mat on her cot. "Did he rape you?"

She shook her head. "I agreed to it, and he paid me well for what he took." Her voice dropped. "'Twas magic. 'Twas more than just a man." She closed her eyes and her face paled. "It's not important. 'Tis well. I can go home now. But Connor—" She hesitated, bit her lip, dropped her voice, and stepped closer to him. "Go. Wake the lady and be gone before first light. He knows ye, lad. He's looking for ye and the lady."

Connor's stomach lurched. "Who was he?"

She dropped her voice further. "I canna tell ye. I canna risk him comin' back. Please lad—go."

"Take this." He turned his dagger around and let her take it. "This blade is as sharp as I can make it."

Her face paled, but she nodded. "I thank ye."

He returned to his room. Mairead sat on the bed, fully dressed with a dagger in hand. She stood. "What is it?"

"We need to go. Now."

They both put on their cloaks and packs and went to the stables. Connor saddled the horses and led them out. They mounted and walked out of the village, tense and alert.

When they had passed the village boundaries, Connor motioned her to run, and they set the horses at a gallop. After a few miles, he reined in, and she pulled up next to him. "What happened?"

"The maid said someone was looking for us."

Mairead's face paled in the moonlight that peeked through the churning clouds. "Who?"

"I don't know, but whoever he was, he terrified Keely. She said he was more than a man. He had some kind of magic."

"Do you think it was the same man who sent the soldiers?"

"Probably."

"How do we fight an enemy we can't see?"

"Carefully." He sat still and listened. "I don't think anyone followed us, but I want to be sure we're safe. We'll ride tonight and rest in the morning if we can find a safe place." They nudged the horses into a brisk walk.

When morning dawned, Connor found a quiet clearing far enough from the road that no one would see them or the horses. He and Mairead both dismounted. "That wasn't much of a rest. I'd hoped you could get a good night's sleep," he said.

She shook her head and yawned. "I'm all right. If I can doze now, I'll be able to ride again soon." She pulled her blanket out of her pack, found a dry patch of ground, and curled up in her blanket and cloak. "Wake me when you're ready to keep riding."

"I will." He untied his own blanket and sat down next to her. "Can I tell you something?"

"Yes."

"When you reached for my dagger that day, I should have seen that. You were quick. You caught me off-guard."

She opened her eyes. "Why do you tell me this?"

"It's something you can use to your advantage. Men don't expect women to wield daggers. Especially women like you."

"Women like me?"

"Highborn women. You can use that."

She closed her eyes. "I'll remember that."

He resisted the temptation to stroke her hair. *She is meant to be a queen.*

CHAPTER TWELVE

> *When history writes my story,*
> *I want it known that I would only change one thing:*
> *I should have married Maeve.*
> — *Journal of Duke Culain Mac Niall, b. 5926, d. 5987*

She was a pretty girl, if young. Fine brown hair that fell in wispy curls to her hips framed a heart-shaped face, and her lips were sweetly plump. She had fair skin, light blue eyes, and a trim figure. *She would be prettier if she weren't so terrified,* Braedan thought. "Do you fear me, Lady Aislinn?"

Red-rimmed eyes darted around the room, and her hands worried at a kerchief as she fidgeted before the Raven Throne. "Y-your m-majesty, m-my husband, Daron—" She gasped a sob.

"I promised you my protection until your father comes to retrieve you. You have nothing to fear."

She nodded, but she sobbed again. Ronan Kerry stood behind her. Braedan motioned him forward. "You did tell her she had nothing to fear, didn't you?" he asked in a low voice.

"I did, but she may not have believed me."

"Did something happen on the way to Torlach?"

"Not that I'm aware of."

I don't trust you. "I will speak with the Lady Aislinn alone. You have my leave." Ronan bowed and retreated from the audience hall.

Braedan descended the dais to Aislinn's side and took her arm. She flinched. "I assure you, Lady Aislinn, I have no intention of harming you." He escorted her to one of the benches in the hall and seated her. He motioned a servant forward. "Bring bread and cheese. And wine." The servant inclined his head and left the hall.

Braedan sat next to Aislinn. "My lady, I am sorry for your grief."

Her eyes jerked up to his. "Sorry? But you ordered—" She closed her eyes. "I saw him. At the Noble Gate."

Braedan grimaced. *I told Ronan to take it down.* "Your husband stood in my way of taking this throne. I had no choice but to remove him."

"You could have exiled him."

"And give you time to bear him a child? Another challenge to the throne?"

She gasped a sob. "You would kill a child, too?"

Would I? "Surely you must see the necessity."

She twisted the kerchief. "We were only wed six months. I barely knew him. He was kind enough, but . . . ." She took a deep breath. "What will you do with me?"

"As I said, you are free to return to your father. Until he arrives, the castle is your home. You are no prisoner."

"Why not send me home with an escort?"

She's shrewd. "I need to speak with your father."

"About what, sire?"

"Do you presume to know your father's business?"

She lowered her eyes. "F-forgive me, s-sire. I have always been too bold."

Bold, true. But curious as well. "Your father has not yet sworn his allegiance to me."

The wine arrived. Aislinn took a goblet, sipped, and lowered it to her lap. "You keep me hostage, majesty."

"You misunderstand. I offer you and your father the opportunity to swear fealty before someone misunderstands his hesitation as rebellion."

Aislinn nodded. "I am young, but I know politics. I know what my father will expect and what he will offer."

"And what is that?"

She sipped again. "My father had no love for your father or for Daron, but he saw the advantage of allying House Seannan with House Mac Corin. We are a small house, and not as wealthy as some, but we are one of the original thirteen seats of Taura. My father will offer you my hand and hope that you provide him with favors to restore our holdings to wealth."

Braedan folded his arms. "You must see that I cannot take you as wife now, my lady. Any child you conceive now would be assumed to be Daron's."

"I understand, but I do not believe I carry Daron's child." Her face colored. "He didn't bed me often." She took a steadying breath. "I'm young and healthy, though. I could give you many sons if I had the chance."

He hid a smile. *Bold and shrewd, and not afraid to speak truth. I could do worse.* "How old are you, my lady?"

"Sixteen, sire."

A child. She's a child. He motioned to a maid and then took Aislinn's hand

and stood with her. "I thank you for your honesty and boldness, Lady Aislinn. The maid will show you to a room where you'll have every comfort."

Braedan made his way to Igraine's chambers. Igraine looked up from a scroll when he entered the room. "Majesty. What can I do for you?"

As usual, the sight of her made him catch his breath. *She really is exquisite. And she doesn't even stand when I enter the room. She makes it clear that I've interrupted her. How rare a woman this is.* He sat across from her. "My cousin's wife—the Lady Aislinn. Do you know of her?"

"Aye. The guards spoke of her. She was to arrive today, wasn't she?"

"She's here. Igraine, I need a favor."

She folded her hands in her lap. "A favor. Kings don't ask for favors."

"This one does. This is outside the realm of your duties."

"What is it?"

"This girl is only sixteen, and she's terrified. I've tried to reassure her that I mean her no harm, but she still fears me."

"I can't imagine why she's so terrified. You've only murdered her husband, seized her home, and brought her here under heavy guard."

He grimaced. "Will you go to her? Reassure her?"

She tipped her head to one side. "Reassure her." She leaned forward. "Tell me what you really want, Braedan."

He shifted in his seat. "She doesn't seem entirely guileless."

Igraine grinned. "You think she is playing you."

"Perhaps." *And who better to uncover her guile than the other woman who plays me so shamelessly?* "She says her father will offer me her hand, but I can't unless—"

"—unless you know she is not with child."

He inclined his head. "She was forthcoming about her father's ambitions. He wishes his house to return to its former glory, so I understand why he would offer her hand. Still, she's so young, and I hesitate to ally myself with a small house when—"

"—you might make a better match with a wealthier house."

He sighed. "I have to wed, and soon. There's no question of that. The crown has little money, and I'd prefer to ally myself with a wealthy house. There is Kiern in the north—Duke Mac Rian's holdings. It used to be wealthy and could be again. Olwyn Mac Rian is shrewd, even if her father is a dolt." He stopped, considering how to continue.

She waited. "Yes?"

He hesitated. "Do I tell you the truth, Igraine? I fear you would use it against me."

"It depends on what it is."

"At least you're honest." He leaned forward in his seat. "I wish to wed with affection. I knew Olwyn before my exile, and she promised to turn into a cruel, conniving woman. And the Lady Aislinn is pretty and bright, but a child. There are other noble ladies, but I long for more than just an expedient alliance." *I want more than my mother got from my father.*

Igraine's eyes softened at the edges. "I'd not realized you'd developed such maturity."

"I've been accused of many things, but maturity has never been one."

She grinned. "Perhaps it's time, then."

"Is this what we've become, Igraine? A class of squabbling nobles who kill our cousins and sell our daughters for alliances and blood?"

"'Tis the way of things, isn't it?"

"I would have thought you would want it changed."

"I do. Why do you think I'm here?" She stood. "We can't change the entire world at once, Braedan, but we can change it here, for us. Show me where the lady is quartered. I'll see her."

He escorted her to the Lady Aislinn's rooms and returned to his study. He wrote orders for Daron's head to be removed from the noble gate and buried with his body on the Mac Corin grounds. *Ronan won't like it, but it's time to end these games. A new era requires new methods, new mercies.*

He hadn't wanted Daron dead. He had barely known his cousin. Daron was a child of a distant branch of House Mac Corin. Braedan's father chose him as heir because he was pious and committed to ruling Taura alongside the kirok. When Braedan prepared to claim the throne, Ronan had insisted that Daron be sentenced to death rather than exile. "Daron is a traitor to the crown," he had said. "Traitors die by beheading."

Braedan scrubbed his face with his hands and rested his elbows on his desk. *I should have insisted on exile. I could have sent him away with his wife to Aliom or some distant place where they could have raised a family and practiced their faith.*

When he opened his eyes, they fell on a skin of oiska. He pulled out the stopper. The smoky aroma reminded him of nights in exile when he first began to gather men around him and they found women in taverns and public houses and slave trains. Logan always kept watch while Braedan and the others drank, gambled, and whored the nights away on Ronan's money.

He put the stopper back in the skin and summoned a guard. "Send for Commander Mac Kendrick."

Several minutes later, Logan opened the door and bowed. "Sire."

Braedan picked up the skin and held it out to Logan. "Take this. I have no need of it."

Logan frowned as he took the skin. "Of course, sire. Is there something wrong with it?"

"No." Braedan leaned back in his seat. "Do you ever miss it? Culidar?"

A grin flickered across Logan's face. "Miss sleeping in mud and relieving myself in a ditch? No, I can't say I do."

Braedan laughed. "You've been a loyal friend, Logan. I appreciate your faithful service."

Logan shifted his feet, and for a moment, Braedan thought it might have hidden a flinch. The commander cleared his throat. "Thank you, sire. Is there some other way I can help you?"

"No. You're dismissed." *And this is how things are now. These men are no longer friends. Now, I'm a king and they're subjects.*

He passed the afternoon answering correspondence and reviewing petitions, and when a maid brought his supper, he thanked her with a distracted wave of one hand. When his guard announced Igraine's arrival, Braedan was surprised at the late hour.

He stood as Igraine entered the room. "Please, have a seat. Wine?"

"That would be lovely." She sat and took the wine he poured for her. "I've seen the girl. I do not believe she is with child. She recently had her bleeding, and she tells me Daron rarely bedded her."

"Oh?"

"Aye. If it concerns you, though, keep the lady Aislinn here for a few more weeks. Assign her a maid or two. If she is with child, they will notice." She sipped her wine. "Your cousin seems to have had little interest in her. Aislinn says he preferred to spend time with the kirons in prayer and supplication."

Braedan thought for a moment. "You're not saying—"

"I don't know. Perhaps it was only prayer." She paused. "I do know that the lady got little pleasure from your cousin. He saw bedding her as a duty only." A hint of anger hovered in her voice.

Braedan grinned. "You rise to the lady's defense, Igraine?"

She lifted her chin. "A woman deserves as much pleasure in bedding as a man, don't you think? The old idea that a woman's pleasure comes with a babe in the womb and squalling infants around her—'tis an idea whose time has faded."

Braedan laughed. "And you, Igraine?"

Her mouth tightened. "I have little desire to have a babe at the breast every turn of the seasons. I'll not be a broodmare for any man, least of all one who seeks only his own pleasure." She sipped her wine. "Lady Aislinn did express her admiration of your stature. She wondered what your intentions are."

He folded his hands. "It is not my intention to wed or bed the Lady Aislinn. I intend to send her home. Her father can make her a good match with some noble son who gives her all the pleasure she deserves." He paused. "Do you think I was wrong to kill Daron?"

Her green eyes sparkled above the rim of her goblet. "Regrets?"

"A king shouldn't have regrets."

"Perhaps a king should have more regrets than most. Perhaps he has more to answer for." She stood and put her goblet on the desk.

Braedan walked around the desk. "You didn't answer my question."

"You did the practical thing, but did you do the right thing?" She shrugged. "In sixty years, when you are old and gray and lying on your deathbed, will singers speak of your coup or of your peaceful reign? Will the people forgive you Daron's death or curse you for it?"

"You think history will decide whether I did the right thing?"

"No. But the deed is done. Now you must serve the people in such a way that history forgives Daron's death."

He folded his arms. "Sometimes I don't like talking to you."

She inclined her head. "Then I have served my purpose."

"Will you stay? Have more wine and a bit of supper?"

"Not tonight. I have plans."

Unexpected jealousy stirred. "Plans?"

Again, the tilted smile crossed her mouth. "Plans. Good night, sire." She left his rooms in a swirl of silk.

He sat down again and thought of the Lady Aislinn. He did need to make a match soon, and there were ladies of wealthy, noble houses who could give him sons and bring money and allies to the crown. *And she would be eager to please. I could show her that all Mac Corin men aren't so reluctant to please a woman. She wouldn't refuse—she'd see it as a way to secure her position.*

He shook the thought away. *I won't play her like that—not a child like her. But there was a time when I wouldn't have thought twice about pleasing myself with a young woman, no matter her age or station. Have I grown up, or am I getting weaker? Besides, affection would be nice. At least compatibility. Someone I can talk with—someone like Igraine.* But Igraine was impossible—a foreign princess with no desire to have children and a tongue that would drive away more allies than it would win.

He wondered about Igraine's evening plans. *She has no qualms about teasing me. She can't be chaste. Does she have a lover somewhere? Maybe Logan would know.* He finished his supper and went to bed early.

He was dreaming of his time in Culidar when he awoke to shouts, cut-off curses, and banging doors. *Is the camp under attack? Logan—Aiden—one of them will get me if they need me.* He pulled a blanket over his face.

"—to Aliom, and if I wish to see him, I'll see him even if he's seducing a goat!"

Braedan blinked as someone pulled the blankets off his head. He looked up into emerald eyes surrounded by unruly red hair. Igraine's hands were on her hips. "How *dare* you! How *dare you*, Braedan!"

He blinked himself awake. *My bedchamber—Torlach—I'm the king, this is Igraine.* "What's wrong?"

Logan stood nearby looking embarrassed and faintly amused. "Forgive me, majesty. I couldn't stop her. She insisted on seeing you, and there was nothing for it."

"What time is it?"

"Just after dawn, majesty."

"Damn." He sat up and rubbed his face. "You can go, Logan. Apparently her highness needs to speak with me." Logan bowed, stepped out of the bedchamber, and closed the door.

Igraine folded her arms and fixed him with a steely gaze. "Explain yourself, Braedan."

He adjusted the blankets to cover himself and tried to clear the fog of sleep. "I don't know what you—"

"You ordered kiroks seized and searched and Holy Scriptures burned. You created dozens of homeless kirons who just ended up in the castle courtyard looking as though they had been dragged through the first mud of creation. I had to hear about all of this from Logan. Explain to me, Braedan, why you treat me as some plaything rather than an ambassador. Any other ambassador would never—"

"Wait. Stop." He rubbed his face again. "Igraine, I'm at a disadvantage here. Can't we discuss this later?"

"We'll discuss it now," she said, and she pulled the blankets off him.

"Damn it, Igraine." He scrambled to pull on breeches.

She scoffed. "Unless it's covered in some kind of foreign pox, it'll not shock me." The gaze fixed on his face. "I'm surprised to find you alone. Could you not find a virgin kitchen maid to indulge you, then?"

"I haven't had time to even consider—" He stopped himself. He went to the stand near his bed and poured water. "What was it you wanted?"

Anger flared in her eyes. "Did you not hear a word I said, lad?"

"You caught me off-guard. I'm not an early riser."

"The kiroks and kirons. Nearly forty men arrived at the castle gates this morning begging for help from the king, and I had to hear from Logan that the king was the reason the men were there." She lifted her chin. "How dare you, Braedan—how dare you not tell me what you ordered? How dare you let me find out this way, when we have almost forty men standing homeless at the front gates? Would you have treated any other ambassador this way? Or do you withhold information from me because I'm a woman?"

He drank again, composing his thoughts. "What were you doing up so early?"

"I often rise before dawn. I was reading Taurin law and composing letters to the kirok elders and—"

"Don't you sleep?"

"I've not the same need for sleep as you, *majesty*."

He wanted to curse again, but drank instead. "All right. Are you angry because of my orders or because I didn't tell you?"

"Both. I told you my first night here that it was foolish to risk angering the kirok. When we agreed that you would keep me here as an ambassador, you should have told me everything. If I had known then about your order, I would have insisted you stop it immediately. But I'm also angry because in the three weeks that I've been here, you've had much time to tell me this and you haven't. I had to hear it from Logan. I don't ever want to hear about anything that concerns Taurin relations with Aliom from the mouth of a guard. Do I make myself clear?"

He tipped his head and ran one finger around the edge of the goblet. "I should have you taken to the dungeons for insolence."

She tossed her head and scoffed. "Best be about it, then. And I'll be writing my father the moment you do." She held out her fists as if waiting to be chained. "D'ye have the shackles here, or will ye be calling a guard?"

He stifled a grin. *The way this woman talks to me. I should be angry, but gods, I can't be.* He inclined his head. "Put your hands down, my lady. Please forgive me. I was remiss. I should have told you, and I should have rescinded my orders. In all honesty, I simply forgot. I've been busy with other things, and it wasn't important enough to—"

"*Wasn't important enough?*"

"Poor choice of words. It was already ordered. I didn't give it another thought. I ordered it done the first night. By the time you took your position, my thoughts had turned to other things."

Her voice lowered. "Can I trust you will rescind the orders now?"

He swirled the water in his goblet. "Yes," he finally said. "This morning. Now can I go back to bed?"

"No. I want full authority to care for the men at our gates and any others who may show up before your messengers reach your men."

"Full authority? What does that mean?"

"I want to find them a place to stay and be certain they are adequately fed and clothed. And they will not be tortured—do I have your word?"

"Yes. Fine. You have my authority to treat them as you see fit."

She pointed to his study. "Go write the orders, Braedan. Now."

He laughed. "You presume to order me, highness? You forget your position."

"I know my position quite well. I am your ambassador to Aliom, and I will not leave your rooms until the orders are in my hands."

He finished the water in his goblet and walked out to his study to sit down at his desk. He rubbed his eyes again. "Gods, it's early."

She sat across from him. "I'm happy to wait until your majesty has cleared his head of drink enough to form coherent sentences."

"It's not drink. It's just early." He picked up a quill and parchment and scrawled orders giving her authority to care for the kirons. He then picked up fresh parchment to write new orders for the men he'd dispatched across the island. He gave them both to her to read. "Will these suffice, ambassador?"

She read each one and placed them back on the desk. "They're adequate." She stood. "Sign them, and I will see to it that the scribes enter them into record and that messengers are dispatched to the men in the field."

"You'll see to it? It is my seneschal's job." He signed both papers.

She smiled. "Why bother Cormac with such triflings, Braedan? I can take care of it right now and allow him to sleep."

Braedan leaned back in his chair. "All right. Go ahead. You'll see to it that he's aware of the orders?"

She inclined her head. "Of course." She picked up the parchment and folded both pieces. "Perhaps this is your first step, majesty."

"Toward what?"

"That history you'll want written when you're old and gray—the one that forgives you for killing your rival."

He stood and walked around his desk to stand next to her, realizing for the first time that she wore only a light blue, silk dressing gown. Her hair was tied with a loose ribbon and drawn over one shoulder, and he folded his arms to control the temptation to touch it. "You don't believe I should be king."

"No, I don't. You stole this throne—I've made no secret of my opinion."

"And yet you're helping me."

"Whether I like it or not, you are the ruling authority in this country. Without some kind of rule, chaos will descend. I have no wish to see Taura fall into ruin. I'm protecting the interests of Eirya as much as I am protecting your interests."

"I didn't think you were such a pragmatist."

"Perhaps I am. Does that bother you?"

"No. But if the saying is true that a man should keep his friends close and his enemies closer, he should perhaps keep the pragmatists in his service closest of all."

She dropped her eyes in a seductive gaze that had no hint of submission in it. Her cheeks colored, but she shifted her feet toward him. "I look forward to that, majesty." Before he could respond, she turned and left his chambers.

He let out a long breath when the door closed. *This woman can play me. This woman can play anyone. I hope to gods she's on my side.*

Igraine walked with a purposeful stride toward the chambers where scribes transferred the king's orders into record. Logan fell in step next to her. "Did you get what you wanted, your highness?" he asked.

She stopped and turned to him. The brooding features, the dark curls, the haunted eyes—none of them could hide the smile that twitched the corner of his mouth. "Do I amuse you, Commander?"

"No, my lady. The situation amuses me."

She put her hands on her hips. "You didn't have to help."

"That's true. I didn't. But I confess—I wanted to see what would happen if you caught him unaware." He held out his hand. "May I deliver these for you, my lady?"

She looked down at the parchment. "They just need to be transcribed into record and then I need a copy taken to Cormac. I had thought to wait and deliver them to Cormac myself."

Logan took one step closer to her. "Let me, highness. You can gloat to Cormac when all the kirons are safely ensconced and fed."

Her eyes jerked up to his. "You were listening!"

He laughed. "It's my job to listen. And if I may be bold, highness, it wasn't hard to hear you. Some of the servants are even now being treated for bleeding ears."

She opened her mouth to retort and then thought better and closed it. She gave him the parchment. "If I ask later and discover these weren't delivered—"

"You won't."

She nodded. "Very well. Then I'll go see to the kirons."

Logan bowed. "Good day, your highness." He strode down the stone corridor.

Igraine frowned. Logan confused her. He seemed to want to be her ally, but when she had flirted with him, she had been met with everything from lack of interest to outright derision. Yet he'd also shown her kindnesses that she never expected from one of Braedan's loyal men, and he had let her into the king's chambers when doing so could have meant punishment. *He risked his own safety for me.*

She started in the direction of the castle gates and then stopped. She turned toward the sound of Logan's footsteps. "Commander."

He stopped. "Yes?"

She caught up with him and folded her arms. "What are you about, lad?"

"Highness?"

"You left a skin of Eiryan oiska on my desk this morning." He started to speak, but she held up a hand. "Don't be denying it was you. I asked my guards. They told me you'd been in my study."

He shifted his feet and cleared his throat. "I thought you might like a taste of home, highness. Nothing more."

"Hmm." She bit her lip. "I'll not be carousing with men beneath my station, lad."

"Of course not, highness."

"And yet this isn't the first kindness you've done."

"Highness?"

She stepped closer. "Eiryan lace? Threads in my father's colors? Even lamb chops for my supper one night? I know you're after bringing these little bits of home to me."

He frowned. "No, your highness. I only sent the oiska."

"Then where did the other things come from?"

He shrugged. "I can investigate if you'd like."

Braedan. Does he think he'll be seducing me with gifts? "No, thank you. I think I know where they came from." She paused. "I do thank you for the oiska."

"I meant nothing improper by it, my lady. I just thought you might miss the Citadel."

Her irritation faded. "I do miss it, aye? Sometimes. The oiska will remind me of nights around my family's table."

He inclined his head. "Is that all, highness? I have duties."

She gestured in the direction of the scribe chambers. "May I walk with you?"

"What about the kirons?"

"The servants will care for them. They can wait."

He hesitated. "I'm going to visit the sayas. I may be a while."

"So early?"

He took a long breath. "I don't want the king to know that I visit them."

She blinked. "Are they well? What are you—"

"They're well," he interrupted, holding up a hand. "But you can't say anything to the king about what you see. Do I have your word?"

She hesitated for a long moment. *This is a good man. This man is better than the king he serves.* She finally nodded. "Very well. You have my word."

CHAPTER THIRTEEN

> *With justice, mercy.*
> *With death, life.*
> *With the raven, the dove.*
> *Balance arrives in the place with no law.*
> — *Songs of King Aiden, Book 15, Verse 3*

The great expanse of the Wilds stretched before Connor and Mairead as they rode at a steady pace past small homesteads and through deep forest. Rain muddied the road with a nearly continuous downpour for two weeks after they left Keely's village in the night. The rough weather made travel difficult and cold, but it kept thieves and brigands away. "It's a two-edged sword," Connor told Mairead. "Thieves are lazy, so they stay out of the rain. We're miserable and they're warm, but at least we don't have to fight them."

To her credit, Mairead didn't complain. "I think I like the rain," she announced one night as it hammered the small lean-to he'd fashioned to keep them dry.

"Liar."

She laughed. "If I keep saying it, I might start to believe it."

"Are you warm enough?"

"I'm all right."

"On the other side of the Wilds there's a fair-sized city called Leiden. A lot of merchants and traders and freelances stop there. It's the only real city between the Wilds and slaving territory. We can stop there, find an inn, and warm up."

"Is there nothing between here and Leiden?"

"Not much."

She was quiet for a moment. "How did he know we would go there?"

"Who?"

"The one who's tracking us. How did he know we'd go to that tavern in that village?"

He turned his head toward her. "I wondered that, too."

"Perhaps it doesn't matter where we stop—perhaps he knows where we are right now. He knew where we were after Aileen and Donal's house, and he knew where to send the Taurins." She turned to him. "How do we fight that?"

Her eyes really are pretty. He rolled away. "Get some sleep."

They slept close to each other that night, wrapped in separate blankets, their small fire smoking and sputtering nearby. When Connor woke in the morning, his arm was draped over Mairead's waist, and she was curled up close to his chest. *She smells like fresh rain. I just smell like wet horse.* "Mairead."

"Hmm?"

"Time to ride."

She opened her eyes, saw where she lay, and scrambled to sitting. "I'm sorry—I don't know what—" Her face turned crimson. "You must think I'm no better than—" She bit off the words.

"I thought you were cold, that's all. It was an arm, Mairead. Nothing more. Your honor is still intact."

She crawled out of the lean-to. "I'll be ready to go in a minute. I need to say prayers."

He wondered how much supplication it would take until her god forgave her for being cold enough to curl up next to him.

Three nights later, they sat huddled separately in a small grove. The trees sheltered them from the worst of the rain, but their wool cloaks were soaked, and they struggled to keep the fire burning all night. Mairead sat with her knees to her chin against a tree trunk, shivering and sniffling, a steaming cup of tea in her hands.

Connor inched closer to her. "Tea not helping?"

"Not much."

"Let me put an arm around you."

"No, I'm all right."

"You're not all right. You're teeth are chattering, and you're nearly in tears."

She wiped her nose on her cloak. "If I weren't so wet, I could tolerate the temperature. I just feel like I'll never be warm again."

He wrapped his cloak around her and pulled the blankets over both of them. She tensed at first, but as he rubbed warmth into her back and arms, she started to relax. She sighed against his chest. "I shouldn't do this. It's not proper," she said.

"Would you rather catch a chill and end up waylaid for the winter?" He put his other arm around her. Her shivering slowed. "I've seen men die from consuming coughs and fevers, and I don't want history to remember me as the man who let the Taurin heir die."

Mairead laughed. "Then I suppose I will suffer your arm around me."

He grinned. "And I suppose I'll suffer a pretty girl next to me. The sacrifices I make for my job."

She laughed again.

The next day, the rain started to ebb and the temperature rose a bit. When Connor smelled a distant cook fire, he directed Mairead off the road. They followed a narrow, barely visible path through thick brush to a grove deep in the trees. A few goats bleated in surprise, and a man emerged from the house with a bow drawn and aimed at Connor. Connor held up his hands and offered to pay for a warm meal and a dry bed, and the man lowered his bow and gestured them to a shabby outbuilding with only three sides. "At least it's dry," Mairead said.

They tied the horses to one end of the shed and went to the woodsman's house. He was a gruff man in middle years with little to call his own, but he'd cooked a thick stew for his supper, and he was willing to share for the coins Connor dropped on his table. When Connor brought out his skin of oiska, the man gave them a brown-toothed grin and suddenly offered Mairead a shabby fur. She tried to refuse, but Connor gave the man another coin and poured oiska into a worn clay cup, and the man draped the old pelt over Mairead's shoulder.

When she settled onto her straw bed later, Connor spread the pelt over her. "It's not what the noble ladies in Torlach are wearing, and it stinks like dead mice, but at least it will keep you warm," Connor said. He moved away to sleep at the other side of the pile of straw. When he rolled away from her, he could still feel her eyes on his back.

The rain held off for the next several days, despite the overcast skies. They finally crested a hill and broke through the line of trees that marked the northern edge of the Wilds. Connor pointed to the labyrinthine sprawl below. "That's Leiden. They say it's the oldest city in Culidar. I've heard there's a well in the center of the city that dates back to when the Western Lands were united."

"How many times have you been here?"

"Dozens, years ago. I used to pick up work here. I ran a lot of these northern routes back and forth until I started getting more work in the south." He dismounted. "We can't make it to the gates before they close at sunset. We'll have to wait until morning."

They built a fire and ate, and she retreated to say her evening prayers. He stirred the fire with idle distraction as she returned to sit across from him.

"Your face is always peaceful when you finish praying," he said.

"I know it's a nuisance to you, but it centers me on what's important. It helps me remember to be thankful."

"Some would say you have few reasons to be thankful right now."

She blinked, surprised. "How? I have my life, for one thing. Some of the sayas cannot say the same. I'm healthy and safe." She gestured at the sky. "It's finally dry and not too cold. We had apples and salted meat for supper, and you made that delicious flatbread. Don't you have any faith in anything?"

"I have faith in myself. When I rely on myself, everything is perfect."

She said nothing.

The silence pressed on him like a pebble in his boot. "I used to pray, but I don't see the point," he finally said. "The gods, the earth, Alshada—they do what they want and I do what I want. My prayers can't change anything."

She worked her hair free of its braid. "What about the ravenmark?"

"What about it?"

"Don't you think it came from Alshada? Don't you think there's a purpose for it?"

"I don't know." He thought. "I've seen the earth magic. I know it's real. There's more to it than just the Morrag. The tribes say that when the chaos grows strong enough on Taura, the Forbidden will return to power and the earth magic will rise to seek vengeance."

"Do you believe that?"

"I don't know. I've tasted the earth magic when I've hunted with the tribes. And after what we've already heard and seen on this journey, I believe more and more that the Forbidden are coming out of hiding. But still, it seems like a leap of faith, and I'm not very good at those kinds of jumps."

They slept across the fire from each other, and in the morning, she practiced her bow and her hand fighting skills. "You're getting stronger," he said, panting. He rubbed his thigh where she had kicked him. "I'll have a bruise here."

She beamed. "When will you teach me the sword?"

"When you're strong enough."

"Do you need me to kick you again to prove I'm strong enough?"

He chuckled. "That's not the strength I mean. I'll know it when I see it."

They reached Leiden at midmorning. Plain-dressed guards let Connor and Mairead through the gates. They held quarterstaffs at the ready and wore swords on their hips, and Connor noticed Mairead glance up at the arrow notches in the towers above the gate. "Graymen," he told her. "They train under the old city walls."

"Under them?"

He nodded. "This city is ancient. Some say the Sidh built it, but even the Sidh queen can't say for certain. There are caves and hideouts under the old walls. Every male youth of fourteen is required to present himself for training for three years. They don't see their families the whole time. The elders keep them locked away under the walls or in the center of the city where they train in the arenas. When they can defend the city, they are free to go. Every man who's completed his training is required to serve at the gates or on the walls for three days of every moon cycle."

"Why do they call them graymen?"

"Because they wear plain clothes so they're hard to see. For every one you see guarding the gate, there are five in the crowd who are on duty, but not posted. And since every man is trained the same way, all of them are ready to defend the city at any moment."

Connor directed Mairead toward the commerce quarter. He found his old favorite public house—the Ciderpress Inn. They rented a room, ate thick porridge and sweet ham, and drank warm, fresh cider. The maid flirted with Connor, but he turned his attention to Mairead and ignored the maid.

When they had finished their meal, Connor stood and took Mairead's hand. "Let's find you some better clothes."

"Connor, I'm fine. I don't need anything."

"I've watched you shiver yourself to sleep for the last time. I'm finding you something warmer."

After a morning in Leiden, Mairead had a new set of bracers and two pair of soft leather breeches. Connor also bought her warmer tunics, a fur-lined cloak, and a wrap made of wolf pelts that didn't smell like dead mice.

As they walked back toward the public house, Mairead stopped and frowned. He turned back. "What is it?"

"Do you hear that?"

He stood still. "I just hear city noise."

"No, there's more. I hear crying. Like a child crying."

He listened for a moment and followed her eyes. "I hear it. It's a faint mewling."

"A baby?"

"I don't know."

She followed the sound down an alley and behind a building. Connor followed, hand on a dagger in his belt out of habit.

Mairead gasped as she rounded the corner. "No."

A woman in thin, ragged clothing lay collapsed against a wall, her open mouth and eyes gaping skyward. She had no shoes or cloak, and the dress she wore didn't cover her legs. The weak mewling sound came from a bundle on her lap. She had been nursing the child, or trying to, when death came. Her shriveled breast was exposed, raw and empty and blue from cold.

Connor knelt and put a hand to her neck, though he knew it was hopeless. "She froze to death. Or starved. She gave the child her shawl."

"But it's not that cold."

"You can say that? As cold as you've been these last nights? Imagine if you'd been underdressed and hungry and perhaps sick."

She closed her eyes. "No. You're right." She knelt and picked up the baby. "He can't be more than a couple of months old. And he's so cold." She wrapped her cloak around him. "He needs food. We need to find a wetnurse."

Connor stood. "Where?"

"Is there a kirok in this town?"

"Across town. But the inn is closer than the kirok."

She bit her lip. "Sayana Muriel had to give a babe goat's milk once. Perhaps they have some at the inn."

He carried their purchases as they walked back to the Ciderpress Inn. Connor asked the innkeeper for fresh goat's milk. The man blinked in surprise. "Goat's milk?"

"We found this child," Mairead told him. The baby fussed weakly from her arms. "His mother was dead. He needs to eat. Do you know any wetnurses?"

"No, but the baker's wife just had a baby. She may be willing to help."

"Would you send her to our room?"

"Aye."

"Is there someone who can care for the mother's body?" Connor asked.

"I'll send word to the gravedigger and the elders. We'll see if we can find the lad's father."

Connor took Mairead and the baby to the room. She cradled the baby and fell into a natural swaying rhythm where she stood. She smiled at the bundle. "He's beautiful."

"Is he well?"

"He looks well, but his cries are so weak." She stepped closer to Connor.

"Please, take him for just a moment?"

Connor stepped back and held his hands up. "No, this is your business."

"I need to use the chamber pot."

"Just set him on the bed."

"Connor SilverAir, are you telling me you're afraid of a baby?"

"Not afraid. Just not fond of them."

She rolled her eyes. "He needs warmth. It won't kill you to hold him for a moment." She thrust the bundle at him, and he took it rather than let her drop him. She stepped behind a partition with the chamber pot.

The baby's eyes were sunken with lack of fluid. He had a dark complexion and brown curls, and his eyelashes were long and thick. He fixed Connor with a brown-eyed stare. "Sorry about this," Connor told him. "It's been a long time since I held a babe. You look like you could be Sidh. Was it your father? Your mother didn't look it." The child yawned. "I know. You need food. I wish I could help." A song came to mind. He hummed in a low voice. He summoned the air and wove braids around the baby. A smile passed over the tiny mouth, and the child fixed his gaze on the braids. "You have a touch of it, or you wouldn't see the braids."

"You big liar." Mairead's voice startled him, and he turned. She stood near the partition, adjusting her tunic. "You said you weren't fond of babies. Look at you—humming a lullaby and entertaining him."

He gave her the baby. "My sisters. I had nieces and nephews."

"Were they—"

"All of them died in the attack on Kiern."

She touched his arm. "I'm sorry. I didn't realize you lost so much."

"It's in the past."

She settled into that rocking sway with the baby again, but she kept her eyes on Connor for some time. He turned away from her gaze, grateful for the knock on the door that saved him from answering more painful questions.

The woman was older than he remembered, but the upswept brown hair and hazel eyes were unmistakable. "Linna!"

"Connor!" She put her arms around his neck. "Lad, it's been years. Where've ye been?"

"All over. I had no idea you lived here."

"We just moved here a couple years ago. My husband—he's the baker for the inns around here."

"The baker's wife? You're the woman who just had a baby?"

"Aye—another girl, just about six weeks ago." She smoothed her skirts and stepped into the room. "Three girls, now."

"You know each other?" Mairead asked.

Connor gestured to Linna. "This is Donal and Aileen's oldest daughter, Linna. Linna, this is Mairead. I'm escorting her to Sveklant."

Linna curtsied. "Mairead. 'Tis a pleasure. Is this the lad?"

Mairead held the boy out to Linna. "His mother was dead and he needs suckling. Can you help?"

"Aye, o' course." She untied her dress and sat down as she put the baby to her breast. "He's a pretty lad, isn't he?"

Mairead smiled. "He's beautiful. Is there an orphanage in this town? Or does the kirok help find homes for orphans?"

"No orphanage. The kirok does help when it can." She smiled. "I'd take him. I wanted a son and ne'er got one. I'll take him if we canna find his da."

"You'd decide so quickly?" Connor asked.

Linna scoffed and waved a hand. "'Tis nothing. 'Tis what we're called for, aye? To help those who canna help themselves?"

Mairead frowned and pulled Connor aside. She lowered her voice and cast a glance at Linna. "Is this really Aileen's daughter? After what we saw—and it's too much a coincidence—"

"I know." He walked back to Linna. "How are your parents?"

"Well," Linna said. Her eyes softened. "They're living with Aine and her husband in the far north. 'Tis peaceful. 'Tisn't far from Svek country."

Connor sat down across from her. He couldn't think how to say the words. "We went through the village where you grew up. We stayed with your parents there."

She frowned and shook her head. "They've been living with Aine for years. Took her north after—" She bit off the words. "After ye left."

"The people we stayed with were Syrafi, we think. After we left, we saw them fly away. There was no sign of the farm."

"The farm burned years ago. Perhaps ye had a blessing from Alshada." She winced and adjusted the baby against her breast. "Lad, there's plenty," she whispered, chuckling.

Mairead knelt next to her. "Will you be able to feed two babes?"

"Aye, 'tis naught. I've ne'er had trouble suckling a babe. I'll take the lad overnight and see if we can find his family tomorrow. If no one turns up, I'll keep him."

When the baby at last fell into a contented doze against her, Linna pulled her dress back up. "Will ye come for supper, Connor? Meet my family?"

Mairead was about to accept, but Connor shook his head. "No, thank you, Linna. Go with the baby, and we'll check on you tomorrow."

She started to say something, but then smiled and nodded. "All right. As ye wish." She left the room, smiling down at the babe in her arms.

Mairead turned to him. "Why did you refuse? I would enjoy visiting with a woman, and it would be wise for us to see where we're leaving this child."

He turned away and started taking off his bracers. "With two young babies, they don't need guests."

"That's ridiculous. I should go help her." Mairead started to put on her cloak. "I can cook for her, perhaps."

He snorted a laugh. "Mairead, you can barely set water boiling when we camp, and she's married to a baker. She doesn't need a cook."

Her face reddened. "Then I'll do her laundry or play with her other children. I'm sure there's some way I can help. Or do you still think I'm useless?"

He stifled the urge to roll his eyes. "You're overreacting. I just don't think we need to intrude on Linna's life." He gave her a tilted smile. "Stay here. Take a bath. I'll take you out into the city."

She folded her arms. "I thought we agreed this was my job."

"Taking care of babies?"

"Rendering aid to the poor and those less fortunate. I can help Linna and her family. You're keeping me from it. Why? Did you bed that woman once and you're afraid she'll tell me?"

"Damn it, Mairead, that's none of your business." He walked to the door. "We're staying here. Bathe or don't bathe—I don't care. I'm going to the common room. Come find me when you can listen to reason." He slammed the door behind him before she could respond.

Mairead didn't follow, so he ordered a bath for her and sat down with ale and a pipe. He was nearly to the bottom of a second tankard of ale when a familiar face caught his eye. The man approached and held out his hand. His grizzled face creased into a wrinkled grin under a shock of gray hair. "Connor Reid. I never thought I'd see ye back this way," he said.

"Declan Kennon," Connor said. They clasped arms. "Still running these northern routes? I thought you'd be in Tal'Amun by now."

Declan grinned. "My wife wishes it so. I canna quite give up the trading life yet."

Connor chuckled. He had escorted Declan's livestock trains from Leiden to the northern edge of Espara in his early days as a freelance. Declan and his sons raised hearty northern prairie cattle; they sent the cattle south to Esparan traders who valued them for their thick, furry hides and rich meat. Connor liked working for Declan. He was a fair boss who paid well, and Connor enjoyed the camaraderie with Declan's hired hands. It wasn't until he took Declan and his wife east to Tal'Amun one winter that he decided he'd had enough of northern snow and ice.

Declan was a rare breed in Culidar—a man who had turned a few head of prairie cattle into a vast, thriving ranch. But despite his success and the dozens of peasants, hired hands, and small crofters who depended on him, Declan refused to call himself anything more than a simple farmer or merchant. He dressed in plain clothes and ran his own routes, preferring the thrill of the road to the drudgery of ranch life.

Declan motioned for a tankard. "What're ye doing back this way, lad?" he asked. "Last I heard, ye said ye'd stay in the south where 'tis warm."

"I was in the south. I was working for an Esparan kanisse."

"Working for her?"

Connor grinned. "Sometimes."

Declan laughed. "I miss ye on the route, lad. 'Twas always fun watching you and the other boys get yourselves into messes with the tavern girls."

"I've outgrown tavern girls." Connor drank. "You taking cattle south?"

Declan hesitated. "Not this time." He leaned forward. "What're ye doing now, Connor? Ye on a job?"

"I am."

"Can ye leave it?"

"Not really. Why?"

The maid set down a tankard for Declan. He took a long draw off it while she walked away. He leaned forward and lowered his voice. "I need a good man to lead some wagons through Nar Sidhe territory. I'd pay ye well, and there'd be more work in it after."

Connor frowned. "You have a good man. Angus can take your wagons south."

Declan's blue eyes darted toward the maid who passed their table. He lowered his voice more. "Angus is one o' the best there is, and with livestock he's fine, but . . ." His voice dropped to a whisper. "There's silver in the mountains, lad. It's hard to get, but I've managed to fill up some wagons. They pay well for it in Espara."

Connor leaned forward. "How much are you paying?"

"Enough you wouldn't have to work again."

"I don't have to work now."

Declan's eyes narrowed. "What do ye want?"

Connor thought. "Your house in Tal'Amun."

He laughed again. "Ye're daft, lad."

Connor leaned back and drank his ale. "You're the one who needs help. I confess I like the idea of sitting on a balcony on the Eastern Ridge, overlooking the sea and sipping maki and eating savories from the fine-fingered hands of Eastern ladies."

Declan considered it. "Ye'd have to give me more'n one trip for that."

"Three."

"Six."

"Five, but you have to give me Angus to finish the job I'm on now."

"Why Angus?"

"I'm escorting a woman to Sveklant. I need a man who can be trusted to keep his breeches laced and get her there before winter, and I know if Angus drops his breeches for anyone but his wife, she'll make him wish he'd been born a eunuch."

Declan nodded. "Done. Do we have a bargain?"

Connor hesitated. A dozen thoughts raced through his mind. *You could go to Tal'Amun, be away from your mother somewhere warm. But if she found out, they'd hear the yelling in Alshada's golden city, and she'd never free me from this binding.*

Then he thought of Mairead. *Angus is a good man, but he'd never teach her to fight as she asked.* He drank his ale, picturing Mairead's fierce gaze and the stubborn set of her jaw, and closed his eyes. *She's stubborn, overly concerned with the downtrodden, and far too curious about my past, but I promised. I don't break my word. I just have to be more careful about what information I share.*

He shook his head. "Sorry. I can't do it. But it's flattering that you'd be willing to give up so much to get my services."

Declan leaned back in his chair. "Is she worth it?"

Yes. The thought came unbidden. He frowned. "It's not that. I promised my mother I'd do this. I won't break a promise."

The scent of Mairead's hair drifted to Connor on a wisp of air. He turned toward the stairs to see her enter the room dressed in a light purple linen dress, her hair tumbling almost to her waist. She smelled clean, fresh, and innocent. His breath caught in his throat, and he stood. Men around the common room quieted. Several pointed and a few started to stand, but then she saw him and smiled, and her eyes fixed on his, and he couldn't look away. "You look like you feel better," he said, hoping she didn't hear the tightness in his voice. *She's always pretty, but I had no idea.*

Her smile was hesitant and her voice stiff. "I do, thank you." She turned her gaze to Declan. "Is this a friend of yours?"

Connor gestured, and Declan stood. "Declan Kennon, this is Mairead. Declan is an old employer and friend."

Declan bowed to Mairead. "My lady. 'Tis a pleasure." He clasped Connor's arm. "I understand why ye turned down my offer. I wish ye the best, lad." He shook his head and left the inn.

Mairead sat in the chair Declan had emptied. Connor drank his ale and tried to ignore the way her dress hugged her slender curves. "Where did you find the dress?"

She smoothed the skirts on her lap. "Aileen gave it to me. When you mentioned going into the city, I just thought—"

"It was a good thought. You look very pretty." *You tempt me to break my word.* He leaned forward. "I'm not very good at apologies."

She laughed quietly over a long exhale. "Neither am I." She put her hand on his arm. "You were right. It was none of my business. Your life is your own. I have no right to pry into it."

He put his hand over hers. "Not everyone needs help, Mairead. Linna and her husband will be fine."

"Perhaps." She gestured upstairs. "Do you want to bathe?"

"I'd rather not leave you alone here. I'll just wash up."

She gave him a nervous smile. "You really could use a bath."

He laughed. "Am I offending your nose, my lady?"

"A bit. And you could shave."

He rubbed his chin. It had been several days since his face had seen a knife. He swallowed the last of his ale. "All right, I'll bathe, but you have to stay in the room."

"Connor!"

"Keep your back to me. I'll behave, I promise, but I won't leave you out here alone." He nodded toward a table where four men sat playing dice.

"Those four—they haven't been able to concentrate on their game since you walked in the room. And that one—the dark one pretending to look at his books? He hasn't taken his eyes off you. I'm not going to risk that one of those men is the man who found us in the last town. It's up to you—let me bathe while you're in the room or put up with the odor until we get to a stream."

She sighed. "All right. I'll keep my back turned."

He stood and took her hand. He asked for fresh water for his bath, and when the servants delivered it, Mairead sat down with her back to the washtub as Connor started to undress. He bathed and shaved, pulled on fresh breeches, and picked up his boots. "I'm dressed."

She stood, turned around, and gasped. "You aren't dressed—you haven't put your tunic on." She turned away from him again.

He laughed. "My being without a tunic will not ruin your chastity. And you're pretty, but you're not my type."

She turned, indignation flickering across her face. "Not your type?"

"You're the type of girl men marry. You're a noblewoman who needs to have children. I have no intention of doing either of those things."

She bit her lip, crossed her arms, and tilted her head. "What did the man in the common room want?"

"You're changing the subject."

"Yes I am."

He laughed. "He offered me a job. He was going to give me his best man-at-arms to take you to Sveklant in exchange for my services taking him to Espara."

"Why did you turn him down?" She sounded surprised.

He pulled his tunic over his head. "I promised I would take you to Sveklant. I don't break my promises."

"Could his man have taken me there safely?"

"Yes."

"Was it a good offer?"

"It was exactly what I wanted."

"Then why didn't you take it?"

He took a step toward her. "I told you. I don't break my promises."

Her gaze weakened his knees and reminded him of an afternoon on a Taurin hill, lying in the heather with a pretty girl who gave him his first kisses and nothing else. "I appreciate that, but I would have understood," Mairead said.

The idea disturbed him. "Did you think I would? I promised. A man has nothing without his word."

She gave him a doubtful look.

"I don't break my promises."

"You just haven't found a promise binding enough yet. All men break a promise eventually."

"Not me." He picked up his sword and belted it around his hips. "And since I promised you a night in the city . . ." He picked up her cloak and held it out to her.

She hesitated, biting her lip. "Are you certain? After our words earlier, I don't expect anything."

He put the cloak around her shoulders and fastened it. "I'm certain." He started to lift her hair out of the cloak.

"I can do it," she said. She pulled her hair over her shoulder and smiled.

His hands twitched to twine into the honey-blond locks, but he offered her his arm instead. *Don't forget yourself. This is just a job. She's meant for a better man.*

Emrys hid in a shadow across the street as the raven and the heir left the inn arm in arm. He followed as they wandered through the marketplace looking at the work of the silversmith, perusing cloth selections, and examining weapons displayed by an armorer of rare skill. The raven bought two more daggers. *As if he needed them. If he knew the power in his blood, he'd not see the need for so much weaponry. But then, I'm still alive because he doesn't know his power.*

He'd spread the word of the raven's arrival in Leiden. Word quickly reached the cattle merchant, and when Emrys saw him enter the inn, he'd hoped the raven's greed would be enough to lure him away from the girl. When the merchant left the inn chuckling, Emrys followed him to his wagons outside of the town. "He wouldn't take the offer," Declan told his wife after relating the entire story. "He said he wouldn't break his promise to his mother."

Emrys seethed at the words. *If Maeve is keeping him bound with her magic, I'll flay every inch of skin from her pretty body.* He disappeared between the elements and returned to the city.

When the raven and the woman finished shopping, they found a public house with pipers and drummers playing for coin, and the raven insisted the heir learn to dance to the folk music of the Culidaran people. She laughed and tried to follow his lead with clumsy steps. "How do you know this?" she asked him over the drums and pipes.

He grinned. "My father. He thought a man should be able to quote poets and dance as much as hunt and fight."

"A wise man." She stepped on his foot again.

He chuckled behind a curse. "How is it you can fight with your fists and feet so well, but you can't learn a simple folk dance?"

"I have no ear for music." She held his hands, tense, and stepped on his feet again. "Why don't you quote me some poetry, and we can try the dancing another time?" The raven laughed and put his face next to the girl's ear. After a moment, she pushed him away and gave him a playful slap on the shoulder as she laughed and her eyes brightened with affection. "I didn't mean bawdy poetry."

The raven grinned. "Be more specific next time."

She laughed again. They stood together and walked to the bar for more ale.

Emrys saw their growing affection blaze as they stood facing each other. The raven put his hand on her shoulder, and she put her hand on his arm. The man pulled her closer. She smiled and stretched up to speak closer to his ear. *It's only a matter of time.* He knew—if they grew too close, if they bedded each other, Emrys' fate was as good as sealed. *He never should have made it this far. He should have died at Kiern.*

Emrys had tried tempting the raven with a woman and money, and neither had worked. The raven had to choose to leave on his own, or the girl would still be protected. If he hated her, he would leave. But watching them together, Emrys knew there were few options left for making the raven hate her. Emrys considered the heir's deep piety. Could he use that to drive the raven from her side?

He slipped between the elements. He floated along the main road until he found the wagon he was looking for and slipped back into the world at the side of the kiron asleep near a campfire.

The man sat up, his graying hair mussed. "Wha—"

Emrys knelt next to the man, his human form casting a shadow over the kiron's face. Several other men snored around the campfire, and Emrys shivered at the sweet sensation of the transgressions they all carried with them. *I could take the kiron now. His transgressions might strengthen me enough to confront the raven.* He shook the thought away. *No. I need one worse than this.* "I need you to repay me."

A small whimper escaped the man's throat. "So soon?" One of the other men shifted and rolled over, and the kiron dropped his voice. "You promised me time," he whispered. "I want more time."

"I've shielded you for nearly ten years. No one knows your true blood, and I've made sure all evidence of your unusual proclivities disappears before anyone knows. It's your turn. You owe me much."

The kiron closed his eyes and nodded. "What would you have me do?"

"It's not a painful duty, Gavin. If you're very clever, you might be able to indulge all of your basest desires."

Lust—for flesh, for dominance, for blood—rose in the man's eyes. "Tell me."

Connor and Mairead returned to the inn late that night. He stopped her hands as they reached for the pin holding her cloak closed. "Let me."

She lowered her hands. He unfastened the cloak and hung it on a peg. "You've been very courtly tonight. Should I be wary?"

"Wary?" He brushed her hair off her shoulder and let his hand linger on her arm. The ever-present ache of the Morrag eased. *Being with her—I haven't felt this at peace in years.* "You think being with me would be so horrible that you have to be wary? I'm hurt."

She laughed. "You are a rake. Telling me bawdy poems, talking me into drinking too much ale—what are you after?"

"Nothing." He reached into his belt for the daggers he bought earlier in the day. "These are for you."

She shook her head. "I saw how much you paid for these."

"Mairead, you need daggers of your own. Take them."

She hesitated, but finally took them.

"Don't mention money to me again. If it were a concern, I would tell you."

"Connor," she started. She sighed and smiled. "Thank you."

"You're welcome." Silence fell around them. He slipped his arm around her waist and spread his hand across her back. Her cheeks colored with a pretty pink flush, and her lips parted. Her eyes fixed on his, and his thumb traced her lips and jaw. "You're a very beautiful woman, Mairead," he said, his voice tight.

She tensed and spun away from him. "It's late. I'm tired."

He held up his hands, stifling the desire to kiss her with thoughts of mundane tasks that he needed to do in the morning. But watching her hair swing unbound against her dress only made him long to pull her back to him again. "I'll wait outside while you undress," he said.

She kept her eyes averted and her arms folded over her midsection. "Y-yes. All right."

He went into the hallway. *What were you thinking? She's not for you.* But he couldn't stop thinking of the feel of his hand against her back and the lure of her untouched lips. He scrubbed his face with both hands.

"Connor!"

He drew his dagger and burst through the door in one motion. Mairead stood in the center of the room in her shift. The bed coverings were drawn back, and a snake lay coiled on the mattress, Mairead's dagger piercing its head.

Mairead whirled. "I was getting into bed. I pulled the blankets back and saw it. I had the dagger in my hand and I just stabbed—"

He prodded the snake. "It's a mountain viper. They live in the southern mountains."

"What was it doing in my bed?"

"The only people who have them in this part of Culidar are slavers. They use them to strike and subdue people they're interested in selling." He turned to her. "I'd say someone in the common room noticed you and thought he'd make some money."

She closed her eyes.

"Do you need to sit down?"

"I'm fine." She picked up the dagger and snake, opened the door, and stabbed the dagger into the oak. The snake dangled from the knife. When she closed the door, she met Connor's eyes. "It can let them know what will happen if they try it again."

He grinned. "You are a surprising woman."

"Thank you." She pulled the blankets back all the way, checking the bed, but there were no more vipers. When he'd pronounced the room safe, she climbed into the other side of the bed, and he lay down on the floor next to her.

After a few minutes of quiet, Mairead leaned over the edge of the bed. "Connor?"

"Yes?"

"Thank you for the lovely evening. I can't remember the last time I enjoyed myself so much."

"Despite the snake?"

"Perhaps because of it." She paused. "You're nobler than you care to admit."

"There's no need for insults, Mairead."

She laughed.

He listened to her drift to sleep and wondered if she'd think him so noble if she knew what he thought of when he remembered how she looked in the linen shift.

In the morning, they found Linna and her husband's shop. Linna stood speaking with three men. She had one baby slung on her back and one on her front, and a tall, sandy-haired man stood next to her with one solicitous hand on her shoulder. "Connor, Mairead—come, meet the elders and my husband, Sean."

The sandy-haired man offered his arm to Connor. "'Tis a pleasure, Connor. I've heard much about ye."

"That's not as comforting as you might think," Connor said.

One of the other men inclined his head to Connor. "Finn Alban," he said, clasping Connor's arm. "You're the man who found this baby?"

"No, the lady did. She heard him crying."

"Did you find his father?" Mairead asked.

Finn shook his head. "The girl was a stranger. We asked around—no one seemed to know her. She may have been a runaway slave, we don't know. She didn't seem to own a thing. We buried her outside of town in the graveyard of unknowns."

"Does the town have a way to care for children like this?" Mairead asked.

"Not officially. The kirok helps where it can. I know Sean and Linna well. Sean is a good man and makes a good living, and he'll likely be an elder one day. And Linna—I'd trust my own children with her. If they want to keep him, he could do no better."

"We want him," Sean said. "Linna's already named him. We'll love him as our own. 'Twill be good to have a son."

"Then I suppose it's settled," Finn said.

After the elders left the shop, Sean took Mairead's arm and led her away. "Let me give ye some bread for your journey," he offered. She smiled and nodded.

Linna waited until Mairead was out of earshot and then spoke in a low whisper to Connor. "Have ye told her, lad? About Aine?"

"She only knows as much as she needs to know."

Linna sighed. "Connor, the lass looks at ye with more affection than ye realize. She'd understand."

"It's just a job, Linna." He looked around the shop. "Your husband does well."

"He bakes for many of the inns in the district. We have everything we need. 'Twould do you good to build a life. Find a girl to settle down with."

"I have a life."

"Aye, and has it brought ye peace?" She took a step closer to him. "Aine is well, lad. She was hurt, and she cried for a fair season, but she's well now. She has a family and a home and all she wanted. She wishes she—" She stopped. "She hates the way it ended. She regrets that she dinna forgive ye."

She has regrets? I have enough for both of us. "Forgiveness is a foolish notion. She owes me nothing."

She put a hand on his arm. "When ye're done with this journey, come back for a bit. See how the lad is growing."

I can't look at you without seeing Aine. "Perhaps."

Linna knew. "Then 'tis goodbye, aye?" She raised on tiptoes to kiss his cheek. "Alshada's blessing's on ye, Connor. And on your lady as well."

Mairead and Connor said their goodbyes and rode out of town in silence. "Linna is a lot like her mother," Mairead finally said as the town faded in the distance.

"She is."

"Was Aine like her mother, too?"

He turned to her. "I don't know what you want to hear, but I have no confession to make to you, Mairead. This isn't the sayada, and I'm not a supplicant." He nudged his horse into a trot. Mairead fell in next to him, quiet. His conscience nagged him, and at last he slowed and spoke again, twisting the reins around his hands and keeping his eyes focused ahead. "What you did for that baby—that was a noble thing."

"Not noble. Necessary. It was the right thing. Anyone would have done the same."

"No, Mairead—not anyone." He paused. "A whore's child. He should have died. Many would wonder if you favored him or cursed him."

She frowned. "He's a child. How is it a curse to save him?"

"You can't save them all."

"But we saved that one." She reined in. "What's really bothering you? You're not so callous that you would have let that child die if I hadn't been there."

He wasn't so sure. *If you hadn't been there, I would have been with a woman or a merchant or a group of soldiers, and I never would have noticed. Or I would have ignored it.* "Why didn't I hear the child before you? I'm the one who's trained to be alert. And why didn't I see that beggar in the last town, or the woman in the alley in Aileen and Donal's village?"

"Perhaps because you are trained to be alert to danger. Your senses are focused on other things. I'm trained to care for the needy. I just see different things."

"It bothers me."

"Why?"

It bothers me because I'm noble, and I was raised noble, and I have lost that sense that my father and sisters had—the one that cares for those less fortunate. But he couldn't say that. "We should stay out of the towns for a while. I want to make sure we lose any slavers who might want to take you."

"I don't think slavers put that snake in the bed. I think it was the one who's following us. I've decided I'm not worried. Alshada has his hand on us."

He grunted. "You won't mind if I keep my sword sharp just in case he lets up for a moment, will you?"

She laughed. "I won't mind. And I hope you'll keep training me. I can be more useful to Alshada if I am well-trained."

"I doubt Sayana Muriel would approve."

"I can live with that."

He laughed, and as the road stretched out ahead of them, they fell into comfortable conversation. Connor thought that they could have been halfway to Sveklant at this point if he didn't have to train her, but he realized that somewhere along the way, he had stopped worrying about the pace. *We should be going faster. Every day on the road is a day she's in danger.* But behind that thought came another. *As soon as we get to Sveklant, I have to leave.*

For the first time since the journey started, it was a thought he dreaded.

CHAPTER FOURTEEN

> *When the Forbidden rise, the earth will call its own.*
> *When evil poisons and chaos returns, the ravenmarked will rise.*
> — Second Book of the Wisdomkeepers

Braedan stretched stiff arms and shoulders as he returned to his chambers. *I've grown soft since I came home.* His entire body ached from the hour-long sparring session, and he bore new nicks and bruises over his whole body. The Dal'Imuri freelance he retained as armsmaster taught more by forcing Braedan to defend himself than by offering instruction. *At least he almost made me forget how early it is.*

He rounded the corner to see his seneschal waiting at his chamber door for their morning briefing. "Cormac."

The seneschal turned. He wore his full green and gold Taurin livery, as usual, including the purple and gold sash that indicated his rank. His pale blue eyes bore dark circles underneath, and his thin, rounded shoulders slumped with weariness. The man was never a picture of haleness, but Braedan wondered if his new duties were too much for him. *If he weren't so competent, I'd look for someone else. Hard to believe he's my age. One would think him a decade older.*

Cormac bowed low. "Sire. Did I have the wrong time for our briefing? I thought—"

"This is the right time. I was up early and decided to spar." Braedan entered his study with Cormac close behind. He removed his thin black linen tunic, poured water from a flagon near his desk, and drank. The servants had delivered his morning meal. He ignored the mead and stabbed a sausage with a knife as he sat down. "What do I have today?"

Cormac placed a pile of parchments on the desk and picked up the top one. "Lord Duncan Guinness has returned from Eirya. He requests an audience with you and the Princess Igraine to discuss her position in your court."

"Coordinate scheduling with her highness and prepare a response. I want to meet with him as soon as possible." He drizzled honey on a poppyseed cake. "How bad is the audience hall today?"

"I've cleared as many petitioners as I could, but you have several lords waiting. Lord Mac Rian of Kiern has been quite vocal. He wishes to discuss trouble with the tribes." He paused. "A tribal chieftain awaits an audience with you as well. I do recommend, majesty, that you call him soon. I fear your men will have trouble keeping the lords and the chieftain separated."

Braedan grimaced behind his goblet. *I knew we should have left them alone.* Ancient treaty allowed the tribes sovereignty over the great forest, but Braedan had violated the treaty in his attempt to find the Brae Sidh. He'd already lost several men to skirmishes along the border. He didn't want to take the battle to the forest where the tribes had the advantage, but he had to find the Sidh even if it meant war with the tribes. *If they even exist. I have to make a show of looking, at least. But what will the dark man demand next? Have I made a deal with Namha himself?* That thought twisted his stomach. "Keep Lord Mac Rian stewing. I'll see the tribesman first—alone, away from the other lords. Mac Rian can wait."

"Forgive me, majesty, but Mac Rian insists that you show him the same courtesy your father showed him."

Braedan set down his goblet. "Tell Mac Rian that I am not my father."

Cormac inclined his head. "Of course, sire. He also wishes to let you know that he brought his daughter Olwyn with him. I believe he wishes to introduce her to your court."

He wants to secure his position by offering his daughter as a bride. "Ask the kitchens to prepare a banquet for tomorrow evening. It need not be extravagant—just enough for Mac Rian and the lords and ladies who are at court."

"Yes, sire. Lord Seannan and his daughter will expect some kind of preference."

"They may sit at the end of the dais." He sipped his water and thought. "Invite Duke Guinness."

Cormac blinked. "Sire?"

He grinned. "Let's not allow Mac Rian or Seannan to think they have any preference at court. Call this a dinner to welcome back our most trusted ally—the Eiryan ambassador."

"And her highness?"

"I'll talk to Igraine."

Cormac cleared his throat. Faint concern hovered on his face.

"Something else, Cormac?"

"Majesty, there was a maid here this morning."

Braedan leaned back. "A maid?"

"One of the princess' maids. She left your chambers while I was waiting for you."

"Yes. She slept here."

Cormac frowned. "Princess Igraine's rooms are quite close to yours, and she is rather protective of her maids. If she were to discover indiscretions—"

"If Igraine is concerned about her servants, I'm sure she will discuss her concerns with me herself. She isn't shy with her opinions."

"Sire, perhaps it would be more appropriate for me to find entertainment for you in the city."

"I think I can deal with Igraine." *I actually quite enjoy dealing with Igraine.* He took another drink. "What else must I attend to for the day?"

Cormac inclined his head and picked up where he left off. "If you could find some time to go through some correspondence with me—"

"After the midday meal." Braedan picked a slice of pear. "I need to bathe before I meet with petitioners."

"Yes, your majesty. I will inform the chieftain and lords of your schedule. May I have your leave?"

"You may."

Braedan finished his morning meal, bathed, and dressed in the clothes laid out by his squires—black wool breeches, silk undertunic, and a green doublet trimmed in ermine and embroidered with the raven in wing on the breast. Last, he picked up the raven crown—a relic of the days over a thousand years before when kings and queens ruled Taura. Logan had discovered the crown in a deep vault beneath the castle while looking for anything that might help them find the Brae Sidh. The crown was carved from a single piece of onyx. The whorls and curves and knots of the piece had no beginning or end, as far as Braedan could tell. He'd lain awake for hours the night Logan found it, staring into the depths of the onyx in the firelight from his hearth, following the curving lines with a finger and inevitably losing track of where he'd begun.

He handed the crown to his squire, who placed it on his head. The weight pressed on him, and he flinched away from his reflection in the mirror. *I have as much right as anyone to wear this crown,* he reminded himself. *This is no different than sitting on the Raven Throne.* "You may go," he told the squire, fidgeting with the collar and sleeves of the doublet.

He left his rooms flanked by guards. Igraine was returning to hers in her riding habit. She pulled leather gloves off delicate hands and inclined her head. "Sire."

"Did you enjoy your ride, highness?" Loose strands of hair escaped from her hat to cling to the faint sheen of moisture on her slender neck, and he fought the urge to tuck them behind her ear, remembering how she'd scolded him about touching her hair without permission.

She offered her hand, and he stepped closer to lift it to his lips. "Aye. 'Tis brisk. Autumn has arrived. I confess I am thankful for your climate. In Eirya, I would be confined to a library with my needlework by now, watching ice and snow pile around the castle."

"I can't see you confined anywhere, your highness—certainly nowhere that needlework is your only option for entertainment." She gave him a tilted grin, and he stepped closer. "I have petitioners to see now, but I'd like some time with you later if I may?"

"At your pleasure, sire." She hesitated, head tipped to one side, and reached up to fuss with the shoulder of his doublet. "Tsk. Did your squires not pass a brush over your clothing, then?" She showed him a small piece of string. "Such finery spoilt by a stray thread. For shame, your majesty."

He grinned. "Perhaps you should dress me."

"I'm not a squire, my lord." But her voice was tinged with amusement rather than irritation for once. She gave him a perfunctory curtsy and walked away with her maids in tow.

He turned to watch her, admiring the stately posture and proud lift of her head, before continuing on his way. In front of these castle people, propriety was all, but when they were alone, formalities were dropped, and they sparred and teased and argued and traded innuendos as he had never done with another woman. Her very presence both disarmed and invigorated him.

Cormac waited in the audience hall with a man dressed in a woolen kaltan that skimmed his knees, dark brown boots, a sleeveless linen tunic, and fur sashes. The man's graying hair was braided into dozens of plaits all over his head and drawn into a single leather cord at his neck. Dark blue dye snaked and coiled across his face in a web that covered the skin from above his left eye to just below his nose.

Cormac's hands shook when he gestured to the tribesman. "Traitha Hrogarth, your majesty. Traitha, the king of Taura, Braedan Mac Corin."

Braedan inclined his head, but Hrogarth stood stoic, arms folded. "Traitha Hrogarth. You are welcome to Torlach and my court," Braedan said.

Hrogarth spat. Braedan's guard put a hand on his sword. "Do not begin our discussion with lies," Hrogarth said. "You do not welcome me. You make me wait as a commoner among men who look upon me with distaste and disrespect. Speak to me with truth, as one king to another."

"Traitha Hrogarth is the chief-chieftain of the tribes. He speaks for all the tribes," Cormac said.

Braedan inclined his head. "Forgive me, traitha. We intended no offense." Cormac wore a tight expression. *He couldn't have known or he would have insisted I see Hrogarth sooner.*

Hrogarth didn't react. He was shorter than Braedan by at least a head, but his tattoos and the veins and muscles that stood out on his arms gave Braedan cause to stand back. Braedan knew he could swing a short sword reasonably well, but he didn't think Hrogarth would even break a sweat if they went up against each other in single combat.

Cormac cleared his throat. "Traitha, may I bring you refreshment?"

Hrogarth grunted. "Oiska. Men cannot treat over this water you call ale."

Braedan nodded to Cormac. "Oiska, then." Cormac bowed and left the room.

Braedan gestured to a small table and chairs near the dais where the Raven Throne sat. "Will you sit, traitha?" The man didn't twitch a muscle. Braedan wasn't sure if he should sit or stand, so he remained standing. *May as well get to the point—he seems to be waiting for it.* "Traitha Hrogarth, you requested audience. How can I be of service to the tribes?"

"Stay away from the great forest."

"Perhaps if you could help me find what I seek—"

"There is nothing within the forest that concerns the Taurin throne, yet your men trample sacred places every day. You violate a treaty that has stood for two thousand years." His eyes narrowed. "I do not come to negotiate. I come to warn: Stay out of the forest, or suffer the sting of a tribal spear in the heart of your country."

If this is the way he wants it . . . "I need access to the great forest. I know my men outnumber yours. I intend to keep searching for what I need, and if I lose more men, so be it."

Hrogarth snorted a laugh. "You know nothing."

Braedan took one step toward Hrogarth. "How many can you afford to lose? How long until we find one of your villages?"

A lazy, menacing smile crossed Hrogarth's face. "You won't find our villages."

"Are you certain?" The question masked his own doubt. *We haven't found a single village yet.* "I can double or triple the men I have in the forest right now and do no harm to my defense forces here in the city and the countryside. Can you say the same?"

Hrogarth stood silent.

"How many sacred spaces do you wish to see trampled?"

Hrogarth didn't move or speak. Braedan waited. Cormac entered the room to set a small jar of oiska and two cups on the table. Braedan poured one cup, sat down, and swirled the drink before he swallowed it. Hrogarth didn't move. "My father was your enemy," Braedan said. "I have enough enemies, but I can make room for one more if need be."

Hrogarth poured oiska, drank, poured another cup, and sat down. "Have you ever seen the west coastline of the island?"

"I haven't had the pleasure."

A languid smile crossed Hrogarth's face. "It's not hospitable, but pirates like it. So do venom runners and slavers. Eiryan forces patrol the Galoch Sea, but they can't catch everyone. Many hide in the coves along the west coast. Some come toward the forest. We drive them back, but we could stop. We could turn away as they come through the forest and bring their venom and the slave trade to your borders." He drank again. "You have a choice as well, princeling. You can leave the tribes alone, or we can break our side of the treaty."

Braedan poured another cup of oiska. "It would seem we are at an impasse, then."

Hrogarth poured another cup. Sat back. And waited.

How can the man drink oiska so early in the day? Hrogarth said he did not come to negotiate, but to warn. The dark man told him that the tribes could find the Brae Sidh. He needed an earth guardian, and Hrogarth could provide one. *There must be something he wants.* "Lord Mac Rian of Kiern awaits an audience with me. He says he is having trouble with the tribes. Would you know anything about that?"

"He intrudes on sacred spaces. He pays the price."

Braedan frowned. "He's sending men into the forest?"

Hrogarth nodded.

Why would Mac Rian be intruding in the forest? "Do you know why?"

"Ask him yourself."

He knows. It came to him. "I might be able to help you rid the forest of Mac Rian if you provide something for me."

Hrogarth drank again and set his cup down. "Ask."

How did he end up in control? "I need an earth guardian."

Hrogarth was still steady, even after the three cups of oiska. "I'll not give up a tribal woman, but there is a woman who has the power of an earth guardian. If I tell you where she is, will you leave the great forest?"

"Yes." Braedan leaned forward. "Where is she?"

Hrogarth shook his head. "Get the Taurins out of the forest and I'll tell you. When all of you are gone, I will come back." His mouth twisted into something like a smile as he stood. "I want to see you keep faith."

Braedan stood. "It will take time to reach all of the men in the forest, but I'll do it, and I'll see that Mac Rian stays on his side of the road. And then you will return?"

Hrogarth nodded. "I keep my word, princeling." He held out his weapon hand with a dagger drawn, hilt side offered to Braedan. "Give me your word."

In a breath, Braedan's guard had drawn his sword and leapt between Braedan and Hrogarth. Braedan stared at the dagger in Hrogarth's hand. "How did you get that in here?" *I shouldn't have said that.*

Hrogarth grinned. "Your word."

Braedan motioned to the guard. "No swords. The traitha comes to treat, not to wound." The guard relaxed, but he didn't reseat his sword. Braedan reached down and drew a dagger from his boot. He stepped around his guard and held out the dagger, hilt first. "You have my word."

They exchanged daggers. Braedan ran a thumb across the carved bone hilt of the dagger in his hand. It contained unfamiliar runes and a murky stone similar to the one he had once seen around Igraine's neck.

Hrogarth leaned forward. "That is a sacred blade. Break your word, princeling, and I will sheathe it in your heart before I take it back."

Braedan met Hrogarth's eyes. "I will keep my word."

Hrogarth stuck the blade Braedan had given him into his belt. "Drink with me. Seal our bargain." He picked up the jar of oiska and poured himself one more cup.

Braedan poured another cup and lifted it to Hrogarth's. "To alliances old and new."

Hrogarth shook his head. "Trade."

Braedan hesitated, but reasoned that he had seen the man pour the oiska—oiska he had already tasted—and he hadn't had time to poison it. *But I didn't see him draw the dagger, either.* Braedan held out his cup, and they traded.

"May the earth's wings shield you," Hrogarth said, lifting his cup.

Braedan lifted his cup. "A tribal toast?"

Hrogarth gave one terse nod. "Drink." They drank together, and Hrogarth slammed the cup down and inclined his head. "You will hear from me soon." He left the room, two guards flanking him. Braedan's guard at last relaxed and sheathed his sword.

Cormac entered the hall. "Majesty, is everything all right?"

"Better than expected." He gave the sacred blade to his guard. "Tuck this away. I have no desire to announce my possession of a tribal artifact. You can deliver it to my chambers later."

"Yes, sire."

Braedan turned back to Cormac. "I'll need some time to clear my head of oiska before I hear petitioners. I need to take a walk."

Cormac inclined his head. "As you wish, majesty."

Braedan left the throne room by the rear exit with guards close on his heels. His head spun. It had been some time since he'd had to shake off a night's debauchery with more of the same. Oiska didn't agree with him at such an early hour anymore. He needed to gather his wits before he met Mac Rian.

Gray autumn gathered around him in thick waves of salty mist as he walked into the rear garden. Few plants were in bloom, and most had been cut back for the winter. His mother's favorite tree, a sturdy oak, was shed of half its leaves, and acorns littered the ground beneath it. The swing he used as a child still hung there, the thick hemp ropes turned slate gray by the weather and years and the flat plank weathered and rotted near the edges. He sat on a wrought iron bench near the tree, put his elbows on his knees, and folded his hands as he thought about how to approach Sean Mac Rian's requests. He frowned, and the oiska churned in his stomach as if to highlight his loathing of the northern duke. *The only thing Mac Rian wants is to be as close to the crown as possible,* he thought. *If he had more money, he'd try to take it himself.*

Braedan's distrust of Mac Rian ran deep. When Braedan was nine, Sean Mac Rian visited Torlach with his daughter, Olwyn. Swayed by the duke's sweet words, Braedan's father gave Mac Rian additional lands and all but eliminated the responsibilities Mac Rian had to the regency, saying that Duke Mac Rian needed all of his resources to rebuild his holdings since his father had squandered most of the family's wealth. *And now he comes to beg help from me. What will he promise me in return?* His stomach twisted again. *His daughter. And gods help me, he knows I need to wed.*

"Considering which chambermaid you plan to deflower next, Braedan?"

He opened his eyes. Igraine stood before him, arms crossed and green eyes flashing with anger. "Is something amiss, your highness?" He stood. "I don't know—"

"You do know, and more importantly, I know." She had changed from her riding habit to a jade green silk gown and bold jewels that would have overwhelmed a lesser woman. Her hair was looped and pinned into an intricate design halfway back on her head and left to swing unbound behind her. "Keep your hands off my maids, Braedan."

Braedan's guard took a step forward, but Braedan gestured him away. "My lady, I don't know what you're talking—"

"You bedded Gwyn," she said in a low, hissing tone. "I know you were with her last night. I spent the morning soothing her tears and attempting to assuage her guilt. I don't give a pig's member who you are, lad—she's a fifteen-year-old girl and you deflowered her without a thought to any needs but your own."

He folded his arms. "She said she was with me?"

"She didn't have to. She's been weeping all morning and the Lady Aislinn said she came out of your chambers while I was riding." She spoke each word distinctly. "Keep your hands off my maids, Braedan."

He laughed. "You presume to threaten me, Igraine?"

She lifted her chin. "You think I've not considered a way to follow through on a threat, then? You think I've nothing to keep from you, lad?" She lowered her voice. "If you want me, you'll keep your hands off my ladies and stop acting like a rutting goat."

He hated that his breath quickened. He forced himself to breathe slower. "Want you? I don't know what you mean. You're an ambassador and a foreign princess. I wouldn't presume to think of you improperly, highness."

Indignation crossed her face. "I'll not believe you've never looked at me and thought about it."

He couldn't resist goading her. He leaned closer to her ear and lowered his voice. "If I wanted a chance with you, lady, don't you think I would have asked for one by now?"

For the breath of a moment he thought she might slap him, but he should have known—he should have realized that Igraine would never do what he expected of her. She lifted her mouth and pressed her lips to the skin behind his ear, teasing him with the tip of her tongue just before she drew away enough to let her breath linger near his neck. "Tonight, when you're alone in your bed and all of my ladies are tucked safely away, consider that if you had waited, you could have had me."

He closed his eyes. "You tease me, my lady."

"I never tease about this." She drew away. "I will see you in the audience hall, majesty." She turned and walked away, the green silk clinging to her hips and her hair swaying with her proud gait.

Braedan let out a long breath. *At least she helped me shake the drink.* "Let's get back. The lords will be wondering where I am."

The audience hall had grown crowded in Braedan's absence. Several lords of the realm awaited him, and at the front, dressed in black and red silks and woolens, stood Sean Mac Rian. The lords all bowed low as Braedan ascended the dais and sat on the Raven Throne. Logan took a place next to him, affecting the easy stance of a man who could strike down a threat to the king and return to his position with no more than a blink.

As Braedan sat, the doors opened again, and his breath caught in his throat. Igraine glided in with two ladies trailing her. *The way she enters a room is the stuff of legend.* He stood again and descended to meet her. She offered her hand and a deep curtsy. He bowed. "Your highness. Do you join us today as an ambassador or as a petitioner?"

She straightened, her face a mask of regal propriety. "I'm here as an interested observer and friend of the court. If it pleases you, majesty."

Cormac called Mac Rian's petition. "Duke Sean Mac Rian of Fox Hill, your majesty. He requests your assistance with some difficulties with the tribes."

Braedan forced his eyes away from Igraine. The duke gave a low bow as he approached the dais. "Majesty. I humbly thank you for your attention to my petition," Mac Rian said.

"My lords are always welcome in my court," Braedan said, struggling to maintain an even, polite tone. "Tell me how I can assist you."

"The tribes, majesty. They have started to make forays across the boundary and into my holdings. I need additional men to help me hold them back. I fear for the peace between our peoples, but I fear more that the savages will overrun Kiern and its environs and penetrate Taura."

Braedan leaned back against the throne. "I've received your many letters, Duke Mac Rian. You still say you don't know why the tribes are encroaching on your territory?"

"No, majesty. I don't know. Their attacks seem unprovoked. I've lost good men to their spears and arrows, and I fear it's only a matter of time before I lose villagers. Already, merchants are using the east road out of fear of using the great road. I fear you will look weak, my lord."

If I deny him men, the tribesmen will make short work of him. "How I appear to other lords and tribesmen doesn't concern me much, Mac Rian. If you don't want to lose men, stay out of the forest. I need all of my men here." He nodded toward the door, dismissing Mac Rian.

"Sire, if I may?"

It was Igraine's voice. She'd risen from her bench, and all eyes turned toward her.

"You have something to add, highness?" Braedan asked.

"I realize it's not my place, my lord—I am your ambassador to the Great Kirok, not to the tribes, and I have little sway in your relations with your lords—but I think you may be too hasty in refusing men to assist Lord Mac Rian."

Braedan lifted an eyebrow. "Hasty? Do you presume to know the business of the tribes and northern lords, my lady?"

"May I speak freely?"

"When have you not spoken freely?"

An amused chuckle passed through the crowd. Igraine even smiled and gave a low, brief laugh. "My lord knows me well," she said in a low, purring timbre. "I wish only to point out that your lord uncle's men are still in the city shoring up the defenses of the army. If you might beg his indulgence and assistance, you could send the men from Stone Coast to investigate this matter."

Braedan glanced at Ronan, who shrugged as if to tell him to do as pleased him. "My lord uncle needs to return to his holdings before winter sets in," Braedan said.

"Then perhaps they could ride north and return to his holdings once this trouble with the tribes is settled." She turned to Ronan and smiled. "As long as you must go north anyway, why not take the great road and help your fellow lord sort out this trouble before you cross over to the east?"

Ronan stood. "If my nephew wishes my assistance in this matter, I am at his disposal—and at yours, my lord Mac Rian."

Braedan stifled a sigh. "And do you think you could get this matter sorted quickly, uncle?"

"Of course."

"My lord—" Igraine smiled again. "If I may, it would be a greater show of your authority if you would accompany your uncle."

"Do you have any concept of how to keep still?" Braedan snapped.

She lifted her eyebrows. "And do you have any concept of how to speak to a foreign royal?"

She gives as much as she gets. And gods help me, I can't be angry with her. He rubbed a hand across his mouth to hide a grin. *It's tempting to goad her just to hear her lilt.* He shook his head. *Pay attention. She wants you away from Torlach. Why?* "Who do you propose would look after affairs here, highness?"

"Your seneschal is a highly competent man. I'm sure he can look after everything. I am, of course, at your disposal as well, and I would be delighted to assist Lord Rowan."

Braedan sat up all the way. "You would assist Cormac?"

"If it please you."

Braedan shot a glance at Ronan, who gave an almost imperceptible shake of his head. "I don't feel comfortable leaving a foreign princess in a position of such authority," Braedan said.

Igraine blinked. "Sire, forgive me. I only meant that I could offer administrative assistance to Lord Rowan—legal research, assistance with correspondence, those kinds of things. I would not presume to govern in your stead, majesty."

Braedan rubbed his chin. The lords listened carefully, watching to see what he did. Mac Rian waited, eager and hopeful. *If I give Mac Rian the help he asks for, the rest of them will expect it as well. Still, I am his liege. If he asks, I should assist him.* He gestured to a servant. "Water." The boy bowed and brought a goblet, and Braedan took a long drink to give him a moment to consider his position. *Mac Rian isn't telling me everything. If I went north, I could find out what's really happening with the tribes and perhaps find a guardian myself. But if I anger Hrogarth in the process, is it worth it?* He glanced at Igraine again. *I can't let the other dukes think a foreign royal has sway over me, either. They'll assume my loins are doing the thinking.* He drank again to hide a grimace and shifted in his seat. *And I confess—they may be right. Damn woman.*

He gave the goblet to the servant. "Her highness speaks eloquently in favor of helping you, but I'm not prepared yet to acquiesce," he told Mac Rian. "Let me have a night to consider your request and her suggestion. I will give you my answer in the morning."

Mac Rian bowed. "Of course, sire." He backed away from the dais and sat. Igraine and Ronan returned to their seats as well.

Braedan turned to Cormac. "Who's next?"

Cormac called the next lord forward, and Braedan dispatched the petitions of the dukes and minor lords quickly. When Cormac signaled the guards to let in the other petitioners, the audience hall filled with commoners and merchants. Cormac introduced the petitioners one by one, and Braedan listened as boundary disputes, minor criminal cases, tax questions, and other matters were brought before him. He found himself stifling or hiding yawns in short order. Igraine's eyes rarely left his face.

When Cormac brought a common woman of middle years before him, he expected another boundary petition. "This woman is from your uncle's holdings, majesty," Cormac said. "She wishes to present her claim for ownership of her property."

Ronan stood. "Majesty, may I?"

"You may speak."

"This woman's petition has been before my court before. Her husband died some time back, and they had no surviving children. By law, without heirs, her property should be mine to claim."

"Sire, please," the woman said. "The farm belonged to my father. He bequeathed it to my husband when he died. I have men to work the land, but your lord uncle desires to put me out of my home." Tears welled in her eyes. "I've lived there my whole life. We've paid our dues—we've given our tenth to your lord uncle every year. We've always lived within the law. Am I to be homeless because I have no heir?"

"You have no one who could take you in, lady?" Braedan asked.

She lifted her chin and straightened her shoulders. "I'm an able-bodied woman capable of taking care of myself. I have no need of a keeper. My only crime is being a woman. I can't keep my farm because of my gender. Is this the king's justice?"

"Majesty, it is the law," Ronan said. "A woman cannot inherit property. I have offered to take the lady into my household as a maid, but she has refused."

"I am not a servant," the woman said. "Majesty, I beg mercy of you—let me keep my farm."

Braedan considered her. *People will follow a vision. I have a woman ambassador in my court. Perhaps it's time to change things.* "Very well. The king's court will be merciful. You can keep your home and lands, and upon your death, they will pass to Lord Kerry."

The woman's face broke into a wide smile amid shocked murmurs of the crowd. Ronan's face clouded. "Majesty, you cannot just overrule the law that way," he blurted.

And now my uncle will interrupt me as well? "If I can't, who can?" Braedan held up a hand when Ronan opened his mouth. "Protest again, uncle, and I'll have you escorted out." He gestured to the woman. "You can go, lady. Find a place to stay. Lord Rowan will draw up papers. Return tomorrow and your deed will be ready."

She curtsied, low, and started to speak, but Igraine stood and interrupted. "Majesty, forgive me again, but I fear you are making a grave error."

The hall fell silent. Braedan's shoulders tightened. *Will this woman ever learn to keep still? Who's king here?* He stood. "I warned my uncle, highness. Do you expect me to be more merciful for you than I was for him?"

"No, I expect you to listen and obey the law you purport to respect."

He motioned to Logan. "Escort her highness back to her chambers."

Igraine brushed Logan's hand away and took a step toward the king. "A moment, sire." She gave him a winsome smile. "Please."

That smile... I know what it does to me, I know why she uses it, and yet.... He sat on the throne again and folded his hands in his lap. "Make it brief."

"Forgive me, sire, but despite this woman's sympathetic argument, the law is not on her side. She cannot inherit property. It is sad and unfortunate, but the law does not recognize her as a separate and distinct person from her dead husband. Only a separate and distinct person can inherit property, and only men are recognized as such."

Braedan leaned back on the throne. Ronan and the common woman stared at Igraine. "I realize the problem, my lady, but I've already overruled the law and granted her request."

"And is it your plan to overrule the law every time you don't like it?" She stepped closer to the throne. "If the king thinks he operates outside the law, he is no better than a common criminal. You are bound, majesty. It is sad, and I grieve for this lady, but she has no legal options. You cannot overrule the law for one woman unless you plan to overrule the law for every woman."

My father would never have stood for this—for a woman speaking this way in open court. I should have her taken away. But . . . His hands tightened in his lap. "Do you argue to change the inheritance laws, my lady?"

"I am simply pointing out to your majesty that the law, as it stands today, is not on the side of this woman. It is on the side of your lord uncle. If the king will not follow the law, then the king opens his justice for abuse and disparity based on the whims of nobles and outlaws alike. If no one follows the law, anarchy will follow in short order." She paused. "But if the law is unjust, it is a matter for the king and his advisors to consider if it might be changed." Her eyes flicked down to his hands, and a hint of a smile twitched at her mouth.

She sees my tension. This woman misses nothing. He unfolded his hands and tapped his lip. She stood with the poise and elegance of a woman raised in a royal court, but she spoke with the wisdom and eloquence of a man practiced in law and leadership. He stood. "Her highness has given me much to consider. Forgive me, lady, but I will have to reconsider my ruling. Please come back to court tomorrow. I will give you my answer then."

The woman's eyes teared, but she swallowed once and curtsied. "As it please your majesty."

Braedan waved away the next paper Cormac tried to give him. "I've heard enough petitioners for today. I have much to consider. You may return tomorrow, and I'll begin hearing cases again." He descended to stand near Igraine. "Highness, a word in private?"

"Of course." She took his arm, and Logan and her ladies fell in behind them.

When they were out of earshot of the lords and petitioners, Braedan dropped her hand and turned to her. "Is this how it is in Eirya? Is this how your mother speaks to your father—interrupting his deliberations and scolding him in open court?"

She lifted her chin. "Aye, 'tis. If ye don't like it, get control of your court."

She had slipped back into her lilt as into an old pair of slippers. The sound of it tickled his ears. "I had control until you arrived."

She snorted. "Your control is an illusion. You speak without thinking, make decisions based on whim instead of the law or even thought. You're no better than your father if ye can't even handle a bit o' dissent."

His composure wavered. *She may as well have slapped me. It would have been easier to recover. Am I so much like my father?* He took a deep breath and lowered his voice. "Of all the people in the room who would argue with my decision in that final case, you are the last one I would have expected."

"D'ye think my desire for equality between genders and classes precludes my love of the law, then?"

"My pragmatic princess has little room in her spirit for mercy and exception."

Her mouth dropped. "Little room for mercy? You can't be serious. It is the role and obligation of the noble class to dispense mercy when and where it is required—as your uncle was doing by offering the woman a position in his household. Her pride kept her from accepting it. She desires only to stay in her family's home."

"And you don't think I was merciful?"

"Aye, perhaps, but you were breaking the law. Once she married, the law saw her and her husband as one person. When he died, it was as if she did as well for the purposes of ownership. Her circumstances are sad, but the law is clear." She smiled. "If the law recognized her as a separate and distinct person from her male relatives, we wouldn't have this issue, would we?"

"We come to the heart of it, don't we? You want the law changed."

"If the law is unjust, it is the duty of the king and his advisors to change it." She paused. "You are the king. You cannot just make exceptions to laws you don't like. You can, however, change the law by royal edict."

He crossed his arms. "I would need a very good reason to change a law, wouldn't I?"

She inclined her head. "I will write one for you." Her eyes softened, and she gave him a hesitant smile—a genuine smile. "I confess, sire, I thought ye'd have me in irons after my interruptions."

One corner of his mouth tilted involuntarily. "I should have. My father would have."

She laughed, low and seductive. "Then perhaps you are a better man."

And like that, I've forgiven her. What does this woman do to me? He offered his arm again. When they arrived at her door, he turned to her. "A moment in your study, my lady?"

"Of course."

Logan opened the door, and they both walked into the room, leaving her ladies in the hall. "Duke Guinness has returned from Eirya."

"I'm aware," she said. She walked to her desk and picked up a parchment with green wax. "He wrote me as well." Her face clouded, and she frowned.

"Something wrong at home?"

She put the parchment down. "Nothing I can't take care of. What of Duncan's return?"

"I want to welcome him back. I'm planning a banquet for tomorrow night."

She smiled. "A banquet. How lovely."

Her tone suggested she'd rather stab herself to death with an embroidery needle than attend his banquet. "You disapprove?"

She sighed. "No. 'Tis proper. I suppose you'll expect my attendance. Will I be there as your ambassador or as the Eiryan Princess Royale?"

"I hoped you would attend as my companion."

Her face turned to cool steel. "Your companion. You would dare to ask after your shameful behavior with Gwyn? To expect that I would sit on the dais near you and laugh at your jokes and pretend nothing is amiss when I know how you treated that girl? You're an ass, Braedan."

He stepped closer to her and forced himself to speak in measured tones. "I am asking a favor of you, my lady. There is an expectation that I will wed, and soon. At least two Taurin lords will be there to parade their daughters in front of me tomorrow night. If I could count on having you at my side for the evening, I could graciously put off a conversation with these lords." *And perhaps charm my way into your graces again.*

She folded her arms. "Do not become accustomed to receiving favors from me."

"I swear I will not."

Her mouth tightened. "I suppose there is no harm in playing this little game. Very well. I'll prepare myself appropriately."

He lifted her hand to his lips. "I owe you, Igraine."

"Rest assured that I will insist you pay that debt."

"It would likely be the easiest debt I'll ever pay."

"Do not be so certain." She removed her hand from his. "If you'll excuse me, majesty, I have work. I'll prepare an argument in favor of changing the inheritance laws for your review."

He inclined his head. "I look forward to reading it, your highness." He left her chambers and let out a long breath in the corridor. "Logan—walk with me."

Logan inclined his head and fell in step with Braedan. "Where are we going, sire?"

"Surprise inspection. Assemble your men."

"Of course, sire." Logan was silent for a moment. "The princess is a complicated lady."

Braedan stopped walking. "Why do you say that?"

"I've watched her. She has a way about her. The servants adore her. She showers them with kindnesses. She is distrustful of most of your guards, but she treats us with respect. She and Cormac get along well, even when she vexes him." He shrugged. "She is complicated."

She's Eiryan. The country was as well-known for its progressive ideas as for its brutal military strategies, for its humble beginnings as for its current wealth. *She's as much a paradox as her own country.* "I need to walk," Braedan said, and they walked the rest of the way to the guard quarters in silence.

Emrys hovered just inside the guardhouse, waiting. A tall, blond guard entered as the last of the other guards left, and Emrys hovered above the guard's shoulder while he removed his sword and boots and took off his livery. At his ankle, a leather strap stretched tight through a murky gray stone. He sat down, crossed his ankle over his knee, and studied the stone.

Emrys shook off the protections of the elements and appeared next to Matthias. "You've done well, Matthias."

Matthias startled and turned to Emrys, hand on his dagger. When he saw the familiar face, he relaxed. "You. I looked for you after you showed me his majesty's camp, but I could never find you."

"I always planned to return when it was time. Now, it's time."

When Emrys had directed Matthias to Braedan's camp from the tumbledown public house where the young man worked, he hadn't been certain his plan would work. He'd been sure his mistress would find this creature before Emrys could gain his allegiance. Now, Matthias was his, and his mistress had no idea of his existence. *As long as he doesn't shift yet, she won't know he's here.* "Do you still wear the talisman I gave you?"

Matthias pulled it from under his shirt. "Always, as you instructed. What does it do?"

"It protects you from harmful magic."

Matthias frowned. "What harmful magic?"

"There are wards around Taura. The talisman keeps them from harming you." He paused. "The woman Igraine—you find her bewitching."

Matthias' eyes grew hungry. "Any man with breath in his body would find Igraine bewitching. Have you seen her?"

Emrys suppressed a grimace. "She does not appeal to me. She has dangerous magic that threatens your king. I want you to kill her."

Matthias' face paled, but under it was the bloodlust of his kind—the longing to shred skin and break bone and tear organs. His voice dropped to a whisper. "You ask me to betray my king. He doesn't want to risk war with Eirya."

Beneath the loyal words, Emrys heard desire. "If you want the woman, that's no concern of mine. As long as she ends up dead, I don't care what you do with her first."

Matthias' fingers twitched and curved into a claw-like form, and his voice turned hoarse with need. "What do you suggest?"

CHAPTER FIFTEEN

May Alshada give you a gentle path,
a light heart, and a boon companion.
— Eiryan blessing

Igraine fidgeted before the mirror, fussing with the neckline of her blue silk gown. It revealed a fair amount of skin, and she wondered if she should risk so much for her first formal banquet in Torlach. She picked up the sheer Eiryan lace her mysterious admirer had left and covered her shoulders. *It helps. A bit.*

Attending Braedan's banquet as his companion wasn't only a favor to him, though she was happy to let him believe so. If Duncan Guinness could see that she had influence over the Taurin throne, he might be inclined to speak favorably of her position to her father. Sitting next to Braedan, laughing at his jokes, and playing the noble lady for a night was a small price to pay for continued freedom. *Besides, it's not a painful price. I can think of worse men to spend an evening with.*

Gwyn opened Igraine's bedchamber door and gave a quick curtsy. "Your highness, it's time. Commander Mac Kendrick is waiting to escort you to the banquet."

Igraine smoothed her dress once more and went to the door. Logan's usually stoic expression softened. "My lady," he said, offering his arm. "Forgive me for being forward, but the king will be proud to have you next to him on the dais tonight."

"Thank you, Logan." She took his arm. "Who has arrived so far?"

He curved her hand around his arm in a familiar gesture that would have earned any other guard a scolding. "The lords and ladies here in the castle are drifting in. Duke Mac Rian and his daughter haven't yet arrived, but they are staying in an inn near the castle."

She nodded and sighed.

"Heavy heart, your highness?"

She laughed. "No. I simply don't care for these functions."

"While there are common folk at the gates who would trade everything they own for a glance from you or the king," he said.

"D'ye think I don't know my role well enough, then?" She scoffed. "'Tis one I've been groomed to play, or couldn't you tell?"

"You play it admirably, my lady." Logan was silent for a moment. "Igraine," he said, quiet. "May I ask why you are doing this?"

"Have we grown so close that you use my familiar name?"

"Haven't we?"

She hid a grin. "Perhaps. What is it you're concerned about?"

"You are letting his majesty believe that you might have more in mind than just working as his ambassador."

She turned to him. "The king is no innocent in these games. He refuses to choose or deny the Lady Olwyn or the Lady Aislinn. He lets them believe they have opportunity to become the next queen of Taura."

"And is that what you want? A crown?"

"Be careful, Commander. Your words have an edge."

"That's my job—keeping the king safe behind sharp edges."

She inclined her head. "The crown I already have is heavy enough. I have no need for another." She put her hand on his arm again. "Take me to the banquet."

The low murmur of voices greeted Igraine as they approached the banquet hall. Guards opened the door, and Logan stood aside as the steward announced her. "Igraine Mac Roy, Princess Royale of Eirya and Taurin Ambassador to the Great Kirok in Aliom."

Logan led her down the steps of the banquet hall to the echoes of light applause from the lords and ladies. Her eyes fell on a familiar face already at the long table on the dais. "Duncan!"

Duncan Guinness stood, his smile creasing his weathered face under black hair salted at the sides with gray. "Grainy." He took her hands and kissed her cheek. "'Tis a relief to see you well and whole."

She squeezed his hands and returned the kiss. "I'm far too cagey to die in some silly political wranglings. Where is Cara?"

"She stayed on Eirya. She grows heavy with child, and she didn't want to risk giving birth at sea. She'll join me after the child comes."

"How does she fare?"

"Well. Very well. She's beautiful when she's with child." He lowered his voice. "I was not meant to be a widower. Give me the joy of a young woman's touch in my home and the sound of children laughing, and I'm a happy man."

She smiled. "It shows."

Logan had retreated to escort more noble ladies, so Duncan seated Igraine and sat at her right hand. "Tell me what this ambassadorship is about, Grainy." He picked up his goblet. "Your father is not happy."

She avoided his eyes and sipped the heavy wine. "Your letter was quite clear about my father's opinions of my choice. We can discuss it tomorrow with the king."

"I'd like to hear more about it without the king present."

She nodded a greeting to a lady who passed by the dais. "I wanted more than the kirok. You know that."

"And you thought squirming your way into an ambassadorship would do that, then?" His voice was edged with an odd mixture of reproach and pride.

The accent of home felt familiar and comforting to Igraine. She took a long drink of wine, set down her goblet, and turned to him. "What would you have me do, Duncan?"

"I would have married you. You know that." His voice was tight.

"You loved Cara."

"I would have put that aside."

She put a hand on his arm. "I care too much for you to see you bound to me when you love another."

"Igraine—"

They were interrupted by the steward announcing another guest. "Ronan Kerry, Duke of Stone Coast."

Ronan Kerry strode to the dais and approached Igraine. "Your highness, what a vision you are tonight." He took her hand and bowed.

She forced a proper smile. *Time to play royal games.* "My lord is kind."

"Just honest. Will you take a turn with me around the room, my lady?"

She tensed. To greet her and offer his hand was entirely proper and appropriate, but to ask for a turn implied he wished for more than a proper greeting. *Still, with eyes on me, I can't refuse. What will the gossips think?* "Of course, my lord." She stood and put one hand on his arm.

He led her off the dais and toward the edges of the hall where only the servants walked. "I was impressed by your eloquence this afternoon, highness. I had no idea you were so well-read in Taurin law," he said, inclining his head toward her ear.

She took a half-step to the side to put more space between them. "I've had little else to do while I wait for the kirok to send ambassadors. I read, I visit the kirons and sayas, and I wait. I like the law."

"That's clear." He lowered his voice and kept his eyes straight ahead. "Be careful though, highness. Don't reach too high."

She stopped. "Too high? I don't know what you mean."

He turned to her and put one hand on the hilt of the dress sword at his side. "You suggested helping Cormac govern while the king is away. A foreign princess has no right to sit on the Raven Throne unchecked."

She lifted her chin. "I have no desire to sit on the Raven Throne at all."

"I would not have thought you would reach as high as ambassador, either, yet here you are. What do you want, Igraine?"

She straightened her shoulders. "I think that's for me to discuss with Braedan. You have no business—"

"He's my nephew, my king, and my heir," he said, his voice turning into a low hiss. "I will make it my business." He paused. "What do you want?"

A purpose. A mission. She gave him a cool gaze. "I wish to return to my seat, my lord, rather than listen to the thinly veiled insults of a man who didn't have the fire to take the throne for himself."

His mouth turned grim. "I had no right. He had the better claim."

"In a coup, swords matter, not claims. Return me to my seat or I will walk there myself and propriety be damned."

A sneer curled one corner of his mouth, and he put a hand on her arm, fingers tightening enough for her to understand the unspoken threat. "You are a fiery one, aren't you? Is that pretty mouth useful for anything besides speaking out of turn?"

For one moment, she considered slapping him. Instead, she stepped closer and lowered her voice. "You have just ensured you will never find out."

Duncan leaned over to her as she reached her seat amid the whispers and covert glances of nobles in the hall. "Are you well, Grainy?"

She smiled at Duncan, picked up her goblet, and sipped her wine. "I'm fine, Duncan. Please, tell me all the news from the Citadel."

When Braedan arrived a few moments later, Igraine stood with the rest of the room as he walked the long banquet hall and approached his seat on the dais. His easy smile and sharp blue eyes greeted the lords and ladies around him. Igraine's stomach fluttered at the sight of him. *By the gods, he's easy to look at.*

When he arrived at his seat, Braedan lifted Igraine's hand and bowed as she curtsied. "My lady. I confess part of me regrets insisting on your presence tonight."

"Have I displeased, sire?"

"On the contrary—I fear I won't be able to concentrate on any matters of state with your beauty to distract me." He swept one hand toward the crowd. "And I confess I do feel a twinge of guilt for the sake of all these ladies. You shame their beauty."

She couldn't resist a smile. *I shouldn't let sweet words go to my head.* She inclined her head. "You are too kind, majesty."

Duncan stood and bowed to Braedan. "Majesty. I thank you for the honor of an invitation."

Braedan inclined his head. "Lord Guinness. I'm pleased you chose to attend tonight, and I'm sure our royal lady is happy to hear news from Eirya."

Duke Mac Rian entered the room, his daughter on his arm, and Braedan's eyes widened. The duke's daughter was a beauty, Igraine thought. Her raven-black hair fell to her waist. Her eyes were heavy and dark, and her skin had the faint coppery sheen that spoke of Esparan blood. She was tall and lithe and walked with a gliding gait. Igraine felt a stab of envy at the woman's tiny waist and perfect proportions.

Mac Rian walked up the dais and bowed to Braedan. "My lord, may I present my daughter, Lady Olwyn Mac Rian."

Braedan took her hand and bowed. "My lady. We have met before, I believe, but we were both much younger."

The lady curtsied. "I do remember, your majesty." She had a low purr to her voice that distracted even loyal Duncan's ear, Igraine saw. "It has been too long. The years have blessed you."

"And you, lady. Every promise in that youthful face I recall is fulfilled in the beauty I see before me." He gestured to Igraine. "I have the honor to introduce you to my companion for tonight, Igraine Mac Roy, Princess Royale of Eirya."

Olwyn turned to Igraine, and Igraine waited for her to curtsy first. Olwyn's mouth twitched into a forced smile, and after one long moment, she offered a curtsy. "Your highness."

Igraine merely inclined her head. *Make me wait, will you? You should learn your place.* "Lady. Welcome."

Olwyn straightened and lifted her chin. She gestured to the food. "Such a lovely meal, your majesty. I do wish I had a larger appetite. I fear I won't be able to enjoy everything here as much as some of your guests." Her eyes flickered over Igraine's body.

Braedan turned his head, but not before Igraine saw his grin. "Please, my lord and lady—be seated." He picked up a goblet and hid his mouth.

Igraine saw the twinkle in his eyes. *Ass. Does he think to play me against Olwyn?* "Something funny, my lord?" she whispered when he sat.

"Not at all," he said.

The steward tapped the floor again, and Cormac entered the hall. He walked toward the dais as his name and titles were called, but when he saw Olwyn, he paled. His breath quickened, and his eyes flickered away from Olwyn. He approached Braedan and bent down to whisper something. Braedan frowned. "Are you well?"

"I-I'm well," he said, loud enough that Igraine could hear. "I just have work. Will you excuse me, sire?"

"Of course, Cormac. We will speak on the morrow." Cormac offered a quick bow and ducked his eyes before scurrying from the hall.

Braedan frowned, but then turned to the assembled guests and announced the feast begun. He sat and leaned toward Igraine. "Do you know what that was about?" he asked behind his wine goblet.

She also hid her mouth when she replied. "No, sire. When I spoke with him earlier, he still had plans to attend the banquet. Perhaps something new has arisen that requires his attention?"

"He didn't mention anything."

She lifted her goblet and lowered her voice to a near whisper. "It began when he saw the Lady Olwyn."

Braedan turned to her, his eyes twinkling. He gave her a crooked grin. "Jealous that he had no such reaction for you, my lady?"

"I have no desire to drive fear into men's hearts."

"No?" He didn't wait for her to answer. "I'm sure he's all right. He usually eats in his chambers and doesn't much care for these kinds of events."

"Neither do I, but I'm here, aren't I?" The servants came with the first course then—a rich beef broth seasoned with leeks. She lifted her bowl and raised her voice again. "Your majesty, in Eirya, it is custom for lords and ladies to share the bowl with those to either side. The bowl offers the warmth of friendship and hospitality and protection. May I?"

He nodded. "Please."

She sipped from her bowl, then lifted it to his lips and tilted it so that he could sip. "Now you."

He lifted his bowl and sipped, then offered her a sip. "A lovely custom." He stood. "We are nothing to our Eiryan cousins if not accommodating." He gestured to Duke Kerry to stand and repeated the ceremony while Igraine did the same with Duncan. Lords and ladies around the hall repeated the process, murmurs of agreement and praise fluttering throughout the room. Braedan put his hand on her arm. "Thank you for sharing that, my lady."

I'm a foolish girl, besotted by sweet words and chaste touches. She smiled and sipped her wine and tried to shake off the sensation of his hand.

As courses came and went, Igraine spent much time listening to Duncan tell her news of home, her parents, and her brothers and their families. She was worried when he said there had been no word from Ian for several months, but Duncan tried to reassure her. "The lad writes many letters when he's asea and sends them all at once when he reaches a port," he said. "Your lady mother will go months without news and then catch up all in one evening when a horse arrives."

"You can't begrudge me my concerns, Duncan. He's my closest brother and completely guileless. Should he fall into something dangerous—"

"He won't. He sails with Robert Dougal now."

That was some relief. Captain Robbie, as he was known, had a girth nearly as wide as his ship, a peg leg, and a temper as foul as a winter squall, but he was shrewd and successful and had been sailing trading ships longer than Igraine had been alive. "I hope my father's anger isn't so great that he would keep word of Ian from me?"

"No, of course not." He drank and picked at the ribs on his plate—leavings from a side of rich grass-fed beef from northern Taura. "Your father worries for you. You are his only daughter. He only wishes the best for you."

We have very different opinions of what that may be, Igraine thought.

When the beef had been cleared and a light salad of bitter greens, sweet apples, and candied walnuts was placed before them, Braedan leaned over to her. His eyes were still alert and bright, and she realized that he had only just started his second cup of wine. Other lords and ladies were well into their cups. Even Duncan and Sean Mac Rian looked flushed and glassy-eyed. "I wish, highness, that I had thought to bring in some entertainment. I fear my haste caused me to overlook such niceties."

"You needn't pay a harper when you have Princess Igraine present," Duncan said. "The lady is well-practiced and greatly gifted in song."

Why did you mention that? "Duke Guinness is too generous with his praise," she said, giving him a harsh look. He grinned behind his goblet. "He praises me because he has much love for my family. In truth, sire, I sing only slightly better than a braying hound and harp only enough to please my lady mother."

"I find that difficult to believe. I must hear this." He signaled for a steward.

"Majesty, please. I am out of practice and—"

"Please, your highness." It was Duke Kerry's voice. He lifted his goblet. "Grace us with a song. Let us all hear if you can sing as elegantly as you speak."

She gave the duke a cool smile. "My lord, we have a saying in Eirya: 'The man who wishes for rain sometimes suffers from flood.'"

Braedan laughed. He whispered to the steward and then turned to Olwyn. "And you, my lady? Do you sing or play?"

She lifted heavy eyes to his. "I sing, majesty, but only for more intimate audiences."

Igraine rolled her eyes. *Why doesn't she just disrobe right here?*

Within a few moments, the steward returned carrying a small harp. Braedan stood and plucked the strings. To Igraine's surprise, he started to tune it and strummed a chord. "It was my mother's," he told Igraine when he passed it to her. His voice was tight and low. "She had a beautiful voice. What I remember of it."

"I will attempt to do it justice, majesty." She stood and descended the dais to stand in the center of the hall. Her hands turned cold and her palms started to sweat, and she feared dropping the harp. A look at Braedan emboldened her. *Why does he affect me this way? I haven't felt this bold since—* She shivered. *I won't think of him.* She tuned the harp and ran her fingers over the carved willow bark and strings. Voices around the hall hushed as she began to pick out notes and chords. The harp was in excellent condition and well-made, the strings still supple and easy to strum. "'Tis been some time since I had an audience, my lords and ladies. If I offend your ears, rest assured that I will understand if you leave." There were gentle chuckles at that.

She tuned for a moment longer and then shot a glance at Ronan Kerry. He met her eyes and lifted his goblet. She began to strum a lively tune, tapping her toe in time. "My lords and ladies, I'm sure you know of the fine sheep of Eirya—those with the red wool flecked with gold. Some poets say Alshada himself gave our sheep the color of sunrise when he saw them on the eastern shore." She dropped her voice. "But, I know the true story."

> *A Taurin lad with hair of gold,*
> *Heigh ho, heigh ho,*
> *Did wash ashore one winter cold,*
> *Heigh, heigh ho.*
>
> *His eyes fell on a maiden fair—*
> *Heigh ho, heigh ho,*
> *With curly locks of copper hair,*
> *Heigh, heigh ho.*

The audience started to clap.

> *The lad gave chase his lass to seek—*
> *Heigh ho, heigh ho,*
> *But she proved timid, mild, and meek—*
> *Heigh, heigh ho.*

When they found the eastern shore,
Heigh ho, heigh ho,
He pled "stay with me evermore!"
Heigh, heigh ho.

Everyone was clapping now and cheering her on. The story wound on, and Igraine kept it rising until the young lad caught his maiden in a dark wood, and she finally succumbed to his amorous advances. When he woke in the morning with his arms around her and his face in her hair, he realized it was a sheep he had caught. By then, he so loved the ewe that he stayed with her and gave all Eiryan sheep the golden cast of his hair.

The lords and ladies laughed and cheered when she finished—all but Ronan Kerry. He clapped politely, but his mouth was drawn into a tight frown. "You sing prettily, my lady, but such a bawdy song."

She raised one eyebrow and affected a sweet tone. "You did wonder, my lord, what my mouth was good for." The lords and ladies laughed, including Braedan. Igraine's stomach fluttered with pleasure. "But lest you think I can only sing bawd, let me sing you another song—if it please his majesty."

Braedan inclined his head and smiled. "It does. Please sing whatever you wish."

She smiled at Duncan. "To honor my lord father's loyal ambassador and my dear friend Duke Duncan Guinness, a song of Eirya." She slowed the pace and began a melody in a minor key.

Where sapphire water meets emerald turf
And rocky shores do rise,
Where silver waves bring mighty ships
There will I rest my eyes.

Eirya, land of songs and dreams
Land of poets fair
Let me rest upon your shore
And free me from all care.

All Eiryan children learned the song. Eiryan people sang it on feast days to recall why their people left Taura. Eirya was a land of beauty and song, hardship and trial. She closed her eyes and remembered home. When a deep, rich baritone voice joined her alto, she opened her eyes. Duncan had descended the dais to join her in the song, his eyes misty.

> *My hopes will rest on emerald hills,*
> *On silver mountaintops,*
> *On sapphire waves and northern fields,*
> *On golden barley crops.*
>
> *When low I join my fathers past,*
> *My soul to heaven flies,*
> *Rest my body on that isle*
> *Where emerald hills do rise.*

When the last note died away, she took Duncan's hand and stretched to kiss his cheek. The entire hall applauded, and Duncan led her back to the dais.

Braedan stood. She started to give him the harp, but he shook his head. "Keep it, my lady. For now. I wish to hear you play again. You have the voice of one of the fabled fair folk, even when you sing the bawd."

She lowered her eyes and inclined her head. "You are too kind, your majesty."

"I speak only the truth." He met her eyes and lifted her hand to his mouth. His lips lingered against her hand.

She stepped closer to him. "Majesty—"

"Forgive me. I have duties." He turned back to the banquet hall and signaled the steward to bring the final course—a tart of pears and apples in a heavy cream.

When everyone had finished, Braedan stood. "Lords and ladies, I thank you for attending tonight. I promise you that the next feast you are invited to will be held with more notice." He lifted a goblet to Igraine. "Perhaps there will be reason to celebrate. Please, stay and enjoy your wine and oiska. I must bid you all good night as I have early duties." He lifted Igraine's hand and kissed it, said good night to the other men on the dais, and bid Lady Aislinn and Lady Olwyn good night. Olwyn stepped very close to him to whisper in his ear. He grinned and kissed her hand again, but then shook his head and left the dais.

Duncan and Igraine spoke for a few more moments as some of the lords and ladies began to leave, and then Logan entered the hall. He walked up to Igraine and bent low to her ear. "My lady, may I escort you back to your rooms?"

"In a moment. I'm speaking with Lord Guinness."

Logan hesitated. "Highness, there is pressing business. May we speak in the corridor?"

She frowned. "Of course. Excuse me, Duncan. I fear I'm needed elsewhere." She bid farewell to the other lords and Lady Olwyn, took Logan's arm, and followed him into the back corridor where servants bustled back and forth. "What is it? The sayas—"

"The kirok people are well. The king requests the pleasure of your company, but he didn't want everyone to know."

A shiver passed through her. Logan held out her cloak, and she let him help her into it and clasp it. "Where is he?"

"He waits on the north wall. Your maid let me into your room to retrieve your cloak. The king wishes to meet you away from prying eyes and ears."

"Of course." She took Logan's arm, and he led her through back rooms and corridors to the north wall of the castle.

Braedan rested his arms on the wall and stared toward the hills in the distance, his profile outlined faintly in the waxing moon. He turned and smiled at her. "Thank you, Logan. You're dismissed. I'll see the lady safely back to her chambers."

When they were alone, Braedan took her hands. "Forgive my clandestine request, Igraine. Tongues wag at court, as I'm sure you know. I didn't want anyone to see us leave together."

"And yet you asked me to accompany you and sit in the place of your queen."

"Did you like that place?"

"I liked it only as much as I enjoyed the company to either side of me." She dropped his hands. "Braedan, I'm tired. I've had enough of courtly games. If there is something you need to ask of me, please be about it. I'd like to be abed."

His mouth curved into a distracted smile, and he lifted one hand to twirl a lock of her hair around his finger. "I spoke at length with my uncle this afternoon," he said, but she sensed that it wasn't what he really wanted to say. "We agreed that I would accompany him north to investigate the trouble with the tribes."

"I'm glad to hear that. 'Twill serve you well to show your authority in the north." *And it will rid the castle of your uncle and his men while you ensure he's not scheming behind your back.*

He pulled his hand away from her hair and cleared his throat. "I'll leave Cormac in charge, but I want you to help him. Your knowledge of Taurin law is admirable. I'd like to appoint you as a legal advisor to the crown."

She lifted an eyebrow. "A foreign princess in such a position? That's not what you wanted yesterday."

"You've given me no reason to doubt your loyalty to me. I read your proposal to change the inheritance laws and found little reason to disagree with your opinion. You have a sharp mind, and your work is flawless. You won't have the power to make decisions—only to offer legal opinions. Do you want the position?"

It's a position I've dreamed of. "I'm honored by the trust you've placed in me, your majesty, but I don't want to lose the ambassadorship."

"Do you think you can do both?"

"Of course."

"Then you accept?"

Gods, yes. Of course. She kept her voice steady. "I would be pleased to serve your court this way. Do you plan to propose a change to the inheritance laws?"

"I am considering it."

"And the woman from yesterday? What of her?"

"I told her she could stay in her home for six more months while I review the law." He hesitated and shifted his feet. He picked up her hand again. "There is a way I could give you more authority."

"Oh?"

He nodded. "If you were queen, you could serve as both an advisor and my regent when I am away."

It took every bit of Igraine's practiced royal training to keep from gaping at the suggestion. *Queen. When he said he wanted affection? Does he feel that way, then?* She cleared her throat. "I-I doubt your uncle would approve."

He laughed. "Did you sing that song just to spite him?"

"Perhaps."

He chuckled. "My uncle offers his opinions, but my decisions are mine alone. A marriage would cement an alliance between our countries and give my reign legitimacy. Besides, as valuable as you are to my court as an ambassador and a legal advisor, your beauty, talent, and wit are wasted in any position less than queen."

Silence surrounded them as she considered what to say. *This wasn't what I expected.* "Are you asking me for permission to approach my father?"

One side of his mouth tilted into a smile. "I suppose I am."

She closed her eyes. "I don't want a political marriage."

He lifted her hand to his mouth. "This is more than politics. I am growing fond of you."

The words softened her heart, but she squared her shoulders. "And yet you still find time to carouse with chambermaids. That's not the behavior of a man who is growing fond of a woman."

"You would have me believe you've never caroused with Logan?"

She frowned. "Logan? Why would you say that?"

"I know he takes you riding out to the lake. And there have been rumors. I've not said anything, but I have wondered what is between you two."

So much, and yet nothing. He is a friend and a stranger at once. And spirits help me, I betray your trust with him—but not in the way you would think. She pushed the thoughts away. "Logan has never been anything but a perfect gentleman."

"Hasn't he?"

"No. He is a friend and a trusted guard only." She put a hand on his arm. "And he is no king."

He took both of her hands. "Am I king enough?"

"You will be, in time." She twined her fingers with his. "I confess, Braedan. I am growing fond of you as well."

The sound of the banquet hovered in the background. Men in the watchtowers murmured in low voices, and in the distant woods, wolves called to each other. Braedan stepped closer to her. His hands went under the cloak and around her waist. His mouth hovered next to hers. Her breath quickened. He tightened his hands on her waist, pulled her closer, and pressed his mouth on hers.

Igraine's knees went weak. She was no stranger to kisses, but Braedan's mouth on hers was so sweet and hungry that she gasped. His hands ran up her sides and back under the cloak. *Don't give up too much—don't let him have too much*—but her body melted against his. She put her arms around his neck. *He kisses as if he hadn't kissed a woman in years.*

It was some time before he pulled away from her. "You make it difficult to believe you are chaste, lady."

He did not take his arms from her waist, and as she slid her hands down from his neck, she found herself regretful. "You make it difficult to deny you, my lord."

"You vex me. I've never been so unbalanced by a woman."

She found that satisfying. "Lady Olwyn—she doesn't vex you?"

"Are you jealous?"

"No. You asked me out here, not her."

He laughed. "Olwyn is not one I would want to share the throne with."

"What about your bed?"

He shook his head. "I've seen Olwyn's true nature. When I was nine, she and her father visited Torlach. I watched her whip a young horse bloody. She was only seven, but she ordered her servants to hold the horse still until she'd torn gashes in the filly's side." He laced his fingers in the small of her back. "What about Duncan Guinness?"

"What about him?"

He lowered his head for a moment and laughed. "You would make me beg? Igraine, tell me what favor Lord Guinness owes you."

She considered withholding the information longer, but his face was earnest and open, and she took pity on him. "Duncan was widowed several years ago. My father was looking for a match for me, and he asked Duncan. I care very much for Duncan, but as a favorite uncle only, and he was in love with one of my ladies in waiting. I released him from his vow by refusing to wed him so that he could marry Cara. My father was furious, but Duncan and Cara got what they wanted. I took the brunt of my father's anger."

He pulled her closer. "Could you be my queen, Igraine?"

She hesitated and stared out toward the lake. "This place—it's not Eirya."

"Do you miss home?"

"I do. I miss familiar voices and the sounds of the market in the city—the accent of my people. I had hoped to go home one day, perhaps." She closed her eyes. "But there are days . . . Sometimes, when I'm in the courtyard, I catch the scent of the sea, and I feel like I'm home, riding past the fishing village. Sometimes the mists hover over the tor, and I think of the low rocky peaks of Eirya. When I hear merchants haggle and one has the accent of home, I almost feel I'm there." She stopped. "I sound foolish."

"No. You sound like a woman who loves her country the way I love Taura." He paused. "Do you like it here?"

She considered that. "I do. Here I have a purpose."

"Then stay. Become my queen."

"Braedan, I don't know. Marriage, children—it's not what I want."

He tipped his head. "You suggested you might want me in your bed."

"And I did and do, but as a lover, not a husband."

"If I promise you more than just the life of a pampered royal, would you consent to marriage? To giving me an heir?"

Her heart raced. "What do you mean by 'more'?"

"I'd let you keep your current positions. I'd never relegate you to serving as a queen who plays court and plans parties." He pulled her closer. "I want to make Taura something better. I think I could do that with your help."

She hesitated. "Such a thing would require more than just me giving my consent. I could defy my father in asking for a position within your government, but for a marriage, he will expect consideration. He will want a formal agreement. I can't just run away and give you my consent."

"We are seeing Lord Guinness tomorrow. We can discuss it with him. If you are giving your consent now, that is."

I want to, but can you promise the one thing that means most to me? "I want your faithfulness. I won't marry a man who can't keep his breeches on when he's away from my bed. No more chambermaids, no more whores. I'll not be a silent trophy for you to trot out when you want to show how progressive you are. You can be a man who honors his commitments and his vows. I deserve nothing less."

A smile twitched at the corners of his mouth. She couldn't tell whether he was mocking her or admiring her. "You want position, power, faithfulness. Anything else?"

"I want the sayas sent to Eirya, and I want the kiroks rebuilt in the duchies and the countryside. I'll do what I can to see that the kirok builds them, but I want your guarantee that you won't interfere with the kirok again once I work out the treaty with the elders."

"Done. Do I have your consent to discuss your hand with Lord Guinness?"

Marriage. It's too much. It's not what I wanted. But though his ascension was brutal, he had listened to her and followed her advice on many matters, not just those surrounding the kirok. *And I can't deny the way he makes me feel.* "I had hoped—if not for love, at least for affection or compatibility if I wed."

He leaned closer to her ear and kissed her neck. His voice was low and strained, and he tightened his grip on her. "We could easily discover if we're compatible, Igraine. And as for affection, I have developed a great deal of it for you."

She closed her eyes. "Compatibility—are you asking—?"

He laughed against her neck. "No. Not tonight. I'll prove to you that I'm more than a rutting goat first."

She lifted her chin, and his mouth traveled along her neck as she suppressed a whimper of desire. "You have my consent."

He raised his head and kissed her once more. "I will ensure that you never regret that choice, Igraine."

He took her arm, and they turned back toward the main part of the castle. When they arrived at her bedchamber door, he kissed her once more and then stepped back and bowed. "Good night, your highness."

She curtsied, tempted to ask him to stay. "Good night," she finally said. Logan stood guard at her door. He opened it as the king walked away, and she stepped into her rooms and sighed. *This was not what I expected. Still, it's not unwelcome. Have I only needed the right man? Perhaps it wasn't marriage I loathed.*

She checked on her maids in the smaller bedchamber and then went into her own room and removed her jewels. A faint rustle from her wardrobe made her stop. *Someone else is here.* She picked up the small knife she kept on her dresser. *Something's wrong.* "Who's there?"

He gave her no time to shout. One hand flicked her knife away and gripped her wrist, and the other went over her mouth in a swift, sudden movement. "Try to cry out, my lady, and I'll snap your neck before the sound leaves your throat." He twisted her arm around behind her back and pushed her toward the wall.

He was dressed entirely in black, but she recognized the blue eyes and golden beard of one of the king's guardsmen at once. She fought to breathe around the rag he held over her nose and mouth. Her free hand struck at him, but he simply stuffed the rag into her mouth and snatched her hand. "I've watched you, lady," he said. "I've heard how you speak to the king." He held both wrists behind her back in one massive hand. She struggled, but his grip was too strong to budge. He pulled a rope from his belt and turned her around against the wall, pressing one knee into her back. "I wonder—how did you convince him to keep you alive, Igraine? Did you open your legs that first night?" She felt the rope slide over her wrists. "Did you tease him, make him *wait*, the way you've made me *wait*?" The rope tightened in one brutal yank, burning her skin and forcing a grunt of pain.

He turned her around again and pulled a dagger out of his belt. A heavy arm held her across the chest while he trailed the dagger's point down her body. "I wonder what the king would say if I told him I saw you with Logan. I saw you in the stables, adjusting your skirts. I *know* you've been with him."

She could only stare at the glint of madness in his eyes. *Made him wait? I've barely noticed him. I don't even know his name!* Her eyes darted around the room, desperate for a weapon, an escape, a way to call for help.

He slapped her. "Look at me. Don't look away. I want you to see everything." He pinned her shoulders to the wall and pushed his body up against hers. The cool steel of his dagger pricked her neck, and she hissed. He used the point of the dagger to slice the dress off her shoulder. "You wore my lace tonight. You know, don't you? You understand. We're two halves of a whole, Igraine. You're the other half of me." He put his mouth on her neck.

She remembered the small stand by her bed where she kept a pitcher of water and a book. She wriggled her leg free enough to kick it, and the stand toppled. The heavy book and pitcher, the goblets and candlestick, the table all fell with a crash.

The guard cursed and struck at her with the knife. She ducked and ran toward the door. She spat out the rag and screamed. "Gwyn, Logan—help!"

She tried to open the latch with her bound hands, but he pressed her against the door, the knife to her neck. "I said I would kill you. I told him I would. I *can't*!" The flat of the dagger pressed into her skin. He closed his eyes, opened them, seeming to steel himself to do it. She tried to fight him again, but couldn't move. He had her pinned.

"My lady!" Gwyn was pounding on the door. "Guards—her highness—the princess!"

A growl rose from the man's chest, and he tipped his head back to howl in frustration. "I have to kill you!" The dagger pressed against her neck again. Blood trickled down her throat. She screamed.

He shoved her to the floor and ran for the window. The door crashed open. Logan was there, and Gwyn. The guard fixed his eyes on Igraine's. "We're one."

Logan drew his sword and took three steps. Glass shattered, and the guard jumped. Gwyn screamed.

But there was no impact. Igraine struggled to her feet. "Where is he?"

Logan swore an unfamiliar curse under his breath. He pointed. "Look."

In the distance, two great black wings rose into the sky to cross the moon.

CHAPTER SIXTEEN

For the man who serves Alshada faithfully,
there is eternal rest in the golden city.
— Proverb of the Kirok in Aliom

Igraine twisted the cup of tea in her hands. Logan's mouth was grim. Duncan's eyes were tense, angry, and defensive. Gwyn's face was pale and frightened. "I want him found," she said. "Tonight."

Logan's hand tightened on his sword. "I've dispatched as many men as I can spare to look for him."

Braedan watched her with a solicitous eye. "Are you certain you don't want a sleeping draught?"

"No, I don't want to sleep. What was his name? Matthias? I want someone to hunt Matthias and his creature down and kill them." She sipped the tea. "What was that thing?"

"I don't know, highness," Logan said. "It looked like one of the Ferimin, but I didn't think—" He bit off his words. "I saw Matthias land on the thing's back. It was waiting for him. He could be in Espara by now."

She grimaced at her tea. It was some kind of herbal infusion Repha Felix had prescribed, and she'd insisted on adding a shot of oiska, but it wasn't what she wanted. "I need straight oiska." She put the cup down and Gwyn started to rise, but Logan put a hand on her shoulder. He fetched oiska and poured for Igraine. "How did Matthias get into my chambers?"

"I think he slipped in during the bustle of activity around the banquet, highness," Logan said. He gave her the oiska.

She tossed the shot back in one swallow. The burn of the oiska soothed and warmed her. "I don't care what you have to do," she said to Braedan. "I want his entrails held high for all to see. Hang the rest of him from the city walls."

His voice was regal and steady when he took her hands and spoke. "I will hunt for him, I promise you."

"And in the meantime, if he comes back?"

"I will post additional guards around your room, including some at your bedchamber door, if you wish," Logan said.

She nodded and let out a long breath. "I haven't taken a bedmaid in years.

I prefer to sleep alone. But until he is caught, I will have my maids sleep with me."

"A wise precaution," Duncan said. "May I have a word with her highness alone?"

Braedan kissed her forehead and stepped out of her antechamber with the others. When she and Duncan were alone, he knelt before her. "Igraine, go home. You aren't safe here. I will ask your father to give you some position of authority in his court. I'll see that he sends you to Aliom to treat for him if you'd like. But please, my lady. Return to Eirya."

He doesn't know—Braedan hasn't told him. "Duncan, I can't. I have given Braedan my consent."

"Your consent?"

"To ask Father for my hand."

His eyes widened, and he stood, slowly, his body tense. "You would be queen here? You would marry a usurper?" His voice carried an angry tremor.

"I would. He's not what any of us thought. I think—I know I could develop some affection for him." She paused. "I already have."

Duncan turned back to her and sat. He laced his fingers together so tightly that the knuckles turned white. "Grainy, you will only bring yourself grief. Wedding him will only cause you tears."

She stood. "You forget your place, Lord Guinness. I do not seek your counsel."

Duncan stood. "This is a foolish course," he started, his voice rising.

She whirled back to face him. "Foolish? You think to know how I feel? What I want?"

"I know you're a pragmatist and a realist, and I know your passions run hot and cold with the tides," he said. He waved away the beginnings of her protest. "No, for once, you should listen. You've already seen something tonight that shouldn't even exist, something that had a hand in trying to kill you, and yet you would stay here? In this—this den of vipers?"

She raised her chin. "And you would have me return to Eirya to wed some lordling who can't keep his breeches laced? To just retreat into the shadows and do my duty? Bear a dozen children for the crown, like a good Eiryan lady?"

He tipped his head toward the ceiling and muttered a plea for mercy. "Listen to me, Igraine. I know you don't believe in unseen things, but after tonight, I feel I should tell you—Cara had a foreboding about this journey of mine for days before I left. When I boarded my ship, she wept. Cara doesn't weep. She stood holding our son and weeping as if she would never see me again. She fears for you so that she cannot sleep."

"You know I adore Cara, but she is with child, and her husband is far from her side. I cannot put too much weight on the fearful dreams of a woman with child."

"Still, after what happened tonight, I would think you might consider returning. My ship can sail on the morning tide. You can correspond with the king from Eirya. If your affections are true, a few months of separation will do no harm. And it will give him time to bring this man Matthias to justice." He paused. "Please, Igraine. I could not live with myself if something happened to you when I could prevent it."

She put a hand on his arm. "I thank you for your concern, Duncan, but I will not be chased away from my duties by one mad guard. I trust Braedan and Logan to keep me safe." She held up a hand when he started to speak. "I will take precautions, I assure you. But I will not go home."

He closed his eyes and shook his head, and a rueful grin crossed his mouth. "You never change, Igraine. I should know better than to assume prudence on your part. Very well. But know that I'll keep my ship ready to sail the moment you say."

"Aye."

"We'll talk more tomorrow. Try to get some sleep."

"I will." She stretched up and kissed his cheek.

He opened the door to the corridor. "Since I cannot speak sense into her, I'll take my leave, majesty. May I trouble you for additional guards to see me back to my ship? I'll stay there tonight. I can't be certain this attack wasn't aimed at Eirya, and I want to have my house thoroughly examined before I take up residence again."

Braedan gave orders and stayed behind as the others dispersed. He poured another cup of oiska for Igraine and one for himself. She took her cup and drank the shot while he swirled his in its cup. "How can I make amends?"

"Draw and quarter the bastard where I can see it, and we'll consider that a start."

He smirked. He lifted his hand to her lip and ran a thumb across it. "He hit you?"

"He slapped me. I'm unharmed."

"Your neck?"

"A scratch only."

He set his cup down. "Duncan is protective of you."

"He is my father's friend of forty years. They once fought for my mother's affections. My father was the upstart merchant and my mother the crown princess." The oiska made her talkative and bold. "She was betrothed to Duncan, but she loved my father. The king proclaimed single combat to first blood to decide who could marry her. My father tricked Duncan, gave him a sting on his arm, and won my mother's hand."

"Tricked him?"

"My father had little training in how to fight back then. He fought like a street child. Duncan was a lord and had all the armor and training. My father didn't even have a sword. He threw aside the one the king gave him and used only his dagger. While Duncan was obeying forms and rules, my father dashed in and stung him on the arm. Duncan shows off the scar as an example of what happens when a man becomes too arrogant in his strengths." She poured herself another shot of oiska, and the warmth at last stilled her shaking nerves.

Braedan grinned. "I can see where you get your upstart nature. It's an inborn trait."

"Perhaps." Silence hovered around them. *He's so close.* She put a hand on his chest. "Perhaps you shouldn't leave tonight."

"No?" He picked up her hand and put his lips against the red rope burns on her wrists. "Don't you think you'll be safe enough with a chambermaid in your bed and extra guards at the door?"

She closed her eyes. He put one hand in her hair, and she lifted her chin. He kissed her neck. *He smells like the sea. Like fresh air.* "Perhaps if you are so concerned for my safety, you should guard me yourself."

One finger of his other hand stroked her skin along the edge of her dressing gown, inching it open. "Perhaps I should sleep between you and your maid to guard you both."

She slapped his shoulder. "Don't be an ass."

He laughed and kissed her neck again. His breath warmed her skin. She pressed herself against him. "You've been through a lot tonight. I don't want to take advantage," he said, low, against her ear.

She put her arms around his neck. His arms tightened around her waist. She tingled from his touch as much as from the oiska. *I shouldn't have had so much to drink.* "What makes you think I'm not taking advantage of you?"

"I want to prove myself to you. I want you to know I'll be faithful to you."

She put her mouth against his neck. He inhaled, sharp, as her mouth moved up to his ear. "I promise you, after a night with me, you'll not want another woman," she whispered.

His voice wavered when he spoke. "A promise like that . . . How can I refuse?"

Her mouth found his. *The way he kisses—* His hands slid up her sides, and his mouth trailed down her neck to her shoulders. "Please tell me you know how to use that tongue for more than just arguing with me," she said.

He laughed. "I think I might."

She laced her fingers with his and led him to the bedchamber. He shut the door. She started to unbutton his doublet as he trailed two fingers along the edge of her dressing gown down to the top of her breasts. His touch sent prickles down her neck. He untied the robe and pushed it off her shoulders, his mouth following the silk as it exposed her skin. "Igraine," he whispered. His hands slid into her robe and tightened against her back. She expected the rough skin of a man used to holding a sword, but his hands were smooth and soft and his grip firm and insistent. He put his mouth next to her ear, and she shivered and closed her eyes. "I don't expect this. You don't have to do this."

"I never do anything I don't want to do." She tilted her head up and met his eyes. She pushed off his doublet, took his silk undertunic off, and ran her hands along his chest. She dropped her robe and pressed herself against him. "I want this."

His mouth was on hers, and she lost the will to speak again.

When they lay spent next to each other, he pulled her close against him, pressing up against her back. "Did I find all the places you wanted kissed?"

By the spirits, yes. "You may have missed a small spot behind my left ankle," she said.

He chuckled. "I'll get that next time." He kissed her ear and nuzzled against her neck. "You were no maiden, my lady."

"Does that bother you?"

"No. I like a woman who knows what she wants." He kissed the nape of her neck. "You certainly know what you want."

She smiled at the sensations of his fingers tracing idle shapes on her thigh and his mouth nibbling at her shoulder. *He makes me shiver. I shouldn't feel this way about him. He stole this throne. But what he does to me . . .* She rolled over, lifted his hand, and toyed with his fingers in the moonlight that streamed through the broken window. The cool night air raised gooseflesh on her skin, but she shunned blankets. She wanted to see him. "Virginity is a silly notion, isn't it? A man's worth is counted by how many women he beds, but a woman's worth is decided by some little barrier between her legs. There's no way to prove if she lost it to a man or a horse."

He snickered. "A horse?"

"I've been riding since I was three. My maidenhead was gone long before I lost my virginity."

He watched her mingle his fingers with hers. "Have there been a lot of horses?"

She laughed. "Three before you. I'm sure you lost count years ago."

He was quiet for some time, his mouth resting on her shoulder. "I did. I should have been pickier. Kinder. A string of maids and whores and a few sayas and camp women—that's all I have to show." He sighed. "I've been selfish. And foolish. I drank too much when I was younger, and it made me cruel. I fear most of those women got little pleasure from me."

She pulled his arm tighter around her middle. "You aren't the man in the rumors. Did exile change you?"

"Perhaps. Living that way—the men called me king, but it meant little. We all used the same waste ditch. I suppose it did tame me."

"Tell me."

"At first it was just me and Cormac. He was a mealy-mouthed commoner that my father hated, so he saddled me with him. We had no money. We begged the indulgence of farms and inns and did odd jobs and survived. I smelled like a pig. I learned to live with deprivation."

"Then your uncle found you?"

"Eventually. Logan found me first. He and his men saw what happened in Kiern. They deserted and tracked me down. They swore fealty to me on a field outside of a broken down village. Just like that I had a small army. They're all still with me—Logan, Ewan, Malcolm, Aiden. Those first twenty men are the core group, the most loyal men I have. I wrote my uncle, and he started sending money. He tried to send men, but I sent them back. I didn't want confused loyalties. I built my own army."

She wrapped one leg around his. His legs were lithe and muscular and smooth against hers. "And somewhere along the way, you grew up."

"I hope so. I want to be a good leader. I don't want to be the man my father was, but I don't want to be the man my uncle wants me to be, either."

"Who does he want you to be, then?"

"Someone merciless. Ruthless."

She wove her fingers into his hair. "That's not you. I thought it was, but you're not your uncle. Or your father. You're Braedan, and you can make this throne what you wish." She kissed him. "I wouldn't be in your bed if I didn't believe you'd be a good king."

He said nothing for some time, his expression serious and thoughtful. "I can be. With you next to me." He traced her lips. "I love your lips. I've wanted to taste these lips from the first night I saw you." He kissed her neck and belly and worked his way down.

"And yet you still bedded my maid."

His lips paused at the top of her leg. "That was not what you thought it was."

"Oh?"

He lifted his face back to hers. "My uncle bedded her. I found her crying in the corridor. She didn't want to go back to her room. She feared facing you. I don't know why—she confessed that you are the kindest mistress she's ever served. I think she didn't want to disappoint you. I let her sleep in my bed, and I slept in the antechamber."

Igraine sat up. "You took the blame for your uncle? Why?"

His eyes twinkled with mischief. "Because I like it when you're angry with me."

She hit him with a pillow. "You ass."

He laughed.

"You mean you let me scold you just because it tightens your groin?"

"Yes. Exactly."

She hit him again; he took the pillow and put it behind his head. "Why didn't you tell me the truth sooner?"

"Would you have believed me? Or would you have thought I only said it to get you into bed?"

She picked up another pillow, but he tackled her and kissed her. She slapped his shoulder even as she surrendered to the kiss. "You great ass." She bit his earlobe.

He bit her shoulder in return. "I love your accent."

She grinned. "You want me to curse you with an Eiryan accent, then? You like my lilt, is it? Aye, and you're an evil, foul, prick, son of a sheep, m'lord." She shivered as his kisses grew more insistent.

He gave her a kiss that awakened desire again. "You're right," he said. "I don't think I could ever want another woman."

Igraine shivered. "Nor would I want another man." Decorum and propriety disappeared, and passion was all that mattered.

Braedan propped his head on one hand and watched Igraine brush her hair. The early light streaming in through the broken window hovered around her as a halo. "That sight might be enough to turn me into an early riser."

She turned and smiled. "Good morning, love." She put down her brush and sat next to him. Her dressing gown fell open to reveal her legs. She leaned down to kiss him, her lips lingering on his a moment longer than he expected. "Did you sleep well?"

"Better than I have in months. What sleep I got, that is." He stroked her hair. "Regrets?"

"None. You?"

"No." He sat up. *Can I be worthy of a woman like this?* "Is this how it will always be? You'll be up for hours before I'm awake, running the country and making councilors flee with tails between their legs until I smooth things over?"

"Perhaps."

He pulled her into another kiss. "Come back to bed."

"I have duties. So do you."

"I'd rather stay in bed." He brushed her hair back from her neck. "The cut—it's already healing."

"I've always healed quickly." She showed him her wrists. "The rope burns are nearly gone."

He kissed her wrists and buried his face in her hair. "Do you think our sons will have this copper hair? And your green eyes? Or your temper?"

"My brothers don't. All three have brown hair and blue eyes, and none of them have my temper." She smiled. "I'll not be a broodmare, my lord. You may as well sire a son first if you want one. I'll not spend my life carrying children in the hopes that I might give you a son. And I'll not stop taking the herbs until we're wed. I'll not be with child until I have your name."

The way she talks to me—my father would never have tolerated this. He grinned. "As long as we're bargaining, give me two sons. One for the throne and one for the ducal seat. Fair?"

She laughed. "All right. Unless I convince you to change the inheritance laws and give your daughters an equal chance."

Daughters just like her. Could I be so lucky? "One argument at a time." Her lilt aroused him. He untied her dressing gown and slipped one hand inside. She didn't push it away. "Half an hour. I'll make it worthwhile."

"Such a high opinion of yourself," she said, but her voice wavered. "Perhaps I should school you a bit, then?"

He grinned. "Please do."

"Braedan." The whisper was silk over steel. "If you'll swear to keep to me always, I'll not leave you. Not for Eirya, not for another man. I'll never leave your bed."

"I swear it. I do." He pulled her down to the bed with him. *How could I want another woman?*

They were talking quietly of Taurin politics, when Logan knocked on Igraine's bedchamber door. "Highness?"

Braedan pulled her close. "Don't answer. I don't want to be king just yet."

She kissed him. "You are king, love. And he wouldn't be here if it weren't important." She stood and pulled on her dressing gown. "One moment, Logan."

"Is the king with you, my lady?"

She smiled at Braedan. "He is."

"He should hear this as well."

Braedan frowned and pulled on breeches. "Do you think they found Matthias?"

"So quickly?"

He put a hand on her arm. "Wear your hair this way." He pulled it over her shoulder to cover a mark he'd left on her neck, and her face turned red. It satisfied him that, despite her boldness, she was discomforted by their passion.

They left her bedchamber to find Logan and Cormac in her study, both of them wearing grim expressions. Igraine sat down behind her desk, and Braedan took a seat across from her. "Well?" Braedan asked.

"There's been an attack, majesty," Logan said. "On Lord Guinness. He was on his way to his house this morning to inspect it. We had the extra guards around him as you requested, and he had his own guards, but they were assassins."

Igraine gasped and put a hand over her mouth. "Gods—Duncan—"

Braedan thought the earth might as well have dropped from beneath his feet. He let out a long breath. "Dead?"

"Yes, your majesty. And his guards, and several of our guards as well."

Igraine put her face in her hands and sobbed. Braedan stood and put his hands on her shoulders. *Guinness, dead. This will surely mean war if Igraine was right about his relationship to Cedric.*

Cormac cleared his throat. His face was pale and his hands shook, but he spoke clearly. "Most of the assassins escaped. Those we killed had no marks to identify them."

"What would lead someone to do this?" Braedan asked. "Do we have any idea?"

"None, your majesty, but—" Logan hesitated.

"Tell me."

"The men who survived can't agree on the number of assassins," Logan explained. "I wouldn't think anything of that, except that one of them says one of the men among the assassins disappeared. The man who saw him said he stabbed Guinness, then vanished."

A cold chill ran down Braedan's back. *He's returned.* The man had told him not to marry Igraine—he had said Braedan's desire would be his downfall. Now, he was trying to ensure that his words came true. "Thank you, Logan." He waved them away.

Braedan knelt next to Igraine as she wept into her hands. He turned her to face him and took her hands in his. "I am so sorry, Igraine. I swear I will do everything I can to find out who did this and bring down the king's justice on his head."

She sat very still, very quiet, tears spilling onto his hands where he gripped hers. "Go. I wish to be alone."

"Igraine—"

"I don't want to say something I will regret. Please, leave before I do."

"I didn't do this."

"If you hadn't taken this throne, Duncan might be alive."

That truth twisted his stomach. *I can't deny that.* "I am going to sort this business out as much as I can, and then I have to go north. I will leave Logan and Cormac to work with you to find out what happened. I will trust that you can try to smooth things over with your father."

Her tears stopped. "Duncan was my father's best friend. This will require more than a smoothing over. Do you trust me to deal with my father over this? Without you here?"

"Yes. I do. If you will be my queen, you will need to govern when I am absent."

"You give me the power of a queen already? Even without a formal alliance?"

He nodded. "I trust you. I love you."

The room was still, silent. She fixed her gaze on his. "Thank you, Braedan. I will not disappoint you."

"Igraine." He stopped and let out a breath. "I am sorry for this. I will do whatever I can to make amends. I swear to you."

She nodded. "I meant everything last night. But now, I need to think. I need time."

"Can I come see you later?"

"I will come to you. When I'm ready."

He nodded again. He stood and kissed her forehead before he left the room. As the guard closed her door, Braedan heard Igraine's sobs break free, and a lump formed in his throat. *I have to rid myself of the dark man.*

CHAPTER SEVENTEEN

We began as two. We end as one.
— Queen Brenna's diary

Mairead's lungs ached. She tried to catch her breath as she fought the hands that pinned her. His legs between hers, he stared down at her with a confident gleam in his eye that said he knew he'd bested her. "Give up, my lady. You're as good as taken."

She gritted her teeth. *I won't let you beat me.* She mustered strength, shifted her weight, and kneed him in his side. The force of the blow knocked him off-balance. One hand let go of her wrist, and she brought her elbow across her body to slam it into his forearm. He yelped and released the other wrist.

She squirmed free and stood. He lunged for her. When he grabbed her wrist, she slammed the heel of her other hand into his ribs. He choked out another yelp. She gripped her hands together, elbowed him in the ribs, kneed him in the stomach, and pushed him over.

Connor held his hands up in surrender. "All right, you win. Damn it, Mairead. I need those ribs."

She wiped her forehead. "So that was better?"

"Yes. I'd say you're getting much better." He rolled to his side, one hand clutching his ribs.

She stepped closer. "Did it really hurt so much?"

He snatched her leg and pulled her down. The air rushed from her body again. Before she could react, he straddled her, his knees holding her legs together. One arm held her down across the chest, and he held a dagger at her throat. He hovered above her with a wicked grin, his face just inches from hers. "No quarter. No mercy."

The flat of the blade felt cool against her skin, but she knew how sharp he kept his daggers, and she wouldn't risk moving more than a swallow. His arm pressed her shoulders tight against the ground. "No mercy," she said with effort.

"How would you get out of this?"

"Don't know. Can't move."

He loosened his arm enough for her to draw a breath. "If he wanted to kill you, you'd be dead by now. But if he doesn't, he has to loosen his grip somewhere. It's probably going to be his arm. What would you do?"

"Strike him in the nose with the heel of my hand."

"Good. What if he moved his legs?"

She didn't say anything.

"Remember, Mairead, no mercy. If you have to get free of a man who's trying to rape you, strike where it will hurt the most." He paused. "He'd have to loosen his legs if he wanted to rape you. Before he gets your legs apart, what would you do?"

She swallowed again. "Bring my knee up between his legs."

"As hard as you can, right?"

"Yes. I give up. You win."

"I know. I'm just trying to decide what the price of your freedom should be." He tilted his head. "I could demand a kiss, but that seems so predictable. Like a rogue from a story."

"You are a rogue."

He laughed. "I could make you fish for our supper, but we'd starve. You can't catch a fish to save yourself."

"Hurry up. It's hard to breathe."

He dropped the knife and put his arms on either side of her shoulders, boxing her in with his elbows. They both panted with the exertion of the fight. His mouth hovered just above hers. *If I stretched up just a bit . . . .*

He sat up and pulled a kerchief from his pocket. "I nicked you. I'm sorry."

The opening presented itself, and she punched him, hard, in the diaphragm. When he tried to catch his breath, she squirmed free from his legs and hit him again, knocking him onto his back. She picked up the knife and turned the blade on him, holding the flat of it at his neck as she boxed him in the same way he'd held her. "I think I just figured out the price of my freedom."

He choked out a laugh. "You wicked woman. That will teach me to underestimate you. I didn't see that coming at all."

"That was the point."

He laughed harder. "All right. You win. Really."

She stood, but she held the knife on him. He stood up, caught his breath, and picked up the kerchief. He waved it. "Truce, my lady, please."

"Really?"

"Yes, I swear. Let me look at your neck. I promise I won't attack again." She let him put the kerchief on her neck. Beads of sweat trickled down the edges of his hair. "I'm sorry for this."

She put her hand over his. "It's all right. I'm the one who insisted on practicing with bare blades."

"You were good today. Your strikes to my ribs were well-placed and painful. Another man might not have recovered as quickly, and you would have at least had time to run."

"If you'd been wearing your jerkin, you wouldn't have even felt it."

"But I wasn't, and many thieves and brigands won't be wearing one, either." He rubbed his side and pulled up his tunic. "How does it look?"

She grimaced at the large welt. "Ugly."

His laugh surprised her. "Good girl. You didn't give me quarter. I'm proud of you."

He's proud of me. It shouldn't matter, but it does. He removed his tunic to wipe sweat from his face, and she found herself wishing she had stretched up and kissed him when she had a chance. *I shouldn't think of that,* she scolded herself, ducking her eyes to avoid looking at his chest. "Thank you for the practice," she said.

He chuckled. "You don't have to keep thanking me. I'm enjoying it, too."

She forced herself to meet his eyes, despite the urge to stare at his chest. "You aren't fighting the way you'd fight a man."

"What makes you say that?"

"You wouldn't lunge at a man the way you lunged at me. And you'd never pin a man down like that. You're going easy on me."

He stepped closer to her. "I'm not going easy. I'm attacking the way most men would attack a woman. Like it or not, men will look at you and see a pretty pair of legs. If they want you dead, that's one defense. If they want to rape you, that's another. If I can just teach you to defend against those two things, you'll have an edge."

He thinks my legs are pretty. I shouldn't think of that. I should just be grateful he's teaching me. She pulled the kerchief away. "Did it stop bleeding?"

He touched her neck. "I think so. It's not bad—just a scratch." His hand lingered against her neck, and his thumb stroked her jaw.

How does he expect me to catch my breath with his hand on my cheek like that? But she didn't step back. The early morning quiet was broken only by the sound of geese in the distance, and Mairead's stomach fluttered. Connor shifted his feet and lifted his other hand to her opposite cheek. Heat crept up her face. *I could kiss him now. I could.*

She dropped the kerchief from shaking fingers. "Oh—"

"I'll get it." A note of regret tinged his voice as he took his hands away from her face. He stepped back and picked up the kerchief. "We should get moving—take advantage of decent weather."

She nodded, reluctant, and went to her blankets to pack her things.

She and Connor had fallen into an easy camaraderie since leaving Leiden weeks before and entering the vast taiga of northern Culidar. The low northern forests went on for leagues, thinning into plains and meadows more often the further east they went. Small villages along Haman's Road offered meager comforts for travelers. When there was a dry copse of trees, they camped in it, and when they found a farmer willing to exchange shelter for coin, they took the opportunity to get out of the rain and cold.

Connor taught her to live the way he did. Soon she could set up and break down their camp, clean fish, prepare rabbits for cooking, build a fire, identify and find edible roots, find deer trails, and watch for signs of predators. He continued to teach her how to fight with daggers and her fists and hands. After they left Leiden, he found two sticks of similar length and began to teach her the footwork and forms for swordplay.

Mairead discovered that she preferred her bow to blades. When she practiced every morning, they measured her rare misses in fractions of an inch. The first time she referred to the bow as hers, he didn't argue. The next morning he put the quiver over her horse's saddle instead of his own.

The landscape of Culidar still bore the scars of the breaking of the Western Lands. Stone ruins fought a losing battle with the forests. Occasional glimpses of ivy-covered spires or mossy towers on the horizons were the only hints of the past. Remnants of cities had faded into villages, and villages had faded into family farms. The people lived with raw determination and an uneasy truce between their livelihoods and the forest.

Mairead grew fonder of the land and people each day. *This is my calling,* she thought. *This is where I'm meant to be, not Taura or Sveklant.* But each time she tried to express her thoughts to Connor, the words stuck in her throat. *Alshada, how can I betray my duty this way?*

She found comfort in caring for people whenever possible. One rare sunny day, she shared bread and cheese with Connor in a small village square. Two small children sat nearby watching them. Mairead broke off a small piece of bread and gave the remainder to the children. She turned away from Connor's gaze, afraid he would chide her for her generosity again. "They need it more than I do."

He took the last of the ripe apples they'd found from his pack and gave them to the children, along with a slab of cheese. "I can always hunt for us."

I wish I could do more. Alshada, care for these babes. "Why are these people so poor?"

"Not enough resources, too many threats. The south is bordered by the Nar Sidhe. There aren't many merchants who can get through either way to encourage trade. A few hired swords like me can guide some of them through, but we're in short supply. That's why we're so highly paid. The only western harbor in Culidar is the Port of Sorrows, and it's controlled by slavers. In the east, Culidar and Sveklant blur into a big expanse of prairie and fields, and in the north, there are just mountains."

"Don't they have anything?"

"Some do. Declan—he managed to build a ranch with his prairie cattle. There are a few others who have enough money to hire good men to keep the slavers away. It's spotty. The wealthiest men are slavers and venom runners."

She shuddered, and her heart ached for the children she'd fed. "Did I feed them today only to have them taken by slavers tomorrow?" she whispered.

He didn't answer.

Another day, they crested a hill and saw a train of wagons in the distance. Connor's face turned grim, his eyes tight with the peculiar pain she'd seen in them before when he fought or they came upon danger. A raven landed near them, its head cocked to one side, and she noticed that Connor studiously avoided looking at the bird. "Let's go into the trees."

"Why?"

"Those are slavers."

A small huddle of people sat near a man with a whip and a sword. Two women held several small children close. Near them, a slaver emerged from a wagon with a young girl who wept as he tied her to the row of captives. Another slave put his arm around her. She flinched, but accepted the comfort.

Mairead put a hand over her mouth. "Is there nothing you can do?"

The raven croaked and hopped closer. Connor flinched. "What do you think I should do, Mairead? Charge in there and risk my life and your safety for people who could be captured again tomorrow?"

Yes. Perhaps. "Where do they take them?"

"Espara, mostly. The empire is huge, and there are many nobles who love having slaves. But there are also nobles in the east who buy them. The Tal'Amuni emperor buys beautiful women for his harem. Sometimes, the slavers keep the prettiest girls and use them in their own brothels here in Culidar. Some of the children, too."

"Children?"

He met her eyes. "Some men and women cannot be redeemed."

Mairead's stomach twisted. "Is there no law here at all?"

"The few nobles who have managed to establish themselves make their own laws, and they control a few cities, but outside of those?" He shrugged. "It's called the Wilds for a reason."

That night, she sobbed into her blankets, trying to stay quiet. Within moments Connor was next to her, one strong hand on her shoulder. "I wish there weren't so many harsh things to show you. But if you will be a queen, you need to know the truth of the world," he said.

She rolled over and sat up. "Have you ever helped any slavers?"

"No. Not intentionally."

"Have you ever been able to help any slaves?"

The firelight flickered across his face. "A few times. I have a client in Espara—she's very wealthy. She had slaves. I convinced her to pay for their freedom."

"A client. A woman you were able to convince to pay for freedom for her slaves."

He gave her a crooked grin. "I can be very convincing."

She laughed and wiped her eyes. "I want to make this place better."

He wound a stray lock of her hair around one finger. "You've already made this a better place to live."

Despite the ever-present poverty and slave trade, Mairead looked forward to each day with Connor. With each mile, she became more reluctant to say goodbye to him. With every sparring session, she sought moments to relish having his body close to hers or his hands on her. The more time they spent together, the more she found herself thinking of things she knew were sinful.

The day brought overcast skies, and they covered a good distance along the main road. When they stopped at a small stream for a midday meal, Connor spread a blanket on the ground while Mairead retrieved flatbread, apples, some leftover pheasant, and their waterskins. He sat next to her, took out his knife, and started slicing apples. "On your back there's a line of script under the wolf. What does it mean?" she asked.

He kept his eyes focused on his task. "It's my father's name in the tribal tongue. I had it put there when he died."

"What was his name?"

"It's not important."

"It was important enough for you to put it on your back."

"My father's name is important to me, not to you." He grinned, but there was pain under his eyes. "If you keep asking about my tattoos, Mairead, I'll make sure you get one of your own."

She smiled, but it masked frustration. *Who are you under the weapons and blue dye?* For weeks, they had traveled together, eaten together, even slept together, and she still knew little about him. He hid his past behind his wit, and every time she asked him about something private, he deflected her question with a roguish answer or a teasing grin. "You know, we've been traveling together for weeks now and I still don't know your father's name. Or your mother's."

"You don't need to know."

"But I want to know."

He said nothing.

She sighed. "You have so many secrets."

He was quiet for some time, focusing on slicing the food and parsing it out. When he spoke, his voice was low and tense. "I don't like to talk about it—about him. It reminds me of what happened." He paused. "I was there that day. In Kiern. I saw the fire. I was coming back from the tribal hunt. The duke's estate was on fire. It was too dangerous to go into the town. We couldn't save anyone." He gave her a slice of apple. "I just watched from the road. I stood with my mother and we watched and knew they were gone."

She reached out to touch his shoulder. "I can't imagine. I'm so sorry, Connor."

"You asked me once if I ever wondered what might have happened if Kiern hadn't been attacked. By then I had already made this life, but I do wonder, sometimes, if I could have made a life there."

"What kind of life would you have made?"

"It doesn't matter. I'm happy with this life."

That's not true. "Are you?"

"More or less." He ate another slice of apple.

"What about the tribes?"

"A tribal life? Perhaps. I go back for the hunt every year, but I hunt with the southern tribes."

"Why not with your tribe?"

He sighed. He drank his water and ate a piece of bread. At last, he spoke. "When the attack came, I was enraged. I was ready to ride to Mac Rian's estates and murder him and his daughter. My mother fastened my will to her own through a spell. Whenever I thought of seeking vengeance on Mac Rian, her will would override my own." He paused again. "She never removed the spell. Mac Rian had the regent's ear, and my mother was afraid of Mac Rian's daughter. I think she was trying to protect me. I left. I haven't been home since."

She understood what he had meant when he said the Sidh queen had promised him something. "So that's why you agreed to do this job. I'm just a means for you to have the bond removed."

"You were, at first."

"What am I now?"

"A friend. A woman I respect and admire." He toyed with his knife. "I thought you would be some pious, sour woman, but you're not. I enjoy being with you."

She smiled. "Is that you talking or the bond?"

He grinned. "It's me. I don't think my mother has used the bond on me since Kiern. She's threatened it, but I think if she had her way, I'd be in the Sidh village married to some little Sidh girl who would give her an—" He stopped.

She frowned. "Give her a what?"

"How much do you know about the Sidh?"

"Not much. What you've told me and what I've read in a few ancient books."

He nodded. "The queens have all had the last name SilverAir. From the beginning. And all but one of them have had only one girl child who eventually became queen."

SilverAir. "All but one. The last one. Your mother?"

He nodded. "My mother. Queen Maeve SilverAir. She has no other children. I think she hoped I might give her an heir someday."

"Can't you rule the Sidh?"

"No. Only a woman can rule the Sidh. Only a woman can be born with all three talents and the *codagha*—the magic that binds the Sidh together."

"Your mother didn't want any more children?"

"She couldn't. She nearly died having me. Most of the Sidh are very small, and my father was a big man. She nearly bled to death when I was born. It took the magic of all the Sidh healers and the skill of a Taurin midwife to save her."

Mairead smiled. "So I know half of your secret—that you're royal on your mother's side. What's the other half? Are you some distant royal cousin of mine on your father's side?"

He laughed. "I've said enough for now. I'll tell you the rest another day." He cleaned his knife and started to pack up their food.

I don't want to go yet. Mairead thought quickly. "So if you won't go back to the tribes or Kiern, where would you go?"

"If I wanted a settled life?"

She nodded.

He shrugged and tossed a rock into the stream. "Espara, probably. It's beautiful there. Warm. The sand is white, and the water is as warm as fresh bathwater and clearer. There are fish in every color. I have a house there."

"A house?"

He nodded. "On a little island where there's only a fishing village. It's right on the water. The balcony off my bedchamber overlooks the sea, and I can swim every morning."

She smiled. "It sounds lovely. Why don't you stay there?"

He tossed another rock into the water. "I've thought about it. I've thought about settling down with a girl from the fishing village, raising a family, having a normal life. I have the money for it."

"Why don't you?"

"I think I'm made to wander. I think the Morrag keeps me restless." His eyes locked on hers. "But if I could settle somewhere, I'd go there."

She twisted a piece of grass. "I'd like to visit Espara someday, but I think I'm made for the cold and rain. I wouldn't know what to do with all that sun."

"So the one who never gets cold wants sun, and the one who shivers constantly wants rain."

She laughed, but stopped when she saw longing in his eyes. *Longing for a woman? For me? Or for permanence? Alshada—* She stopped. How could she pray? She couldn't think what prayer would be honorable. *Alshada, give me wisdom.*

Connor stood. "We should ride." He held out his hand, and she took it and stood. He lingered next to her and squeezed her hand before he let it drop. They remounted the horses and returned to Haman's Road.

When they stopped to camp for the night in a small patch of scrubby northern brush, Connor pulled out his fishing line. "We're still close to that stream. I'll go catch our dinner. Can you set up camp?"

"Yes."

He walked away, and she wandered toward the trees looking for dry wood.

She was kneeling to add a stick to her growing pile when she realized the forest had gone silent around her. Her skin pricked. *Something's not right.* She straightened, her eyes scanning the trees. The hair stood up on her neck and arms, and branches snapped next to her. A low growl rumbled through the air, followed by a grunting sniff. Mairead started to back out of the trees, but fear paralyzed her feet as a brown bear walked from the trees and lumbered toward her.

The horses neighed in panic, and Mairead screamed, dropped the wood, and ran to the horses for her bow. She nocked an arrow. When the bear stood on hind legs, she fired. The first arrow hit the bear's chest, but only angered the animal. She nocked another arrow, fired, and it hit the bear's throat. A choking growl wound out of its mouth. The bear lowered to all fours and started at a rumbling jog toward her as she nocked a third arrow. She focused, aimed, fired, and hit the bear's eye.

Still it lumbered closer, closing the gap. Mairead dropped the bow and drew a dagger. One paw lifted and brushed over her head. She ducked and stabbed, but her dagger glanced off the bear's shoulder. She ran. The bear followed her, roaring in pain.

She tripped, rolled over, looked up. Another roar—hot breath washed over her face. The mouth gaped above her, and she brought the dagger straight up under its jaw and into its head. She twisted the blade and pulled it down across its neck. A spray of warm blood covered her upper body. She blinked and shook her head, trying to clear her eyes, as the bear twitched, shivered, and fell, half of it pinning her to the ground.

"Mairead?"

Connor was calling her, but she couldn't speak. She struggled to pull her body from under the bear. Connor ran into the clearing, sword drawn. He swore and fell to his knees next to her. "Gods—no—Mairead." He pulled her from under the bear, and she struggled to sit up against him. "Thank the gods," he said, pulling her into his arms. "Thank the gods. Are you all right?"

She bobbed her head and found her voice with effort. "Did you see it? Do you see it?"

"You're covered in blood." He drew away from her enough to wipe away blood and check for wounds. He touched arms, shoulders, legs, back, chest to see if she was wounded. She didn't resist. Fear hovered on his face, belying his calm tone. "Are you all right?"

"Fine—bear's blood. I heard it—I ran—my bow—" She struggled to catch her breath.

Connor wiped as much blood from her face and hair as he could with a kerchief. "Can you sit up?"

She nodded. "Not hurt."

He gave her one more searching look and then examined the bear. "Clean shots, all of them. And you hit his artery by sheer luck." He flipped her braid over her shoulder. "If you didn't want trout for dinner, Mairead, you could have said something."

She breathed out a weak laugh and collapsed against his chest. His arms tightened around her. "I heard it rooting around in the trees. It came out at a run and then it stopped and stood up on its back legs, and I shot—I didn't even think about it. I just shot, but it kept coming. It couldn't see, but it kept coming. I had to stab it. I've never killed anything before, except that snake. You've killed everything we've eaten. It's one thing to shoot at a target, but this—" The words tumbled out in a rush as she started to shake. "All the blood—it just sprayed everywhere and I—"

He cradled her head against himself. "Are you sure you're all right?"

She pulled away and nodded. "Is this what it's always like? Killing something? Is this what it's like to kill a man?"

"The first time I killed anything on a hunt, I was seven years old. I was hunting with my father, and I shot a small deer. I didn't think I'd ever stop shaking." His eyes grew wistful, as they always did when he spoke of his father. "I've killed all kinds of animals, and it gets easier. I don't think much about it anymore. But killing a man is different."

"How?"

"I can't describe it. I can justify killing a man when I'm defending myself or someone else, but it never gets easier. There's always an ache."

"You were so hardened about killing the Taurins that day. You didn't seem to care about any of them."

"I didn't, not really. But they were still men."

The feeling started to come back to her feet and hands, and her head slowly stopped buzzing. She sat taking slow, deep breaths as she thought about what he'd said. "Have you ever killed a woman?"

"No. But I would if she threatened me or someone else."

She gestured to the bear. "What are we going to do with it?"

"We'll carve some of the meat for food, and then we'll move our camp. Tomorrow, we'll bathe. I can keep our scent away from the camp with my air talent. No other animals will find us."

She nodded. "It seems like such a waste—all that meat."

He tipped his head. "We passed a farm not far from here. We could take it there."

"Could we?"

"Yes. I hate wasting things, too, and I'm sure the people on the farm will be grateful for the meat." He held out his knife to her. "You want to help dress and skin it? It's your kill."

She took the knife. "Show me what to do."

They worked together in the waning light, carving as much meat as they could cook and eat before it spoiled. When they finished, Connor showed her how to make a travois, and he attached it to the sorrel's saddle. They pushed the bear onto the travois, mounted the horses, and turned toward the farm they had passed.

As they approached the farm, a woman ran from the small cabin with a pitchfork in hand. Dim firelight framed her body. "No closer, mind. My husband's not far away. He'll be returning soon."

Connor held up a hand. "Lady, we've not come to harm you. We're traveling, and my companion killed a bear. It's far too much meat for us to take on our journey. We've taken what we want, and we wish to leave the rest of the meat and the pelt with you." He pointed at the travois.

Her eyes widened. "What d'ye want in return?"

"Just a little water to wash up," Mairead replied.

She hesitated before she lowered her pitchfork. "All right. Water's inside." She nodded toward the house.

They entered the broken down cabin to find three children huddled in a corner. Mairead knelt in front of them. "It's all right. We're not here to harm you."

The children relaxed. The oldest, a girl, stood. "What're ye doing here?"

"We brought you some meat. We killed a bear, and it's too much for us. Could you eat the rest?"

The girl's eyes grew wide. "A bear?"

"They've not had much meat since their father passed," said their mother as she entered the house behind Connor and Mairead. A flicker of pain crossed her face. "He's been gone two years. Was a good hunter. Brought home deer and elk and whatever else he could find."

Mairead touched her arm. "I'm sorry."

"We've done all right. We have goats and chickens. The animals provide us with much."

"Why don't I finish butchering the bear for you?" Connor asked.

"Oh, lad, ye needn't—"

"I insist."

She crossed her arms. "A wet rag won't do ye any good, lass. I'll draw ye a bath. The two o' ye can sleep in the barn, if ye wish."

Mairead smiled. "We're grateful, lady."

She nodded once and started to bustle around her house, giving instructions to her oldest daughter to help draw the bath. Connor went outside.

After Mairead had bathed and Connor had cleaned himself of the animal, the woman, Tarah, spitted the bear steaks and cooked them over her hearth. Mairead ate and watched the children feast on second and third helpings of meat.

When they had finished eating, Tarah showed them to the barn and returned to her house. Connor spread their blankets on fresh straw and retrieved the skin of oiska from his horse. He sat next to Mairead on one blanket and gave her the skin. "To congratulate you on your first kill," he said.

She grimaced. "I'm not sure it went down very well last time."

He removed the stopper of the skin and took a long drink. He nudged her arm. "Try again."

She lifted the skin to her lips. The burn of the liquid felt oddly soothing, and she shuddered as it spread warmth through her body.

He grinned. "Was that so bad?"

She shook her head and took another drink. "It does feel good, doesn't it?"

He took the skin back and drank. He set it down long enough to drape her cloak around her shoulders. "Warm enough?"

She nodded. She leaned back against the straw, warm and sleepy, and stared at Connor as dim light from an oil lamp flickered over his features. "It's nice to be out of the elements for a night."

"It is." He reached into the pocket of his jerkin and held out three bear claws. "Here. I saved these for you."

"For what?"

"You should wear them. It's not easy to kill a bear. You fired true and performed under pressure. These will help you remember."

She took the three claws. "I couldn't do this without you. I didn't know anything when I started this journey. You've been so patient and kind." Her voice sounded far away, and her vision had grown fuzzy.

He took the skin, drank, and handed it back to her. She drank again. He put one arm around her shoulders and pulled her close. She felt his lips on her head. "It's been easy to teach you. I've enjoyed it."

She sat up to look at him. *He's so handsome—those dark eyes. What was Muriel thinking sending me with this man?* She traced the tattoos on his arm, let her fingers drift up to his shoulder, then down to his chest, just inside the opening of his jerkin. *What if I offered? Would he turn me down?* "I'm glad you're the one the Sidh queen asked to come with me. I like being with you."

His breath quickened. He put a hand in her hair. "I like being with you, too."

Mairead leaned forward. "Connor . . ."

He took her hand away from his chest and squeezed it. He picked up the oiska. "I think it's time to put this away." He helped her lie back on her blanket and took the bear claws. "I'll put these somewhere safe until tomorrow." He covered her with her cloak.

She closed her eyes and sighed. "Will you lie here with me?"

He patted her shoulder. "That's the oiska talking. Go to sleep."

"You're right. Thank you, Connor."

"Good night, Mairead."

He blew out the lamp and moved to the other side of the stall. Sleep drifted in and overtook her, and she dreamed that night of bear pelts and fires and oiska and Connor's arms tight around her.

When she woke in the morning, Connor's things were already packed. She started to sit up and groaned. Her head pounded and her stomach lurched. "Gods." She fell back into the straw.

Connor's laughter pierced her head, dagger-sharp against the pain. "Good morning, Mairead," he said, his brown eyes sparkling with satisfaction. He wore only breeches, and his skin had a faint sheen of sweat. "Need some help?"

"How much did I drink?"

"Not that much. You just aren't used to it."

"You are a little too happy about this." She pulled her cloak over her face. "Bachi's teeth, it's bright."

He crouched next to her and slapped her shoulder. The vibrations sent waves of pain through her head and body. "Get up. We need to ride."

She threw the cloak off and blinked, trying to open her eyes all the way. "Help me up?"

He held his hand out and helped her to standing.

She let out a long breath. "Everything hurts."

He handed her a waterskin. "Drink."

Her stomach reeled, but she sipped some water. It helped, so she sipped a little more. She blinked again.

His face came into sharper focus. "Better?"

"Yes." She gestured to his bare chest. "Why aren't you dressed?"

"It's sunny out, and Tarah needed a few repairs to her house. I fixed a few things up for her." He gestured toward the house. "She rinsed out our dirty clothes for us last night. Everything's clean and ready to go."

"Last night? Did you go back to the house after I fell asleep?"

"I couldn't sleep."

She opened her mouth to ask him what he'd talked about with Tarah, but they were interrupted by Tarah's son entering the barn. "Is the lady up? I need to milk the goat."

Connor grinned. "I think she lives. You can milk your goat, Dylan."

"You've learned the children's names?" Mairead asked.

"It's hard not to when you're conscious and paying attention." He laughed at the dark look she gave him. "It's all right. You were a little shaken last night at supper. Come on. Tarah will feed you. We'll say goodbye and be on our way." He walked out of the barn.

Mairead folded her blankets. She found Connor in the house, pulling on his tunic while he talked with Tarah. *What was wrong with me yesterday that I didn't see how pretty she is?* Her brown hair was swept back off her neck and face, revealing fine-boned features and soft blue eyes. Her figure was trim, and if her face had some wrinkles, they only served to reveal her hardships and joys.

Tarah offered Mairead a chair. "Sit, lady. I'll bring ye porridge. Your things are washed and dried." She pointed to a pile of folded clothes.

"You didn't need to do that," Mairead said.

"'Twas nothing. I'm grateful for the meat and the pelt. My boys will share it next winter."

Though her head and stomach resisted the idea of eating, Mairead forced herself to have some eggs and porridge at Connor's insistence. He moved about the cabin with familiarity, talking with Tarah and teasing the children.

When they prepared to leave, Connor lifted Tarah's hand and kissed it. "Thank you for your hospitality, my lady. It was a true honor to meet you."

Her face colored and she brushed his hand away. "Such formality. I was glad to help ye."

Mairead gave Tarah a brief embrace, despite her hunch about why Connor had returned to the house the night before. "I thank you as well. You were a great blessing to us."

Connor and Mairead both mounted their horses and started to ride away. Connor stopped at the barn. He pulled a heavy kerchief from his saddle and dismounted. Mairead heard the clink of coins as he tucked the kerchief inside the barn door.

"What was that for?" Mairead asked when he mounted.

"They need it. I don't."

She was quiet as they started to ride. "You could have given it to Tarah directly."

"I didn't want her to get the wrong idea."

"What do you mean?"

Connor sighed. "I thought she needed some money, and I didn't want her to think I expected something in return. She's a struggling farmwife with no husband and only a few friends. I didn't want her to think I expected bedding in return for coin."

Mairead's stomach plummeted with shame. "You didn't bed her?"

"No, of course not." He turned to her. "If I'd wanted bedding last night, I could have had you."

A warm flush crept up her cheeks. "Connor, don't—"

"You were in no state to stop me. You even asked me to lie down with you. But I didn't, because a woman who consents only because she needs money or because she's drunk isn't a bedpartner I want."

She met his eyes. "I'm sorry." She bit her lip. "That was a noble thing—leaving that money."

"Not noble. Necessary." He spurred his horse into a trot.

Mairead's face burned with shame, and she regretted her assumptions. *I waver between wanting him closer and pushing him away, between trusting him to believing the worst of him. Will I ever figure out how to feel?* She shook her head. *A few more weeks—just a few more weeks, and he'll leave, and then I can settle into an appropriate life without all of these questions.*

But as she spurred her horse ahead to catch up, she thought of his arms around her, and she couldn't help thinking that if he'd only settle down, he'd be a completely appropriate man for the Taurin heir to wed.

CHAPTER EIGHTEEN

The village was a waste. The estate, the shops, the homes all gone. The people—Mac Rian's men brutalized the women and tortured the men. I couldn't serve a man who could turn a blind eye to that.
— *Letter of Logan Mac Kendrick, Year of Creation 5987*

As evening started to verge, Connor stopped and held up a hand. "Did you hear that?"

"Hear what?"

He motioned for silence and sat very still. "Someone's in trouble."

Her heart raced. "Connor—"

"Shh." He set his horse at a slow, quiet walk along the road. He held up his hand again and dismounted. "Through those trees—hear it?"

Muffled grunts and cries came from not far away. "What is it?"

"Don't know. Keep an arrow nocked. I'll go see."

She dismounted. "I'm coming with you."

"All right, but be sure you can fire that thing if you need to." He walked into the trees.

She followed with the quiet, creeping steps he'd taught her. He crouched at the edge of a clearing and motioned. She peeked through the trees. Three men in brown kirok robes were tied together near a wagon with a team of two horses. Five men were taking belongings from the wagon and sorting what they wanted. She started to move forward, but Connor held her back. He shook his head and frowned. She waited.

He straightened, drew his sword, and stepped out of the trees. "You can keep the books. I'll take the holy wine."

All five turned and dropped the items in their hands. A big man with a sword stepped forward and swung a few times, and Connor parried easily and stabbed him through the belly. Mairead gasped as the other four rushed forward. She took aim and fired, hitting one thief in the shoulder. He cursed and fell as Connor stabbed another. Connor swung back to finish the man she'd wounded. Her hands shaking, Mairead nocked another arrow and took aim, but by the time she was ready, the final two were dead at Connor's hand.

He turned to her. "Nice shooting."

She stepped out of the trees. "Not so nice. I hit his shoulder, and I should have had another. I froze."

"But you fired when you needed to, and you disabled him. It's a start." He knelt.

Her knees threatened to crumble. "Are they all dead?"

"Yes." He sliced one man's throat. "I like to be sure."

She couldn't look at the bodies. Instead, she approached the bound men and sliced their ropes off. "Thank you, my lady," the oldest kiron said, bowing. He had wispy gray hair and a stern, lined face, but his voice was deep and soothing. "They were preparing to haul us away to slavers. I feared I'd never see my country again until you and your champion came along."

The kiron's two companions stretched and rubbed their wrists. One was tall, lank, and plain with a dark, pock-marked face, and the other had a muscular build and a charming smile. His eyes skimmed Mairead quickly, and she crossed her arms and cleared her throat. "I'm glad we could help. Are you all well?"

"Yes, thank Alshada. They hadn't done more than surprise us and tie us up."

Connor joined them then. "What did you have that they could want?"

"I don't know. I'm a member of the Order of Sai Johan. I can't imagine they would want my books. Perhaps they thought I was a merchant."

"Perhaps." Connor sounded doubtful. "If you're all right, we'll be on our way."

"Connor." Mairead drew him to one side with a hand on his arm. "We could camp with them one night, couldn't we? I haven't spoken to a kiron in so long. It would be nice to pray for those men who died."

He frowned and leaned down to her ear. "I don't trust this, Mairead. There's something not right. I have a bad feeling."

"What kind of feeling?"

"I don't know." He hesitated. "How do you know the man who's been following us didn't send these to kill or capture us?"

"They're just kirons. I'm sure one as vile as the one who's been tracking us wouldn't want anything to do with kirons."

He didn't look convinced.

"Please?"

His mouth tightened. "All right. But I want you close tonight—no sleeping across the fire or the clearing. I don't trust these men."

Her heart raced. "They'll think we're—" She couldn't finish the thought.

"Pretend to be my wife if you must."

The men had started to pack up their wagon. *If I want to spend time with a kiron, I need to decide now.* "All right. I'll pretend to be your wife, but only until we part with them."

"Tomorrow," he said.

"If it makes sense."

He nodded, grudging. He turned back to them. "Where are you going?"

"Where Alshada takes me." The kiron smiled at them. "I don't have a permanent kirok. Men of my order travel and minister to the needy and the faithful wherever we are led."

"It's nearly night. Why don't we camp together?" Connor asked.

The kiron bowed. "We would be grateful for the protection. I'm Gavin."

Mairead felt heat rise in her face. "I'm Mairead and my husband is Connor. We'll be happy for the company." *Lying to a kiron. Alshada, forgive me.*

Connor and Mairead fetched their horses, and Mairead started to pull food out of their packs. Connor put a hand on her arm. "Nothing we have to cook," he said, low.

"Why?"

"I want our supplies to stay packed in case we have to run. Just take out fruit and jerky. And the bread Tarah gave us, if you'd like." His eyes narrowed. "Keep your daggers on you, too."

She scoffed. "You're being overcautious. They're just kirons."

He frowned. "No, they're not."

The kirons cooked their own supper and offered some to Connor and Mairead, but Connor turned them down. He did offer his oiska, however. All three men turned it down. "Alshada demands our abstinence," Gavin said.

Connor shrugged. "As you will. It's some of the best."

Mairead frowned. "You know servants of the kirok don't drink," she whispered.

"I know."

She grimaced. *He wanted to see if they'd drink it because he doesn't trust them.*

When supper was finished and prayers spoken, Connor spread his blanket on the ground and took off his jerkin, tunic, and boots. "We should get an early start tomorrow," he said, laying his sword next to him. "This weather is too good to waste."

Mairead sat next to him on the blanket and took off her boots and weapons. She stared at his bare chest. *I don't know if I trust myself. I think I trust him more.* She worked at unbraiding her hair. "You don't think you can leave your tunic on tonight?"

He laughed. "You should be happy I've kept my breeches on at night since we started this journey. People were meant to sleep naked."

"Don't you ever get cold?"

"Not really. I get warm and I sweat, but I don't get cold like other people do."

"Does it have something to do with your blood?"

"Some Sidh have the same resistance to cold, but they're all stone talents."

"Is it the ravenmark?"

"Perhaps." He grinned. "You're stalling."

Yes, I am. She swallowed, ran her fingers through her hair, and lay on her side facing him. "I think these kirons are honest enough. Don't you?"

"No. Something isn't right with them. I can't place it."

She sighed. "You just don't want to be around kirok people."

"Have I made a secret of that?"

"No. I just thought—"

"That you could change me? Save me?"

She couldn't answer. She rolled to her back and pulled another blanket over her. "Good night, Connor."

He inched closer and propped his head on his hand. "This will never do."

"What?"

"You just lying over here, ready for sleep, without so much as a good night kiss for your husband."

"You're such a rogue."

He laughed. "I'm serious. Do you want them to think we aren't really wed?"

She rolled away from him. "Let them think we're fighting."

Silence, and then his breath next to her ear and his hand on her hip. She closed her eyes and shivered. "Do I make you nervous, Mairead?"

"Yes." She rolled to her back again to look up into his eyes. His hand slid across her belly, and he hooked his thumb into the top of her breeches. "Connor . . ."

"Just one good night kiss. Just to make it look real." His face hovered over hers with a teasing smile. "You still owe me a kiss for that bruise."

She sighed. She raised her head and kissed his cheek. "Will that do?"

"It was a much bigger bruise than that." He lowered his head, and she drew a sharp breath in as his mouth met hers.

His lips were soft and practiced; she tasted the oiska on his mouth. He kissed her first with a lingering flutter, drew back to look at her, and leaned in to kiss her a second time. His hand slid down to her thigh and tightened. She lifted her hand to his head and ran her fingers through his coarse hair as he pulled her closer. Without her permission, her body pressed itself against his. His tongue teased the inside of her mouth, and his teeth pressed with gentle, insistent pressure on her bottom lip before he drew away.

His voice was rough and low when he spoke. "That's how I would say good night to my wife. If you were my wife."

She pursed her lips. "Is that all?"

He kissed her once more, quickly, his lips fluttering away just when she wanted more of them. "No."

"What—"

He leaned down. The scent of him—leather and sweat and steel and oiska and magic all together—made her head reel. He bit her earlobe as if he were savoring a very sweet, ripe plum. "Do you want me to tell you? Or would you rather I show you?" His leg slid up her thigh and between her legs.

Yes, show me. She hated that her voice shook when she spoke. "C-Connor, you sh-shouldn't—"

He put his lips on hers again. She whimpered. Her arms felt weak, but she forced them around his neck. *Keep doing this!* He pulled her close, one hand holding her firmly against him. She felt a warm ache between her legs. *This is what Sayana Muriel warned me about. He makes me want to sin. How can he—?*

He finally drew away, a wicked grin planted firmly on his mouth. "Good night, Mairead." He rolled to his back next to her.

There are no words . . . She lay staring at the stars for some time, unable to sleep, her heart racing. She prayed he couldn't hear it. She finally rolled to her side and propped her head up. In the dim light of the fire the tattoos on his arm wove together in a sensuous dance. "Do you . . . How do you . . . I mean, what makes you pursue a woman?"

He rolled to his side and propped his head on his hand. "Why do you ask?"

Because I want you to pursue me. How can I say that? "I'm curious."

"I'm not a book for you to study, Mairead. It's not something I can put into an equation or a map or formula." He grinned. "I think you want to know if I'd take you to bed."

"What if I did?" *Where did that come from? When did I become so bold?* She clenched her hands together to stop them from shaking as heat rose in her face.

He laughed. "I don't know. Ask me and we'll find out."

She closed her eyes. "If I were some other woman, would you?"

"A woman like you? Beautiful, educated, kind? It would be a great privilege to have you in my bed." He leaned closer and his mouth hovered near hers again. "If you were some other woman, of course."

Some other woman . . . "How can you go from woman to woman—"

"It's only with their understanding and consent." He chuckled. "Don't feel sorry for the women I've been with, Mairead. I assure you they have no regrets."

Even Aine? He wouldn't say what happened with Donal and Aileen's daughter. She didn't want to think him capable of siring a child and leaving, but he said he didn't want a wife or children. Still, Donal and Aileen were grateful to him. *If I knew what he did, if he'd tell me, maybe I could . . . Gods, how can I think of that? But he feels so good. Did he feel good to Aine, too? Why won't he tell me what happened?*

He put a hand on her cheek. "What are you afraid of?"

"You. This. I can't—shouldn't—"

"There's no sin in a kiss." His lips found hers again.

Mairead's stomach lurched, and Muriel's cautions tumbled through her thoughts. *Men think only of bedding a pretty girl. Men think of satisfying their basest desires. Alshada has given women the greater strength for the greater duty—to remain chaste until marriage. You, Mairead—you are the last of your line. You must remain chaste until you wed.*

She bolted upright and put her hand over her mouth. "This isn't right. This isn't—"

He sat up next to her. "Mairead—"

"No." She turned to him. "This is wrong. This is sinful."

He laughed softly. "This isn't sinful. I've hardly touched you."

"But you would if I let you."

He shrugged. "Most likely, yes."

This man! "You really don't have any respect for anything do you?"

He lifted an eyebrow. "Respect?"

"Yes, respect. For me, for the kirok, for Alshada. Why do you hate the kirok so much?"

"I don't hate the kirok."

"You do. You hate everything it stands for." She paused. "It makes me wonder what you really think of me."

The kirons stirred on the other side of the fire. Connor lowered his voice. "Can we talk about this somewhere else?"

She stood. "I think we should talk about it here. I don't mind if they hear. Are you trying to hide something?"

He cursed, and she flinched. "I've not hidden a thing about my feelings toward the kirok since we started this journey," he said. "You're the one who keeps trying to change me."

"Perhaps you need changing," she said. "You don't follow kirok teachings. You drink, you kill, you bed any woman you want. You say Alshada doesn't care what you do."

"I really don't want to talk about this in front of them," Connor whispered, one hand on her arm and his mouth close to her ear. "Can we go somewhere else?"

Heat rose in her face. *This is what you do—you hide yourself from the truth so you can have what you want. And right now you want me, but what about in the morning?* She shook her head. "No. I won't let you distract me and try to cajole me into your bed." She stepped back when he reached for her. "I'm a fool. To think what I almost gave you—" She bit off the words as Gavin stepped closer. "I need to walk away. Don't follow me."

He put a hand on her arm again. "I'm not leaving you alone."

She pulled away. "You don't have a choice." She stalked into the trees, brushing away angry tears as she walked deeper into the forest. *Foolish, foolish girl. To think I wanted to go to bed with him! He's nothing but a rogue, and he'd bring nothing but tears.* She shook her head. *I'm better off keeping my distance. No more sparring, no more training. He can deliver me where I'm supposed to go, and then I'll say goodbye.*

Connor watched Mairead walk away, his jaw hanging open. *Where did all of that come from?* But he knew. Her kisses weren't as chaste as she wished, and he'd been surprised and aroused by the passion in them. *I didn't intend any of this. I just wanted to tease you. I didn't expect to enjoy it that much.*

He paced, watching the trees. He knew it was unsafe to let her go into the forest alone, with the other men not asleep yet, but he couldn't follow her. A raven landed in a tree at the edge of the clearing and cawed. Connor grimaced. *You could help me.* He directed his thoughts to the Morrag. *You could give me some clue how to deal with this woman. Or at least tell me why I distrust these men so much. A raven croaking at me? That's as likely coincidence as anything.*

Gavin put a hand on Connor's shoulder. "Let me talk with her."

No, not you. "She just needs some time alone."

"Connor, I was married once. I remember." He smiled. "I'll speak with her."

Connor clenched and unclenched his fists. *She'd rather talk to him than me. She trusts him more than she trusts me, all because of a brown robe and a smattering of kirok language.* "Good luck. She's strong-willed, and she doesn't much care for advice."

Gavin chuckled. "Just like my wife was." He followed Mairead.

Connor pulled out his skin of oiska and sat near the fire. His hands shook with anger, and he took a long drink to calm himself. He wiped his mouth. *What was I thinking? A pretty girl smiles at me, I do what she asks, and then she thinks she can change me? I'm a fool, too.*

One of the other men, Kef, gestured from across the fire. "Aye, boyo. Will ye still share?"

Connor passed the skin over. "You aren't so abstinent after all?"

"No." The man took a long drink. He passed it to the other man, Owen.

"We're not kirons, either. He has us pretend—makes him look better, seem more important."

"Do you really do as he says? Minister to the downtrodden all over Culidar?"

The men laughed. "Aye, that's it. Minister to the downtrodden." He drank and set the skin down. "No, lad. We've better ways to pass the time."

Connor saw the fist coming just before it hit his jaw. It knocked him backward. He staggered to his feet and drew a dagger from his boot. "What—"

"There be some things we need to know about your lady and your mother."

"My mother?" He shook his head. "My mother's dead."

The men laughed. "No, lad. We know who ye are. And we know your mother isn't dead."

Three men came out of the trees. *They've been tracking us.* Panic set in—*Mairead.* Kef lunged at him with a dagger. Connor deflected the blade, but the edge sliced his forearm. He hissed in pain, and the raven took flight near him, cawing and flapping around the scene. Connor drew his other dagger. *Focus on the fight. Don't let the anger draw you into her grasp.*

A big, greasy, bearded man in black leathers approached swinging a flail, and another man crept up behind Connor. Blades glinted in the firelight on either side of him, and Kef struck toward him again. Connor focused on defense, strategy—he pictured his battle training, the armory at Kiern, the sparring sessions with Edgar, previous fights—anything that would keep him alive. He parried, spun, sliced. One man fell screaming, blood spurting from a wide gash in his neck. Another swore and stepped back, cradling a fingerless hand.

But there were too many, too close. The man with the flail swung as Connor spun back toward him. Connor's hand connected with the flail and turned to porridge with a crunch. He roared. Pain blinded him long enough for two men to grab his elbows from behind. He went to his knees. *No defense—Mairead—gods, they'll kill her.* Fighting to stay conscious, Connor tried to form braids of air, but the big man drew up his own talent and flicked the air braids away. Connor gasped in pain and disbelief. *Damn it—how did I miss it?* "You're Nar Sidhe," Connor said. *That's what I sensed. They were far enough away to keep me off-balance. They must be shielding their magic—animstones?*

"Aye, lad. And we're needing a bit of something from ye about your people." He signaled to the men behind Connor. One kicked him in the kidneys and pushed him down to bind his legs. They lifted him to his feet to face the greasy man. The man picked up a stick and hit Connor across the face. Light flashed and pain erupted as bone shattered around his eye. "Ye'll tell me where to find your mother, lad, or we'll be turning ye over to the kiron. He likes a big boyo like you, and then we'll all be having a turn." He swung the flail a few times and then connected with Connor's torso.

Connor gasped as ribs cracked. He tried to draw air, but couldn't. The blow should have caved his chest in. *They don't want me dead.* He doubled over, but they pulled him back up by the hair.

The man hit him again from the other side. Bone crunched. "Call up your magic if ye want. Let the raven take ye. 'Tis what you're afraid of, aye? That it'll take ye? Make ye something wicked? Let the Morrag save ye." Connor couldn't count how many fists pummeled him. "We'll stop if ye tell us where to find your mother."

Connor spit blood. "Fuck you. Find her yourself."

"Your little lassie's a pretty one. The kiron, he'll enjoy that one. Ye want to watch? Ye can watch us all have a turn—see her pretty little legs splayed for all of us, hear her scream, watch her bleed." He grinned. "Mayhap if ye play nice, we'll leave ye a bit of her. 'Twill be a ragged bit, mind. Ye'll not get that sweet bit ye been wanting."

Don't listen. Focus. There must be an out. There's always a way out. But only pain answered.

Kill them, raven.

Something flared in Connor's chest. *The Morrag—no—don't—* But he couldn't stop it. It swelled, sweet and powerful and strong, as the men pounded him. The pain only served to feed the Morrag. Strength gathered in his arms, legs, shoulders. Muscles that had lost feeling answered again. He tugged against the hands holding him. *I could escape. I could fight, but at what price?*

I will give you strength, raven, the Morrag said. She laughed, a high, cackling, exultant sound. *You'll be mine.*

No—I won't! Connor pressed her voice aside. He tried to draw a full breath. His ribs protested every move, and every blow sent agony through his limbs. Strength faded as he pushed the Morrag back. "No." He spit blood.

The man laughed. "No? Ah, lad, we're just getting started." He swung and hit again. "Tell me how to find your mother."

Connor gasped, spit more blood. Strength retreated. His knees crumpled and his arms went limp. *They'll kill me and rape Mairead and find my mother. Is this it? How it ends?* And then, the thought he hadn't wanted to acknowledge. *This is what you wanted. You wanted someone else to kill you—destroy you and keep you from the raven.*

Tears stung. *It's what I wanted. I wanted to die.* He thought of Mairead. *I should have promised you everything.* He closed his eyes. Weakness overtook him. "Fuck all of you." *At least the raven won't have me.*

The men laughed. "To the end, eh? All right—if ye must."

"The kiron'll want his chance. Just make it so he canna fight."

Connor fell. Fists and feet pounded him. Sounds faded. *Mairead, I'm sorry. I'm sorry.*

Above, the raven's caw faded into the distance.

By the time Mairead talked herself down from her anger and stopped walking, there was no sign of the camp. She slumped against a fir tree, sliding down to curl her knees to her chin. She closed her eyes and took several long, deep breaths. Only the subtle sounds of the forest surrounded her—night bugs, an owl, a raven in the distance. She folded her hands. "Alshada, give me wisdom. I care for him. Forgive me, but I do. Show me how to speak your truth to him." Only crickets answered, but Mairead rested her head on her knees, finding comfort in the words and the ritual.

Footsteps approached. Mairead readied herself for words with Connor, but smiled when she saw Gavin. *Perhaps he can pray for Connor with me.* "Gavin. I'm surprised Connor let you follow me."

"Forgive me, Mairead." He knelt before her. "I thought perhaps you might wish to have a sympathetic ear." He offered her a thin smile. "Connor is protective, isn't he?"

"We've had a few close calls since we started our journey. He fears losing me, I think." *I should tell him we aren't married. I don't like lying to him. But then Connor will be even angrier.*

"You have such a strong faith. How did you find yourself wed to a man with a faith so weak?"

She thought for a moment. *No more lies—I can't lie anymore.* "Gavin, I should tell you something."

"Yes?" He shifted his weight.

Overhead, the raven's cawing grew closer.

Mairead tensed. *He wants something from me.* She put subtle hands on the hilts of both knives in her boots. "Nothing. Never mind." She started to stand. "We should—"

But there was no time to finish. Gavin's placid face turned cold. He lurched toward her. She scrambled to one side of the tree, and his hand fell on her foot. She kicked with her other foot, hitting him in the face. He jerked back, blood streaming from his nose, while she drew both knives and jumped to her feet. "Who-who are you?"

His arm came toward her, and she slashed. Blood sprayed from the slice in his forearm. "What do you want from me?"

He flicked blood aside and lunged toward her again. She slashed. He grabbed her arm and swung a fist at her. She ducked and stabbed toward his side, but the knife bounced off a rib. He howled in pain and let go of her, clutching his side.

Mairead hesitated. *He's wounded—I can run. But what if he chases me? Can I make it back to Connor in time? Oh gods—Connor was right! What if they're attacking him?*

Gavin straightened, preparing to lunge. Mairead gritted her teeth, took one step toward him, daggers crossed before her in an X, and slashed his throat open with a quick slice in two directions. He screamed and clutched at his throat.

Mairead stepped back, horrified, as Gavin's blood sprayed out onto her and his gurgling cries echoed through the trees. He clawed at his neck, frantic at first, then slower. Her heart thundered against her chest. *Finish him. Stop the screaming.* She stepped toward him and stabbed between his ribs, and his arms went slack.

Connor—what have they— She started toward the camp, but another man appeared out of the trees—a large, heavy mass of muscle and hair. "Oh, lassie. They dinna tell me ye'd be such a lovely."

She stabbed, but he grabbed her forearm and unbalanced her. She struck his thigh with the blade in her other hand. Instinct told her to twist it and slice as deep as she could. He cursed and went to one knee, holding her arm. She sliced through the muscles in his arm—once, twice—until his hand went slack. He howled. "Bitch!" He looked down at the blood staining his breeches. "Fucking bitch! What did you—"

She didn't give him a chance to finish. With every ounce of strength she could muster, she stabbed her dagger straight into the base of his skull. He shuddered and fell, and she drew the blade out and ran toward the camp again. Overhead, the raven flapped and cawed and croaked, diving and rising. Voices drifted through the trees—cursing, grunting, wicked laughter. *Connor!* She stepped closer to the clearing and saw the four men gathered around him, beating him. *The horses—* They were close, and her bow hung from her saddle.

Connor wasn't making any noise. *Hang on. I'm coming.* She shushed the horses and took her bow and quiver down. She nocked an arrow and shielded herself between the horses. *Nock, aim, release. How many times have I done this?* Her hands shook. She steadied herself. *Don't miss. You have one chance.*

The arrow landed with a *thunk* in the back of one of the men holding Connor. The others stopped, but she already had another arrow nocked. She aimed, fired, and took down another man who ran toward her. *One more— nock, aim, release.* Another man fell.

The fourth was too close. She dropped the bow, drew a dagger, and threw it. It landed in the grass. The man flicked her other dagger from her hand in a single swipe, but she twisted his hand away and grabbed his forearms. Her knee came up hard into his groin, and he groaned and fell. She picked up her dagger, pulled his head back, and slit his throat.

Blood soaked the ground as she straightened and whirled, looking for more of them. Connor lay on the ground, bound at hands and feet, choking out ragged, desperate breaths. "Connor." She ran to his side and cut the ropes. She turned him to his back. "Can you talk?"

He gasped, trying to draw breath. His eye was blackened and shattered, and a seeping welt marred his jaw. A ragged cut ran across one forearm. She could barely make out his tattoos with all of the welts on his torso, and his sword hand was swollen almost beyond recognition. "Mairead—you're all right. I thought they'd—"

"Just tell me how to help you."

"Make sure they're dead."

She picked up his sword and stabbed the three she'd shot, then returned to his side. "Now what? What can I do?" She pulled him against her lap.

He groaned. "Just need a few minutes." He coughed and winced. "Ribs broken. Hard to breathe."

Gods, we're nowhere! There's no help! "Connor, I don't know where to take you—"

"I can help, yes."

A tall woman with a long gray braid, freckled skin, and fierce golden-green eyes stood at the edge of the trees. She surveyed the dead men, hands on her hips and mouth in a tight line. "Well, I suppose they got what they deserved."

"Who are you?" Mairead asked.

"Bah. I knew this mulehead in his youth." She folded her arms over her chest. "It's like looking at your father, yes? You've grown up."

Connor's body went limp against Mairead's lap. "Rhiannon. It's good to see you."

"And it's good to see you alive—Connor Mac Niall."

CHAPTER NINETEEN

*In the Keep of the Syrafi lies the source of the animstone.
Those who wear it bear the mark of creation in their souls.
— Legend of the Syrafi, oral tradition*

Igraine stood in the castle courtyard wrapped in a fur-lined cloak as Braedan prepared to leave for the Mac Rian holdings. Surrounded by his personal guards, the soldiers standing in formation, the horses, the stablemen, the supply wagons, and various other servants, she was starting to regret her decision to see him off. "Perhaps I should return to my chambers and wave to you from the window," she said.

"I want you here. Stay."

"I'm merely an obstacle." She stepped aside for a stableman rushing past with a piece of repaired tack for one of the king's guards.

"You're not an obstacle." He tugged at the wool doublet he wore, loosening it around his neck. "Are you certain I need to dress in such finery just to ride?"

"Would you rather look a servant, then?" She adjusted his collar for him. "You fidget like a new-made squire, love. Stand still."

"Silk and wool just to lead men out of the city? This is the kind of foppish finery my father enjoyed."

She put her hands on his cheeks. "You are king. I know you want to lead by vision, but even the best visions need to catch the eye first." She brushed a smudge from his shoulder and ran her fingers through his short black hair. "I suppose you'll suffice."

"Should I find a maid to dress me each morning to make sure I portray the proper image?"

She leaned closer and dropped her voice. "Only if you never want to return to my bed."

He laughed, and his eyes twinkled. Her heart skipped. *He makes my knees weak. What a foolish girl I am.* But as she stepped away to watch him give final instructions to his captains and reject, once again, Cormac's suggestion that he take a carriage, she realized once more how much affection had grown between them. *He is not the man I expected when I came here.*

The week since Duncan's death was colored by grief, filled with frantic preparations for Braedan's trip north, and accented by Igraine's own new duties as a legal advisor to the Taurin crown. During the day she maintained an uneasy truce with her emotions, presenting her usual practiced cool competence to the lords and ladies in the castle, but at night, with Braedan, she abandoned decorum.

Braedan's arms welcomed her whether she cried, raged, opined, or seduced. He pleased her the way previous lovers never had. They shared his bedchamber, occasionally beginning to undress each other even before they reached his chamber door. She all but forgot Matthias' attack when she was in Braedan's bed.

She developed a grudging admiration for how he managed his army, his guards, and the castle affairs. In the calm aftermath of his ascension, he let designated leaders handle their own affairs with only casual oversight. He took Igraine's advice and appointed men to help him govern—judges who could hear disputes in his stead and dispense the king's law fairly—and the appointments freed him to pursue some of his other visions.

Unfortunately, one of the men he appointed was Ronan Kerry. Braedan had decided not to take him north and instead appointed his uncle Lord High Chancellor, only one level below a regent. When he told Igraine, she sat up in bed and slapped his shoulder. "You fool, Braedan. You've just handed him your throne."

Braedan sat up and leaned against the pillows, one hand behind his head. "He is my uncle. He's no threat to me. He practically raised me."

She stood up and pulled on a robe as anger rose. "And so you waited until now to tell me—when you leave tomorrow and I have no chance to sway you and you've already bedded me? You ass." She poured wine and stood near his window, facing him. "I gave you a way to rid the castle of him. I told you to send him north, and I told you to go with him so that you could watch him, and now this? D'ye not see what he's doing, lad?"

Braedan laughed and stood. "You're angrier than I thought you'd be. Your Eiryan is showing."

"Damn it, pay attention. Your uncle has designs on your throne."

Braedan folded his arms across his chest. "It's no secret that you and Ronan don't like each other. But unless you have some proof that he's plotting against me, this only sounds like the anger of a woman scorned or a jealous noble." He paused. "Do you have some proof?"

Her jaw tightened. "I don't need proof. I'm not wrong about these things. He has too much power."

"Jealous?"

"No. I have no right to a position as chancellor. I'm not Taurin. But surely there are other men as competent and more trustworthy. Why not give Ronan some high foreign post where he can't make any moves against you—an ambassadorship to Espara, perhaps? He could take his lady wife home to her family."

"He says he doesn't like it there." Braedan put his hands on her arms. "Don't worry. Ronan won't hurt your position or my power. He helped me get here."

But watching Ronan's men in the courtyard gave Igraine pause. The men from Stone Coast milled around the gate, ramparts, and courtyard. None of them were assigned to Braedan's contingent. *Kerry has managed to stay here with all of his men, while Braedan leaves with all of his closest guards.* She spotted Logan. *Well, almost all of them.* Fortunately, Logan had insisted on remaining behind to command the men from Stone Coast and the remaining Taurin troops. Still, Igraine could not resist an uneasy shiver. *This will come to blows.*

Braedan noticed. "Cold?" He took a piece of parchment from Cormac.

"No. Anxious."

"There's nothing to be anxious about. This is what kings do." He opened the parchment and started reading.

Leave their thrones in the care of men who would usurp them? The cool autumn breeze teased his hair, and Igraine pursed her lips. "Braedan."

"Hmm?" He stood between his horse and Cormac, staring at a piece of parchment. "What is it?"

"I wondered if we might have a moment before you go."

He wrinkled his brow.

She cleared her throat. "Alone." She gestured to the chaos in the courtyard.

He blinked, surprised. "Yes. Of course." He handed Cormac the parchment. "Reply to Lord Seannan and tell him the crown doesn't owe him or the

Lady Aislinn anything more. I will not offer restitution for the loss of his son-in-law. I will consider making some small public improvements to his holdings in the spring, but his defenses and his wall are his responsibility. I'll not pay for them." Cormac inclined his head, and Braedan turned to Igraine. "Inside the great hall?"

She nodded and twined her arm around his. "The atmosphere in the courtyard is not conducive to a final goodbye, Braedan."

"Ah, I'm sorry." A guard opened the door to the great hall, and when they entered the relative quiet, Braedan pulled her into his arms. "Didn't we have enough privacy this morning? I thought we took care of everything."

"We did. I just wanted one more moment with you," she said.

"For what purpose? If I had the time, I would gladly find a quiet room to indulge you once more."

"It's not that." *He'll think me a fool.* "Forgive me, Braedan. I shouldn't have . . ." She started to go.

He stopped her with a hand on her arm. "Igraine, I should not have neglected you. I'm sorry for that."

She took a deep breath. "In Eirya, it is customary when lovers must be apart for the lady to give her lord something to remember her." She pulled a small scarf of blue silk from the silver belt she wore and held it out to him. "I took this from the scraps of the blue dress you care for so much. I thought it might remind you of me. It's silly, Braedan. I shouldn't have bothered you with it."

He took the silk. "It's not silly. I like when you share Eiryan traditions with me."

She draped the silk around his neck and pulled him closer. "This week has been difficult, but it has also been delightful. Passionate." She closed her eyes. "I'm as besotted as some foolish shepherdess in a story."

He lifted her chin, and she opened her eyes to see him smiling. "As am I." He lowered his voice as a servant bustled past. "This is an unfamiliar role for me—the doting lover and future husband. I don't know how to act."

"Act as if I am your entire world. Act as if I am more important to you than your kingdom."

"You are."

She smiled. "Don't ever say that to anyone but me."

"Do you ever stop thinking of politics?"

"Only when I am thinking of the law."

He grinned again. He held the blue silk to his face. "You've scented it with your perfume."

"I hope it reminds you of me while you are away."

"Perhaps I can think of some unique ways for us to use it when I return." The thought of that made her shiver. "You render me speechless, majesty."

"I doubt that, highness." He twined the silk around both their hands, joining them in an imitation of the kirok handfasting. "Are you certain you won't join me? The nights will be cold without you."

"I have no wish to travel north at this time of year. I'm enjoying my autumn without ice and snow. Besides, Cormac is ailing, and I don't trust your uncle. You need someone here to watch the kingdom."

"I suppose I knew you would say that." He untied the silk and put his arms around her waist. "One more kiss?"

"If I must." His arms tightened around her, and he kissed her. His hands slid up her back, under her hair, and his mouth drifted down her neck. She sighed. *He is very good at this.*

At last, he pulled away from her and stared down, satisfied. He smiled and lifted the blue silk. "Thank you for this. I will think of you every time I hold it."

If it keeps you away from Olwyn Mac Rian, it will serve its purpose. "I am pleased that you like it."

They walked out of the great hall arm in arm. He mounted his horse and reached down to grasp her hand. "Commander, I'm trusting you to be at the lady's service while I'm gone. Please escort her wherever she'd like to go."

Logan bowed. "As you wish, your majesty."

Igraine met Braedan's eyes. *He trusts me.* "Safe journey."

He squeezed her hand and winked at her with a roguish grin. The drumroll began, and the king led the retinue out the castle gates.

Igraine's eyes stung. Logan held out a kerchief. "Damn cold air," she said.

"Of course, my lady." He offered his arm, and together, they wound their way back to the castle.

Her days fell into an easy routine once the king's retinue left. She heard petitioners with Cormac and Ronan, and together, the three of them conducted the business of the state and the castle. She wrote letters and waited for responses. She wandered the city, Logan and her ladies at her side, and greeted the merchants and commoners alike. The more she knew of them, the more she could picture herself as queen of Taura.

A week after the king's departure, Logan came to her study one afternoon. One of her maids let him in, and Igraine looked up from her work.

"Commander. What can I do for you?"

"I thought I might be able to offer you something, highness. It's a beautiful day. Would you like to go riding?"

"I have a fair bit of work to do. Petitioners are trying to get home before winter snows hit. I don't want them held up."

"Perhaps you will find it easier to concentrate after some fresh air."

His voice carried an urgency she'd learned to recognize. He gave a barely perceptible nod. "All right. Let me change."

"I'll have the horses saddled."

When she arrived in the stables, he was waiting with a white mare and his own gray stallion. They rode toward the north gates of the castle and reined in near a large round stone building with a high roof.

The former smokehouse was one of the first buildings erected at the castle site. When the earliest kings and queens of Taura needed a place to stay while the great castle was built, they had used the building for living quarters. In later years, it was used for a smokehouse and then a storage building. At Igraine's insistence, Braedan had ordered it made hospitable for the sayas.

Igraine didn't relish the idea of seeing Sayana Muriel. "Must this be done today?"

He nodded as he helped her off her horse. "I wanted to send this lady off some while ago, but you were busy with the king. The lady has family in the north. If she leaves now, she can reach them before the snows are too heavy."

"Who is it?"

"Saya Cait."

Igraine nodded. She let Logan open the door for her and entered the building as she removed her riding hat and gloves.

The sayas had turned the interior of the building into a warm, inviting home. Logan had ordered bunks and modest furniture built for them, and the women had used every bit of it. Beds lined the curve of one side of the building, and other portions of the interior were dedicated for washing clothing, preparing meals, and storing food. A small door led to a fenced yard where they could walk on sunny days, and Igraine knew they were making plans to plant a small garden in the spring.

Sayana Muriel approached Igraine as the door closed. "Your highness," she greeted. "It's been some time. Have you brought us any news from Aliom?"

Igraine turned over her hat and gloves to another saya and shook her head. "Taurin ships are slow in autumn, sayana. If they were Eiryan, perhaps

I would have some answers for you."

Muriel's calm smile creased her weathered cheeks. "It is well. Alshada protects us."

I protect you. But Igraine stifled her irritation and smiled. "We've come for Cait today, I believe. Is she prepared?"

The dark-haired woman came forward. She curtsied. She'd lost weight since Igraine saw her last, and her robes hung from her in loose folds. "Your highness. You are a blessing from Alshada. I thought I'd never see my sister—"

"'Tis well, Cait," Igraine said. "You can go see your sister."

Logan cleared his throat. "I'll wait outside." He left the smokehouse.

Igraine undressed. "You know how this works?"

Cait nodded. "He'll take me to the main road?"

"Aye. A man waits there with one of my maids, Deirdre. You'll trade clothing with her, and the man will take you to an inn where the owners will give you supplies to help you go home." She pulled off her riding habit and traded it for Cait's linen underdress. When Cait had donned Igraine's riding clothes, Igraine helped her bind her hair atop her head and hide it under the riding hat. "Keep the hood of your cloak up as well," she told Cait. "The guards expect to see red hair. If they see black, they will question you."

Cait swallowed hard and nodded. Her eyes were tired and drawn. "I can't thank you enough, your highness."

"Don't thank me. This is Logan's doing. I would see you safely to Eirya or Aliom in due course. He insists that you will be safer away from the castle."

Cait nodded again. She embraced Muriel and a few other sayas and opened the door to find Logan waiting. He helped her onto Igraine's white mare, and they galloped out of the north gates.

Muriel gestured to a chair. "Please, highness. Have a seat. We've just made tea. Would you like some?"

Igraine took the chair and arranged the saya's white robes around her legs. "That would be lovely, sayana."

Muriel nodded toward one of the younger sayas and then sat next to Igraine. "How do you fare in the castle, my lady?"

"Well, thank you." She hesitated. "Sayana, there is some news, though not from Aliom. The king has made me an offer of marriage. I've accepted."

Muriel's eyes widened for a moment, but then she nodded. "Then you will refuse the kirok permanently."

"The kirok was never my first choice, sayana. You knew that. I chose it to avoid an unwanted marriage."

"And the usurper has convinced you that his cause is just?" Rare anger tinged the older woman's voice.

A saya brought tea, and Igraine poured herself a cup and stirred honey into it. "He didn't have to convince me of anything. I saw for myself. He is a better king than we expected. I can do good in this position."

"He stole his throne," Muriel said in a low voice. "He had his cousin murdered and—"

"And he has done nothing that other conquerors haven't done all through history, even conquerors the kirok has endorsed," Igraine said. "Do you think I haven't told myself all of these same things, then?"

"Saya Hana died fleeing his hand, and you would wed and bed the man who ordered it done."

"He didn't want anyone to die. Killing Hana was a mistake."

Muriel shook her head. "No, your highness. I cannot endorse this."

Igraine stood and pulled up the white hood of the saya's robes. "Then it's fortunate for me that I don't need your approval. Excuse me." She walked out the rear door of the building and into the yard, keeping her hood high so that no one would see her hair.

The time passed slowly under Muriel's tense observation, though Igraine managed to avoid further conversation with the sayana by chatting with some of the remaining sayas. She counted eighty women remaining of the original one hundred four. *We've helped more than twenty get free of this place*, she thought. *Seven weeks, twenty lives, and dozens of lies to the man I love.*

When Logan finally returned with Igraine's maid, Igraine was happy to exchange the sayada robes for the riding habit that Deirdre wore. The maid dressed in a simple serving dress and slipped out the door with a basket of linens to be laundered in the castle.

Igraine left the building without saying goodbye to Muriel. "Logan, let's go riding."

He blinked. "You said you had too much work."

That was before I suffered Muriel's glare. "I know. I need some air."

He nodded. "Very well."

They turned back to the north gate. The guards frowned in confusion. "Commander," one said, holding out his hand. "Didn't you already pass through with her highness?"

Igraine lowered the hood of her cloak. "Do you question the desires of your future queen, lad? Would you care to answer to the king?"

The man dropped his hand and bowed. "No, my lady, of course not. I—"

"I dropped a scarf. 'Twas a gift from the king and I'd like it back. You will let us pass."

"Of course, your highness." He stood aside, and Igraine and Logan passed through the gate.

When they were well away from the gates, Logan glanced at Igraine. "It might have been better to wait until the shift change," he said. "They wouldn't have questioned you."

"I didn't want to wait."

Logan nodded. "Tension with the sayas, your highness?"

"I prefer not to discuss it."

"As you wish." He rode in silence for some time. "It's been some time since we rode together. I've missed your company."

She twisted the reins around her hands. "I've spent more time with the king."

"As you should. As his betrothed."

"Not officially." She cleared her throat. "You're still certain the sayas are in danger?"

"I am, especially after the attempt on your life."

She sighed. "I don't know how many more of these escapes I can manage," she said. "My duties are expanded with the king away, and now that he isn't here, Cormac and Ronan watch my every move. Can't you use Deirdre? Dress the sayas in her servant dresses and let them find your man by themselves?"

He shook his head. "The guards are instructed to question any servants coming or going. They would not recognize the sayas as servants, and I doubt that any sayas could lie convincingly enough to get past the guards."

"Then put men you trust on the north wall."

"I can't. Most of them went north with the king. I want him protected. The rest are in positions where I need their eyes and ears."

She frowned. "Are there so few that you truly trust?"

"Yes."

She tightened her hands on the reins. "There is much suspicion about what is between me and you. I can't give Ronan more reason to speak against me to Braedan."

Logan fixed his eyes ahead. "I will speak in your favor to the king. I will protect you from Lord Kerry." He gestured ahead. "Let's ride out to the lake."

Before she could answer, he spurred his horse northward, and she followed.

Cantering across the fields through the crisp autumn air cleared Igraine's head. They rode around the lake, past the foot of Macha Tor, and back toward the castle. Logan indulged her in a race, laughing when she reined her horse in long after he crossed their agreed upon finish line. "Don't go up against this one," he said, patting the stallion's neck. "He's big, but he's fast."

"You cheated."

"I did not," Logan said over an indignant laugh. "You were distracted."

She scoffed. "Well, let's see how he does if *I* have a head start." Before he could answer, she had spurred her mare into a full gallop toward the castle.

The pain struck suddenly. Her leg seized, and her hand flew to the arrow stuck in her calf. "Damn it!" Another arrow flew over her back. Igraine tumbled onto the ground and dove behind a tree. Blood stained her boot and skirt, and pain radiated up her leg. "Logan!"

The world spun with a sharp crack to her skull. A man's hands and legs pinned her on the ground. She struggled to reach the knife in her boot. His hands tightened on her throat. She choked and writhed under him.

Blood sprayed her face, and the man fell off her. She shook her head to clear her eyes. Gentle hands helped her sit up. "Igraine. Are you all right?"

She nodded. The man lay next to her, dead, his head nearly severed. He was nothing—a lowborn thug dressed in plain homespun—but near his hand lay a royal-issue dagger. "Who is he?"

"I don't recognize him. He's not one of Braedan's men." He touched a raw place on her head. "You'll have a good black eye. Are you hurt anywhere else?"

"My leg—an arrow. Did you find the other one?"

"No." He tied a long piece of cloth around her leg. "First an attack on you in the castle, now an attack in the king's own forest. Where did you make such determined enemies?"

"I don't know." Her head spun and warmth drained from her arms and legs as she started to lose control of her muscles.

He examined the arrow, and she winced. "I can't touch this. If it's barbed, it will tear your leg up. I need to get you to Repha Felix."

She nodded, but she was growing dizzy. "I don't feel well."

The world went dark.

Waking was a slow, tricky business. She tried to open her eyes, but she thought it would have been easier to dance in lead slippers. She heard herself moan from some incomprehensible distance. *So thirsty.* "Wa—" Her voice was barely more than a croaking whisper.

"Highness?" The repha's voice. "Are you waking?"

She couldn't nod. "Water."

He fussed around her, and then a strong hand held her head up while cool liquid touched her lips. The fire in her throat faded with slow sips from a goblet. "My thanks."

"Can you open your eyes?"

She tried again. Focus returned as she blinked and lifted her lids. The repha's face hovered over her. "Castle."

Relief tinged his smile. "Yes. Logan brought you back. The arrow was poisoned. I gave you an herbal remedy."

She nodded. "Leg?" Talking seemed such an effort.

"It will be fine. Your boot stopped much of the blow. Thank the king for his insistence on buying you the finest leather."

She tried to smile.

"Lie still, highness. You're in the king's bed. Your ladies are here. Logan and Lord Kerry are looking into what happened."

"Cormac?"

"He went into the city this morning. No one has seen him since."

She closed her eyes again. "Rest."

"Of course." He didn't move away. "Highness, you wear a stone on your ankle. May I ask where you got it?"

She cleared her throat and rasped an answer. "Mother. Why?"

Silence. "No reason. We can discuss it further when you wake."

She drifted to sleep as if lulled by the mere suggestion of it.

When she woke again, she wasn't alone. She struggled to sit up. "Repha?"

A heavy arm fell on her chest, knocking her back against the bed. She screamed. Steel flashed. She pushed the hand away, the sting of the blade fresh against her neck. The man was on her bed, straddling her. "Repha—Logan—help!"

"Shut up!"

Her hand gripped his forearm and she locked her elbow, trying to keep the knife away from her. She pushed at the arm on her chest with her other hand, but he shifted it to press against her throat. Breath came only in choking gasps. The blankets and his body had her trapped. She opened her mouth, trying to breathe or speak, but nothing came out.

The door crashed against the wall. Another flash of steel flickered through faint light from a torch. Warmth soaked her blankets and night clothes as the man collapsed on top of her in death. Breath rushed back into her lungs, and she pushed the man off herself.

One of Ronan Kerry's guards stood over her. "Highness, get up. The castle is under attack."

She dragged her body to standing. "Who—what—"

"We don't know. The sayas and kirons are dead."

Her stomach lurched. She tried to put weight on her injured leg, but couldn't. The man put an arm around her. "What happened?"

"We don't know yet." He supported her weight. "I'm taking you down to the dungeons."

"The dungeons?"

"It's the most secure part of the castle. There's a room down there for this kind of thing." He helped her hobble out of the bedchamber.

"My maids—"

"We've secured them in the servants' quarters. They're fine."

"How did he get in here?"

"I don't know. The guards outside your room are dead."

"Where's Logan?"

He opened the door to the corridor. "The king's commander? I don't know." He hesitated, looking both ways. He dropped his voice. "It's quieter, but stay close. We can't say if everything is safe yet."

Igraine's stomach roiled at the sight of the two crumpled Taurin guards. *I insisted on Taurin guards, and my insistence got them killed.*

The guard helped her down the corridor and several flights of winding stairs to a clean, cool room furnished with comfortable chairs, a table, and several cots. Repha Felix was already there, as were several lords and ladies who had been in the castle for court matters. Felix came to her side and helped her to a chair. "Highness, are you all right?"

She nodded. "I'm fine. I just want to know what's happening."

"As do we all." Repha Felix pulled a kerchief from his pocket and put it against Igraine's neck where the man's blade had stung her. "Are you hurt anywhere else?"

"No, but my leg throbs. What do you know?"

"Little. I left your chambers to retrieve some more poultice for your leg. Before I could return, everything was in chaos. The men were racing out of the castle toward the outbuildings. One of them brought me down here." He dabbed at her neck. "It's not deep. You are very fortunate, highness."

She closed her eyes. "Kerry's man said the sayas and the kirons are all dead."

"So I heard." He lifted her hand to the kerchief. "Hold this on your neck while I check your leg."

She leaned back in the chair and held the kerchief. "Sayana Muriel, all those women, the kirons—who would attack people of peace and service?"

Felix said nothing. He treated her leg with fresh poultice and propped it on a chair. The cut on her neck had stopped bleeding, but he dabbed a strong-smelling ointment on it and gently pressed a wad of linen over the ointment. He gave her a goblet. "Something for the pain," he said.

She shook her head. "I want to stay awake."

"It won't make you sleep." He offered the goblet again. "Drink, highness."

She took it and sipped, but when Felix turned away, she set the goblet next to her and leaned back to wait.

The door opened, and a guard brought a wan-looking Cormac in. Looking at him in the faint light of the room, Igraine was certain that he had lost weight in the last weeks. *Where does he go so often? And why is he so sickly? What's he hiding?*

"My lady, are you all right?" Cormac asked.

"Everything will heal with time. Do you know what's happening?"

"No. I don't know anything." He found a seat away from the rest of the crowd and leaned over to put his head in his hands.

Time crept by as they all waited for news. One of the guards was able to bring some food, water, and wine for the group. Igraine, still aching from her wounds and the poison, rested on a cot. Cormac remained in the same position.

Felix knelt next to Igraine and picked up her goblet. "You didn't finish this."

"I didn't need it."

He frowned, but he set the goblet aside. "May I check your wound again?" he asked, gesturing to her neck.

She nodded. "You asked me earlier where I got the stone around my ankle. Why did you want to know?"

Felix replaced the linen on her neck and looked around at the other people in the room. He pulled a chair close to Igraine, his back to the others. When he spoke, his voice was barely more than a whisper. "It's an animstone.

They are very rare. They are found in the mountains beyond Sveklant."

"I wear a rare stone," she said, dropping her voice to match his. "I fail to see why that's significant. I'm a royal lady. I've owned many rare stones."

"You say your mother gave it to you?"

"She made me swear never to remove it."

He opened his mouth, then closed it and took a deep breath. "Does your mother have magic blood? Or your father?"

She scoffed. "No one in my family has magic blood," she said, her voice rising. Felix gestured her to speak more quietly. She rolled her eyes and lowered her voice. "Magic is a foolish notion—myths and legends from tapestries woven hundreds of years ago and stories written by the earliest men."

"Not myths." He leaned forward. "The animstones are often worn by people of magic blood who wish to suppress their magic for a time. The stones were formed at the creation. No one knows exactly what they are. Some say they came from the world before this one. The Sidh queen wears one in her crown that augments her magic, but for other Sidh, the stones suppress the talents."

The Sidh queen? "Are you saying I must be Sidh?" *There are no Sidh.* But doubt started to creep in. Felix spoke with assurance. *Even if he's wrong, he speaks as one who believes what he's saying. What if he's right?*

"There are two magicked races—those who have elemental talents, like the Sidh, and those who wield supernatural gifts, like the Syrafi and Ferimin. You don't have the look of someone with Sidh blood. It runs true. If you were Sidh, you would be dark. But the Syrafi—I don't see how it's possible." He paused. "Whatever you do, lady, you must not let the king or Cormac find out. If they knew—"

At last, the door opened, and Logan, Ronan Kerry, and three of Ronan's guards entered the room. Logan's face was drawn, tired, and grim. Ronan Kerry shadowed him, arms crossed and face equally grim. Igraine sat up on her cot to hear what they had to say. Ronan spoke. "My lords and ladies, the castle is secure. Most of you can return to your rooms. My men will escort you."

"Can you tell us anything yet?" a lord asked.

"I need to speak with her highness and Lord Rowan before I can tell you anything more." The guards led the lords and ladies back to their rooms in the castle, and Ronan turned to Cormac. "Lord Rowan. We need to speak."

Cormac nodded and took a deep breath. "Yes. What have you discovered?"

Ronan put one hand on Logan's shoulder. "Tell them."

Logan's eyes flickered from Cormac to Igraine and back. Two guards entered the room, and Logan removed his sword, the gold cord around his livery, and his insignia of rank. He placed them all on the table. "It was me. I surrender myself to your mercy, Lord Rowan."

CHAPTER TWENTY

The One Hand holds all that was, is, and will be.
— Proverb of the Tal'Aster Sect

"He's a Mac Niall?" Mairead gasped. Connor groaned in her lap. "He's Culain Mac Niall's son?"

The woman with the gray braid—*Rhiannon, he said*—stepped closer. "He didn't tell you?"

"He tells me as little as possible," Mairead said. Connor made another sound that sounded like an attempt at a laugh, but it turned into a cough and painful spasm against Mairead's legs. He rolled his head and spit blood. Her chest tightened. *Please, Connor. Please don't die!*

"Well, he'll need some healing, I expect. Let's get him to my house." Rhiannon knelt and touched Connor's forehead. "I can't carry you, boy. Can you walk?"

Mairead felt his head twitch in a small nod against her lap. She and Rhiannon helped him to standing. Her legs shook as she lifted his weight, but she gritted her teeth. *He needs me. I can do this.*

His knees buckled, and he stumbled. "Damn it—can't. I can't."

Mairead tightened her grip around his torso. "Connor. Lean on me." *Alshada, please—please don't let this be the end for him. Please help us!*

His knees buckled. "I can't." He turned his head. She swallowed bile at the sight of his swollen, battered face. "Mairead, I should have—" He coughed.

She put two fingers on his lips. "No more. Let us help you."

His good eye turned glassy, and he grunted. "Mother," he whispered. He fell.

Mairead knelt next to him and pulled him close on her lap again. "Connor, please," she whispered.

The hair on her arms rose. She lifted her eyes to see orange and yellow stone braids weave a small hillock next to them. Mairead had to blink several times. The smallest and most beautiful woman she'd ever seen emerged from the hillock, hands on hips and mouth drawn into a tight line. "What happened?"

His mother! She didn't have time or inclination to think of manners and how to greet the tiny queen appropriately. "We were attacked," Mairead said. "I got free, but he—" Her voice choked and she composed herself. "Please, can you help?"

"Your house is nearby?" Maeve asked Rhiannon.

"Just a few hundred paces."

Maeve nodded. "Lead me. I can bind him in air and bring him along."

Violet threads wound around Connor's body, and he sighed in relief as the braids lifted his body off the ground. Rhiannon led the group toward her house.

Mairead stifled a gasp. *She's carrying him on the air. How is this possible?* She stepped next to Connor's body, stretched out flat on thin violet strands that she could only barely see in the darkness, and took his good hand. *Focus on Connor, not the magic. Not the Sidh queen. This is about Connor.*

"Mairead," Connor whispered.

She squeezed his hand. "I'm here."

"You're safe?"

She nodded. "I'm safe. I'm here. We'll help you."

They stepped through the forest to a small cabin, and Rhiannon opened the door. "There's a bed behind the curtain. Put him down and let's see what we have," she said. Maeve brought Connor's body to rest on a soft mattress behind a patchwork curtain. Rhiannon started to prod the welts and rising bruises on his torso.

Mairead put a hand over her lips, but a sob escaped.

"Now, lass—he'll be all right, yes," Rhiannon said, but there was doubt in her voice. She pressed on his belly, sides, and chest. He grunted.

"How bad is it?" Maeve whispered.

"Bad. He bleeds inside, too. I can treat broken bones, bruises, but the bleeding?" She shook her head. "We can only wait it out. Unless you can conjure some skill with healing."

"I have no talent for it," Maeve said, her voice on the edge of panic. "I'll call the Sidh ladies."

"No." Connor opened his eyes. He tried to sit up, but fell back and moaned. "Mother, they're looking for you. Don't risk—"

"Is there any other way?" Maeve asked, her voice rising and all royal composure gone.

"I don't know of any," Rhiannon said. "We could wait out the night, see how he is tomorrow, but by then it could be too late."

Tears spilled onto Mairead's cheeks and down to Connor's arm. He turned his head toward her and opened his good eye. She sniffed. "I'm sorry, Connor. I should have trusted you," she whispered.

His eye fluttered closed, and he lay motionless.

Mairead gasped. "Connor, don't—don't let it take you." She shook his hand, but he'd faded, leaving behind a bruised, battered husk.

"He lives, but not for long," Rhiannon said. "The Sidh are safe here. Call your healers, Maeve."

Maeve's eyes turned glassy, and gooseflesh rose on Mairead's arms. A translucent blue braid skimmed her ankle, and she jumped. Within moments, violet, green, and orange braids swirled around the room. The violet braids deposited a small woman dressed in sheer sky blue silk. A second woman stepped out of a thin waterspout and waved the liquid out the window amid green braids. Rhiannon's dirt floor undulated for a moment, and then a third woman slid up from a pile of soil the size of a molehill. She gestured the dirt back into place. All three women turned to Maeve.

The Sidh queen pointed at Connor. "My son," she said, her voice cracking under the regal authority. "Heal him."

The Sidh women pushed Mairead out of the way. "He asked me to stay," Mairead said.

"He can't know now, lass," Rhiannon said, her hands on Mairead's shoulders. "Come. You need tea. You can't wait on a thing like this without a cup of tea, no."

Mairead's eyes burned with desperate tears. *Alshada, don't take him—don't let me lose him.* She let Rhiannon lead her to a small table near a hearth, and the older woman put a kettle over the flames.

Maeve sat at the table as well. "Mairead."

Mairead closed her eyes. A memory returned. *I've been in this woman's presence.* "You know me."

The queen didn't speak. Rhiannon moved small pots and jars around behind them as she prepared tea and food. The Sidh magic in the air raised the hair on Mairead's arms as the healers ministered to Connor. *I've felt it before, even before the night Connor took me away.* "You were there when I was anointed," Mairead whispered. "You saw—you watched. I felt you there."

Maeve's mouth was drawn into a somber line, and her brown eyes brimmed with tears. "Macha Tor is the most sacred place on Taura. I was crowned there, as were all of the Sidh queens back to the creation of the world. For a human to be crowned there—such things are felt in the web. I sensed a ripple, and I responded to it." Her hands remained folded in her lap. The deep mauve silk she wore shimmered in the pale light from the hearth, and the murky gray stone in her silver circlet caught the light and sparkled. "You were so small," she whispered. "Such a pretty child, with your blond curls and your rosy cheeks. I wanted a daughter, and when I saw you—" She pursed her lips and shook her head, composing herself. "Do you know who anointed you?"

Mairead shook her head. "I thought it was just a vision or perhaps one of the Syrafi."

"It was Alshada himself. Muriel prostrated herself, but you danced up to him without fear, without worry. And when he knelt and wiped the oil across your forehead, you giggled. He said your line would bring peace to Taura."

Alshada himself. And she was there. "How old was Connor then?" *Fool. Of all the questions you could ask, that's the one you choose?*

Maeve gave her a wistful smile. "Eleven, perhaps twelve. Old enough to prefer his father's company, young enough to still want his mother's attention." She took a deep breath. "What happened to my son?"

Mairead told her everything from the time they met the kiron and his companions to the point when Maeve arrived, leaving out the details of their kisses and intimate conversations. "I don't know what they wanted with him—why they didn't just kill him," Mairead said.

Rhiannon doled tea leaves into three cups. "Well, it's clear, don't you think? He said they wanted the Sidh. They wanted you because you're Queen Brenna's heir."

The reliquary—that's why. "They needed me to carry the reliquary," she whispered, her heart racing. "And they wanted Connor to help them find you," she said to Maeve.

"How do you know she's the heir?" Maeve asked Rhiannon.

She poured water over the tea leaves and brought over bread and cheese. "I see things, you know. Hidden things. I see a crown on the girl's head and black wings around the lad. Always have, yes."

Mairead closed her eyes and put her face in her hands. "This is my fault. I asked him to bring them along. I convinced him to let them travel with us. If he dies because I was an idiot—"

Maeve reached out and put a slim hand on Mairead's arm. "I think he is stronger than you think."

"He's a Mac Niall." Mairead couldn't look at Maeve. "You were Culain Mac Niall's mistress."

A hint of humor tinged the queen's voice. "A plain way to say it, but accurate."

Mairead opened her eyes. "And you?" she asked Rhiannon.

"I was his nanny, yes. I delivered him, in fact. I ministered to the lady when she nearly died. Now I can minister to him in his pain. The earth brings her will around, yes."

"Forgive me, Rhiannon, but how did you come to be here? Just when we needed a safe place?" Mairead asked. *What if this is another Syrafi illusion, like Donal and Aileen's farm? Will healing work if it's all an illusion?*

The old woman shrugged. "I live, I hunt, I heal here. You came to me. Coincidence, perhaps." She bustled away.

Time passed with agonizing sloth. The Sidh healers stayed behind the curtain, the vibrations and aura of their magic hovering around the small rooms. Mairead couldn't stand the wait with Maeve's eyes on her. "I need some fresh air," she said, and walked out of the cabin before the other women could respond.

Once outside, she wished she had her cloak. The autumn chill hit her full on after the warmth of Rhiannon's cabin, and her breath hovered before her when she exhaled. She wandered toward a small barn near the cabin. Against one outside wall was a stack of chopped wood under a short overhang. She sat on the ground near the wood, drew her knees to her chin, and fell into shaking, gasping sobs. She couldn't even form the words to pray. *What if I never get to tell him how I feel? If he wakes up, I'll tell him. If I can figure out how I feel.*

When her sobs at last started to abate, she lifted her head and tried to compose herself. A barn cat sidled next to her, rubbing her legs and purring, and Mairead lowered her knees to give the orange tabby a place to nestle. The cat kneaded her legs and curled up in a warm ball, and the autumn chill didn't seem as bitter. Mairead stroked the cat's ears and head idly. She sniffed and wiped her nose on her sleeve. She leaned against the woodpile and closed her eyes as the cat warmed her.

"Mairead."

She startled, disturbing the cat, and turned to see Rhiannon. "Is he all right?" She stood quickly. The cat mewed a complaint. "Are they done?"

"No. We should go get your things, yes?" Rhiannon stared at the cat. "You think she is one of you, eh?" The cat mewed and sat down to lick one paw. "Heh. The lioness knows, yes." She strode away, and Mairead hurried after her.

The bodies were stiff when Mairead and Rhiannon arrived at the camp. Wolves and other wild dogs called to each other in the distance, but the fire had kept them away. Flies were already gathering, and the horses whickered and stamped nervous hooves at the sounds and smells. Mairead turned her face away from the bloody scene. She picked up blankets and packs and put them on the horses. "What about the animals that belonged to the kirons? I mean—"

Rhiannon took the reins of the wagon team. "I'll take them. Leave them, and the wolves will get them."

When everything was packed, Rhiannon stamped out the remainder of the fire. They left the wagon. "Leave the bodies," Rhiannon said. "Food for wolves and crows and worms, they are. Let the earth care for her own." She walked past Mairead toward her cabin.

Faced with the prospect of leaving, Mairead finally stopped and stared at the dead bodies in the faint moonlight. "I killed those men," she said. Rhiannon stopped and put a hand on her shoulder. "I killed them. Six of them. How could I do that?"

"He taught you, eh? He's good. His reputation is well-deserved."

Mairead shuddered. "How could he be caught so off-guard?"

"Distraction? No man is perfect, even a raven." She waited. "You want to offer up prayers, eh?"

The question was an honest one, if brusque. Mairead shook her head. "I can pray from your cabin." *And I don't know if I can offer prayers for these.*

They walked in silence, Rhiannon directing them through the forest, her eyes fixed ahead as she walked. Her graceful frame picked over brush, and her pale gray dress stood against the dark of the forest as a faint beacon. The moon cast dim shadows through the trees, and soon, Mairead saw the light of Rhiannon's small cabin ahead.

Rhiannon stopped and lifted her eyes. "Hmm. Harvest moon soon. Dark creatures rising, yes. They'll have need of souls."

Mairead shivered. *Whose souls?* They tied the horses outside and went in the house.

Maeve still sat at the table twisting her teacup in her hands, her eyes red-rimmed. "They're still working on him."

Mairead sat down again. "I was so angry with him. I shouldn't have been so cruel. If I hadn't walked away, they might not have . . ." Her voice caught on a sob.

Rhiannon stood. "I'll check on him. They may need something." She went behind the curtain.

Maeve cleared her throat. "You and my son. Has he behaved nobly?"

Mairead bit her lip. *He taught me to fight and shoot a bow. He bought me suitable clothes and daggers. He told me about constellations and tried to teach me to dance. He's kind and funny and proud and strong, but he has a soft side. He sang to a baby. He's kept me warm and kissed me and touched my hair.* "Your majesty, he's a man you can be proud of. He's noble in every way."

Maeve sat very still, very quiet. "You're in love with him."

Her voice had a strange mix of shock, pity, and maternal protection. Mairead straightened in her chair. *She's his mother, but she stole his will. She keeps him bound.* "Would it matter if I were?"

Maeve's eyebrows lifted in subtle chiding. "Do you realize what you are, child? Your loins are not your own. You belong to Taura."

"I'm not a child. And your son is noble. He would be an acceptable match for a queen."

"He has no certificate of nobility in Taura," Maeve said, and Mairead heard regret and pain under the truth. "He is not recognized as noble. His father gave him the Mac Niall name, but Connor burned the paper that acknowledged even that much. And when Culain died, his name was attainted in the royal court. There is no Taurin law that would recognize Connor as legitimate or noble." She paused. "Even if he were legitimate and recognized, he is not a man to marry. He'll ruin you and leave you."

Mairead thought of the longing in Connor's eyes the afternoon when he told her of his house in Espara. *Could I make him stay? Could I convince him?* "Forgive me, majesty, but that's none of your concern. What is between Connor and me is our business. Not yours."

Maeve's eyes narrowed. "You speak as a queen, but you have no crown. I'm not your subject, child."

"No, and neither are you my queen."

"You may not be my subject, but he is."

"And what did that earn him? A binding you've forced on him? You expect as much from him as I want—more, perhaps. You wish him to live a life you carve for him. I wish him only to share the life he has with me."

Maeve's jaw tightened. "I've lived in his head for six years. He is my son and I love him, but I also know more about what he is than you possibly could." She stopped, abrupt, and shook her head. "He's not for you. You are the heir to the Taurin throne. You cannot bed a half-Sidh, bastard son of a tainted duke."

"Did anyone tell you not to bed a Taurin lord before you conceived Connor?"

The magic pinched Mairead's skin, and she gasped and found herself unable to move. She could only focus ahead as her arms and hands and feet and legs were bound, tight, by violet braids stronger than rope. The braids tightened, cutting into her skin. She resisted the urge to grunt or whimper. *I will not give her the satisfaction.*

"You will never mention Culain Mac Niall to me again," Maeve said. Her voice rang with the sharp crack of a northern wind. "I will not be taken to task for my choices by a kirok-raised whelp who thinks only of warming my son's thighs."

Mairead could only gasp as Maeve's icy stare penetrated her. She struggled against the bonds, angry and frustrated but held tight. *She binds me like she binds him. Can't she find any other way to deal with people who disagree with her?* "Let . . . me . . . go. My . . . choice," she said, gulping air between the words.

"Maeve, stop." Rhiannon's voice cracked through the cabin. Maeve frowned, and the braids disappeared. Mairead gasped air into her lungs as she could breathe and move again. Rhiannon went to her side and steadied her in the chair. "You will not, Maeve. Not here. You can fight destiny in your own home."

"Destiny? I'm fighting a child with an insolent mouth."

"No. You fight destiny." Rhiannon stared Maeve down until Maeve finally turned away.

The healers stepped out from behind the curtain. The woman in blue—the air talent—curtsied. "Majesty, we've done what we can. We've repaired the bleeding inside and knitted his bones. The bruises will take some time, but he will live."

Mairead and Maeve both let out a long breath of relief. "Thank the gods," Maeve said, her voice cracking again.

Alshada, thank you. "You couldn't heal the bruises?" Mairead asked.

The stone talent took a step toward Maeve. "Majesty, there's something different in his blood. Something not right. We could only repair the tissues.

His blood wouldn't cooperate with us."

Maeve's lips tightened into a stern line. "Yes. I'm aware."

How can she seem to love him one moment and care not a whit the second? Alshada save me from becoming this cold. "It doesn't concern you—this problem in his blood?" Mairead asked.

Maeve raised an eyebrow. "Consider your tone, girl."

Mairead's spine stiffened. "Don't tell me—"

"I know what this problem is. It's nothing to worry about."

"But—"

"Mairead." Maeve fixed her with an expression of regal authority. "It's nothing to worry about."

Mairead bristled. "You keep more secrets from him? You and Connor—you and your damn secrets!"

"Girl," Rhiannon said. She put a soothing hand on Mairead's shoulder. "As well you fight the tides as fight the Sidh queen. Come, see the boy."

Mairead and Maeve entered Rhiannon's small bedroom. Mairead sat and took Connor's sword hand. It was still swollen, but he could move his fingers again, and he didn't wince when Mairead lifted it to her lips and kissed it.

He opened his eyes and forced a smile in Mairead's direction. He lifted a hand to her cheek. "You're all right?"

She nodded. "I'm fine. But you—"

"I'll be all right." He turned to his mother. "Even now you can't leave me alone?"

She grimaced, but there was relief on her face. She swiped her eyes with an impatient hand. "You should thank the spirits I felt you being beaten. Otherwise, you might not be alive."

A flicker of a grin crossed his mouth. He turned to Mairead. "You stayed with me?"

"As much as they would let me. Connor, I'm so sorry. I'm so sorry. I should have listened to you. I should have trusted you."

He smiled. "It's all right. You just see the good. You always see the good." He closed his eyes again. "Mairead, will you stay with me?"

He wants me to stay, not her. Mairead kissed his hand again. "Yes. Of course, yes. I'll stay," she said, sparing a quick glance for Maeve.

Maeve pursed her lips in a stern, displeased grimace, but she stood. "I'm going to go talk to Rhiannon," she said in a tight voice. "Call me if he needs anything." She went to the other side of the curtain.

Mairead stroked Connor's hand. She edged closer to him, tempted to lie down but afraid of hurting him. *I almost lost him. My foolishness almost cost him his life.* She put one hand on his chest, and he struggled to lift his other hand to cover hers. She sniffed and stroked his battered eye with two light fingers. "This is what it took for me to find out that you're the wild Mac Niall son I always heard about?"

"Right now, I'm just the broken Mac Niall son."

She let out a weak, breathy laugh. "I'm just so glad you're alive I can't even be angry that you didn't tell me."

"That was my plan all along. Wait until I was abused beyond recognition and then let you find out." He winced, but he held his arm out for her. "Lie next to me?"

She was too grateful and tired to argue. She removed her boots, weapons, and jerkin and lay down, pulling a thick quilt over them both. "I killed those men. Six of them. I killed six men."

"You saved my life."

She closed her eyes. "There was so much screaming. When I slit Gavin's throat, he screamed and screamed."

He rolled his head to put his lips against her forehead. "Men scream when they're dying. Death isn't pretty."

She sighed. "Is that what battle is like?"

"No. Battle is worse. You did the right thing. We survived—that's what counts."

She watched him drift to sleep. She couldn't shut out the screams of the men she'd killed, but neither could she conjure any regret. *I can't feel sorry for them. I can't be sad that I killed them. What am I becoming?*

Emrys stormed around the clearing, pausing only to kick the dead men several times before he walked into the forest. The heir had shown faith in the kirok over faith in the raven, and it still wasn't enough to chase the raven from her side. *Another man would have turned her over to the kirons and left.* If Emrys was right, the raven's choice had only strengthened their bond, and now he had more work to do.

He sensed them in the old woman's house. Some in the surrounding farms and villages called her crazy. Others called her healer. Emrys knew she was neither—she was more. Practiced in herb lore and wards, the woman had woven spells around her house that kept him from getting too close. *I could get the girl and Maeve if it weren't for the spells.*

The old woman walked outside muttering to herself and cut several sprigs of holly. She arranged them over her door, stopped, and cackled. "You're here," she said, turning to face him. "Their bond grows stronger. Her blood draws him closer every day and binds her closer to this land. She rises in her power and strength before she even knows what she is. Your time draws near, forbidden one."

He knew she could only see his shadow, but her eyes and her words chilled Emrys to the deepest part of whatever soul he still had. *There is yet time. Until she conceives, I have time.*

She pointed at the house. "That boy has more power in his veins than you do with all of your stolen souls combined. And the girl, she's the lioness you fear. The sons and daughters that come from this union will bind the three lands and restore peace between the races, yes."

The words weren't hers. They came from the One Hand. He shuddered. *This isn't over between us.*

"Ha. You think I fear you? Come test me. See how old Rhiannon can hold up under the fires of Namha's minions. I'm not afraid to see my transgressions, no. I'll look at them and laugh. I stand firm, yes." She stood straight and tall, arms folded and her shawl draped around her shoulders.

Emrys wanted to test her. He wanted to flay her skin, show her the transgressions around her soul, and make her cry for the earthspirit. *There are so many ways to bring me pleasure and you pain.*

She took a step toward him. For a moment, her voice rang with the Voice of the one he feared more than any other. "I fear no man or spirit, demon or god. I am held by the One Hand. You have no power here." The old woman smiled. "Enjoy your remaining days, forbidden one. When the raven comes into his power, you will have no peace left."

Emrys clenched his fists. He needed time. He needed to think. He slipped between the elements again and returned to Taura.

Mairead woke to voices on the other side of the curtain. "—tell him what he is, then perhaps I will." Rhiannon's voice was low, angry, and tense. Outside, night still covered the cabin. Mairead shivered and pulled the blanket tighter over herself. Connor snored softly, the steady rise and fall of his bruised chest reassuring her. She lay very still and listened to the conversation in the main room.

"You swore an oath," Maeve said, equally tense and angry. "You swore you would not. If you break your word, I will—"

"Do as you will, Maeve. You think I fear Sidh magic? Bah." The rhythmic creak of her rocking chair and the click of knitting needles gave cadence to her words. "I will not let the boy go from here without knowing what he is."

"What do you think he is then?" Maeve's voice rose a bit and then quieted. Mairead had to strain to hear. "I've been trying for almost thirty years to figure out what he is. I did what I did to protect him. Can you give him some assurance or guidance that I can't give him?" The room was silent. "Your visions don't show you what I've seen. I've been inside his head for six years. I've sensed it every time he's fought, every time he's killed, every time he's been injured."

"I know more than you think. Your friend, the Syrafi, she speaks to me, too."

"Bronwyn has been here?" Maeve's voice sounded confused and surprised. "When?"

"She's the one who told me to wait here, years ago. She said he would need me."

Maeve let out a long breath. "She protects him."

"The One Hand promised, yes?"

Maeve's voice was barely a whisper. "Yes." Her voice cracked. "Rhiannon, if he knows everything, how can I protect him?"

"Do you think you've protected him this way? Do you think the Morrag has no power over your bond? No. If the Great Mother calls her ravens, the ravens will come. He will follow her, and if you are bonded to him when he does, it could very well kill you. Then where will he be, eh? Who will guide him then?"

There was a long pause filled only with creaking and clicking. At last, Maeve sighed. "This little queen. She thinks she can tame him."

Rhiannon laughed. "That boy isn't meant to be tamed, no."

"At least we agree on that," Maeve said. "She does seem to care for him, though. Do you think she—"

"I think their destinies are twined. There is much they are meant to do together."

The silence hovered again. "What do you keep from me, old woman?"

Rhiannon cackled, soft. "Not now. The girl is listening."

Mairead's heart thumped against her ribs, and she closed her eyes. Maeve pulled the curtain open, allowing a sharp shaft of firelight to pierce the shadows of the small bedroom. Mairead tried to breathe slow and heavy and deep. *I did this a thousand times in the sayada.*

Maeve stepped closer to Connor. She bent, kissed his head, and returned to the other side of the curtain. "If she's awake, she's very good at feigning sleep," she told Rhiannon.

Rhiannon laughed again. They fell into conversation of old days on Duke Mac Niall's estate, remembering Connor and his sisters, and Mairead drifted back to sleep.

In the morning, the aroma of baking bread and another, bitter odor woke Mairead. She stirred, rubbed her face, and opened her eyes to see Connor on his side staring at her. He smiled. "Good morning."

She sat up. "You're awake."

He nodded. "Rhiannon is making kaafa. I always wake when I smell it."

"How do you feel?"

The swelling on his eye had gone down enough that he could open and close the lid now, but the bruise around it was black with purple shades. Even the white of his eye was red from the blood. He tightened his swollen right hand around hers. Along his ribs and sternum, his tattoos were obscured by purple and red mottling. "Awful, but alive."

Her chest tightened and her voice quivered. "Connor, I'm sorry. I should have trusted you."

He put two fingers on her lips in an echo of what she had done the night before. "No more. It's over. You're forgiven."

She wiped her eyes. "Your mother will want to see you. Can you walk?"

"I don't know. Probably." With Mairead's help and much wincing and grimacing, he stood, and they shuffled to the other side of the curtain.

Maeve sat at the table holding a steaming cup under her chin. "Connor. You look—" She bit off the words.

"Such flattery."

She pulled out a chair for him. She kissed his head when he sat. "I'm just glad you're all right."

Rhiannon came in the house with a basket of fresh eggs. She grunted toward Connor. "You look like someone used you for a tribal drum, boy."

"I feel that way, too." Rhiannon set a mug of the steaming bitter drink in front of him. "Rhiannon, you jewel. How did you know I drink kaafa?"

"Your father always drank it, yes. I have friends. They bring me things sometimes. I'll brew something for your pain, too." She turned to Mairead. "Tea for you?"

"Yes, thank you, Rhiannon."

Rhiannon returned to her ministrations. She hummed an idle tune as she worked; it reminded Mairead of some forgotten song her mother might have sung.

Maeve sat back in her chair. "Mairead told me what happened. I assume those men were looking for the Sidh because they want the reliquary. They must want Mairead because she can carry it. Rhiannon thinks one of the Forbidden was behind the attack."

Rhiannon placed trenchers of food in front of everyone—boiled sausage, eggs, fresh bread, dried tomatoes for Connor, Mairead, and herself. She set a trencher of bread, tomatoes, a handful of hazelnuts, and a few preserved and warmed roots in front of Maeve and sat down. "He waited outside my house last night. I talked to him." She adjusted her shawl, calm and unruffled, and started to eat.

Mairead's mouth dropped. "He was *here?*" *It must be the one who's been tracking us.*

Connor put a calming hand on Mairead's, and some of her tension faded. "One of them has been tracking us. Do you know which one you saw?"

"He had a male presence, yes. The cat was frightened. She doesn't like men." As if summoned by the conversation, Rhiannon's gray tabby jumped into her lap. Rhiannon scratched the cat's ears. "Never fear. The holly will protect us."

Maeve drew in a sharp breath. "You knew he was tracking you, and you didn't contact me?"

Connor waved her concerns away with his uninjured hand. "We've had a few close calls, nothing more."

"It is not up to you to play games with the life of this girl," Maeve said, anger rising in her voice.

Mairead bristled. *I'm a queen, too. She won't treat me as if I'm not even in the room.* "Connor hasn't played games with my life," she said. "He's been diligent and faithful to complete the task you gave him. You should trust your son."

Maeve frowned. "Then I hope he has a plan to deal with this."

"With the Forbidden? Sorry, no," Connor said. "But I will continue to keep Mairead safe to the best of my abilities." He sipped his kaafa. "I don't think we'll make it to Albard before the snows hit now. I have to stay here for a while and heal. I can't sit a horse like this."

"Where will you go?" Maeve asked.

"Galbragh."

Maeve's face hardened. "You'll hide her in the midst of slave territory?"

"I can't go to some little village. Slavers are too unpredictable. At least Galbragh is defended. She'll be safe in the palace district for a winter. I'll hide her with Prince Henry."

Maeve considered that. "And where will you go?"

"I'll stay with her. I won't leave her until I see her to Albard. That was the job, right?" He squeezed Mairead's hand. "Besides, I'd rather spend the winter in a palace than fight ice and snow back to Espara." His thumb brushed across Mairead's knuckles.

Mairead's stomach lurched with hope. *A whole winter with him? Could I be so lucky?*

Maeve's gaze flitted from Connor to Mairead and back again. She finally stood. "Since you don't seem to need my input in this decision, I'll return to the village. Rhiannon, thank you for everything."

Rhiannon stood, and the cat protested its unceremonious dismissal with a sharp yowl. "It was good to see you, yes."

"What has it been—fifteen years? More?" Maeve put a hand on Rhiannon's arm. "Thank you for caring for Connor."

"Bah. I suckled him and changed his pants. He's like a son to me as well."

Connor grimaced.

Maeve embraced Rhiannon. "When this is over, I'll come back for a long talk over tea."

"Yes. Some tea." Her eyes narrowed. "You're ready, yes. I think so. Some nettle, red clover, raspberry leaf—I think you're ready for some tea. Soon."

Maeve frowned. "Yes. Well. I'll visit soon." She looked at Connor. "We should speak privately for a moment. Can you walk outside?"

"I need my boots."

Mairead fetched his boots from behind the curtain and helped him into them. She held the door for them and watched as Connor leaned against a tree and spoke with Maeve. "Rhiannon," she said. "What did the Sidh healers mean when they said there was something wrong with Connor's blood?"

Rhiannon busied herself with clearing food Maeve had ignored. "The Sidh speak of elements and magic, yes. The elements are in all of us—stone, water, air. They run through us in our blood. If they say his blood fought them, they mean they couldn't use the elements within it to heal him."

"Then how did they heal him?"

"Elements outside his body," she said. "It must be, yes. But they have to take away for everything that is added. Balance. It took them quite some time."

Mairead sat down again and sipped her tea. She screwed up her courage. "Did Queen Maeve do something to Connor's blood?"

Rhiannon sat down at the table and leaned close to Mairead. Her eyes flashed with anger. "I am many things, but not an oathbreaker, no. You will not get me to say."

Mairead lowered her voice. "You know I heard you talking last night. I heard her say that she's afraid of what he is. What is he?"

Rhiannon shook her head. "Not for me to tell." She drank her tea and averted her eyes. "He will come into his power when the time is right. She cannot keep him from it."

"You mean the ravenmark?"

Rhiannon put down her cup and turned a steely gaze to Mairead. "You think you'll tame him, girl? Eh? That boy isn't meant to be tamed. You have a great destiny, and it's twined with his, but if you think you will keep him tame and staid and in one place, only grief will come to you."

"I haven't—"

"You have, lass. I see the way you look at him, and he has affection for you, yes. Bed him, have his children, enjoy what he can give you, but do not expect to tame him."

I can't give my heart to someone who won't stay. Mairead blinked back tears. *How can I feel so divided? How can I want him so much, even knowing that even his own mother doesn't think he can commit to me?*

"Mairead." Connor's voice called her from outside the cabin. She walked outside to see him alone, bent over, his hands bracing himself on his knees as sweat trickled down his neck. "Help. I need to lean on you."

She put his arm around her shoulders and helped him back in the house to the bed. She pulled his boots off and sat next to him. "What did you and your mother discuss?"

"The bond. The Sidh village and the tribes. You."

"What does she think of me?"

"Probably that you're a poor unsullied girl I'll defile the first chance I get."

After the words we had, I suspect her feelings are much stronger than that. "Did she remove the bond?"

"No. I haven't finished the job yet."

It stung. *He'll ruin you and leave you.* "Am I still a job to you?"

"No, that's not what I meant." He lifted a hand to her face. "Of course you're not just a job to me. But, I agreed to get you to Sveklant, and until I do, I have to live with the bond."

She took his hand in hers. Rhiannon said she couldn't keep him tame or staid. *But I want a home. I want a husband and a home. I could have his children, but I would never have him.* She swallowed her tears. "Do you need anything?"

"I just need rest. Sleep." He stroked her cheek. "Mairead, what is it?"

"I'm tired, too." She leaned down to kiss his forehead. "If you need me, just call." He closed his eyes, and she walked to the other side of the curtain and leaned against a wall. *The ravenmarked never have balance,* he'd told her. *He'll ruin you and leave you,* Maeve said. Mairead swiped her eyes. *No. He won't ruin me. I won't let him. He's not for me.*

CHAPTER TWENTY-ONE

I've watched the forest for some time.
For every raven I see, there is a dove.
I think Aiden is my dove.
— Queen Brenna's diary

The first few days at Rhiannon's house blurred together for Connor. He would wake, eat, try to move around, and then go back to bed. It didn't help that Rhiannon insisted on giving him various brews for the pain and stiffness that also made him sleep. He tried to refuse her, but she would hear none of it. "I'll get fat just lying around, sleeping, and eating," he said in a futile attempt to refuse her one morning.

"You'll get well, yes. Drink." She gestured to the cup before him and checked his bruises and cuts while he drank. When he finally finished the brew, she pushed him away to bed again.

Mairead slept on the floor next to the bed every night. Every morning, she was up before he woke, helping Rhiannon with farm chores and work around the house. "I may as well. It keeps me busy," she told him one night while she brushed out her hair after a bath.

The familiar scent of her stirred longing. "Are you still practicing your bow?"

"Yes, and my daggers. I practice the forms and the exercises you taught me every morning." She smiled. "I've never taken care of pigs and goats and chickens before. Is this what you did for the Mac Raes?"

He laughed. "That brings back memories. Slopping pigs was not my favorite chore."

"I've decided that chickens are more pleasant roasted over a fire than pecking around a barnyard," she said.

He laughed again and winced. She tensed, but he waved a hand. "I'm fine. Just sore." He reached for her hand.

She stood before he could touch her. "Go to sleep. I'm going to finish a few chores." Before he could protest, she was gone.

On the fifth day, he woke before dawn and sat up. Mairead still slept, and he didn't hear Rhiannon. The tenderness in his face and torso had faded, and he fidgeted with restless energy. *I need to hunt.* He slipped out of bed, pulled on breeches, boots, and tunic, and left the house, bow in hand and knives in his boots.

The sky bore the dark purple of pre-dawn as he picked his way through the forest. Elk trampled the distant underbrush, but he knew he was too weak to carry an elk back to Rhiannon's house. *A yearling deer at most,* he thought. He sniffed the air, and his stomach lurched. *Carrion.* The sky ahead swirled with black shapes. *Damn. The Morrag.*

Memories of his initiation flooded back. The skin on his thigh tingled again as if it recognized her presence. Odors of rotting flesh and death hung in the air. He nocked an arrow. The ravens circled. "I know you're here. If you want me, take me," he said.

The ravens descended one by one, merging eyes, wings, talons into the feathered woman with the smooth coal-black face he recalled. She approached with an undulating glide, her wet, black eyes fixed on his face. "You refused to heed me. You ignored my warning and fought me. Why?"

The voice rang with familiarity, but the experience of hearing it aloud again made him shudder. "What warning?"

"My messenger."

The raven in camp. He frowned. "Why didn't you just talk to me? You aren't shy about invading my thoughts."

"If you were mine, you would have seen them as they were." She held out one undulating arm. "Why did you refuse me? I would give you strength."

He stretched he bowstring taut. "I don't want it—not with the price you demand."

She stepped closer. "What price I demand would come back to you a thousandfold. Give yourself to me, and you will be rewarded beyond your imagining."

His mouth twisted in disgust, and he scoffed. "That's a lie. That's something men tell themselves when they justify stupidity. They sell themselves to magic or religion and justify wars and atrocities by saying they'll be rewarded in this life or the next."

"Then you will refuse the girl?"

His grip on the bow wavered. "What does Mairead have to do with this?"

"She bonds you. She holds your heart. Pledge yourself to me, and she will be yours."

He stood resolute. "No. You can't tempt me with that. I won't do that to her."

"She will be another man's bride if you refuse her."

"I know that."

"You would willingly give her up for her good, even if it destroys you?"

"Yes."

"Then she would not be in the way of you coming to me."

"Damn you." He raised his bow and drew back the arrow, aiming it at the heart of the form. "They should have killed me. I'll die before I let you take me." He fired.

Though her body appeared solid, the arrow flew through her chest as through a vapor and landed in a tree behind her. Her satisfied cackle rose into the trees. "You cannot harm me, raven," she said. "You belong to the earth. You will come to the earth, and you will lead many men to do my bidding." She reached for him again.

He stepped back, his stomach twisting in fear and anger at once. *No. Not this time. She won't touch me again.* He dropped his bow and drew his sword, fighting weakness in his arms and shoulders. "I may not be able to wound you, but I'll destroy as many of your birds as I can before you take me."

The Morrag drew her arm back. "You will come to me, raven."

The sun slowly lightened the sky around them. Her body dissolved into ravens. One by one, they fluttered skyward and disappeared.

The spirit's voice hung over the clearing with one final warning: *You will be my first.*

Connor sheathed his sword and let out a breath, clutching his aching ribs. He leaned against a tree for several minutes. A deer tiptoed from the wood. He picked up his bow and drew an arrow, but realized he'd grown too weak to haul the animal back to Rhiannon's house. He slung the bow over his shoulder. "I guess it's your lucky day." The deer twitched an ear.

Mairead looked up from her chores when he returned to Rhiannon's farm. She smiled. "You must be feeling better."

"Much." He stepped close to her. He tried to kiss her cheek, but she bent to pick up a wooden bucket. He stepped back. "You look pretty this morning. The autumn air agrees with you."

She averted her eyes and affected a bright tone. "Flattery so early in the day? I don't know if I'm ready to spar with you just yet."

"It's not flattery." *She holds your heart,* the Morrag had said. *She has no idea.* "What can I do to help?"

Connor felt better each day, and he offered to do some small repairs to Rhiannon's house before they left. He also moved to the loft in her small barn so the women could sleep in the bed. It reminded him of hiding in the hayloft to escape his tutors when he was a young man. The scent of the hay and sounds of the surrounding forest comforted him.

One morning, Mairead woke him in the middle of a dream. "Connor," she said, shaking his foot from where she stood on the ladder. "It's morning. Rhiannon sent me to wake you."

He rubbed his face and sat up. "I was dreaming about you," he said.

Her face flushed pink. "What about?"

The thought of his dream made him shiver. "It's not important. I'll be down in a few minutes."

She frowned. "Rhiannon has breakfast ready."

"All right."

She disappeared down the ladder. He lay back against the straw pillow, closed his eyes, and returned to the dream.

By the time he'd washed, dressed, and joined the women in the house, Mairead had already eaten. "What took you so long, boy?" Rhiannon asked as she put warmed kaafa and a trencher of food in front of him.

"Just a little sore this morning."

She narrowed her eyes and stared at him. "Mairead, will you go gather eggs for me?"

Mairead stood. "Of course." She picked up the egg basket and left the house.

Rhiannon sat at the table as Connor started to eat. "A little pent up need, yes?"

"Gods, Rhiannon. You may have changed my pants when I was a child, but you can stay out of them now."

She scoffed. "You could have the girl, you know. She wants you as much as you want her. She'd make you happy, and not just under the blankets."

He pushed bits of sausage around on the trencher. "She's made it clear this week that she doesn't want me."

Rhiannon shook her head. "She fears what she feels, but make no mistake—she's in love with you."

He set down his knife. "I won't ruin her that way. Not with what I am."

"And what are you, then, eh? You think a bit of blue dye means you can't give that girl your heart? Bah." She cuffed his ear. "You're a mulehead if you think you'll find anything better. That girl is meant for you, yes."

He sipped his kaafa. "The throneless queen and the tainted duke."

"What?"

"Isn't that a line from something?"

She frowned. "Where did you hear it?"

"I dreamed it. I was dreaming about her, and I told her that's what we'd be—a throneless queen and a tainted duke. It seems like it's something from a story or a legend."

"The songs come around sometimes, bringing wisdom." She paused. "I've seen the eddies of your future swirl around you since you were born. You have a great destiny, yes, and that girl is part of it."

He couldn't look at her. He couldn't eat. "I can't ruin her. I can't give her the hope of a future and then leave her that way."

"You think she's weak?"

"No, she's the strongest woman I've ever met."

She lowered her voice. "You love her. You don't want to hurt her. But you're hurting both of you by refusing her."

"And when the Morrag takes me? What then?"

Her eyes narrowed. "How many did you kill when it quickened?"

He flinched. "I lost count."

"Hmm." She put her hand on his forehead and closed her eyes. "She blocks it. She keeps her own counsel, this Morrag. All I can see is your future with that girl. She is meant to bear your sons and daughters."

He pushed his food away and stood. "I have to go. I'll bring you some meat." He picked up the bow and quiver near Rhiannon's door and walked out of the house.

He heard Mairead in the barn and stopped to look in on her. She soothed the chickens, petted the barn cats, and even stopped at the goat's stall to offer a gentle hand. The stubborn nanny butted her hand. "Stop that. I offer you a scratch behind the ear and you repay me with a headbutt?"

Connor put down the bow and walked up behind her. "If you scratch behind my ear, I promise I won't headbutt you."

She startled and turned around, smiling. She put her hand in his hair and scratched. "How's that?"

"Better." His hands twitched, longing to touch her. "Mairead—"

"I have to take these eggs to Rhiannon." She picked up her basket and started to leave the barn.

"Mairead, wait."

She stopped. "Yes?"

He thought of dozens of things he could say, but none seemed adequate. "I'm going hunting. Want to join me? There are deer and elk in the forest here. I'll show you how to cure the meat, and we'll stock Rhiannon's larder for the winter."

Her face flushed. "Yes. All right. I'll get my cloak."

When they brought a deer back to Rhiannon's house, Connor and Rhiannon taught Mairead how to cure the meat and prepare it for winter. "You'll turn me into a tribal woman yet," she said.

"Ha, tribal." Rhiannon wiped her forehead and her stern eyes fixed on Mairead's face. "You already are tribal, girl. You have the lion in you."

Connor saw the flicker of confusion on Mairead's face. "Your wits are addled, Rhiannon. There is no lion tribe," he said.

"The lion is in this girl, make no mistake." She walked away muttering, leaving them to ponder her words.

They left Rhiannon's house two days later. Connor wasn't completely healed, but he assured Mairead he could sit a horse and defend her. "Besides, we know you have no problem defending us, don't we?"

"True, but there may not be another Rhiannon next time." She folded her arms and surveyed him with a critical eye while he readied the horses. "Are you sure about this? We can stay longer if you need to."

"No. I'm sure. I want to get to Galbragh before the snows get heavier in the north."

They finished packing and said goodbye to Rhiannon. She pulled Connor aside and lowered her voice. "The throneless queen and the tainted duke—I remembered, yes."

"Oh?"

She nodded. "It's Svek. It's from a song. I don't recall the entire thing, but there's a verse—

> *I dreamed I dwelt in castle walls*
> *With steward, maid, and page,*
> *With throneless queen and tainted duke*
> *And silken-covered mage.*"

Connor frowned. "Why would I dream of a Svek song?"

"Your destiny is written in that song. The songs come around."

He scoffed. "A tavern song proves my destiny? You've lost what few wits you had. I probably heard it on one of the two trips I've made to Sveklant. Besides, I've never met a silken-covered mage—a few Tal'Amuni eunuchs, but no mages."

Her mouth tightened. "There's more to the song than that.

> *I dreamed of distant warhorn's call,*
> *Of steadfast lion's pride,*
> *Of sunset over blooded isle,*
> *Of darkened raven sky.*
>
> *But whence came vict'ry sweet and true*
> *I dreamed of bounties wide,*
> *Of sons who ruled the kingdoms three*
> *And daughters by their side.*
>
> *From fields where ravens feasted well*
> *Come grasses tall and bold,*
> *From stone-ridged mountains bright with fire*
> *Come waters pure and cold.*
>
> *Shed no tears for me, my heart,*
> *For though my bones lie cold*

My soul will feast with Syraffair
And dance in streets of gold."

He thought she would begin singing it true if he didn't stop her. "I thought you said you didn't remember all of it."

"There's a lot more than that, yes. Those are just the verses the Great Mother gave me."

"It's a pretty dream—victory and bounty after war. I'll have to sing it to some Svek girl when I get to Albard and see if it warms her icy blood."

She cuffed his ear. "Stubborn boy. I should send some jasmine with the girl, yes. Or some vanilla oil. You need her. She's got a heart of pure gold and a spine of steel."

"I'll consider it."

She sighed. "A potion for listening. That's what I need. A potion to make men listen to reason. Great wealth lies down that path, yes."

"You'd have nothing to do if men listened to reason." He chuckled at the smile that tempted her mouth, and he bent to kiss her. "I'll come back to visit now that I know where you are."

"Yes. You will." She strode over to Mairead's side and pushed a small package into her hands. Mairead's face turned red, and she tried to refuse the package, but Rhiannon insisted. Mairead finally took it, embraced the older woman, and tucked the package in her saddlebag.

When they were out of earshot, Connor turned to Mairead. "What did she give you?"

"It's a package of herbs. Nothing important."

Did she send some kind of love potion? Crazy woman. "For pain?"

"No." She hesitated. "She told me to brew a cup with them every day to prevent conception."

"Are you going to use them?"

She kept her eyes forward. "I don't know."

That night, he found himself staring at Mairead as they ate, memorizing the way the flames accented her face. "This is nice," he said.

"What is?"

"Traveling again. Camping under the stars again." *I've missed being alone with you.*

"Rhiannon's house was warmer."

"I could keep you warm."

She shook her head. She'd not eaten much, instead picking at her meal with nervous fingers. "I don't think it's a good idea." Her voice broke on the words. She stood and went to her blanket. "Good night, Connor."

Mairead kept her distance for the next week. They hunted and went about their old routines, but she affected a stony demeanor that kept them from the easy familiarity they'd shared before they were attacked. She refused to spar with him, instead practicing her bow and the blade forms alone, and she spent more time in prayer, hunched over with her face low to the ground and her shoulders shaking. When she returned to the fire, she always wiped her eyes and curled her knees up tight. He tried to tease her out of her mood, but his best efforts were met with only a cool, regal posture. *She's becoming my mother,* he thought. *Only without the shouting.*

One morning, they woke to thick, wet snowflakes and slate gray skies. He suggested they look for somewhere warm to spend the night. "I think this will turn to rain—it's not cold enough for a real snowstorm yet—but a night off the ground would do us good," he told her.

By midday, heavy skies cloaked their surroundings in a thick, continuous stream of wet snow mixed with cold rain. Mud splattered up from the sodden road, and Mairead's teeth chattered so loudly that Connor could hear them over the horses and the rain. The dreary weather all but hid the next village from them, and Connor didn't see it clearly until they were nearly upon it.

No gate or guards greeted them as they veered off the main road. Rather, the village gradually emerged from the muddy pastureland as a series of hovels and tumble-down animal pens of stone. A heavy peat odor mingled with the scent of pigs, chickens, and goats, and Connor buried his mouth in his elbow to cough. Unwelcome memories stirred, and he closed his eyes for a moment. *I can't stay here. This is too much like—*

"Th-there's a t-t-tavern," Mairead said, pointing a shaking hand toward a low-roofed building boasting the name of The Twisted Broom. "W-w-we can at least w-warm up."

Connor shook his head. "I'm not stopping here. We'll find some trees and set up camp." He spurred his horse forward.

She reined in. "N-no. I need s-s-something warm." She dismounted and led her horse toward the tavern.

He caught up to her and took her elbow. "Mairead, please. Not here."

"Wh-why?"

"Because—" *You can't tell her.* "I swear I'll find another place to stop. Just not here." Anxiety constricted his chest, and his breath quickened.

She shook her head. "We haven't seen a tree in miles," she said. "I—"

But she cut short her sentence with a muffled grunt and she fell against Connor's chest. He steadied Mairead and then took the arm of the girl who'd bumped into them. "Careful—"

She recoiled and held up her hands. "I'm sorry. I'm sorry." Her eyes darted to the side, and she cowered near the horses. "Help me," she whispered. "Please."

Connor scanned the street around them. Three men stood outside a sprawling shack, pointing and talking quietly while the anguished cries of a woman drifted from the open window behind them.

Pain twisted Connor's stomach. *No. I won't do this.*

The Morrag cackled in his head.

He shifted his body so that Mairead and the girl were behind him. "Put a blanket around her," Connor murmured to Mairead. "Don't make any noise or do anything to draw attention to us."

He saw her terse nod from the corner of his eye. "What is it?" she whispered.

"If I'm right, the girl came from that brothel over there. She's trying to run away."

Mairead sucked in her breath. "Is that true?"

The girl whimpered. "Oh, please, please. Don't take me back."

Connor's mouth tightened. *I can't do this,* he told the Morrag. *Not now—not with these women to guard.* "We won't take you back," he said. He ducked into the alley between the tavern and another hovel and turned over his horse's reins to Mairead. "Can you find your way out of town?"

"Yes, but—"

"Go. Ride as fast as you can. I'll go back through the village and make sure you aren't followed."

Her eyes widened, and she grabbed his arm. "How will you find us?"

"Walk around the south edge of the village until you don't hear voices anymore, then kick him into a gallop. Pick up the main road once you're past the houses. I'll find you with the air talent. You remember what it feels like?" She nodded. "I'll weave the braids around you when I find you." He put the reins in her hands, but she stared, open-mouthed. "Go, Mairead. Take her and go."

She finally nodded and took the reins. He helped the girl mount behind Mairead. Mairead looked down at him and wound the reins around her hands.

Her mouth worked as if trying to find words, but she only said, "please be careful."

He nodded, and she clucked the horse into a walk.

Connor edged his way back to the main streets and watched the men standing outside the brothel. They pointed and talked, gesturing in several different directions, until one of them mounted a horse and started to ride south toward the main road. *Shit—he'll find them.* Connor stepped out of the shadows and blocked him. "You looking for a girl?"

"Aye. Ye seen her?"

Connor pointed toward the north edge of the village. "Saw a woman run in that direction a few minutes ago."

The man nodded. "I'm obliged. We'll look for her." His eyes narrowed, and he gestured to the horse. "Didn't you come into town a bit ago with another horse and a woman?"

Damn it. Connor shook his head. "You're mistaken."

"I know what I seen." He dismounted and stepped closer to Connor. "Ye had a woman. Ye stopped at The Twisted Broom, aye?" The slovenly brothel owner and two other burly men stepped into the street toward them.

Connor resisted the urge to fight. The Morrag surged desperate anger through him, righteous and seething and hungry for blood. *Stay calm. Focus on the task. You can get out without spilling blood. Don't spill blood for her.* He pulled a foot of his sword out of his scabbard and put another hand on a dagger. "I said, you're mistaken." *Gods, my voice croaks like hers.*

The man looked down at the sword and took a step back. "Now, lad," he said. "We don't want a fight. We just want our girl, aye?"

"She ran north. You'd better hurry if you want to catch up with her."

He nodded and took another step back. "Be careful, aye? Even a man traveling alone isn't safe in these parts. Thieves everywhere."

The words were couched in a warning tone, and Connor closed the gap between them and took the man's tunic in one powerful fist. He pressed the end of his dagger against the man's throat, and the man whimpered. "I'm leaving now," Connor said in a low growl. "If I even think anyone is following me, I'll be back to gut you. Understood?"

The man swallowed hard and twitched a nod. "Aye."

Connor shoved him into the mud, sheathed his dagger, and mounted Mairead's mare. He turned and galloped out of town just as the other men reached their companion. No one followed him. He slowed several times, but the road remained silent except for the steady rain.

He focused on the road ahead and wove braids of air in front of him as he nudged the palomino into a hard gallop. The braids brought back scents of mud, peat, rodents, but it took some time before the familiar odor of wet horse came back to him. He concentrated until the braids picked up Mairead's familiar scent. Ahead, a horse ran hard with one large huddled mass on its back. He spurred his horse forward and teased Mairead's head with the braids of air. She sat straight up and reined in.

He caught up. "You're all right?" he asked. "Am I the first person you've seen?"

She nodded, her eyes wide with fright. "What happened?"

"I'll tell you later. We need to get off the road."

They rode at a quick walk until the sun began to set. Connor paused several times to weave braids and check for pursuit, but he smelled no one. *Cowards, all of them. It's easy to chase a terrified girl. Not so easy to pursue a warrior.*

There were few options for shelter on the treeless plain, but Connor found a small ravine where they could duck out of sight. A small outcrop of rocks provided a bit of dry ground, and they found enough scrubby gorse to build a sputtering, smoky fire. Mairead and the girl dismounted, and Mairead pulled her pack off her horse. "I'll give you my fresh traveling clothes. They aren't much, but they'll be better than what you're wearing," she said. "I'm Mairead. My companion is Connor."

The girl ducked her eyes and flinched away from Connor. In the fading light, he saw the large welt and ragged cut on the girl's cheek. Blood trickled from a gash in her lip, and angry red and purple blotches mottled her neck. "What happened?"

She ducked her eyes away from his. "Please, I just want to go home. I'll do whatever you wish—just don't hurt me. Just let me go home."

"Where do you live?" Mairead asked.

"A day's ride from here. My parents—" A sob caught in her throat, and she clutched at Mairead's arm. "Oh, please, lady. Help me get home."

Mairead put an arm around her. "Of course."

Connor's throat tightened when he saw the thin, short skirt and torn clothes the girl wore. He reached out to touch her cheek and take a closer look at the cut, but she cried out and shrank back from his touch. "It's all right," he said, holding up his hands. "I won't hurt you. I promise. What's your name?"

Her chest heaved with terror. "K-k-kenna."

He forced a pained smile. "Kenna. We're going to help you." *If I can hold off the Morrag long enough.*

Mairead put a hand on his arm. "She's terrified. You're big and muscular, and you have a sword and tribal marks."

Aine wouldn't let me touch her, either, and she knew me. He nodded. "I'll build a fire."

Kenna changed into a tunic and breeches while Connor built a fire. Mairead unpacked meat and roots for cooking. She offered him the bag of meal. "Will you make some flatbread?"

"Not tonight." He walked away to stare back toward the village. A dark blur of feathers fluttered down toward him, and three ravens landed near their camp.

"They're looking for food," Mairead said.

Connor flinched. *Is that it? You want feeding?*

The croak stabbed through his consciousness. *I want justice,* the Morrag said.

Connor stalked away. "You eat. I'm not hungry."

Mairead cooked for herself and Kenna, and then the women huddled together under blankets and cloaks in an attempt to keep warm. Connor returned to the fire, but he could only fidget and pace with restless need.

Mairead finally stood and walked to his side. "What is it?" she asked.

He rubbed his temples. "I can't stop it," he whispered.

"Stop what?"

"The Morrag. The raven. She wants justice." He rounded on Kenna, and she scrambled backward. "What did he look like? The man who did this to you?"

"Connor!" Mairead tugged at his arm. "Don't shout—"

He shook himself free and knelt next to Kenna. She yelped and curled into a ball. He snatched up her arm to hold her steady. "What did he look like? Tell me!"

She cried out again. "He-he was big and dark. Greasy. H-he smelled like pigs." Her other hand drifted to the welt on her face. "He wore rings."

The Morrag laughed. *Yes, raven. You feel it. You remember. You remember.*

Connor stood. "I have to go."

Mairead held tight to his arm. "What are you planning?"

His stomach twisted in anticipation of embracing the Morrag again. *It's just this time,* he promised himself. *Just one more time.* "To mete out a little justice." He shook himself free of her hand and went to his horse.

"Connor, don't do this. Don't go—don't leave us here alone." She snatched for his arm again.

He swatted her hand away, and she stared, stunned. "You don't understand," he shouted. "You don't see this for what it is. I can't stop this, Mairead. If I don't follow this, it will kill me."

"And you leave us here to be stolen? Sold? All because you have to satisfy your blood lust?" Panic rose in her voice. "What if someone comes after her?"

Words caught in his throat. The Morrag tugged him back to the village, but his promises, his duties, his desires pulled him toward Mairead. He swallowed hard and stepped toward her, lowering his voice and drawing up his last vestige of restraint. "You don't need me," he said. "You know everything you need to know. You have the bow and your knives. Keep quiet, keep the fire low, and you'll be fine." He turned toward his horse.

"Is this how you left Aine?"

This is how I saved Aine. He turned back. "Never mention Aine to me," he said, his voice a low croak.

Her face paled in fear. She took a half-step back, swallowed, and recovered her position. "Did you leave her with your child? Did you give her money to raise your bastard and then leave her? Is that what you'll do to me?"

He mounted and looked down at her. *No more time. If I open my mouth now, all she'll hear is the rage of a vengeful demon.*

The Morrag burned inside, exulting in the sensation of his righteous anger. It rose in a swell of sweet agony, begging to be released. Her voice caressed his spirit with a lover's touch. *My raven.*

The world disappeared, and he could only think of finding the man with the rings and letting him taste steel.

Maeve sat up, her breath tearing at her, the strength of Connor's will ripping at her spirit. She struggled to her feet from her bed. "Evie—"

Evie was already there, black hair in an unruly mass around her shoulders. She gasped. "Majesty, what is it?"

Maeve's breath came in gasps and fits. She collapsed, struggling to hold onto life. *Claws. Raking.* "Get . . . healers . . . now."

A flutter of wings drew her vision to the window. Bronwyn melted out of her owl form and entered the hut through the back door. "Maeve, you have to break the bond with him. Now."

Maeve shook her head, but the pain tore into her, shredding her spirit, her soul. She fought it. Her heart was slowing, and she couldn't draw a full breath. Icy fingers of pain needled her body. Her transgressions were laid bare before her, and the guilt of what she had done, the freedom she had stolen from her son, loomed large in front of her. "No—have to save him—"

"*Maeve!*" Bronwyn's voice cracked the air. "Let him go now! If you hold onto this bond, it will kill you."

Maeve rasped a breath. Another. Her arms stretched for Bronwyn.

Evie fell to her knees. "Majesty," she whispered. She crumpled on the floor.

Warming stones faded, cooling and dimming as the magic of the Sidh weakened before Maeve's eyes. Anguished cries welled up inside Maeve's consciousness. *My people.* The *codagha* tightened, pulling the spirits of hundreds, thousands, into the darkness that consumed Maeve's vision. All around, life faded. *The Sidh are dying.*

"If you die, the Sidh die," Bronwyn said. "Let go of Connor."

A chasm opened before her, a jagged pit of rock and shadow and agony, gaping, ready to close around her, to declare judgment on her. A woman waited, anticipating bone and flesh and muscle tearing.

Maeve struggled, pushed back from the edge, fought the maw of death. "Connor, stop."

"He *can't.*" Bronwyn knelt next to her, her voice ringing with desperation. "Your magic is not powerful enough. The Morrag is stronger. She demands these things of him. If you don't let him go, she will kill you."

The light of the village dimmed. Maeve closed her eyes. *Is this what he lives with? Is this what you've made him?* The maw pulled her closer, and she could no longer fight. She found the bond within her mind. *Connor. I wanted to keep you from this.*

The bond snapped. The chasm disappeared, and Maeve's heart beat normally again. She took a deep, racking breath. Evie struggled up to her knees. "He did it," Maeve whispered. "He broke it himself."

"He was never yours to bond," Bronwyn said, one gentle hand on Maeve's shoulder. "Alshada allowed the bond for a time because it gave you peace in your grief, but it was always Connor's to break."

Maeve's chest ached, and her limbs tingled with warmth as the elements renewed her. "This path will destroy him. The Morrag will consume him. Was he never meant to have a normal life?"

"He was meant to be what Alshada intended him to be," Bronwyn said. "Trust your son to Alshada, Maeve."

I can't. Tears stung Maeve's eyes. "I can't. I have to go—"

"Maeve." Bronwyn's hand tightened. "This is for him to do."

Maeve's chest tightened in agony. "He's my son," she whispered.

"And he is also the raven." Bronwyn's voice remained firm. "I cannot stop you—that is not my role—but I can tell you that your place is here, with your people. You are the Sidh queen. Your duty is to protect the Sidh."

Maeve straightened, clenched her fists, raised her chin. "Do not lecture me on duty."

"Do not force me to remind you." Bronwyn pursed her lips. "Leave now, and the Sidh will suffer. Your place is here."

Evie crawled closer. "Majesty, are you well?"

Maeve closed her eyes and shook her head. *My place is here. Alshada, protect my son.* She stood. "I will check on the village. Fetch my gown."

Pigs and grease. Connor's senses were heightened and channeled. He focused on finding a man with rings. *Pigs and grease.*

Wicked laughter and the pained cries of brutalized women echoed around Connor when he reined in at the door of the brothel. He jumped off his horse and kicked open the door, his sword already drawn. Women screamed and men stood with daggers in hand. One ran toward Connor. Connor drove a dagger into the man's chest. He looked around the common room. "Which of you bastards wears the rings?"

The slovenly brothel owner Connor had seen earlier cowered and cried out. He gestured to a room. Connor kicked the door open. The odors of stale bodies and dirty chamber pots threatened to gag him. From the tangle of naked legs and buttocks, a greasy man with a greasy brown beard looked up. "What—" But Connor grasped him around the neck and knocked him to the floor before he could finish.

The man tried to scramble to his feet. He was a big man, tall and well-muscled, but he had indulged in too much drink and too many whores to be a match for Connor. "Fuck—who are you?"

"Vengeance," Connor said. He twisted his hand into the man's hair and dragged him to the main room. "This bastard likes to beat women." One hand around the man's throat kept him on his knees.

The Morrag swelled inside Connor, controlled and sweet, begging him for blood. *He hurt the girl. He's killed others,* the Morrag whispered. Connor's fingers gripped tight around the man's windpipe. Pinpricks of blood appeared near his fingernails as the man choked and gagged. *He's raped them and beaten them to death. Claw him. Rake him open, raven. He deserves death.*

A low growling snarl came from somewhere inside Connor's chest. "You think it's fun? You like hearing them scream, beg for mercy?" He brought the hilt of his sword down across the man's cheekbone. Bone cracked and blood splattered. "How does it feel, jackass? How do you like being the victim?"

The man yelped. "She was just a whore! I paid—"

Connor brought his hand across the other side of the man's mouth, cracking his lip open. "Now you look just like her. Except she will heal. You won't have time to." He picked up the man's hand and cut it off. With the man's howls hanging in the air, Connor kicked him to the ground and silenced him with one broad stroke down the center of his body.

Claw him. Rake him open.

He twisted his sword and pulled up bowels from the man's belly. They hung from his sword in a grizzly stink of waste. "Any more of you feel like beating up a woman tonight?" Frightened whimpers answered him. "Any of you women want to leave, now's the chance." He threw the severed hand down on the ground. "Use his rings to buy your freedom. It's the least he could do for you. And if any one of you decides to get your 'property' back, know that what I just did to him was merciful." He flung the entrails into the center of the room. The stench of the dead man's belly and bowels filled the air. "You've been warned. Next time, it won't be quick. It'll be slow, painful, and humiliating, and I'll stick your carcasses to the ground for the birds."

He turned to the owner of the brothel. The man quailed under his gaze. Connor pointed at him with the befouled sword. "Give me your money purse." The man hesitated. Connor leapt at him, grabbed his hand, and held the sword over his wrist. "Your purse, jackass."

The man yelped and pulled his money purse from his belt.

"You, the blond in red," Connor said, and a woman near the door stopped, shaking, fear on her face. He threw her the purse. "Take the others with you." She caught the purse, swallowed hard, and signaled to the others. They ran for the door, one of them carrying the severed hand with the rings.

Connor looked back at the owner. "If I ever hear that you've bought a woman or kept one here against her will again, I will be back to cut you apart one piece at a time for every coin you've earned off the backs of these women." The man's face paled. Connor's sword point drifted down. "We'll start with the parts you hold most dear."

Death and fear filled the room. Grim satisfaction hovered at the edges of his awareness, and his breathing started to slow. He retrieved his dagger from the first man he'd killed and returned to his horse to gallop back to the camp.

By the time he arrived, the Morrag was satisfied. He'd quelled the need. He was rank with sweat and covered in blood and bits of body, but he didn't care. He'd embraced the raven, and it hadn't been like before. It was sweet and powerful. It was justice.

When he got back to camp, Mairead stood, an arrow nocked and pointed at him. Kenna slept. Mairead lowered the bow when she saw him. She set it down and ran to him as he dismounted. Her eyes were tight and red-rimmed, but her jaw was set in a stubborn line. She crossed her arms. "Are you satisfied?"

"It needed to be done." His voice seemed far off, as if heard through a canyon. *From the depths of the Morrag's lair.*

"How many?"

"Two. One who attacked me, and one who attacked her."

"Is that it? Are you hers now—the Morrag's?" Her voice cracked on the Morrag's name.

"No."

"How do you know?"

He pointed to his head. "I never told her yes. She won't take me until I tell her yes."

The fire hissed behind her. "Then it will always be like this?" She waved a hand at the horse. "You dashing off to slaughter someone when you can't fight it anymore?"

"He deserved to die."

Her voice rose, tinged with righteous anger. "You don't get to judge that. You are not Alshada." She swiped her eyes and turned away. "We'll take her home, and then I want you to find someone else to guard me. I can't do this anymore."

Gods, no. I can't— He reached out to take her arm. "Mairead, wait."

She turned back. Tears spilled over. "You will always leave," she whispered. "You left your people, your name, your mother, even Aine. You can blame the mark or the Morrag or just your foolishness, but you will always leave."

Her tears glistened in the firelight, and Connor put his hands on her cheeks to wipe them away. "I don't want to leave."

She closed her eyes and whimpered. "Please don't say that."

He tipped her head up to his and slid one arm around her waist. The Morrag faded to a distant echo in the furthest part of his spirit. "I need you."

Her hands pushed against his chest in one weak attempt to walk away, but then she slid them up around his neck and pulled his head down to kiss him.

He pulled her against him, aching to feel skin against skin, desperate to keep her close. *I need this woman—by the spirits, I need this woman.* After death, her kiss gave him life. His hands tightened on her body.

Mairead mumbled "no" between kisses. She wrenched out of his arms. "No." She turned away, and her hand went to her mouth as she started to walk back to the fire.

"Mairead—"

"No." She shook her head. She held her hand out to keep him away. He stepped toward her, but she turned and held him at arm's length. "I can't, Connor."

"Mairead, I want you. I need you. Please, don't walk away."

"Do you love me?"

Time paused. Aine had asked him that same question once. With Aine, he didn't know. With Mairead, he knew—without hesitation—the truth. The question hung between them, waiting for acknowledgement. The fire crackled, keeping random time. The horse stood close, panting. Mairead's brilliant green eyes demanded honesty, commitment, everything she deserved—more than he could offer. *I do love you.* He wanted to say it, but the words stopped in his throat. Desire warred with what he knew was true—that whatever else she had done to change him, he was still ravenmarked. He would still leave. "I don't know."

She nodded and swallowed hard. Her voice cracked again when she spoke. "I don't want less than your whole heart." She went to her blanket and sat down, drew her knees to her chin, and stared into the fire.

Emptiness rushed into the gap where the Morrag had been. Connor returned to his horse and slumped against it, drawing up slow, even breaths until he felt steady again. *You will always leave,* she'd said. He couldn't deny it. In a numb daze, he unsaddled his horse, rubbed him down, and gave him water. He walked to the edge of the ravine and wrapped their camp in braids of air to hide their scent.

For the first night in eight years, the Morrag folded her wings and fell silent.

CHAPTER TWENTY-TWO

> *Give me your cup, Alshada.*
> *Let me drink even to my death.*
> — *Songs of King Aiden, Book 30, Verse 12*

Igraine held a kerchief to her nose as she descended the stairs into the prison cells beneath the castle. The guard, Aiden, showed her to Logan's cell. "Her highness begs a word," he said.

Logan looked up. They'd taken his livery, and he sat on the small cot in a homespun tunic and woolen breeches. His eyes were drawn and tired, and the dark curls on his head were unkempt and greasy. "You shouldn't be here," he said.

"Let me in and then leave us," Igraine told Aiden.

Aiden glanced at Logan, who sighed and nodded. The guard opened Logan's cell and ushered Igraine in. "You still have some authority with them at least," she said.

"They're used to obeying me." He leaned back and stretched his long legs in front of him. "There's little point in coming here. I have nothing more to say."

"Why are you doing this? I know it wasn't you."

"Ronan Kerry thinks it was."

"Why does he think that?"

He shrugged. "He saw me letting a group of people out of the castle gates. He'll say they were assassins and that I was helping them escape."

"Were they?"

"No. They were the few kirons and sayas I could save." He paused. "He will also accuse me of plotting to kill you."

"Me? Why?"

"The royal issue dagger on the assassin in the forest. I'm the one who issues those. When you were under Felix's care, I went to the armory to count the knives. There were three missing. I had the one we found on the assassin. We haven't found the other two."

"What does that prove? Someone stole them—probably Matthias."

He shook his head. "The first thing I did after Matthias attacked you was count weapons. Everything was there. This happened after he left."

"What else does he think he can use against you?"

"Your maid—the one who is sharing Kerry's bed—she told him I asked you to go riding with me. He thinks I tried to get you away from the castle to have you killed."

She knelt on the rushes on the floor and took his hands. "What possible reason would you have for killing me or the kirons and sayas?"

"Kerry wants the throne. He sees me as an obstacle. Braedan's men obey me, not him. If he can get me out of the way, he will gain control of the royal guard."

She frowned. "But why would you confess? With a confession your life is forfeit. The law is clear. A confession means there can be no trial. You will suffer the immediate consequences of this. Why not let there be an investigation and trial?"

His hands were slack around hers. "For a promise. For assurance."

"What—"

"Igraine. Please." He leaned forward and put his forehead against hers. His voice dropped to a whisper. "I'm not afraid of death. I'll die in service to those most important to me."

Igraine didn't know how to answer. She steeled her will. "Tell me who you think truly ordered this done."

"I can't say. No one in the castle died but your guards. It appears you were the only target inside these walls. The ones we killed were assassins, like those who killed Duncan Guinness. They were shadows. Untraceable. They had no markings to identify them."

"Who would want me and the kirons and sayas dead?"

"I don't know. Not Kerry. He wouldn't want to anger your father, and he wouldn't see the kirons and sayas as a threat." He shook his head, frowning. "Kerry is subtle, and this attack was anything but subtle. This was someone who wanted to send a strong, bloody message that the kirok isn't welcome on Taura."

She nodded, slow. "What about Cormac?"

Logan blinked, surprised. "Cormac?"

"He's been acting so strangely, and have you seen how pale and sickly he's become? And where was he that night, or the night Matthias attacked me? Did we ever find out?"

Logan's mouth drew into a tight line, and a muscle twitched in his jaw. "Cormac has many secrets, but he's not a murderer. And as competent as he is as a seneschal, he's a follower, not a leader. I can't see him masterminding something like this. He is unswervingly loyal to Braedan. Unless Braedan ordered him to do this, he would not even consider it. As for where he was, I can't say."

Igraine reached for his hands again. "I will find out who did this. I will clear your name, I swear it. And I will not allow you to come to the court to confess. I will hold your case aside until I can learn what happened."

He shook his head. "You can't do that. I've confessed to two nobles and a seneschal. My life is forfeit. There is no recourse. You know the law. You've read every book and scroll in the castle. My confession will stand, and I must be executed." His eyes were drawn and pained.

She stood, angry. "This is foolish. You would shame your king, shame your guard, shame your own family name for a lie? To be executed for something you didn't do?"

He gave her a sad smile. "Haven't you figured it out yet? I don't use my real name—I haven't in years." He stood. "Follow the law in this. Let me take the blame. Put the kirons and the sayas to rest, and let the kirok curse me."

"This isn't over. You may be resigned to this, but I'm not."

"It's too late. Kerry has already signed the execution papers. I'll be dead by morning."

She shook her head. "No, Logan—I'll find you a way out of this. I swear it."

Ronan agreed to see Igraine that afternoon. He sat at his desk with a goblet in one hand and a parchment in the other. He wore the indigo of his house with the gold sash of chancellor across his chest. He stood and beckoned her in. "My lady. Have a seat. What a delightful treat to see you outside of court."

She let him seat her near his desk. "Lord Kerry—"

"Please, we're to be relatives, highness. Call me your uncle. Or Ronan, if you prefer." He sat behind his desk.

She smiled coolly. "Lord Kerry, we need to discuss Logan's confession and trial."

He spread his hands. "Of course, highness, but I don't know what you would have me discuss. He's confessed. The law is clear." His voice held an edge. "And as you have pointed out, my lady, if the king and his agents do not follow the law, who will?"

Her stomach tightened. "His agents—such as his chancellor? I'm curious about something. Why would you want this position? Don't you wish to return home to your wife and your holdings?"

He leaned back. "Have you ever been to Stone Coast? Nothing but rocks, gulls, and ice in the winter, and in the summer, we don't even have ice to break the monotony. My inland holdings are green, at least, but little grows there except highland cattle, and that's only because they thrive on the scrubby gorse." He waved a hand around the room. "I prefer the amenities in Torlach. Politics, scandals, beautiful women . . ." His eyes drifted down her body.

She suppressed a shiver. "And has your wife given up on faithfulness, then?"

A cruel sneer tempted his mouth. "She never made me promise it. I see no reason to deny myself the company of a beautiful woman." He steepled his hands near his chin. "Do you think you'll get faithfulness from my nephew, highness? You're fooling yourself. He's king. He doesn't need to ask. You can protect your little chambermaids all you want. They will still throw themselves at him for the chance to say they've fucked the king."

You want to play vulgar? I can play vulgar. She leaned forward; his gaze flickered toward her breasts. "And you get his seconds? Is that what you're hoping for? A turn with me?" She leaned back. "You'll not get one."

He laughed. "Shouldn't I evaluate the woman my heir wishes to marry? Perhaps I could teach you something."

"I doubt that."

He stood and walked around the desk to loom over her. "Your friend, Logan. What is your relationship with him?"

She stood. *I won't be intimidated by this ass.* "He's a guard. A friend. And he's never been anything but a proper gentleman."

"That's not what I heard. I heard that Logan had his hands all over you in the stables. According to a witness, your dress was around your waist and his breeches were down before you noticed his presence."

Her heart raced. "Did Matthias tell you that? He saw us there when we came back from riding. Logan was helping me with my cloak, that's all. Braedan knows all about it."

"Truly? The only person to speak for you is a disgraced guard in prison for treason and murder."

"And your only proof is the word of a man who tried to kill me and then fled." She lifted her chin and squared her shoulders. "What do you know about Logan? Why is he doing this? You know he didn't commit this crime. Why would he confess to it?"

"The evidence points to him."

"Hardly any evidence—a royal-issue blade and words of a foolish maid who runs to your bed every time I scold her."

"And what I saw—your lover letting assassins out of the gate." He paused. "Why would you share the bed of a man who kills those you were asked to protect?"

"I don't share his bed. I am the Princess Royale of Eirya and the betrothed of King Braedan. I would not sully his name or mine by bedding a guard."

Ronan folded his arms. "You really believe he loves you. How naïve are you? He sees your blood, your potential to give him an heir, your title—that's all. He'll give you faithfulness for a year, perhaps, and then you'll squeeze out a son, and he'll lose interest in you. You'll get fat, and he'll find some trim little tart to warm his bed. Igraine, I thought you were smarter than that."

"I have no need to prove anything to you. Braedan's faithfulness or lack of it is between me and him."

"Your lover, Logan—"

"He's not my lover."

"Whatever he is, he's a dead man. He's confessed. There is no recourse."

I have to find something—some proof of Logan's innocence—but I have to buy some time. "I demand that you give him a trial."

He shook his head. "My apologies, highness. The execution is scheduled for dawn. I expect you there."

Igraine clenched her fists, fighting for composure. "I will not sit by and watch a travesty—"

"Yes, you will." He leaned close enough for his breath to warm her cheek. "You are the future queen of Taura, are you not? You will see justice carried out in the king's absence. You are an ambassador of the holy kirok. To avoid the execution would be snubbing your nose at those you claim to represent."

The room spun and her leg still ached, but she gritted her teeth against the discomfort. *Time. I need time.* "You're a bastard."

"Be careful, your highness. I may be a bastard, but you answer to me until the king returns." His mouth curved in a sneer. "If he returns."

Her stomach plummeted, and she no longer trusted her legs. She put a hand on the chair. *Braedan—I have to warn him. But how?* She swallowed hard and inclined her head. "Good day, chancellor."

He opened his door and gestured to one of the guards from Stone Coast.

"My lady, you appear a bit pale. My guards will show you back to your rooms. You'll need your rest before tomorrow." He nodded to the man. "Take the lady to her rooms and be certain she stays there."

Her mind raced. "You wouldn't deny me my ladies, would you? And I need to speak with Cormac about some cases. He needs to know about the research I've done." She put a hand on his chest and lowered her voice. "Please, Ronan."

He hesitated. A muscle tightened in his jaw. "I have no objection to you meeting with Cormac, and I would never deny a highborn lady her maids."

He counts on Cormac's loyalty. But Logan says Cormac is unswervingly loyal to Braedan. Will Cormac help me, or has he joined Kerry?

By the time the guard ushered Cormac into her study, Igraine had come up with a plan to help Logan and Braedan. *If Cormac will help.* She gestured to a seat and smiled at him. "I would stand, Cormac, but my leg requires rest."

He sat. He had a bit more color to his face this day, and he wasn't sweating as he had been. "Is your leg bothering you? I can send Felix up."

She shook her head. "It's healing well. I've always healed quickly." She hesitated. *How to approach this? I can't trust him, but he's the only hope I have of helping Logan.* She bit her lip. "Where were you during the attack, Cormac?"

"I was here, my lady. In the castle. I was in my chambers."

She leaned forward. "You weren't. The guards couldn't find you until they'd almost secured the castle. Where were you until then?"

He closed his eyes. "Please, highness—"

"Cormac, I don't care what your proclivities are. If you were in a brothel or a venom den, fine. I just want to help Logan. He didn't have those people killed. He was not the one who let the assassins into the castle walls. I don't want to see him die for someone else's crime."

He said nothing for some time. He simply sat with his eyes closed, his breathing shallow, his face pale. "My lady." His voice was barely above a whisper. "My lady, I don't know how to help Logan. He confessed. His life is forfeit."

Her stomach plummeted. "You can't believe that."

"It doesn't matter what I believe. It's the law."

"Then I hope you can serve Ronan Kerry as capably as you have served Braedan."

His eyes snapped open. "What?"

"I'm convinced he has designs on the throne. Getting rid of Braedan's most trusted guard is just one step." She shrugged. "Follow the law and Kerry, or do what's right. Your choice."

He gritted his teeth. Color returned to his face. "I will not serve that man," he said, low and lethal. "I will not. I will see my king's throne secured." He leaned forward. "Tell me what you would have me do, your highness."

Igraine gave up on sleep long before the horizon began to lighten. She called her maids and dressed in dark, subdued colors, bundling herself in black fur and refusing any jewels. *Fitting for an execution,* she thought, surveying herself. "Fetch the guards," she told Gwyn.

"My lady, won't you eat?"

"No. I have no appetite."

A guard from Stone Coast escorted her to the courtyard, where a small crowd of guards and soldiers had begun to gather. Anywhere Braedan's men gathered, men from Stone Coast found some excuse to hover nearby or break them apart. Igraine's mouth tightened. *He will send Braedan's men away one by one, unit by unit, until he has control of the castle. Then he'll make his stand.*

Word had spread that the king's High Commander would be executed, and the lords and petitioners in the castle gathered in the pre-dawn light for the spectacle. In the center of the courtyard, a hooded figure leaned on his ax near a stained wooden block. Cormac stood near the castle doors, his hands twisting in front of him. He bowed to Igraine. "My lady."

She let go of the guard's arm and stepped close to Cormac. "Were you able to accomplish everything?" she asked in a low voice.

"Yes, highness. It wasn't easy. Kerry has been watching me carefully since yesterday." He dropped his voice even lower. "Duke Kerry has barred the castle gates. He refuses to let anyone but a few servants in and out, and those only after being searched. And he informed me yesterday that he will no longer allow me to correspond with the king unless he reads my messages first."

Ire rose. "By what authority does he—"

"As chancellor, lady. He justifies himself by saying it is necessary for your safety and the safety of the lords and ladies within the castle."

At least it keeps the crowd down to manageable limits. She straightened her shoulders and lifted her chin. "This isn't over, Cormac. If this is the way Ronan Kerry will have it, then so be it."

The castle doors opened, and Ronan walked onto the steps flanked by guards and various lords who hung on the chancellor's every word. Lord Seannan and Lady Aislinn were in the group. Ronan approached Igraine. "A rather somber choice of colors, my lady, given that we execute the man who tried to ruin your efforts here in Taura."

She lifted her chin toward Aislinn, who wore a deep red gown and gold jewels. "It would appear the lady Aislinn brought enough color for all of the ladies present at this obscene event," she said. She stepped toward Aislinn. "Tell me, my lady: what did he promise you for your presence here? A crown?"

Aislinn's cheeks flushed, and her father put himself between her and Igraine. "See here, your highness—"

"Forgive me," Igraine said. "I wouldn't wish to sully your daughter's good name." She turned her back and faced the wooden block. "I want his body," Igraine said, low, to Ronan. "I want to see that it's cared for properly."

"The headsman will take care of it."

She clenched her fists. "No, Ronan. As the only legitimate agent of the kirok in this castle, I will see to his proper burial."

A long silence hovered around them. "Very well," Ronan finally said. "As an act of goodwill, I will let you see to his burial."

Igraine let out a long breath. *I still have some small sway with him. I can't squander it.*

The sun crept toward the horizon, a slit of orange prying the night away from day. Ronan paced away from Igraine and back again. He motioned a guard toward him. "I told them to have him here at sunrise," he said. "Find out where they are."

Igraine's heart raced. She squeezed her eyes shut. *Please, Alshada.*

The sun climbed higher. Murmurs flitted around the courtyard. Men from Stone Coast huddled together in conversation. Cormac and Igraine exchanged glances, and then Cormac bowed to Ronan. "My lord, perhaps I should see what's keeping them?"

A muscle twitched in Ronan's jaw. He started to nod, but a general clamor erupted from the guard towers, and three men from Stone Coast ran across the courtyard to Ronan. "My lord," one said, bowing. "My lord. We don't know how it's possible. We can't find Logan Mac Kendrick anywhere."

Ronan's face turned red with fury. "Escaped? How is this possible?"

Igraine's heart raced. *Make this convincing.* "Is this some trickery? Did you do something with Logan in the night?"

Ronan whirled toward her, his mouth a grim, angry line. "Perhaps I should ask you the same, my lady."

She gave him a thin smile. "When would I have had the time or ability? My lord kept me confined to my rooms all day yesterday."

Ronan swore. He strode back and forth, fuming, one hand clenched on his sword, the other clenching and unclenching at his side. "What do you know?" he asked the guard.

"Not much, my lord. One of the royal guards was on duty. We found him tied up in the cell with a black eye. Mac Kendrick seems to have treated him mildly. We haven't figured out how he escaped the castle."

Ronan's voice carried the cold fury of a man bent on vengeance. "Find this man. Now. I want him back here in irons by the week's end. If you have to bring him back dead, so be it. I want his head on a spike at the Traitor's Gate."

"Yes, my lord." The man bowed and left the room.

Ronan turned to Cormac. "What do you know of this?"

"Nothing, Lord Kerry. I thought he was guilty as well. I was prepared for an execution this morning."

Ronan swore and paced. "The court will hear no petitioners today," he said finally. "I will unleash the dogs and drag this coward back to face his crimes." He returned to the castle in a fury.

One of the men from Stone Coast took Igraine's arm and began to lead her back to her rooms. "Wait," Cormac said. He took Igraine's arm. "I'd like to escort the lady back to her rooms."

The man bowed aside, and Cormac led Igraine through the castle doors. "He has a letter for Braedan," Cormac said, barely moving his lips as he spoke and keeping his eyes straight ahead. "With luck, the king and his men will return before winter sets in."

Igraine nodded. "We have a long road."

Later in the day, when Igraine sat in Braedan's bed with her leg propped on pillows, Gwyn announced Repha Felix, and Igraine ushered him in. "Thank you for checking on me, but I don't know what you can do," she said. "It's sore, but it's healing well. It needs time, I'm thinking."

He sat next to her and picked up her leg. "You may perhaps know the law, but I know healing," he said, opening the bindings around her calf. He prodded the wound, frowning. "There's barely more than a thin scar."

"'Tis always this way for me," she said. "I broke my ankle once. It mended in two weeks."

Felix said nothing as he reapplied a poultice and bandage. He stood and took a book from the pocket of his long apron. "Some reading for you, your highness."

She took the book. *A History of the West*, by Xinias zha Astr. "A book of history written by a Tal'Amuni?"

He inclined his head. "I thought you would find it interesting. If you read it carefully."

She opened it with cautious fingers. The brittle parchment was worn and stained on the edges, but the ink was still dark inside. "'The rending of the Brae Sidh people came at a great, but necessary, cost to the geography of the west. With the help of the Syrafi . . .'" Igraine looked up. "This is written in Amuni. How did you know that I speak it?"

"When I treated you in your chambers the night Matthias attacked you, I saw your pile of reference books. One was in Amuni." He nodded toward the book and picked up his bag of supplies. "When you've finished it, perhaps we might speak again?"

She forced a smile. "Perhaps so. Thank you, Felix."

He bowed and left.

Igraine leaned back against her pillows. *Braedan, I will hold this place for you as long as I can, but I need you here. Hurry.*

CHAPTER TWENTY-THREE

He will bring justice. She will bring mercy.
— *Second Book of the Wisdomkeepers*

Morning with Kenna and Mairead consisted of sparse conversation and unspoken emotion. Mairead cast Connor subtle glances, but she said nothing more than was required for travel. He offered to look at Kenna's bruises and cuts, but she shook her head and ducked her eyes. *It's an improvement*, he thought. *At least she's not flinching.* "The man who hurt you is dead," he told her.

She averted her eyes. "Th-thank you."

Mairead and Kenna mounted the palomino while Connor took the bulk of the supplies on the sorrel. They continued west toward Kenna's home, arriving late in the afternoon amid a heavy, cold rain. Kenna slipped from the horse to run to her father's arms, and Mairead spoke quietly with the man before she remounted. "She'll be well," she said.

Memories tugged at Connor's composure. *Donal held Aine that way.*

They rode wide around the village and finally came to a small stand of trees late in the day, well after sunset. Connor built a fire, and they ate in silence. When they finished, Mairead pulled out her blanket and curled up close to the fire. "No evening prayers?"

She shrugged. "I don't know how to pray anymore."

He sat down next to her, and she tensed. "It's time to tell you about Aine."

"All right."

Where to begin? "I was close to her at the farm. We never shared a bed, but she thought she loved me. But I knew the Morrag—" He broke off the thought. "I told her I couldn't stay. She didn't believe me. I left one night. I didn't know she followed me. Donal caught up with me on the edge of Nar Sidhe territory. He'd found her, but he needed my help—" The words stuck.

Mairead waited. Memories tugged at his resolve not to grieve again. He pinched the bridge of his nose, forcing back the sting in his eyes. "She was in a brothel—the worst kind," he said. "She was a slave, like Kenna. She'd been beaten and abused. She was with child. Someone had found her on the road, beaten her, and deposited her at the brothel, and she was too broken to escape."

Mairead let out a long breath. "And you rescued her?"

I should have kept it from happening. "That was the night the Morrag quickened. It drove me to kill every man in that place. I didn't even know if any of them had anything to do with what happened to her, but it wasn't quelled until every one of them was dead." His throat swelled with emotion, regret and grief and guilt fighting with the satisfaction of having killed so many in the name of the Morrag. "I had no control over it. I just killed. When the rage retreated, there were bodies, limbs, brains everywhere. Some of the men were still alive. I had to finish them. To leave them alive was worse."

"And Aine?"

He squeezed his eyes closed. "She sat in a corner, weeping and screaming, covered in blood. It scared her so much to see me that way that she wanted nothing to do with me anymore. I took her and Donal home, and then I left."

"So that's why Donal and Aileen are so grateful?"

He said nothing for a long time. "If I had been more faithful, she wouldn't have been hurt."

"You've carried this guilt for that long? You can't be blamed for her choice." Mairead took his hands. "Your only crime was leaving without saying goodbye."

"Tell that to the men in the brothel. How many innocent men did I kill?"

The grip on his hands tightened. "They weren't innocent. They were in a brothel—as you said, the worst kind."

"But you're right. I'm not a god. I'm not even a very good man. It's not my job to decide who gets to die and who gets to live—not unless I'm defending someone else."

A long silence fell. "Are you the one the stories speak of? The raven-marked one who will defeat the Forbidden?" she asked finally.

"I don't know." He put his hand over hers. "You want to know why I do the work I do? Because I can defend people with my sword and convince myself that I'm doing the right thing. You want to know why I won't marry? Because I won't bind a woman to me with children or marriage or home. I don't want to destroy her or my children or anything I build with her." He took a deep breath. "The stories say the earliest men with the ravenmark killed their own kinsmen, wives, children. If I let this thing go—if I let it have control of me—I have no idea what I might do. I can't risk it."

She shook her head. "Don't resign yourself to this hopeless path, Connor. Do you really want to spend your life roaming from woman to woman and job to job with no real peace?"

He avoided her eyes. "There is one place I've found peace." He paused. *Should I say it?* "There is comfort in being with you."

The fire crackled behind them. She let go of his hands and sat up straight. Her fingers worried the bottom edge of her tunic. "I don't know what to call this," she said finally, quietly. "I have no experience with men. I don't know what you feel for me. But I know that I don't want to say goodbye to you."

"I don't want to say goodbye to you, either. If it weren't for this thing, I would never leave, Mairead, I swear it. I'm—" He stopped short. *If you tell her you're in love with her, you can't leave. You take away your options. You can't do that.* "Do you still want me to find someone else to guard you?"

She shook her head. "I want you to stay with me."

A wave of relief shivered through him. *There's still time, then. Maybe I can find a way to stay with her. Maybe I can find a way to just serve her—be close to her.* "I will be more careful with your affections. If we're to spend the winter in Galbragh, I'll be more careful when we're together."

She laughed, a sad, rueful sound. "I think it's too late to be careful with my affections." She touched his arm, and he took her hand again. "What will I do without you? When you leave?"

I don't know. "I promise I'll be certain you're with someone safe if I have to leave."

Her mouth quivered into a sad smile. "I wish—" She bit her lip and turned her head.

I wish I could be with you. I wish I could hold you, feel your skin against mine, hear you whisper my name. I wish I could stay with you for the rest of my life. I wish I didn't have this damn demon inside of me. "I wish it, too."

She squeezed his hands and stood. "You sleep. I'll keep watch." She picked up her bow.

"You shouldn't—"

"I'm not tired, and you'll sleep better if you know someone is awake." She pulled her cloak tighter around her. "Besides, I learned from the best." She walked to the edge of the camp and sat down, the bow slung over her shoulder.

He pulled his blanket from his pack and spread it on the ground, but he couldn't sleep. He could only watch Mairead. *One winter isn't enough. A lifetime wouldn't be enough. I need this woman.*

In a large, rambling house surrounded by slave camps, Emrys watched a grim-faced steward read a wrinkled parchment. The man's face paled. "Ye're certain this is true?"

The messenger nodded. "Got that straight from the man what saw it happen. Rode three horses into the ground to deliver this."

The steward muttered a curse. He folded the paper. "I almost pity the man who did it."

Save your pity, Emrys thought.

He'd felt the Morrag awaken days before when the raven finally heeded her call. He'd awakened with her need for blood—*his* blood—tearing at his chest. *Claw. Rake. Maim. Kill. You're not safe, Forbidden One. He comes for you.*

Emrys clutched at his chest, his hands clammy and his heart pounding fiercely against his ribs. *I have time. I still have time. I must have time.*

He slipped in and out of the elements for days, finally tracing the raven to the brothel where he'd killed in the Morrag's name. He hovered in shadow while the slaver's men and the brothel owner tried to trace the man who'd left a bloody streak of death in the common room and freed several of their best whores. He even searched for the raven and the heir himself, but by the time he found them, they had too much of a start for the brothel owner and his men to catch up.

But the trail led him here, to the slaver Seamus Allyn. The slaver had long been a source of pride for Emrys. He kept Allyn alive, relishing the vile touch he brought to all of his endeavors. Emrys settled into the shadows of a corner and waited. Allyn read the letter, cursed, and threw the parchment on the ground. He poured a generous shot of oiska, drank, and poured another. "What am I going to tell his mother?"

"Perhaps the truth this time."

Seamus grimaced. "It doesn't matter what a worthless piece of shit he was, she's still his mother. She won't want to hear that he died in a whorehouse with his bowels on the floor."

The steward inclined his head. "I realize that, sir, but there is little you can do to hide the truth. It's only been a week, and word is spreading."

Seamus put down his cup. Emrys knew he had no love for his son. Seamus complained that he should have killed the woman who bore him once he was done using her. Emrys had been near Seamus long enough to know that the slaver had tried to give his son opportunities to buy into the slaving family, but his every attempt was met with the aggressive incompetence of a man who would rather indulge his base desires.

"Sir," the steward said.

Seamus looked up.

"We should respond."

Seamus nodded. "I won't have the Mac Mahons thinking we can't avenge our own. Do we know who did this? Did he know who he was killing?"

"I've got men looking for answers. They captured several of the women who left the brothel and got descriptions after applying a bit of pressure. The brothel owner gave a description as well. Nothing special—big, dark, heavily armed. The brothel owner said it was the spawn of Namha himself. The women said he was a warrior of Alshada."

"So I should tell the men to look for either a demon or an avenging angel? Fuck."

"There was one other thing. He had tattoos."

Seamus frowned. "Tattoos?"

"He had several blue rings around his upper arm."

Seamus leaned back in his chair and tapped his chin. "It's something. A start. Find him. I want his head. He used my son as an example. I'll use him as one."

The steward inclined his head and left the room. Seamus drank another shot of oiska. He went to his door. "Go to the camps. Find me a woman who hasn't been used too much." The guard inclined his head and walked away.

Emrys emerged from the shadow and sat in Seamus' chair. Seamus spun around and pulled a dagger from his belt. "Who are ye?"

Emrys leaned forward. "You want the man who killed your son? He'll be in Galbragh tomorrow."

His eyes narrowed. "How d'ye know that?"

"I have sources you don't have. Do you want him?"

The dagger twitched in his hand, but he didn't sheathe it. He finally gave a slow nod. "All right. Tell me."

"Promise me one thing. The girl he's with—deliver her to me."

"Fine. Who is he?"

"His name is Connor Mac Niall. He'll be at Prince Henry's palace tomorrow with a girl he's escorting. Do what you want with him, but deliver her to me."

Seamus straightened and thought it through. "In the palace? It won't be easy."

"I'm sure a man of your means has ways. Mac Niall doesn't like to be quiet. He's quite confident in his abilities, and he has money. He'll be in the open in the palace district at some point. He'll probably take his woman shopping."

"*His* woman? Not just a woman he's escorting?"

Emrys frowned. "I've seen how you get men to talk. I've seen what you do to their women. I need her alive and sane."

"Not unspoiled?"

"That doesn't matter. Beat her, fuck her, pass her around—just make sure you don't leave her a babbling idiot."

Seamus folded his arms. "This is too easy. What else d'ye want?"

"Give me the woman, and you'll never see me again."

Silence cloaked the room, as thick as Allyn's transgressions. "All right. How will I find you?" Allyn finally said.

"I'll find you." Emrys slipped back into the elements and hovered in shadow again to watch.

Seamus let out a breath. He fingered the dagger in his hand, sheathed it, and slumped in his chair. He started to pour another shot of oiska and stopped. Instead, he picked up parchment and quill and started to write.

Emrys let a slow sneer cross his face as the words ordering Connor Mac Niall's death appeared on the parchment.

CHAPTER TWENTY-FOUR

Strength. Valor. Truth.
— *Motto of the Mac Niall House*

Winter arrived between Kenna's home and Galbragh. With each day, the snow grew heavier, and with every mile, the mountains became whiter. It took a week of cold travel to reach the city, and though Connor made sure Mairead was covered and warm, she couldn't stop thinking how much she wanted to eat a hot meal in a warm room and fall asleep on a soft bed covered in furs. *With him next to me.*

The cold weather tempted them to sleep close to each other. They huddled together most nights, talking until the fire lowered and their eyes grew heavy, but when it came time to sleep, Connor always walked away to lie down on the other side of the fire.

On the last night, the snow fell thick and heavy, and they stopped in the driest clearing they could find. Connor made her a bed of fir boughs and built a lean-to over it. They huddled together inside it for some time, talking and watching the small fire sputter. When he started to leave, Mairead tugged on his hand. "You don't have to go. You can sleep here."

He shook his head. "It's not a good idea."

"I just want to sleep. Nothing more."

He chuckled. "You do want more, and so do I."

"But—"

"Mairead, I'm disciplined, but not *that* disciplined."

She lay down on the boughs. "You slept next to me before."

"I know. But that was before I—" He paused, thinking. "You know how much I want you. If I lie down with you, I'll start kissing you, and I won't be able to stop." Snow landed in his hair; the firelight lent it an orange sparkle. He covered her with a blanket and her wolf pelt.

She closed her eyes. "Will you really stay with me all winter?"

He squeezed her shoulder. "Yes. I promise."

By morning, the snow had stopped, and a rising sun cast a glow over the vast northern plains. In the distance, a faint white, gray, and brown outline rose from the horizon. Connor pointed at it. "Galbragh."

Mairead sucked in her breath in awe. "It has no end."

He laughed. "Henry would like to think so. It's not the largest city I've ever been in, but it's close."

They entered the city late in the morning, and Mairead's mouth dropped as they went through the gates. She'd never seen a place so large. Even Torlach didn't compare to Galbragh. "It's built on the slave trade," Connor told her. "And the venom and drug trade. Prince Henry tries to keep the city clean, but there are pockets of illegal activity all over. He lets the slavers and venom runners do their business in the countryside. In return, they keep wealth flowing into the city. It's not ideal, but it works."

"Who are these slaving families?"

"The Allyns and the Mac Mahons are the two native ones. There's a smaller operation from Tal'Amun, but it mainly buys women for the emperor and his nobles. The other two families fight for control of the northern territories and have underlings all over the Wilds." He pointed north. "There are camps to the north where they board the slaves onto riverboats and take them down to the northern seas. Taurin ships keep them out of the channel since slavery is illegal in Taura. Eiryan ships patrol the Galoch Sea and stop who they can, but it's a big place. Most of the ships make it through and get to Espara with about half of their cargo alive."

Mairead's stomach lurched. "Half alive? Half of the ones they capture die?"

"Usually. They stack them into the ships on top of each other or chain them together. If the rats don't kill them, starvation or thirst will. Sometimes they throw them overboard alive when there's a storm and they—" He stopped. "I'm sorry. It's too much."

Mairead fought the urge to dismount and vomit. "I didn't know any of this. What a horrible place." *How long will Kenna and her parents be free? Alive? How long before Tarah and her children are taken and sold?*

Connor spoke with a forced cheer. "The palace district is nice. And Prince Henry is a decent man. He'll like you. His wife is only a bit older than you, and he has a sister about your age."

As they rode toward the palace district, the streets and buildings grew cleaner and more refined. Ladies in silks and feathers riding in carriages drawn by matching teams of horses replaced the peasant women in linens who carried baskets of their wares. Men with well-trimmed beards and multiple rings replaced merchants in aprons and soiled tunics. They left behind tumble-down thatched houses packed together along the wall and entered a world of new construction, where rough-hewn timbers and whitewashed walls housed the wealthy elite beneath tiled roofs. Mairead had to force herself to keep her mouth shut, but she couldn't stop her eyes from their frantic attempt to take in everything she saw.

Connor directed her to an inn called the Golden Goose. They turned their horses over to the stableboy, and Mairead watched her roguish man-at-arms melt away and a duke arrive in his place. Connor stood straighter and prouder, and his air changed. *He expects to be served.*

A slight, balding man in fine linen and wool looked up from his work at the front desk. He sniffed at Connor. "Are you the blacksmith? Go around to the stableyard. We have three horses that need shoeing and—"

"I'm not a blacksmith." Connor's voice carried a noble air edged with irritation. "Show some respect."

The man sucked in a breath and bowed, low. "Forgive me, my lord. The attire—I thought you—"

"You thought because I wear leathers I'm used to mucking in horse dung or slaving over a forge? Do I smell like a stable?"

He bowed again. "Of course not, my lord. Please, forgive my assumptions. I will see to your every need personally."

"We'll need a room," Connor said. He glanced around the common room with disdain. "A good one. With guard quarters."

The man nodded. "We have a very nice room in the corner. You'll have a view of the hills."

"Fine. Prepare baths for both of us and send word to Prince Henry that Connor Mac Niall has arrived and would like an audience with him."

"Of course, my lord." He motioned for a boy to bring their packs along and showed them to their room.

Mairead tried not to gape while she looked around the room. Furs covered the large bed, and scattered rugs warmed the timber floor. The furniture was made of rough-hewn wood polished to a smooth, bright finish. Tapestries woven in the colors of the forest, browns and deep greens and dark reds and oranges, decorated the walls. Thin, snowy light streamed in through the glass windows. "Every place I've ever stayed before has had shutters or oiled skin in the windows," she said, touching the glass.

The innkeeper sniffed again. "If anything is unsatisfactory, please call me at once, Lord Mac Niall." He bowed and shut the door.

Within moments, servants arrived and filled a washtub with steaming water. Connor excused himself to wait for his own bath in the guard quarters. Mairead bathed, dressed in a green linen peasant dress that Aileen had given her, and brushed her hair out until it was nearly dry. When Connor knocked on her door, she smoothed the skirt and the nervous flutter in her stomach with sweating hands.

Connor smiled down at her. "You look pretty."

Her knees went weak at the sight of him. He'd bathed, shaved, and brushed his leathers clean, and he wore a dark blue tunic under his jerkin. "I think you mistake clean for pretty."

He laughed. "Henry already sent a reply. He says he'll expect us at the palace this afternoon, at our convenience."

"I don't think I'm ready to meet a prince."

He fetched her cloak and fastened it around her. His hands lingered on her shoulders half a breath longer than they needed to. "You'll be fine." He offered her his arm. "We'll have some spiced wine downstairs, and I'll call for a carriage."

"A carriage? Can't we walk or ride?"

He shook his head. "Only beggars and servants walk to Henry's palace. Invited guests are expected to arrive in a carriage."

They warmed themselves with spiced wine while they waited for the carriage. Merchants and self-styled nobles passed through the room or sat to eat. More than one cast a disdainful look at Mairead. "I don't fit in here," she said in a low tone when one powdered and perfumed lady sniffed and cleared her throat as she walked past.

"It's all right. Neither do I."

"You do, though. You have that noble air. They know you're one of them. They must think I'm—" She stopped and bit her lip.

Connor leaned forward and took her hand. "You're what?"

She lowered her voice and leaned closer to him. "Your paramour. Or worse."

He tilted his head, his eyes kind as he considered her. "You don't have the look of a brothel, and if you were my paramour, I'd dress you in silks and jewels befitting the rank of a duchess."

She didn't know what to say to that. "Connor, I don't think I'm made for this world. For what I'll have to do. I don't know how to be a queen."

"There will be people in Albard who can help you." Pain hovered in his voice.

"I don't want other people."

He poured more wine into her cup. He drank again and rested his arms on the table. "What do you want, Mairead?"

She leaned close to him and lowered her voice again. *Stay with me. I want you to stay with me.* "Does it matter what I want?"

His eyes were tight when he spoke. "It matters. It's just not possible."

She was spared from having to respond when the door opened and a footman in a fur-lined cloak entered the common room. He stamped snow off his feet. "Someone called for a carriage?"

Connor signaled to the man. The footman bowed and offered his arm to Mairead. They walked out into the snow, and Connor helped her into the carriage while the footman put their packs in the wooden trunk. He climbed in next to her, put an arm around her, and leaned down to her ear. "Please don't worry, Mairead. They will love you."

The ride to the palace was a short one, but Mairead's stomach twisted and flipped with every moment that passed. When they arrived at the gates and the guards ushered them through, she gasped at her first close glimpse of the palace. "It's beautiful."

The castle in Torlach was an ancient, rambling stone structure built over the centuries by monarchs and regents who adapted it to their needs. This prince's palace was a new structure. Wood and stone combined to create a magnificent building unified in a common style. Broad-beamed accents, glass windows, and spires that rose high above the turrets and peaks gave the building symmetry and elegance. The cobbled courtyard featured a pool and garden, and the carriage rolled through the gates and around the pool to halt at the front door of the palace. The light dusting of snow and random icicles accented the delicate features of the building as if someone had sprinkled a fine coat of sugar across it.

Connor waited for the footman to open the door, stepped out of the carriage, and helped Mairead out. She suppressed another nervous flutter. He put her hand on his arm and escorted her through the doors into a large open hall.

A steward wearing dark red livery edged in black piping stepped forward and bowed. "Lord Mac Niall. It's a pleasure to see you again."

"And you, Rhys," Connor said.

Rhys led them through the hall to a library where a blond man in a red doublet with a black hawk emblazoned on each shoulder sat behind a desk. "Your highness, Lord Connor Mac Niall," Rhys said.

The blond man grinned. He stood and held out an arm, and Connor met him to clasp his arm. "My old friend," Henry said. "Where have you been? It's been—what—nearly four years?"

"Since I took you to Espara. Where's Lydia?"

Grief flickered across Henry's face. "She died last winter. In childbirth. She and the child."

"Henry, I'm so sorry." Connor put a hand on his friend's shoulder. "I know how much you loved her."

Henry gave him a pained smile under his close-trimmed blond beard. "Introduce me to this beautiful woman on your arm. Don't tell me you've finally married?"

Connor shook his head. "I haven't. This is my ward, Mairead. Mairead, my friend, Prince Henry Brannon of the northern territories."

Henry took her hand and bowed. "A true pleasure, my lady."

"Likewise, my lord." She gave him a clumsy curtsy. Connor steadied her with his hand on her back. "Forgive me, my lord. I fear I'm not used to skirts. We've been traveling. I've worn breeches for weeks."

Henry smiled. "You can grace my court with your presence whenever you wish—in skirts or in breeches."

Connor cleared his throat. "Henry, I've come to ask you if you can return that favor."

Henry frowned. "All right. Please, have a seat. Rhys, see to wine." The steward bowed and left the room as Henry, Connor, and Mairead all sat. "I'm not sure what you need, Connor, but this isn't the best time. The Allyns are at the Mac Mahons' throats right now. I don't have a lot of extra time or money."

"I don't need much. We just need a place to winter. Mairead has family in Sveklant, but I don't want to keep traveling this late in the season. I need a place where she'll be safe until we can leave again. Can we stay with you?"

Henry blinked. "Of course. It's as good as done. And that's all you want from me to clear my debt?"

"That's it. Keep us sheltered and safe until spring, and we're even."

Henry let out a breath. "You're a good man, Connor. It would be an honor to host you and your ward for the winter. Where are you staying now?"

"The Golden Goose."

"A lovely inn, but I can do much better for you. I'll send for your belongings and horses. Might you be able to advise me on some matters while you're here?"

"I'd be happy to."

Henry smiled. "I'll arrange for a meal and have Rhys send for Elizabeth. I believe she's in the city somewhere. She'll enjoy the company of another woman in the palace, I'm sure. Tell me how you ended up escorting such a beautiful young woman."

Connor smiled. "I was in Torlach with my mother. Mairead was a member of her household, and she needed someone to take her to her family in Sveklant."

Henry blinked in surprise. "She's a serving girl?"

"No," Connor said. "She's a daughter of merchants my mother knew years ago. Her family sent her to Torlach for a time to live with my mother."

"Why send her home now, with winter coming?"

"The Taurin government is in disarray right now. My mother feared that Mairead might be stuck there indefinitely. She asked me to get her back to her family as quickly as possible, but we've run into a few delays."

Henry turned to Mairead, his blue eyes curious. "How long has it been since you've been home, lady?"

She licked her lips and tried to calm her breathing. "Six years, I think. I've lost track."

"You have parents in Sveklant? Or someone you're betrothed to?"

She raised her goblet and sipped wine. "My parents are dead," she said, recalling the story she and Connor had discussed. "I have an aunt and uncle. Cousins."

Henry raised his goblet to Mairead. "I look forward to sharing your company this winter, my dear."

She raised her goblet. "I look forward to yours as well, your highness."

Connor and Henry fell into conversation, and Mairead listened as she sipped her wine and servants tended the fire in the hearth. "Tell me about what's happening with the Mac Mahons and the Allyns," Connor asked.

Henry sighed. "It's more of the same—just louder and bloodier. One family accuses the other of stealing slaves or ambushing a train or ruining a brothel, so the other family strikes back, and on it goes. Now we heard that Seamus Allyn's son was killed in a fight in a brothel. Allyn is on the warpath—says he's going to skewer the balls of the man who did it."

Mairead frowned behind her goblet. *A fight in a brothel? But there must be hundreds of brothels in Culidar. And these men run most of them. It couldn't be the same man. Could it?*

"Who does he think did it?" Connor asked.

"I don't know. I hired a man to keep an eye on the slavers for me. He's up there now. I'm hoping he'll be back soon to tell me what's going on. I don't need them bringing this into the city." He rubbed the bridge of his nose. "Tell me again why I fight this?"

"Because slavery is wrong. You believe that. So do I."

"It feels futile. Every step forward is met with resistance and fighting. I free ten slaves to see a hundred more taken. What difference am I making?"

"You're making a difference for those ten," Mairead said.

The door opened, and a stunning young woman entered the room. The men stood and the woman smiled. "Henry, I'm sorry it took so long. The servants had to find me in the city. I was shopping." She smiled and approached Connor. "Lord Mac Niall, how lovely to see you again."

"Lady Brannon." Connor took her hand and swept it up to his lips. "You look well."

"So perfunctory, Connor. Surely there is room for relaxed formality between us, isn't there?" She kissed his cheek and stretched up to whisper something in his ear.

He patted her hand and stepped back. "My lady, let me introduce my ward, Mairead. Mairead, this is Lady Elizabeth, Henry's sister."

Mairead stood and curtsied. "Lady Elizabeth. It's an honor to meet you."

"And you, Mairead." Elizabeth's auburn hair was twisted into braids and loops that accentuated her station, and Mairead was conscious of the simple wooden combs that held her hair back from her face. The lady wore an elaborate dark green silk dress trimmed in ermine and gold thread. Mairead's simple linen seemed plain by comparison.

Elizabeth surveyed Mairead as if studying a peculiar piece of art that didn't quite suit her. "How long will you and your ward be with us, Connor?"

Connor cleared his throat. "Through the winter, I think. Your brother has agreed to house us."

Elizabeth smiled coolly. "Then you will need some more appropriate clothing, Mairead. I have a few things that might suit you." She turned to Connor. "And I expect you dressed appropriately at my table, Connor. No leathers."

He chuckled. "If it makes you happy."

"Wonderful. Mairead, join me, won't you? We'll take tea, and I'll help you find some appropriate evening wear."

"Oh, my lady, really—I don't—"

"Nonsense. You will. I have more gowns than I can wear in a year of suppers. Come."

She left no room for argument, turning to walk out of the library with the full expectation that Mairead would follow. Connor merely shrugged. Mairead took a deep breath and fell in step behind Elizabeth.

Elizabeth led her to her chambers and ordered tea and pastries. As the servants poured and served, she opened her wardrobe, and Mairead gasped at the opulence. There were silk and wool gowns and dresses of every color and style, riding clothes, boots and slippers, furs, cloaks, hats, and even lacy, scanty undergarments that made Mairead blush to see. "Let's get you dressed appropriately, shall we?" Elizabeth said. "And while we do, you must tell me all about your time with Lord Mac Niall."

Mairead felt the heat rise in her face, and she turned to look at a dress of white samite trimmed in silver. "There is little to tell, my lady. He's escorting me to my aunt and uncle in Sveklant."

"But surely there's more to it than that." Elizabeth pulled a red scarf from a basket and held it to Mairead's cheek. "Perhaps a deep lilac," she murmured.

Mairead stepped back. "Connor is my guard and escort only."

Elizabeth lowered her hand. "Connor is never just a guard. He couldn't keep his hands off a beautiful woman any more easily than I can say no to a new scarf." She waved the red silk at Mairead to drive home the point.

Perhaps Connor's changed. Perhaps I know him better than you do. She forced a smile. "What would you like me to wear to supper?"

Mairead spent the afternoon trying on gowns and dresses with Elizabeth's help. When night started to fall, Elizabeth called maids to help her change into a gown of deep blue. She found suitable clothes for Mairead as well, a gown that shimmered from the faintest lavender to the deepest violet depending on the light. The maids piled Mairead's hair in loops and braids and gave her soft palace slippers and simple gold jewels as well. Mairead was exhausted by the time they joined the men in the dining hall.

Connor and Henry both stood when the women entered the room. Connor had changed into woolen breeches and a dark blue doublet. When his eyes fell on Mairead, she saw a raw hunger in them that made her shiver. He paused before he said anything. "Elizabeth, you've made a very pretty girl into a lovely royal lady. I commend you." He never took his eyes from Mairead.

"It wasn't difficult. Your ward is a beautiful woman," Elizabeth said, a twinge of jealousy in her voice.

Connor took Mairead's hand and seated her next to him. "You are stunning, Mairead," he whispered next to her ear. She shivered again at the sensation of his breath near her neck.

They dined on duck and small red potatoes and too many side dishes for Mairead to recall later. She sampled everything from the first course of a simple broth to the last course of a rich cherry tart. By the time she finished, she feared she'd burst the seams on Elizabeth's gown.

Connor leaned over to her when the meal was finished. "Would you like to see your room?"

She caught a faint scent of wine and cherries on his breath. "Yes, please."

A servant led them to a private bedchamber with a sitting room that overlooked the rear garden. Moonlight reflected off the snow on the marble statues in the garden, casting a faint glow up to her room. Her bed was elevated on a dais and covered in linens and furs. Plush chairs in muted hues dotted the room, and to one side, a fire crackled in the hearth. "It's beautiful," Mairead said. "It will be nice to be warm again."

The servant left the room, and Connor tucked a stray lock of hair behind her ear. "I'm finding it very difficult to keep my promise right now," he said in a strained voice.

"What promise?"

"To be more careful with your affections."

Her stomach flipped. She knew she shouldn't, but she put her hand on his chest. "Was there something between you and Elizabeth?"

"She'd like to think so, but no. The last time I saw her, she was seventeen. I don't take advantage of young women." He lifted her hand and kissed her palm. "Besides, as pretty as she is, she pales next to you."

She laughed. "This isn't me. I'm happier in breeches with a bow on my shoulder."

"I know. That's one reason I find you so beautiful."

She leaned closer to him. "I don't want you to go."

He put his hands on her shoulders. "I don't want to go."

"Will you stay?"

The silence pressed on her chest. She ached for his answer, as afraid he'd say yes as no. He bent down and kissed her head, his hands tightening on her shoulders. "Good night, Mairead." He turned and left the room.

She sat down on her bed, fighting tears. "Alshada," she whispered. "If you aren't going to let us be together, then end this. I can't stand this. It hurts too much to be close to him and not be able to have him. Please, either take him from me or let us be together."

The only answer was the crackle and pop of the fire. Mairead's tears turned her gown the color of the sky the morning they left Donal and Aileen's house, and her prayers hung unanswered in the air.

CHAPTER TWENTY-FIVE

The best way to a woman's heart is through a promise kept.
— The journal of Culain Mac Niall

Connor shut Mairead's door and let out a deep breath. The Morrag fluttered, awakening slowly in his chest. He shook his head and rubbed his temples. *I need to fight.*

You want the girl.

No, this is you. This is you making me fight again.

She stirred as if preening. *You could have the girl,* the Morrag whispered. *Submit to me, and she'll be yours. You want her. She wants you. Why do you resist? I would give you strength. I would tell you when to fight and when to rest.*

He stalked to his room and changed into leathers. *I don't care what you promise me. I will never submit.* He offered the guards at the gates a skin of oiska in exchange for letting him out of the palace grounds and then made his way toward Galbragh's commerce district.

The Morrag's presence grew stronger as he walked, as if his tension over leaving Mairead's rooms awakened her fully. *Submit. Submit, raven.*

He pushed the thoughts away and walked faster, flexing his hands in anticipation of tasting blood. *I'm not yours. I won't be yours.*

You already are. You can feel the bloodlust. You want to kill. Submit to me, and I'll make sure you only serve justice.

He shook his head. "No." A couple strolling through the snow stepped out of his path, and the man put his hand on a dagger in his belt. Connor walked faster.

He walked until he heard the sounds of shouting, cheering, and fighting rumbling into the street from the lower floor of a brothel in the commerce district. A pretty brunette in silks and feathers met him when he entered the room. He gestured to the men fighting in the center of the floor. "Who's taking the bets?" he asked.

She pointed to a stout man in woolens who stood leaning on a cane to one side of the makeshift ring. "Fat Flynn handles the lads."

When the night was over, Connor had bested six men and made a lot of money for Fat Flynn. He was sweaty and bloody, but the men who'd taken him on were no match for his tribal training and size, and even the fair amount of oiska he'd had didn't affect him. *Cursed Sidh blood. Can't even get drunk when I want. At least I know I can still fight.* The Morrag rested, calm and settled in his chest. *And at least I subdued you,* he told her.

She cackled. *I rest when I wish. I rise when I must.*

The brunette brought his tunic to him. "The men are leaving. No one else wants to take ye on." She winked. "Except me."

He wiped his face with his tunic. "I only came to fight."

"Ye're certain? Ye can have your pick of the girls. We've been eying ye all night."

He shook his head, but then he saw a girl with honey-blond hair and green eyes a few paces behind the brunette. He nodded toward her. "What about her?"

The brunette grinned. "Ye like blonds, eh? She's a pretty girl. One of the new ones, too."

Connor stepped toward the blond. "How much?"

She shrank back at first, but then straightened and swallowed hard. "For how long?"

"The night."

"A silver."

He thought about it. The soft curve of her neck tempted him. *I could lose myself with her, call her any other name.* He took out the handful of silvers he'd won fighting. "Take this."

Her eyes widened, and she nodded. "For how long?"

"Go home. You're better than this." He pulled the tunic on and left the brothel.

"Lad, wait." Flynn puffed and panted to catch up to him. "Lad, ye've got a wicked punch and good footwork. Ye'd make a fair bit o' coin if ye stay."

"A fair bit of coin for you or for me?"

"For both of us."

Connor shook his head. "Not interested." He walked away before Flynn could say more.

When he arrived back at the palace, he fell onto his bed fully dressed, tossing and turning in restless sleep till morning. When he finally rose and went to Mairead's room, she gasped at the sight of him. "What happened?" she asked, putting her hand up to a cut above his eyes.

He flinched. "Lucky punch. I'm fine."

She ushered him into her room, retrieved a clean cloth, and poured water over it. "Where did you go?"

He sat down on the bed. "Just walked around the city."

"You don't get punched when you're just walking around."

"You do in some parts of Galbragh."

He closed his eyes as she dabbed at the cut and cleaned it. She stood between his legs, his head just beneath hers. "It's not bad. It just needs cleaning. Why didn't you clean it last night?"

"I was too tired." He sat very still, struggling to push away the lure of Mairead's scent and the feel of her breath in his hair. "I don't like keeping secrets from you anymore," he said, quiet.

She lowered the cloth. "What secrets are you keeping?"

"Last night, I drank myself as stupid as my Sidh blood would let me. I fought for money and to prove to myself I can still best a man with my fists. I almost took a prostitute to bed, but I changed my mind."

She waited, quiet, her hands resting on his shoulders. There was no condemnation in her eyes.

"Do you think less of me?"

"No. You're still Connor."

He put his hands on her hips and closed his eyes. "That life—drinking and fighting and bedding any woman I want—it's not enough anymore." His hands tightened, and she wove her fingers into his hair. "I know how pure you are, how much you have before you. I'm just a hired sword with a little money and a little magic. And then to have this thing in me . . . this ache, the Morrag . . . But all I want is to be with you."

Her voice was a nervous whisper. "I'm nothing, Connor. Not a queen. Just a girl with the right blood."

"You will be a queen."

"A throneless queen." She smiled and ran her fingers through his hair. "And you're my tainted duke."

He opened his eyes. "Where did you hear that?"

"I don't know. I just thought of it. Why?"

The last thing I need is a damn Svek song to confuse everything. "No reason." He stood. "I need to clean up, and then we can have breakfast."

He returned to his room to wash and dress. Mairead waited for him, and they walked to the dining hall together. Henry and Elizabeth waited before a table heavy with the bounty of Galbragh and the countryside. Another man dressed in black leathers stood watching out a window, and Connor frowned. "Melik?"

The man turned and flashed a sharp grin. Four earrings glinted in the muted light behind him. "Connor! Good to see you again." He offered an arm.

The Morrag stirred and fluttered in Connor's head. *Kill, raven. Maim. Claw him.*

He forced himself to swallow. *Why?*

You know him of old. You know his transgressions.

Connor suppressed a grimace. Melik was an assassin, and a good one. Connor had heard his name whispered in association with some high profile deaths, but no one could ever prove his involvement with any of them. *He's not assassinating anyone right now.* He focused on the task at hand—greeting Melik and maintaining control. "And you. What brings you to Galbragh?"

"I work for his highness now."

"You know each other?" Henry asked.

Connor nodded. "Melik and I met in Espara. How do you two know each other?"

"He was here asking for work at the Three Crowns. Do you know it?"

The Three Crowns was on the edge of the commerce district. A place where slavers and legitimate merchants alike gathered, freelances regularly went there to find work. Connor hadn't been there in several years. He hadn't needed to, and for that he was thankful. He hated the place. It smelled of desperation and money and dishonesty. As his reputation spread, he'd been able to attract clients without going to such places. Most of his clients came to him through referrals, and he preferred it that way. "I've been there a few times," he said.

"I was asking around for work. Someone mentioned the prince, so I came here," Melik said.

"Melik's been a great help," Henry added. "He's found holes in my defenses that I didn't know were there, and he's been able to keep an eye on what the slaving families are doing. He just got back this morning with a report about the Allyns."

Melik turned to Mairead. "But Connor, we neglect your beautiful lady. His highness tells me he's housing you and your ward for a time?"

"Yes. Mairead, this is Melik d'Nostrius, an . . . associate of mine. Melik, Mairead."

Melik lifted her hand, and Mairead curtsied. "A true honor to meet you, my lady. Perhaps in time we will have the pleasure of some private conversation?"

Mairead smiled, but Connor caught the hint of steel in her expression. "Perhaps."

Melik picked up a goblet with his gloved hand and turned to Connor. He was dressed entirely in black leather. Only his head and the tips of his fingers were uncovered. At his side hung the bags of his trade. "How is Helene? Last I heard you were with her."

"Your aunt is well. You should visit."

Melik snorted. "Yes. I should. Perhaps one day."

Henry stepped in. "Please, Connor, join us." Connor seated Mairead and then sat between her and Henry as Elizabeth and Melik sat. "Melik was just telling us some of what he discovered in the Allyn camp. Seamus Allyn discovered who killed his son."

"Oh? Who?"

Melik lifted a goblet. "I couldn't discover a name, but Allyn was very specific about what would happen to individual parts of the man's anatomy."

"It is his son. The desire for vengeance is natural," Mairead said.

"Perhaps under normal circumstances, but Allyn had no love for this child. He was an illegitimate son sired on one of his own . . . ah, slaves. Allyn tried to take care of the boy with money and opportunity, but they never got along. This is a grudge issue. He doesn't want to appear weak to the other families or to Henry. He only wants blood to make it clear that he can have blood."

Mairead's hands tightened around her goblet. "How does Allyn plan to find this man?"

"The rumor is that he knows the man's name and where he is. I doubt it will be a quiet assassination. It will be loud and bloody, and Allyn may even kill those around the man just to let it be known he can."

The Morrag fluttered again, rising into Connor's chest, twisting and croaking. He frowned and set down his knife. *I thought I satisfied you enough last night.*

But she didn't answer.

Mairead watched him. "Not hungry?" she asked in a whisper.

He shook his head and forced a smile. "I'll be all right."

Elizabeth gave a loud sigh. "Let's speak of something more pleasant. Mairead, perhaps we can go into the city and do some shopping today? We would have the two most handsome guards in the city if Connor and Melik agree to accompany us."

Mairead grimaced, but Connor took her hand and leaned toward her ear. "We should get out into the city. It will be fun." *If you'll keep silent,* he told the Morrag.

Her wings pounded against his consciousness, but she didn't speak.

They finished eating, and Henry called for a carriage. Elizabeth drew Mairead aside to finish preparing for the day. Connor waited at the palace entryway, trying to still and settle the Morrag. He couldn't remember another time that she had been so restless. The effort to keep her stilled was starting to drain him. He paced and took deep breaths of cool morning air, but the Morrag wouldn't stop stabbing at him. *What is this? Is this a warning?* She flapped and fluttered as a bird before a storm. Another thought dawned on him. *Is this the day you take me?*

She didn't respond.

Melik joined him on the steps as the carriage pulled up. "Fine weather for a day in the city, eh?"

"It's clear, but I don't think it will warm up much. I'm glad for Elizabeth's insistence on spending the day out, though. I chafe inside the palace when the weather is good, and Mairead needs some things in town."

"The lady seems reluctant to indulge herself."

"She was raised poor."

Melik adjusted his gloves. "Does she know about you? What you do, how much money you have?"

Connor turned to him. "She knows I have money."

"Good. A solid foundation of honesty is important in a relationship."

Connor narrowed his eyes. "There's no relationship."

"Does she know that? Her eyes rarely left your face."

"What do you think you know, Melik?"

"Nothing, I assure you." But when Melik met his eyes, Connor saw secrets there.

They took a carriage to the center of the palace district, and Melik and Elizabeth took the lead in exploring the shops. Mairead walked with her hand on Connor's arm, and he urged her to look at the same things Elizabeth perused, but she only smiled politely and watched Elizabeth shop.

When they all stopped to eat in a small public house, Elizabeth commented on Mairead's lack of purchases. "You should have taken Connor's offer to buy you that lovely blue silk back at the tailor's shop. With a few small alterations, it would have been perfect for you."

Mairead sipped tea and shook her head. "No, my lady Elizabeth. I'm not yet accustomed to such finery, and once I'm in Sveklant, I'll have no opportunities to wear something so grand."

"Perhaps you just need a man to spoil you, Mairead," Melik suggested with a grin. "If Connor isn't up to the task, I'd be happy to try."

Elizabeth gave him a gentle slap. "Melik, I thought your attentions were only for me."

"My lady, I assure you, I have only your pleasure and indulgence in mind," Melik told her with a rakish grin.

Connor took Mairead's hand. "Let me buy you something else if you don't want dresses. Let's look at the jeweler's."

"If it makes you happy."

He squeezed her hand. "It does."

When they left the public house, Connor put his arm around Mairead to steer her toward the jeweler's when the hair on his neck stood up. The Morrag flared, fluttering a sudden warning through a stabbing ache in his chest. He only had time to shout before an arrow whirred toward them. He shoved Mairead away as it thunked into the door behind her. He flung open the door of the public house and pushed her and Elizabeth back inside. "Stay here."

Mairead clutched his arm. "Connor, don't leave—"

He yanked away from her. "Do as I say!" He turned back to the street, sword drawn, senses attuned.

The Morrag beckoned him. *Submit. Let me strengthen you.*

Stay out of this!

Melik stood with a dagger in one hand and his back to Connor. "They haven't gone—I can sense them."

"The arrow was our warning. Do you think—"

The world erupted in fire. All around, flaming pots shattered. The wooden public house caught fire, and men and women who'd never seen more than a heated argument raced into the street amid panicked screams. Connor and Melik ushered them past the flames and into the relative safety of the open square.

Connor found Mairead and Elizabeth and pulled them toward the door, but bodies clad in dark leathers and masks blocked the way. He shielded Mairead and Elizabeth as Melik stabbed and punched the men at the door. Connor sheathed his sword, unable to swing in the close quarters, and drew his daggers. One man broke through Melik's defense and swung with a short sword. Connor blocked the blow and brought his other hand into the man's chest. Flesh and muscle parted, and the Morrag sighed in contentment as the man bled out on the floor.

Melik defended the door. Connor coughed into his arm. "Melik, get a carriage!"

"Can't—too many!" Another man fell to his knife.

Mairead and Elizabeth were coughing. The smoke stung Connor's eyes and throat. *There has to be a back way.* He led the women toward the back of the public house and found the alley door. He held them back for a moment, listening, looking, and stepped out with caution.

Six men melted out of shadows, all of them dressed in black leathers and masks. Mairead drew her daggers from her boots. One of the men struck at her, and she stabbed him in the chest, pulled out the dagger, and cut his throat as he fell. Elizabeth drew in a sharp breath.

Connor stabbed and parried and whirled. The Morrag clawed at his soul, begging for control. *I would give you strength. I would help you.*

He resisted it. *I don't need you. Stay out of this!*

Stab, parry, slice—the men fell, one by one, four to his sword, two to Mairead's knives. He took her hand and Elizabeth's and led them to the front of the alley.

The public house was engulfed in flames. A building next to it had caught fire, and citizens had started bringing water. Connor and the women slipped away in the other direction. "Where's Melik?" Elizabeth asked, panic rising in her voice.

"Melik can care for himself." A troop of Henry's men ran past, and Connor grabbed the arm of one. "Lady Elizabeth and my ward—get them back to the palace."

Mairead turned. "Connor—no—I'm not leaving."

"Get to safety. I have to find out who did this."

"Connor—"

"Do it, Mairead." He ran back toward the fire before she could object again.

Melik stood outside the public house, daggers in hand, his black leather covered in the faint sheen of wet blood. He turned to Connor. "Are the women safe?"

"I found some of Henry's men. They're taking them back to the palace. Who did this?"

Melik picked up a shard of one of the shattered pots. He wiped the grease from it and showed it to Connor. "Seamus Allyn. This is his trademark."

Connor took the shard. "Animal fat?"

"Slave fat. He could use pitch." Faint disgust tinged his voice. Melik put a hand on Connor's arm and led him away from the crowd. "You were the target. You killed Allyn's son."

"What are you—" Connor's hands and feet went cold, and his stomach lurched. *The brothel. He was the man who raped Kenna.* "Gods. The brothel."

Melik nodded. "You made an example of Allyn's son, whether you knew his identity or not. Allyn intends to make an example of you. You need to run. If you stay in the city another day, your head is as good as rotting on a spike."

"Did he send you to do it?"

Melik shook his head. "If he had, you'd already be dead and I'd be gone and there wouldn't be a fire in the palace district. As I said, this is to be messy work—bloody and brutal. He wants to send a message."

"I can't leave Mairead—"

"As long as Allyn's alive, if she's with you, she's in danger. Allyn wants the Mac Mahons to know what happens when his blood is shed."

"Fuck."

"Indeed."

Connor threw the shard at the wall and roared in rage. *This is your doing,* he told the Morrag. He paced, hands on hips, his breathing ragged and quick with anger. *You sent me to kill, and now this is the price—Mairead.* He pounded the door of the public house and then put his forehead against it and closed his eyes. *I will never be free of you, will I?*

You will be my first. My raven.

Connor's mind raced. *I have to leave her. She has to be able to deny that she knows where I am. She's safer in the palace than with me. I have to get free of Allyn, and then she'll be safe.* He turned to Melik. "Do you know how they found out it was me? Or how they found out I was here?"

"Don't know. You aren't quiet, though. They caught some of the women who ran, and they described you fairly well. Every time you show off those obscene marks on your arm, you announce yourself."

Connor closed his eyes. "If I make a lot of noise and shed more blood, will I call him out? Will he come after me?"

"Probably. He'll only tolerate so many losses before he comes after you himself."

"You've been in his house. You've heard his plans. If I travel alone, she'll be safe?"

"If you go alone, he'll follow you."

Connor nodded. He ran to the palace, where he found Mairead with Henry and Elizabeth in the prince's study. Mairead stood and flew into his arms. "Don't do that. Don't send me away again," she whispered against his neck. "I was so worried."

"I just wanted you safe." He squeezed his eyes shut. "Mairead. I just wanted you safe." He pulled her away. "Are you all right? You and Elizabeth?"

"We're all right." She wiped her eyes. Blood splattered her sleeves and the front of her dress. "Who was it? What did they want?"

"Allyn. He's after me. Turns out I was the one who killed his son."

Henry's face paled. "You?"

"He was raping and killing women. I made sure he wouldn't do it again." He took Mairead's hand. "I need to talk to you alone."

He took her arm and led her toward her room. He tried to think of what to tell her—how he could say goodbye—but he couldn't think of anything that would make the blow easier to bear. *This is your doing,* he accused the Morrag and Alshada and his mother all at once. *All of you. Her broken heart will be on your heads.*

When they reached her room, he ushered her in and pulled her into his arms. "I'm sorry," he said.

"It was the man in the brothel, wasn't it?" she said. "The man who raped Kenna—that was Allyn's son. And now he wants you dead?"

"Yes." He closed his eyes. "Mairead, I have to go."

She pulled away from him. "Of course—we'll go right now."

He shook his head. "As long as you're with me, you're in danger."

Her voice dropped. "What are you saying?"

"I have to go. I have to leave. Now. You have to stay here, with Henry. You're too valuable to the Taurin throne and the future of this land to risk your life."

Her face paled. "Haven't I proven myself capable of keeping up with you?"

He forced a smile. "Yes. And you saved my life in more ways than one."

"Then don't leave me. I'll go wherever you go."

He took a deep breath. "Mairead, our paths don't align. We can't do this. As much as I care for you, your path leads in another direction. I'm not part of it. This threat only proves it."

She folded her arms. "What does it prove? You did what the Morrag demanded. I'm coming with you."

"No." He took her by the arms. "You have to go to Sveklant. Your destiny lies there."

Tears welled in her eyes. "Don't do this. Connor, don't do this."

"I'll speak with Henry. He'll send you to Albard in the spring with a heavy guard. I'll try to contact my mother, see if she can help guide you to the right people. But I can't be part of your life. I put you in too much danger."

Her voice broke. "Will you find me? Later?"

The ache of what he had to do welled up and competed with the Morrag for space inside him. "I can't come back. It's taking me, Mairead. The Morrag. She's been rising all day, and I can barely control her. What if the next man I kill is someone with even more power? What if someone comes back from my past when I'm settled with you in Sveklant? I can't risk your life that way."

She put her hands on his cheeks. Tears lined her face. "I don't want to lose you. I don't want to say goodbye."

"Neither do I." He pulled her into his arms.

The Morrag teased him to submit. *You can have her if you submit to me.* *This is what happens when I follow you. I won't submit to you.*

Mairead drew away and wiped her eyes. She lifted her chin. "You promised your mother you'd take me to Albard, and now you got what you wanted when the bond broke, and you're breaking your word. You promised me you'd stay here through the winter, and you're breaking your word. You told me you never broke a promise. I guess we found one binding enough, didn't we?"

It stung harder than if she'd said she hated him. *I've become an oathbreaker. I shame my father's name.* He squared his shoulders and put a hand on his sword. "You are the Taurin heir. Act like it."

An angry flush rose on her cheeks. "How dare you dictate to me what I should do or be?"

"You are the last of your line. You owe it to your country and possibly the world to marry and bear children and raise them to take back the Taurin throne."

She straightened. "Go back to your life, Connor. Your women and your money and your sword. I'm sure they'll all welcome you. But when there's no woman to warm your bed and money doesn't satisfy and your sword is just a cold piece of steel, remember what you told me this morning—that it's not enough anymore."

I won't be whole without you. "This is the way it's supposed to be."

She turned away. "You're wrong."

He couldn't think of what else to say. He reached into the pocket of his jerkin and pulled out the three bear claws that he had strung on a leather lashing. He put a hand on her shoulder, and she turned back to him. "I made this for you."

She took the claws. "Why?"

"You should have them. You should wear them to remember what you did to earn them."

She pulled a dagger out of his boot. She sliced the lashing between two claws and handed one back to him. "You should remember, too."

He took the dagger. His fingers brushed hers, and it was almost enough to make him change his mind. "You're the strongest woman I've ever met, Mairead."

"Then let me come with you."

He put a hand on her cheek and bent to kiss her. She turned her head away. He inhaled the scent of her hair. "Mairead, I can't risk you."

"Go."

He left the room. As the door closed, her sobs broke free, and only the resolute conviction that leaving would save her made him walk down the corridor.

Emrys was standing on a rooftop several buildings away when he saw the raven ride south out of the city on a gray horse, galloping as if pursued by death itself. The irony of the thought brought a rare smile to his lips.

Emrys had waited for the heir to be unprotected. He had sent thieves, slavers, Ferimin, even a bear, and nothing had worked. The raven remained steadfast and loyal to his duty.

But now—he was riding south, alive still, making enough noise that the slavers would follow and she would be safe. *Could it be this good? Could he have left her?* Though she was in the palace, there were ways to penetrate that barrier. Now that she was unprotected by their bond, it would be a simple thing to capture her.

A flash of light, and once again his mistress stood next to him. "You have finally succeeded in breaking their bond?"

"It appears that way."

She turned her cold eyes on him. "We no longer need her. There is another one of her blood, and he is unprotected on Taura."

"Another? How?"

"The father remarried and sired a son before he died. The boy is a young man now, living with his mother on a farm in Taura. He has no idea of his blood. We can let him live in ignorance until we know where the reliquary is and then use him to carry it."

"And her? What will we do?"

She turned her gaze toward the city. "Once the raven is dead, she won't matter. Alshada still has his hand upon her, though. Find a way to change her course. I don't want her showing up later when we have the boy in our control."

The sneer crossed his face. "I think I know how to get rid of her."

"Good." She paused. "I have work to do on Taura. Contact me when she is put off course."

"Yes, mistress."

She disappeared again, and Emrys slipped between the elements and found Seamus Allyn raging in his study. "You seem angry."

Seamus rounded on him, a dagger already in his grip. "Someone warned him. All I did was set a few buildings on fire." He took three quick steps toward Emrys and reached for him.

Emrys caught the slaver's fist in one hand, and the man started to choke and gasp at the touch. The swirl of transgressions around his head tempted Emrys to draw more of Allyn's soul, but he resisted. *Not yet.* He let go, and the slaver stumbled back toward his desk. "You can salvage this. He's riding south alone. He'll try to lure you away to confront him. Let him tire himself, and then fall on him and do what you will."

Seamus drew heavy breaths and reached for his oiska. He took a long drink from the skin and wiped his mouth with a shaking hand. "What about the girl?"

"Use her to set the prince against your rival."

It took a moment. He had the brutality to maintain his empire, Emrys thought, but not the intellect. As the idea dawned, a slow smile crept across his face. "Take her and make it look like Mac Mahon did it."

"You know a man named Melik?"

"Yes."

"He can be bought. He owes much money in Espara. He'll deliver her to you for the promise of a fair sum."

"How much?"

"Make up a generous number. You need never pay it. I can take care of Melik."

"All right. And the girl?"

"Keep her for yourself. She's a pretty thing, and she's young. Haven't you earned the right to have more than a ragged whore around your legs? Perhaps she could give you a son to replace the one you lost. Or, sell her. She'd fetch a good price from the Tal'Amuni."

Seamus nodded slowly. "It's as good as done."

CHAPTER TWENTY-SIX

A woman with power is a two-edged sword.
— Tribal saying

Braedan reined in at the crest of the hill above Kiern. Malcolm, the commander of the Taurin forces in Logan's absence, signaled to the drummers, and they sounded a beat to rein in the entire retinue. As the group halted, Malcolm sidled over to Braedan, his big warhorse pawing the ground in anticipation. "Sire?"

Braedan gestured. "This is why I love Taura."

The hill sloped west into the great expanse of forested tribal territory and east onto the wide pastureland and fields of northern Taura. Shaggy red and black cattle with long, twisting horns dotted the plains in small groupings. Rough fences and stone corrals carved out pastures and property lines. In the distance, the wild hills of the highlands sparkled with scant early snow. In the summer, they would be bright green and purple from the grasses and heather.

The great forest lay to the west, a solid canopy of fir that stretched as far as Braedan could see. Thousands of tribesmen called the forest home. Braedan didn't know how many tribes existed or how many people they claimed. For all he knew, there could be tribesmen hovering within the trees just thirty paces away. *It's more than likely,* he thought.

It had taken three weeks to get to Kiern. They ran into foul weather more than once, and traveling with a large retinue proved challenging. The supply wagons slowed them down. When the roads became impassable, they had to beg the hospitality of eager nobles, and he found it hard to extricate himself from their presence once they had his ear. He found the diplomacy it required tedious. He promised nothing and took his leave as soon as the men and wagons could travel.

Along with the challenges of politics and weather, Braedan had found himself missing Igraine more than he thought he would. When they camped each night, he ached from her absence. He could distract himself during the day, but at night, only Igraine would have satisfied him. Women were plentiful. Anytime the retinue stopped, it attracted a large following from the neighboring towns. He found himself uninterested. One pretty girl was especially eager to say she had been with the king, but she was a pale comparison to his lady in Torlach. It was easy to turn her down, even before he noticed the blue silk scarf and remembered the words "rutting goat."

He twisted and untwisted the silk around his hand for a long time that night and fell asleep frustrated, thoughts of Igraine filling his head. *It was too soon to be apart from her. Had I known I would have her in my bed, I would have planned to send someone else.* But he knew he couldn't. He needed to fulfill his promises to Hrogarth and the dark man, and if he proceeded carefully, he thought he could accomplish both on this trip.

He gazed down the slope of the main road. The city of Kiern sprawled across the fields in the haphazard array of many of Taura's most ancient towns. The manor house and central town had a wall, but beyond that, houses tapered off into small individual farms and cattle pastures. The city presented an easy target for conquest. He wondered if it had been so haphazard and unprotected when Mac Niall was alive.

He tightened his grip on the reins and shifted in the saddle. He had refused livery for most of the trip, but this day, knowing they would arrive in Kiern, he had dressed in his best green and gold doublet and the finest cloak he owned. He wore leather gauntlets trimmed in ermine, and his squire had polished his boots to a bright black sheen. He had fastened a formal dress sword at his side. *All to impress a man I hate.* He took a deep breath. "Let's go," he said to Malcolm. The captain signaled to the drummer, who struck up a marching beat, and the men started forward again.

Mac Rian was waiting for them on horseback with his own small guard when Braedan's men arrived at the front gates of the estate. The slight, graying man fidgeted in his saddle. He put on a practiced smile and bowed from the seat of the regal gray warhorse he sat. "Your majesty. I welcome you to our meager estates."

Braedan reined in his horse, irritated that Mac Rian's mount was finer than his own. *The man doesn't even try to humble himself.* He returned the bow with a very slight inclination of his head. "Mac Rian. I trust you have accommodations prepared?"

"Of course, majesty. My seneschal awaits your arrival in the great hall. Your men are welcome to encamp on the south field beyond the city wall." He surveyed the retinue. "I had hoped Princess Igraine would accompany you. Has she remained in Torlach?"

"She has. She is assisting my uncle and seneschal with the administration of my duties while I am here taking care of your dilemma."

Mac Rian's jaw twitched. "We heard a rumor, majesty," he said.

"Oh?"

Mac Rian nodded. "There is talk that you are negotiating with Princess Igraine's father for her hand. Is it true?"

Braedan pulled off his gloves. "The lady has given her consent for me to ask for her hand." *Let him stew on that. He'll have little hope of getting close to the throne with Olwyn if he knows I'm to wed Igraine.*

Mac Rian seemed to cringe, his face twisting for a moment before he recovered. "Well, your majesty, my daughter will be disappointed. She was much anticipating the lady's arrival, if only to hear her beautiful voice once again. But let us not tarry here in the cool air. My men will escort you to the great hall. There are stablemen waiting to take your horses."

"You won't mind if my own men escort me, will you, Mac Rian?" Braedan gestured to his personal guard.

Mac Rian's thin mouth narrowed, and his fists tightened within the leather gauntlets he wore. "Of course, majesty. But let me assure you, you are safe within our walls."

"Of course," Braedan replied. He nodded toward the buildings in the distance. "Lead the way."

In the great hall, Mac Rian's servants seated Braedan and his men and offered wine, mead, and food. Mac Rian's thin smirk revealed his satisfaction with the hospitality offered by his estate. Braedan found it lacking. He didn't expect the castle at Torlach, but the lords who had given him lodging at the last minute had been better prepared for his arrival than this petty duke. Braedan wondered how much of the duchy's wealth he had squandered.

As the guards sat at the long table to drink and eat a light meal, Mac Rian gestured to the chairs near the hearth for himself and Braedan. They both sat, and Mac Rian swirled his wine in a silver goblet and held it up to Braedan. "I welcome you again, your majesty. To a long and peaceful reign."

Braedan raised his own goblet, but he didn't drink until he saw Mac Rian drink. The wine's aroma had a bitter cast, and Braedan detected a faint vinegar flavor. *I had better wine in exile.* He set his cup down next to him on the hearth. "Tell me the latest with the tribes."

Mac Rian drank again, but before he could answer, they were interrupted by Mac Rian's seneschal, an older man who shuffled into the room with a gait born of grudging obligation. He cleared his throat. "The lady Olwyn wishes to greet the king."

Mac Rian nodded. "Of course, Lewis. Send her in." Lewis bowed as Mac Rian turned to Braedan. "Forgive me, sire, but my daughter has spoken of nothing but her time in your court since we left. She wishes to greet you."

"I would be delighted to see your daughter once again."

Mac Rian gave him a thin smile. "I fear I've been too indulgent with Olwyn, but then, she has suffered so for such a young woman. My wife died of a wasting illness several years ago. She was always a frail woman. Giving birth to our Olwyn taxed her body near to death's door. Olwyn has turned into a gracious young woman despite my best efforts to the contrary." They both turned their heads and stood as the door opened again. "And here is the lady herself to prove me right."

As much as Braedan adored his fiery Eiryan princess, Olwyn took his breath away. Raven-haired and lithe, Olwyn walked with a smooth, gliding gait, and she wore dark blue and silver that clung to her body as a second skin. Dark skin and dark eyes gave her an exotic appeal. He wondered whose secrets hovered behind that mouth. *Keep to yourself. This one would take all of your secrets, gore you with them, and make you thankful for it.* He bowed. "Lady Olwyn. How lovely to see you again."

Olwyn rose from a deep curtsy, and Braedan took her hand to kiss it. "You grace our home, your majesty." Her voice had a low, even tone. She addressed him eye to eye. "Your Eiryan lady didn't accompany you?"

Braedan shook his head. "Someone had to stay in Torlach to administer my affairs. The lady Igraine is assisting my lord uncle and my seneschal to ensure that our kingdom doesn't fall to pieces while I am here."

She affected a sad tone. "Ah, majesty, I am disappointed." She offered him a seductive smile. "I hope I can fill some small part of her role for you while you are in our home."

Be careful. He smiled at her. "I appreciate your consideration, but no one could replace my princess."

She turned to her father. "I've checked with the kitchen. All is prepared for the feast tonight."

"Feast?" Braedan turned to Mac Rian. "This wasn't an excuse for a celebration."

Mac Rian bowed. "We wished to welcome you properly. And, as I mentioned, we had hoped the lady would accompany you so that we might show her northern hospitality."

You'll be glad you didn't catch the sharp side of her tongue. Braedan wished again that Igraine had joined him. As vexing as she could be, it would have been fun to watch her spar with Mac Rian. *And it would have been entertaining to flaunt our affections in front of Olwyn. Igraine would have given her much to think about and enjoyed every moment of the game.* "Keep it to a minimum, will you?" he said, giving his voice a purposeful edge. "I'm here to help you with the tribes. I have duties in Torlach, and I have no wish to end up wintering in the north because you wish to carouse with the crown."

Mac Rian inclined his head. "As you wish, sire."

Braedan turned back to Olwyn and bowed. "My lady Olwyn, if we are to feast tonight, I fear you'll have to excuse your father and me. We have much to discuss."

She curtsied again. "Of course, my lords. I will await your pleasure elsewhere." She left the room with fluid grace, attracting the eye of several Taurin guards. Malcolm rose and followed her from the room.

"Your daughter is a rare beauty," Braedan said to Mac Rian.

Mac Rian gestured to their chairs. "I do thank you, majesty. I believe that when she heard of your ascension, she had hoped to win your affections."

I'm sure she did. "You were about to tell me about the tribes."

"Yes." Mac Rian drank. Braedan had the impression that it was an act designed to make him appear thoughtful. In truth, he was certain Mac Rian had known what he wanted to say since he left Torlach a month ago. "The tribes. I fear that the difficulties with the tribes have increased since I left Torlach. We have skirmishes every few days now. They continue to encroach on the main road, preventing my men from coming and going, and have even gone so far as to attack a merchant wagon two weeks ago. My men were able to save the man and his goods, but I've had to insist that all traders take the eastern road. They aren't happy, but it's a choice of dealing with tribesmen on the main road or thieves on the eastern road."

It's not as simple as all that, Braedan thought. Before he left Torlach, Braedan sent three of his best men north to gather information on Mac Rian and the tribes in preparation for his arrival. Two days before arriving in Kiern, he had met with one of the guards, and he now knew that Hrogarth's words were true: Mac Rian had been sending men into the great forest. According to the guard, the tribesmen teased Mac Rian's men, leading them into traps, down dead ends, and in circles throughout the forest. "They play cat and mouse with the Taurins," the man said. "It amuses them. They've even seen me—you can't hide from a tribesman—and they just let me watch it all."

What is he after? Is he looking for the Sidh too? Braedan swirled his wine. "I'm curious. Why is it that your predecessor's family lived here for generations and amassed great wealth and never had trouble with the tribes? What has changed so much in less than a decade?"

"I do not know, majesty. Of course, Mac Niall was in league with dark forces. His paramour was a sorceress. Perhaps he was in league with the tribes as well."

Braedan cut him off with a sharp gesture. "Rumor and gossip. I've no wish to recount all of that. I just want to know what you've done that has angered the tribes so much."

"I swear to you. I have done nothing to bring this on."

Braedan set down his goblet and stood. Mac Rian followed suit. "I'd like to see your grounds, if you don't mind."

"Of course, majesty. I'll accompany you," Mac Rian said.

Braedan held up a hand. "No need. My guards will join me." He inclined his head. "See that my rooms are prepared. I won't be long. If we'll be feasting tonight, I'll need to wash off the dust and mud of the road. I'd like a bath prepared when I return."

He found the tightening of Mac Rian's mouth rewarding. The man didn't appreciate being treated as a servant. He bowed. "Of course, your majesty. Lewis will see to it."

Malcolm waited outside the doors of the hall and fell in step next to the king. As they walked into the cool afternoon air, Braedan spoke in low tones. "Mac Rian is lying to me. He's brought this on himself. I need to find out what he's after. I need evidence, not just hearsay. Eavesdropping won't be enough."

"Yes, majesty. I'll see what I can find out."

"Did you speak with the lady Olwyn when you left the hall?"

Malcolm nodded. "She was happy to speak with the king's guard. She assured me that your quarters would be prepared to your liking, and she was very insistent on finding out what your liking was."

Braedan nodded. "It was clear that Olwyn would like to have the ear of the crown."

"More than just an ear, from the questions she asked."

Braedan smirked.

"Don't trust her, majesty. That one has her eyes set higher than you know," Malcolm said.

"What do you mean?"

"Logan was right. Olwyn wants a crown. I fear for the lady Igraine. Olwyn asked a lot of questions about her, and after the attempt on her life . . ." He shrugged.

"That was just one mad guard's obsession."

"Was it?"

Braedan's mouth tightened. "What did you tell Olwyn?"

"I told her that you and the lady have great affection for each other, and she seemed disappointed. She asked about your wedding plans. I didn't know what to say. I told her that you were still negotiating with the Eiryan crown, and that such things take time with the autumn rains and the sea weather getting rougher." He frowned. "She wants a crown, but I think she'd be nearly as happy if you took her back to Torlach to serve Lady Igraine. I think she would make herself available to serve you whenever you wished. If something happened to befall the lady Igraine, why, she would be right there to comfort you."

Braedan grunted. "I'm sure she would."

They walked through the gates and past the scattered houses to the west of the estate, stopping when they reached the main road. Both men stared into the trees, hands on the hilts of their swords. "I can feel their eyes on me," Malcolm said. "How can they be so well-hidden so close to the road?"

Braedan didn't answer. Even the most elite Taurin soldiers or his own personal guards would be hard-pressed to hide so close to a major road. But Malcolm was right—eyes hovered on them. *Predators slavering over a full table,* Braedan thought. He suppressed a shudder, but he wanted them all to see him. They should know the king had arrived in Kiern. "Come on. Mac Rian will be expecting us for his feast."

The king's men certainly make more than their share of noise, Maeve thought. She rubbed her neck and stretched her shoulders in a futile attempt to relieve the tension carried by the Sidh. What had started as a mere twitch of discomfort weeks before had grown nearly unbearable in recent days. *First Mac Rian intrudes on the forest, and now the king. Will we ever know peace again?* She knuckled her back and sat down to evening tea.

Shouts and curses rang through the air, and Maeve flinched and rubbed her temples. *Gods, not more trouble.* The strain of so many Taurins near the village put all of the Sidh on edge, and the normally peace-loving people had fallen more and more to fighting among themselves. "Go see what it's about, will you, Evie?"

But when Evie opened the door, Maeve stood and sucked in a breath at the sight of the slim, well-muscled, graying tribesman before her. He stepped into her hut and spoke in his low rumbling voice. "Maeve. It's time to talk."

Before he could react, Maeve summoned the air and wove it into violet braids as strong as steel. She wrapped the braids around him. He shot her a self-assured grin, and she tightened the braids. "You are not welcome here, Edgar."

"So I was told when the earth guardian I brought revealed the village. I regret I had to hurt a few of your people to get your attention. They didn't want to let me through."

"They have been told not to allow any tribesmen access to the village."

"That might mean something if they were willing to fight."

She turned to Evie. "I'll be fine. Go see to those who are injured. Make sure the healers can take care of everyone." Evie curtsied and left.

Maeve tightened the braids around Edgar again. He grunted, but his eyes twinkled and his grin widened. "Something funny?"

"I was just picturing another time when a fierce young Brae Sidh queen decided that she'd had enough of hunters near her village."

The memory softened her anger. "You and Culain were taken a bit off-guard, weren't you?"

He grinned with a wicked edge. "There is nothing more comely than a woman with the kind of power you have."

"Don't try to charm me, Edgar."

"I'm not. I envied him. I still do."

A smile threatened the corners of her mouth as she remembered the day. "You were cocky beasts—him sputtering about his nobility and connections and you grinning because you knew exactly where you'd chased that stag. What were you thinking?"

"I was thinking I wanted to meet the woman whose beauty I'd heard so much about. Can you let me go now so we can talk like civilized people?" He sensed the retort that hovered on her lips, and he stopped her. "Or at least, like people who have a common enemy?"

She sighed. She let the magic retreat, and he let out a long breath. She didn't realize how tight the braids had been until he rubbed his wrists and forearms. "I'm sorry."

"You bested me fairly."

"The years have been kind to you," she said. *More than kind.* They had been good friends once, thirty years before. She had met Edgar and Culain when they had chased a stag into Sidh territory. Culain was in his late thirties, married, with a family and a duchy to run, and Edgar was in his twenties, a man brimming with confidence and self-assured bravado. Only two years later, Edgar found himself burdened with caring for an entire tribe when the previous traitha died on the hunt. The earthspirit selected the traithas, and though older, wiser men also entered the vision hut with Edgar, the earth had branded Edgar chieftain by the time they all emerged the next day.

The echoes of that young boy still hovered on Edgar's face beneath the snaking blue lines of his brand. He still brimmed with confidence, but it was wiser—mellowed with age. His face was still handsome, the grace of his bone structure smoothing the edges of age that encroached. She still found his dark green eyes bewitching with their long lashes and mischievous twinkle. He wore a leather jerkin and breeches. Both arms were covered with the tattoos of the many hunts he'd been on, and she wondered if he'd started tattooing his legs yet. His braids were still dark with occasional gray streaks. She found herself reminded of Culain. A pang of loss went through her. In Connor's absence, Edgar was the one link she had to Culain. *This is the man I might have chosen once. How could I have let so many years go by?*

Edgar appraised her with a gentle, appreciative gaze. "You are the same as you were thirty years ago. Time stays his hand for you. Even he respects your beauty."

Despite her bitterness, Maeve's stomach lurched at his flattery. *I won't be demure before this man.* "You still have the eyes of a wolf and the tongue of a bard."

He stepped closer to her. "Maeve, I should have been more insistent about watching over you when Culain died. After we fought, I was hurt. I shouldn't have let it stop me. I should have been here. He was a brother to me."

"I wouldn't have seen you. I was so angry. I still am. I am struggling with this—with forgiving you for taking Connor."

"I didn't take him. He wanted to be a tribesman."

"You and Culain didn't have to make it all so appealing."

His tone matched hers, steel for steel. "Did you never forgive Culain, either? He gave his blessing."

I tried. "Connor rejected everything about the Sidh once he tasted the life of the warrior. He didn't want to use his talent. He drank the blood of the animal. He refused to even consider a Sidh girl—"

"He wouldn't look at a tribal girl either—not for more than a night—if that's any consolation."

"It's not."

Edgar folded his arms. "Maeve, Connor sought the tribal path, but he has a calling. His purpose is bigger than either of us know. There's something he's meant to do or be, and we couldn't stop it if we tried. His Sidh blood and the tribal training are both part of that calling." She started to respond, but he held up a hand. "Culain couldn't have stopped it either, but he wouldn't have tried."

Anger dissipated at the thought of Culain, and she lowered her voice. "I know. He was a good father. When I let him be."

Edgar took a deep breath. "Where is Connor? He didn't make it back for the hunt this year."

"I thought he didn't hunt with you."

"He doesn't, but I always hear his name. He's the best hunter in the nine tribes. Everyone talks about him no matter which tribe has the honor of hosting him."

Despite her distaste for the hunt, maternal pride swelled in Maeve's chest. *Culain would have been proud, too.* "He is on an errand for me. The heir is gone. He is taking her to safety."

Edgar smirked. "Are you sure you trust him with that? She needs to remain chaste, doesn't she? He's not a wolf for nothing."

Oh, believe me, I know more about Connor's indiscretions than I'd care to admit. "Connor knows that if he abuses her he'll have me to answer to, and I am the only person he still fears."

"Is he still bound to you?"

She hesitated. The truth of it struck her as she considered how to answer. *If I tell him no, he'll think I let Connor go, and it will soften his heart toward me. And it's not a lie. But if I tell him the whole truth, he'll know that the ravenmark is taking Connor.* She closed her eyes. "No. He broke the bond." She pursed her lips. "The Morrag called him. He answered."

Edgar took a step toward her, and she opened her eyes. He reached out with one hand. "Maeve—"

She stepped back. "Don't. I won't have you prowling around me like a desperate cat."

"What if I were prowling? I'm still unattached. So are you." He unlaced his jerkin and pulled the left shoulder aside, revealing the unfinished marriage tattoo. He pulled the shoulder back up, but left the jerkin unlaced. "You interested? I'd hate to mar that perfect Sidh skin with a tattoo. We wouldn't have to make it permanent."

She put her hands on her hips. "I can see where my son learned all of his bad habits. Why are you here?"

He grew serious. "Mac Rian is in the forest. We've been holding his men at bay for weeks now, but today the unbeliever king arrived in Kiern with a retinue that could storm the forest and give us a real battle. And I think Mac Rian has more men than he's revealed as well. He's too confident. I came to ask for your help. If we work together, we can send these fools running and rid the world of Mac Rian's poison." He paused. "They'll try to get an earth guardian who can reveal your village. They think if they reveal the Sidh village, they can get the reliquary. They're counting on our hatred of each other to ensure that a guardian will do their bidding."

Olwyn controls her father. She wants it. What is that woman? "But the heir is gone. How would they carry it? Only one of Brenna and Aiden's line can even touch it."

He shrugged. "Perhaps they want to reveal it and guard it until they find a way to carry it. It doesn't matter, does it? Your home is still in danger whether they can accomplish what they want or not."

She thought carefully before she responded. *It's time to let the anger go.* "If I do this, this is not a new alliance. This is not peace or forgiveness between our people. I will not pursue a formal treaty with anyone but Hrogarth."

A muscle twitched in Edgar's jaw. "Then what is it?"

"It's two old friends protecting their homes. Two leaders protecting their villages."

"Mac Rian killed Culain. I want him gone."

"I want to taste vengeance, too. I have no love for Mac Rian. But, I will not risk my people more than necessary. With the king here, I will be cautious. I don't want him to know any more about us than he already does."

"Then we'll do this? We'll get rid of Mac Rian and give the Mac Corin whelp a good drubbing?"

Maeve took a deep breath. "What do you have in mind?"

CHAPTER TWENTY-SEVEN

The Forbidden then joined the field of battle, and the Syrafi could not stand against them. Cuhail and his ravenmarked warriors heard the call of the earth, and they answered it.
— Legend of the Syrafi

Minerva folded her hands in her lap and pursed her lips. Edgar sat across the fire from her, his legs crossed, his hands folded in imitation of hers. The earth guardian called Nedra stirred the fire into life again and settled on her knees, the brand across her face snaking and twisting in the faint light. "This is no small request," Nedra said. "She is an outlander and an oathbreaker. And she's part Sidh. If they realize—"

"They won't," Edgar said. He pulled a small murky stone from the pocket of his jerkin and gave it to Minerva. "The Sidh queen offers this animstone to shield your Sidh talent. Should you choose to do this, that is. It won't shield the power of the guardian."

Minerva took the stone and turned it over and over in her palm. The light of her wisdommark shone through the gray and lent it a faint blue hue. "If Braedan finds out I was a saya, he will kill me," she whispered.

"That is possible," Edgar said. "And I will not force you to do this. It is your choice."

"Let me do it," Nedra said. She gave Edgar a feral grin. "I'll take a few of the thief's men to the grave before they take me."

"You're too valuable to the village," Edgar said. "And your power can reveal the Sidh. Minerva's power isn't strong enough, but it might be enough to fool Mac Rian and the king." He watched Minerva and waited.

Minerva shifted her gaze from Edgar to Nedra and back to the stone on her palm. The weeks with the wolf tribe had been more tolerable than she expected. As the head earth guardian in the tribe, Nedra gave Minerva the privilege of serving the earth guardians as an apprentice—a position usually reserved for young girls who wanted to become guardians. Minerva went about her duties silently, busy and grateful to be alive. Still, guilt nagged at her. *I forsake my vows again*, she thought daily. *Alshada, forgive me. Forgive me for serving the earthspirit again. I will return to the kirok as soon as I can. This was the safest place.* Her palm itched and burned almost constantly, and at night, she sometimes cried silently into her sleeping mat in Nedra's tent. Nedra never mentioned whether she heard or not.

Now, Edgar sat before her, waiting. *I don't have to do this. I don't have to face this king, this duke. I can quietly wait out the winter here and then go to Lord Dylan's estate.* She scratched her palm and cringed. *If I were to die doing this, it would free me from this magic—from the pull of the earthspirit. And perhaps this is why Alshada brought me here—to give me freedom from pain through sacrifice. If I help the Sidh and protect the relics by doing this, it will be worth it to die.*

She closed her hand around the animstone. "Tell me what to do."

Braedan found cleansing comfort in the autumn chill that filled his room after the feast. The flattering and fawning of eager nobles and merchants made him feel sullied, and he now lay on his bed undressed, covered from the waist down with a thin linen sheet.

The feast had been less than he expected, but more than he wanted. Mac Rian had invited anyone with any kind of money or position in the town to meet him. He'd managed to excuse himself early in the evening, and the others dispersed soon afterward. They had come to meet the new king. No one wished to share Mac Rian's company any longer than necessary. He could be gracious and courtly, but if someone said something he didn't care for, he grew brooding, waspish, and unreasonable.

The door creaked open, and he reached under his pillow for the sacred dagger Hrogarth had given him. He had thought at the last minute that the sacred blade might be useful in treating with the tribes and had slipped it into his belongings almost as an afterthought, but there was something comforting about holding the bone hilt. His grip tightened on it. "Yes?"

"Sire." Malcolm's voice greeted him from the bedchamber door. "Lady Olwyn begs a word."

Braedan stood and pulled on breeches. "Send her in."

Olwyn entered without Malcolm and shut the door behind her. The moonlight streaming in through oiled-skin window coverings illuminated her dark features. "Majesty. I thought perhaps you might like some company in the absence of your foreign princess."

"Company," he said, unhappy to hear his own voice hoarse with desire. "That's the sort of thing that happens over afternoon tea, my lady."

She gave him a tilted, exotic smile and approached him. One elegant hand traced his chest and belly and hooked the top of his breeches. "What would you prefer to call it?"

You promised Igraine. This woman can please you for a night, but you promised faithfulness. And this woman is no Igraine. He put his hands on Olwyn's arms. He couldn't decide whether to push her away or pull her closer. "I'd call it an ambitious woman who sees a crown on her head trying to seduce her king."

"Your princess is ambitious, too." She put her mouth against his neck, raising gooseflesh. "I merely use different means to power. More pleasant means, I believe." Her hand loosened his breeches.

He turned his head and saw the blue scarf on the table next to the bed. He pushed her away. "I'm sorry, Olwyn. I am faithful to Igraine." He stepped back. "Unless you had something else to discuss, you should go."

"Majesty," she said, an air of gentle chiding in her voice. "If you have not yet wed your princess, what harm is there?" She tipped her head. "Does your princess please you?"

"Igraine pleases me in more ways than you could imagine."

"I doubt that." She closed the gap between them and put her arms around him, pressing herself up against him. "Your princess need never know."

He pulled her hands off him and pushed her arms down to her sides. "I think you should go, Olwyn." He opened the door for her.

She paused next to him before walking through the door. "This is not over," she whispered against his ear.

He grabbed her arm. "Do you threaten your king, my lady?"

Her mouth curved in a languid smile. "You misunderstand, majesty. I would never threaten my king." She tipped her head in the smallest nod proper and walked past Malcolm with her head held high.

Braedan waited until she was out of earshot to motion Malcolm into his room. He shut the door. "Have you found out anything more about her?"

Malcolm shook his head. "The servants are either bewitched by her or afraid of her. I haven't had time to go into the town yet, but perhaps someone there will say something." He nodded toward the bed. "The princess will appreciate your devotion."

Braedan turned away. "You can go." He picked up the blue silk and lay down in his bed. *I'll marry her the moment I'm back if she'll let me—alliance or no.*

In the morning, Braedan woke from a fitful sleep and dressed in simple breeches and tunic. He pulled on his boots and splashed cold water on his face, then strapped on his sword and slipped the dagger that Hrogarth had given him into his belt. He took a deep breath and strode to the door.

Malcolm bowed. "Sire."

Braedan noted the lines under Malcolm's eyes. "Did you sleep?"

"A few hours. I just relieved Ewan a short time ago."

"Do you know where Mac Rian is this morning?"

"He's waiting for you in his study."

Malcolm led him through the long corridors of the estate to a small room at the far end of the house where Mac Rian waited near a table laden with food. He greeted Braedan with a smooth bow. "Your majesty. I thought we could break our fast while we discuss the problem of the tribes."

Braedan sat. "An excellent suggestion." *The sooner we can get this over with, the sooner I can go home.* A servant poured mead for Braedan and portioned food onto a trencher. "I don't want mead. Bring water," Braedan said.

"I was pleased to see how many men you brought with you, sire," Mac Rian said. "We should be able to dispatch the problem with ease."

Braedan leaned forward. "Is that what you thought—that I came to slaughter some tribesmen for you? I have no intention of drawing the tribes into a battle unless I must. I don't intend to lose my men in the forest because you refuse to obey the treaty."

Mac Rian's face paled. "What do you mean, majesty?"

"I know you have violated the ancient treaty between Taura and the tribes," Braedan said. "I just don't know why. If you have a good reason, please tell me. I will defend you as your liege lord if the cause is just. But Mac Rian, if you are making trouble or seeking something that isn't yours, tell me now. I will not humiliate myself or the crown before the tribes."

The man's face was ashen, and his hands shook. "Seeking something? I don't know what you mean."

He's dug himself into a hole that he wasn't prepared to be in. "Who are you in league with, Mac Rian?"

"I am in league with no one other than my king."

Braedan opened his mouth, but a breathless servant burst into the room. "Majesty, my lord, you're needed right away."

Both men stood and followed the young man to the great hall. Two of Mac Rian's men stood in the hall holding a woman between them. She was dressed in furs and leather; one cheek bore a fresh bruise, and blood dripped from a cut on one arm. Her hands were bound behind her back. She stood still and calm, her head bowed in demure acceptance of her captivity.

Mac Rian stepped toward the woman. "Who are you? Why did you venture across the road?"

She lifted her head, and when she saw Braedan, she flinched. She seemed to force herself to straighten. "I didn't. Your men found me performing an earth ritual in the forest. They brought me here."

Mac Rian's eyes glowed with excitement. "Is she an earth guardian?"

One of his men nodded and turned her around. He forced open her right hand. Braedan saw a brand in the shape of a circle with a cross through it. Faint silver light glowed under the mark. "We found her performing an earth ritual on this side of the great road."

Mac Rian stepped closer to her as his men turned her back around. "What were you doing? Cursing my estates?"

"I cursed nothing."

Braedan frowned. *This isn't right. This isn't the kind of woman I'd expect in the tribes. This woman fears me—I saw it on her face—and she seems to have already accepted defeat.*

Mac Rian motioned to his men. "Take her to the prison. Chain her and put a heavy guard around her." He turned to Braedan. "I trust, sire, that we can use some of your men to guard her as well?"

"You don't speak for me, Mac Rian. And you won't order my men," Braedan said.

Mac Rian stared at him, his lips tight. Malcolm and another guard flanked Braedan. "Do you see? The wolf tribe has nothing but hatred for me. They wish to ruin my holdings, and now they are even sending their earth guardians across the road to curse me with their magic."

Braedan folded his arms. "I saw a woman kidnapped from the forest where she was doing what is her right to do on her land. You're a fool, Mac Rian. Don't you see what they've done? They put one of their women out for you to capture to draw you into a fight. Do you really think you would hold her if she didn't want to be held? She could have escaped your men in the forest. She was bait. They will thrash you and send you back here limping, if you're lucky. If you're not, they will kill you."

A muscle twitched in Mac Rian's jaw. "This is an act of aggression against my holdings. I am within my rights to defend myself. I will ready my men to attack the wolf tribe at dawn tomorrow. If you care to join us, your majesty, we will welcome you."

He can't see past whatever bargain he's made. "Before I commit to anything, I will speak with the woman alone. Leave us."

A shocked silence pressed in on them. Mac Rian's lips had gone nearly white. He finally bowed. "As you wish, sire." He motioned his men from the hall.

Malcolm stepped forward to take hold of the guardian, but Braedan motioned him away. "If I make him leave, will you speak with me peaceably?" he asked the woman.

She gave him a slow nod. "Yes, your majesty." She flinched again.

She calls me majesty. She's not tribal, and she knows she made a mistake. "Leave us," Braedan told his guards. Malcolm hesitated. "I'll be fine, Malcolm. She has promised a peaceful conversation. The tribes do not break faith." He dropped his voice. "You can keep Mac Rian's men away from the door, though. I'd rather he not hear any of this." Malcolm nodded and left the room, closing the heavy oak door behind him.

"You know something of the tribes?" the woman asked.

"Just a bit." He gestured to her hands. "If you wish, I will remove the ropes."

She eyed him, still distrustful.

"You promised me a peaceful conversation. I have no reason to doubt you."

She turned and offered her hands. He drew his dagger and sliced through the ropes. She motioned to the dagger when he stepped back. "You have a sacred blade."

"Hrogarth gave it to me. What is your name?"

"Esma."

"And you are an earth guardian?"

She swallowed hard. "I-I am."

"Were you on this side of the boundary?"

"No. I was in the forest, in a sacred grove, and Mac Rian's men surprised me. They brought me back here."

Braedan put the dagger back in his belt. "What were you doing?"

"I was performing a sacrifice that is required of us. It is a sacred ritual."

He stepped closer to her. She tensed. He dropped his voice. "What does Mac Rian want?"

She hesitated, her eyes steady on his.

"You must know. You were left there, weren't you? You baited Mac Rian's men. Why?"

"He seeks the Brae Sidh. He wants an earth guardian to reveal the Brae Sidh village."

That bastard. His belly clenched. *He's after the same thing I am.* "Is he working with someone else? Do you know?"

"I don't know. I only know what we have heard his men say as they've trampled through our holy places."

"Do you know why he seeks the Sidh?"

"For a treasure he cannot touch or use. It's a fool's quest. Our prophecies say that a god must wield it and a man with the blood of Aiden and Brenna must carry it. I don't know why he seeks it." She paused. "I don't know why you seek it, either."

His heartbeat quickened, and he fought to maintain composure and resolve. "I don't know what—"

"You seek Cuhail's Reliquary, but you must know—it holds only death for you. Abandon your search and return to Torlach. You are not the rightful heir, but if you return now, before you do more damage to Taura, you might yet be a good king."

The rightful heir. Pieces clicked into place. *This is why the dark man said he would find the heir. He never said he would kill her. He believes she exists, and he wants her to carry this reliquary for him.* He shuddered. *I destroyed the sayada and imprisoned servants of the kirok for him—for a promise of help in gaining my throne. I am no better than he.* "What is this reliquary?"

"It is the key to healing the earth. It holds the relics of sacrifice from the great battle between Alshada and Namha—Cuhail's sword, the tears of the Syrafi chieftain, and the animstone of the first Brae Sidh queen. In the wrong hands, it is chaos and death."

Gods. I thought it was a fool's quest. I thought I'd never find it. I thought I could make a show of looking for it and eventually he'd give up. "Who would want this reliquary?"

"The Forbidden," she said. "The creatures who live off human transgressions. If they control the relics, they can release Namha and enslave all humanity." She tsked. "How does a man become king of Taura without knowing these things? These are all written in the kirok scriptures and the tribal wisdom books."

He crossed his arms and turned away. *I'm no better than my father. I've betrayed the tribes for ambition and greed. I've put the very existence of the Sidh at risk. And if this woman is right, I've put my country, my people, even the world in danger. All for a throne.* "Esma, I have to leave you here, but I'll get you out. And I will leave my own men to guard you to ensure that the Mac Rian men don't abuse you. Will you promise me you will stay here? Don't try to escape?"

"Because you carry Hrogarth's blade, I will trust you."

He went to the door. "I'll return as soon as I can."

Malcolm waited outside. Braedan drew him aside. "I want my own guards on her door. No one goes in or out of there without my permission, and we'll feed her with food from our stores. Nothing of Mac Rian's goes in there."

Malcolm nodded. "Yes, sire."

"Mac Rian intends to go to battle with the wolf tribe tomorrow. I need to know before then what happened here six years ago."

"Why?"

"Because if I'm going to abandon one of my nobles, I need a fucking good reason. Treason, preferably. Gather the guards and captains, and all of you see what you can find out. I'll meet you in the camp later."

"Where are you going?"

"Hand me your cloak." Malcolm removed it, and Braedan threw it over his shoulders and pulled the hood up. "I need to disappear for a while."

"Majesty, I don't think that's wise."

"I'll be fine. I'll go by the guard tent and get something else to wear, and I'll send Ewan over to relieve you. You can relay my instructions. Where did Mac Rian go?"

"I strongly suggested he and his men might want to wait for you elsewhere."

Braedan nodded. "If I'm not back by the evening meal, come looking for me in the forest. Bring her with you."

Malcolm frowned. "I don't like this."

"Trust me."

Braedan dressed in common peasant clothes and wove through Kiern to the woods on the north edge of town, hiding in alleys and behind houses to avoid Mac Rian's men. He found a quiet copse of trees far from prying eyes and curious ears and lowered his hood. "I know you're here," he called. He drew Hrogarth's dagger from his belt. "I know you're watching this. I need to talk to you."

Birds erupted from the trees in a sudden rush, flapping and fluttering in panicked flight. The brush at his feet rustled as some small creature dove away from the clearing. Not even a beetle stirred. *As if a mountain cat approaches,* Braedan thought. The hair stood up on his arms.

"You have an earth guardian. What are you waiting for?"

Braedan startled and whirled around. The man stood in a shadow, his hood drawn up to hide his face and his arms crossed before him. "You lied to me. You betrayed me to Mac Rian. You set him to the same task. Why?"

"I need the reliquary."

"You need a bunch of molding artifacts from two thousand years ago?" Braedan shook his head. "I can't see what power they could give you."

The man's face betrayed no emotion. "You owe me. You don't need to know why I want them. I helped your men into Torlach, and I told you where the heir was hiding. You need only repay me."

"Or what?"

"Or it will cost you your life."

A chill ran through Braedan. "Have you found the heir yet?"

He didn't miss the flicker of irritation that crossed the man's face. "That is none of your concern."

"It is my concern. If there is an heir to the Taurin throne, she is a threat to me. It's my right to know where she is."

A muscle twitched in the man's jaw. "I have not succeeded in capturing her yet, no. But I know where she is."

Fury rose in Braedan's chest. "And when you find her, you plan to use her to carry this reliquary for you—to get this power for you so that you can unseat me?" The man said nothing. "Damn you."

The man sneered. "The status of my soul has never been in question. I will have the reliquary. Whether you find it or someone else finds it is no concern of mine."

"I'm done with you. You broke our agreement. This is a fool's quest, and I will not pursue it."

The man lunged at him and knocked the dagger from his hand. Skin met skin, and the man held his wrist in a fierce grip. Braedan's throat constricted, and the air around him thinned to nothing. The pain drove him to his knees. Visions of evil things he'd done hovered around him—a girl he'd threatened into bed, a man he'd falsely accused of theft, drunken moments he couldn't remember. Over them all, Daron, his head on the Noble Gate, convicting Braedan of murder. *I shouldn't have ordered it done. I should have exiled him.*

The man's mouth curved with casual, detached amusement. "I will not kill you today. But if you break faith with me, I will come back. Your soul is lost, princeling. Your body is just a matter of time. And if you want a noblewoman in your bed, take Olwyn. Your father enjoyed the pleasures of her body. She knows how to please a man, I assure you. Take her, and your descendants will rule in Taura for generations."

He released his hand, and Braedan gasped as air, welcome and sweet, rushed to fill his lungs. He collapsed onto his side. "I'm . . . done . . . . No . . . more . . . ."

"You've made your choice." He disappeared in a flash of light.

Braedan rolled onto his back, grateful for the autumn air. *Igraine. He'll go after her.* But no—he once said she had powerful protection. *But what could protect her from him?*

He needed help. He stood on unsteady legs and set out at an easy walk on the north side of Kiern, gaining strength with each step. He would go around the city to the forest. He needed to find the traitha of the wolf tribe. He needed to know the relics were safe, and he needed the tribe's help. Mac Rian had to go.

Finding the wolf tribe wasn't difficult. In fact, they found Braedan the moment he stepped into the trees. He heard the rustle of brush moments before someone tackled him, and then rough hands hauled him to his feet. The next thing he knew, a massive, leather-clad tribesman had bound him to a tree.

The ropes cut into Braedan's arms and legs, tightening every time he moved, and he grunted as one of the wolf tribe's warriors pulled tighter. "I'm not going anywhere," he said. "I sought you, remember?"

The man sneered. "Our traitha gave orders: any Taurin in the forest is to be captured and executed. I assume he meant pretender kings, too."

Braedan's mouth twisted. "Fetch your traitha. I would speak with him."

"He's here."

Braedan turned. A lithe, graying tribesman stepped out of the trees, arms folded. The blue lines over his face were similar to Hrogarth's, but Braedan thought this man's seemed more graceful, more subtle. *He could still kill me without breaking a sweat.* He bowed his head as low as the ropes would allow. "Traitha, I beg an audience with you."

The man spat. "Your friend has one of our women. Why should I waste my time listening to you?"

Braedan kept his head low. "I've spoken with your earth guardian. I want to treat with you."

"Speak."

Braedan straightened, working stiffness from his jaw. "They say the enemy of my enemy is my friend, but I wouldn't presume that much on you. Not yet."

The traitha frowned and grunted. "You and Mac Rian are enemies?"

"Can we speak privately?"

The man signaled to the warriors, and they melted into the surrounding forest. He stepped closer to Braedan. "Say what you have to say."

Braedan wet his lips. "You know I seek the same thing Mac Rian seeks. Help me rid Taura of Mac Rian, and I'll abandon my search."

He tilted his head. "How can I know you won't break faith with me? How do I know you won't just lure us into something and take what doesn't belong to you?"

Braedan nodded toward his weapons. "Look. I carry a blade given to me by Traitha Hrogarth."

The traitha crouched to pick up the blade. He frowned. "Hrogarth gave you this blade?"

"Yes, along with the promise of a tribal spear in Taura's heart if I didn't get all Taurins out of the forest."

He straightened and pressed the point of the blade to Braedan's neck. "I could rid Taura of all its problems right now."

Braedan's heart raced, but he fought the urge to turn his head away from the knife. He stared the traitha in the eye. "Do it, then."

The tribesman stood very still, the blade steady against Braedan's neck. For a moment, Braedan expected to feel a warm rush of blood drain from his body, and he resolved not to scream.

The tribesman lowered the blade and sliced through the ropes. He stepped back as Braedan stepped away from the tree. "I could ask you to pick up your sword now. I could insist that we fight to the death."

"You could, but it would be a death sentence for your earth guardian. My men have been told to kill her if I am not back by sunset." *Lies on top of lies. At least that one was for a good purpose.* He paused, rubbing his wrists. "May I know your name, traitha?"

"Edgar Wolfbrother."

Braedan bowed low. "I have no wish to remain your enemy. Mac Rian threatens my throne, and he sits in a seat that he stole. He deserves to die. I wish for you to help me rid Taura of his poison. In return, I offer the tribes opportunity to renew relations with Taura."

Edgar sneered. "Do you not realize the irony? You threaten the tribes and the Taurin heir and sit in a seat you stole."

Braedan's jaw tightened. *I realize more than you know.* "We can discuss my sins later. Right now, let's discuss our shared enemy."

"How many men will he bring?"

"Five hundred, at dawn tomorrow. He says you sent Esma across the road to curse his estates. He'll use it as an excuse to attack."

"How many did you bring?"

Braedan hesitated. "Another thousand."

"Do you intend to join him?"

Braedan crossed his arms. "That depends on you."

Anger flashed across Edgar's face. "We have abided by the treaty, unbeliever. Your father pushed the tribes away from Taura. He made us unwelcome in the cities and refused to see our traithas, so we retreated to the trees. We seek nothing but the freedom of the forest. You threaten us. Why shouldn't we slaughter every one of you?"

You should. You should at least slaughter me. I deserve it. "You're right, traitha. My father treated you shamefully. I have compounded his sins. I beg your forgiveness."

Edgar considered him. "I have no authority to treat with you for the tribes, but those words will have much weight with Hrogarth."

"Then I will share them with him." Braedan paused. "Esma says Mac Rian stole the Mac Niall estate. Is it true? Did he bring false accusations against Culain Mac Niall?"

"Your father wanted to break the treaty and take tribal land. Mac Rian supported him. Culain Mac Niall petitioned his fellow dukes to sanction your father as was their right as members of the Table. They could have unseated him as regent and chosen another. Instead, your father and Mac Rian accused him of treason, branded him a traitor, and attacked his holdings in the night."

"Why?"

"Your father claimed it was to have access to timber, resources, the west coast, but Mac Rian and his daughter were so close to his ear that I think they wanted the reliquary even then. Your father promised the Mac Niall holdings to Mac Rian in exchange for his help and his daughter."

A shiver skipped down Braedan's spine. "My father and Olwyn Mac Rian?" *It's true?*

Edgar nodded. "She sank her talons deep into his heart, boy. She was only sixteen, but once your father had a taste of her, he couldn't put her aside. He would have given her a throne if the law had let him."

Braedan closed his eyes, composed himself, and opened his eyes again. "Who would you have me put in Mac Rian's place? Someone must run the estate."

"Connor Mac Niall."

"There are rumors about him."

"You can see what rumors have wrought. Connor believes Taura has nothing for him. Give him something to come home to."

"Who is his mother?"

"That's none of your business."

Braedan swallowed hard. "My men will not come into the forest. When Mac Rian is committed, we will stay on the road to protect the people of Kiern. We will not threaten any tribal warrior unless he comes across the road to the town. Will you be able to take care of Mac Rian?"

Edgar scoffed. "A game. What about the holdings?"

"I'll restore the Mac Niall name and give the estate to Connor Mac Niall once Mac Rian is dead. But until he returns, who should be the steward of the estate?"

Edgar twisted the dagger, turned it hilt first, and handed it back to Braedan. "I'll trust you to choose someone who will run it well. But promise me this: you'll get the sorceress Olwyn off these lands. She poisons them with her presence."

And to think I was tempted by her body. "Sorceress?"

Edgar nodded. "She has sought Namha since her youth. She desires power, and she is not afraid to conjure dark magic to get it."

"Once Mac Rian is dead, I can make her a ward of the crown and marry her off to some distant duke. Will that do?"

"The land will not be happy until she is dead."

"I can't murder her. I am the king."

"Then we'll do what we can." Edgar glanced at the sky. "The sun is lowering. I promise you, Mac Rian will not live out the day tomorrow. Return Esma to us after the battle."

"I will."

Edgar turned away to join his warriors. He scrambled into a tree, and Braedan gathered his things and returned to the estate.

Maeve stood at the edge of the Sidh village as the sun dropped below the horizon. Edgar had promised to bring news of the earth guardian, but Maeve couldn't still the fluttering of her stomach. *I'm a foolish girl. But it's been almost seven years since I've had a man's arms around me.* She shook her head and drew a deep breath. *There are dozens of Sidh men who would make appropriate consorts,* she thought, and then felt heat creep up her face. *But no Sidh man looks at me the way Edgar does.*

"Maeve."

She spun, her hand flying to her chest, as Edgar dropped down from a tree next to her. "Edgar!"

He chuckled, a mischievous twinkle in his eye. "That was fun."

She waved away the comment. "Did they find your guardian?"

"Yes." Edgar's eyes flickered over her body and back to her face. "Mac Rian's men will be here at dawn."

"We'll be ready." A long silence fell. "You should go get some rest."

"I can never sleep before a hunt or a battle." He tipped his head at her and grinned. "Perhaps I should find something else to do."

He's testing me. She straightened her shoulders and affected her best regal air. "I'm sure some tribal woman can help you pass the time."

He stepped even closer and leaned down just enough to let her feel his breath near her neck. She shivered, and her breath quickened. "Good night, Maeve."

Decades of memories flooded her thoughts. *I could have chosen him. I could have lived with him, here in the forest, my whole life. I wouldn't have had the divided life I lived with Culain.* But then she remembered Culain's blue eyes and roguish smile, and she shook her head. *I loved him, too. I loved two men, and I chose one, and I don't regret it. But now, Culain's gone and Edgar is here.* She stared at his tattooed arms and imagined them around her, and her feet took a hesitant half-step toward him. She caught herself and stepped back.

His hands twitched toward her, but he reined them in. He stepped back, bowed, and disappeared into the trees.

Maeve released a deep, shuddering breath. *I should not want him. I should not be thinking of him that way. He's tribal, and I'm Sidh. If she could see my thoughts, my mother would bind me in braids until spring!*

But the trees rustled around her, and Maeve thought for a moment that she could feel a pair of piercing green eyes staring down at her. Her hand went to her neck, and she laughed softly at the frantic beat of her heart. "Good night, Edgar," she whispered. *Perhaps the next time I say it, you'll be next to me.*

CHAPTER TWENTY-EIGHT

Not all myths are untrue,
And not all legends fade.
— Wisdom of the earth guardians

Braedan returned to the camp to find Malcolm and Ewan waiting in the guard tent with a villager dressed in homespun servant clothes. The woman had a humble beauty under several scars on her face. She held a dusty book in her lap. She ducked her eyes when Braedan entered the tent, and Malcolm stepped close to the king. "This woman is a servant to the lady Olwyn. She has something to say about what happened here six years ago."

"Where did you find her?"

"On a farm outside the city. She lives there with her family and serves the lady during the day." His face was tense. "She's terrified that Olwyn will find out we're speaking with her. I promised her your protection."

Braedan stood in front of the woman with arms folded. "You know something about what happened here six years ago?"

She nodded. "I was with the lady when she brought the assassins to the estate." Her voice rasped, and then Braedan noticed scars on her neck as well. "Duke Mac Niall—he came out of his estate with his sword in hand, and his men fought, but she did something to them. She spoke strange words, old words." She frowned. "I didn't understand it."

Braedan crouched and took one of her hands. "Why were you there?"

She gestured to the scars on her face. "She said she needed strength. I don't know what she did, but when she touched me, I couldn't breathe. And I saw things—memories, horrible things I'd done."

Braedan's knees went weak, and he sank all the way to the ground. *Just like the dark man did to me. What are these creatures?*

The woman swiped at her eyes. "When I was too weak to stand, she gave me to one of her assassins. He cut me." She closed her eyes and shuddered. "She said I was unquickened. She needed unquickened blood."

Braedan frowned. "Unquickened?"

She nodded. "I don't know what that meant, but when she had enough of my blood, she told him to bind my wounds and take me back to her father's estate."

Braedan's mouth was dry, and the men around him had fallen into a sickened silence. "Did she say what she was trying to do?"

The woman shook her head. "If she did, I didn't hear. They killed Mac Niall and his children—all but his son. They couldn't find him." She took a deep, shuddering breath. "Olwyn watched it all. She seemed to . . ." She bit her lip.

Braedan forced himself to swallow over the lump in his throat. "Tell me, even if it doesn't sound possible."

She closed her eyes. "She seemed to feed off it. Not the people dying. That didn't bother her. She seemed more interested in what the assassins did—how they hurt people, the things they did to the women."

Braedan's stomach twisted. He hated that he had to ask the next question. "How can I know you are telling the truth? How can I know you weren't sent here by her?"

She lifted the book in her lap. "I found this when Mac Rian started to rebuild the manor house. There was an old stone vault that wasn't destroyed in the fire. I found Duke Mac Niall's journal in it, and I hid it from my mistress. He wrote about Mac Rian's treachery, about his attempts to encroach on Mac Niall holdings. He saw the lady Olwyn performing dark magic once. He recorded how your father wanted to take tribal lands." She started to hand it to him, but paused and bit her lip. "He wrote about his private life as well, majesty—about his son and his son's mother. I would not wish to damage his family name further."

Braedan closed her hands around the book. "I need the words in this book, but I swear to you, I will not use this against the Mac Niall family."

She nodded and let go of it. "Sire, I knew his son. Connor. He was kind to me once. Please, don't believe the rumors."

"I don't." He took the book and turned to Malcolm. "Find some men to take her back to her family. Help them gather what they can, and then take them somewhere that Olwyn can't find them—east, perhaps. Tell the men they can return to Torlach when they have settled her family." Malcolm bowed and left the tent. Braedan turned back to the woman. "Thank you, lady. You have done a great service to a good man today."

Braedan found a guard to escort him to the small town prison. He found Esma sitting in a pile of fresh rushes on the floor of a tiny stone cell. She stood when the Taurin guard unlocked the door. "What have you chosen?" she asked.

"I've seen your traitha. We've reached an agreement."

She nodded. "Then what do you want with me?"

He hesitated. "I want to know what Olwyn did here six years ago. I want to know what she is."

Esma bit her lip. "I don't know it all. I was not here six years ago. But I can tell you that there are two kinds of power—supernatural and natural. Within natural magic are all of those things created by the One—by Alshada. The Brae Sidh practice elemental magic and some spirit magic. Long ago, the tribes practiced totem magic, and now we practice earth magic, which means we give the earth our sacrifices and she gives us life. And some practice blood magic. Olwyn is one of those."

"What does that mean?"

"Blood is powerful, but it is neither good nor bad. It gives life, and when spilled in sacrifice, it can create powerful wards and connections. But Olwyn is one of those who knows how to use blood to weaken wards, destroy bonds, bind victims to herself, create glamours, even conjure Namha from his prison." She shuddered and rubbed the brand on her palm. "She must die. She poisons the earth."

Braedan found his hand on the hilt of the sacred dagger, and he shifted his posture. "Where were you six years ago?"

She blinked and looked away. "I have not always been a guardian. I have only just returned to the tribe."

He nodded. "You are Taurin."

She didn't move. "I am many things, sire. For now, I am Esma."

He waited, but she didn't say anything more. "I will do what I can to defeat Olwyn."

She gestured to the blade in his belt. "Keep that close. There is power in the sacred blades."

He nodded. "I'll return you to your tribe after the battle." He returned to the Taurin encampment and fell into a restless, anxious sleep.

When the men around him stirred in the morning, Braedan stood and started to dress for battle. Groans and complaints about the hour rippled through the tent, but the men all stood, shook off sleep, and dressed for battle. One of the cooks brought food, and the men ate and drank.

They all emerged from the tent to an unnatural darkness. Malcolm shivered. "There's magic here."

Braedan's skin tingled. "Look—fog."

Malcolm frowned. "That's not fog—that's oremist."

"What's the difference?"

"Fog is natural. This is magic. The Brae Sidh are creating it. It's water bound with the elements of the earth."

For the first time, Braedan believed the Sidh were real. The fingers of oremist drifted low along the ground, weaving around their feet. Braedan hoped he had not misplaced his trust in Edgar. His hand drifted to the dagger. The bone hilt reassured him. "Let's go."

Braedan walked through the lines of his own forces. They were putting on greaves and bracers, belting themselves with blades, and stringing bows. His captains called orders and formed up lines.

Braedan and his guards approached Mac Rian. "Majesty. Have you decided to join us?" Mac Rian asked.

"We are only here to defend the town," Braedan said. "If the tribesmen come across the road, we'll engage them, but the fight in the trees is yours."

Mac Rian's mouth tightened. He stepped closer to Braedan. "You are my liege. You owe—"

"I owe you nothing," Braedan said.

"I supported your bid for the throne. I supported your father. You would abandon your duties now?"

"You stole this seat. I never agreed with my father when he gave you these holdings. You violated Taura's most ancient treaty." He paused. "The throne will not be yours. Olwyn will not be my queen. There is nothing to gain from this. Leave it now, and I'll help you restore the Mac Rian estates."

Mac Rian gripped his sword and took a step toward Braedan, but Malcolm stepped between the two men. He put his hand on Mac Rian's chest. "This is your king, my lord," he said in a lethal tone. "Reconsider your posture."

Mac Rian's straightened his shoulders, his mouth twisted in an angry grimace. He tugged on his gauntlets. "The sun is rising. Let's go."

Mac Rian walked to the front of his line and signaled his captain. A drumroll started. Mac Rian's men advanced into the forest with swords held high, shouting the house motto: *For glory and victory!* The oremist swallowed Mac Rian's men as it rose in a thick curtain high into the trees, obscuring everything in the forest.

The world held its breath in a long pause broken only by the drumroll. A shout, a thud, steel on steel, and the battle was begun, the sounds magnified by the mists.

Far to the north of the line, something caught Braedan's eye. Several figures pulled a struggling person into the fog. Lagging behind was a tall, lithe figure wearing a dark cloak and gliding with unmistakable grace. *Olwyn. I said I wouldn't enter the forest, but if she's taking someone in there for one of her spells, I can't sit by and let it happen.* He nudged Malcolm. "Let's go."

"You would break your word to Edgar?"

"To destroy Olwyn? Yes."

Braedan led Malcolm, Ewan, and two other black-clad guards into the forest behind Olwyn. As they drew nearer, they could hear the muffled cries of a woman and hushed orders as the figures disappeared into the mists. A faint, unnatural light illuminated the group's path. The mists clung to the dark underbrush like a silken veil. Braedan pushed leaves and branches aside as he crept forward. He brushed the mist out of his eyes. *It's like spidersilk,* he thought, flinging it aside and brushing his hands on his breeches.

The group had stopped, and the voices grew louder as Braedan and his guards approached with silent steps. "—can't see a thing—this mist—can't you do something?" a man's voice complained.

"This is Brae Sidh magic." Olwyn's voice held a tone of disgust. "I have no skill against elemental talents." A woman grunted in pain. "Bind her tighter," Olwyn said.

Braedan inched closer, the mists parting a fraction at a time as he moved. He pushed aside the branches of a scrubby bush and suppressed a gasp of horror.

The light Olwyn conjured illuminated the small clearing with a sick yellow hue. Olwyn had Esma stripped naked and tied to a tree, her hands bound behind her.

Olwyn nodded to the four men who had tied Esma, and they moved away. She removed her cloak and stepped closer to Esma, toying with a curved blade in her hand. Esma's eyes were wide with undisguised terror. Olwyn glanced over Esma's body and fixed her eyes on the guardian's foot. "An animstone. For what, I wonder?" She knelt and sliced the stone from Esma's ankle. She held up the stone in the light. "Are you Sidh?"

Esma blinked furiously, and tears rolled down her cheeks as her breathing became more panicked.

Olwyn touched Esma's throat, and Esma started to choke and gasp under the gag. Olwyn took her hand away. "You are Sidh, but just barely." She tapped her lips with the curved blade. "If we cannot reveal the Sidh village with your earth magic, then perhaps we will find a way to reveal the village through your blood. I'm sure you'll tell us where to go once you and I have become better acquainted." She stepped closer, the blade shimmering in the unnatural light, and held up the blade near a tattoo on Esma's chest. A thin, red line trickled down Esma's breast. "Your tattoos are repulsive. I think I'll remove them one at a time until you reveal the Sidh village."

Braedan's throat constricted. *How did she get Esma?* And then, as his heart started to race, *I've never done more than brawl in a tavern or spar in the armory. How will I take on a sorceress?* He gripped the hilt of his sword and prodded Malcolm with an elbow. "Ideas?" he whispered.

"Just leap out and take them," Malcolm murmured.

Braedan swallowed fear and nodded. He drew the tribal blade from his belt, nodded once to his men, and charged.

Olwyn whirled around. A sneer curled her mouth. She clutched Esma's neck again, and the guardian choked and wheezed. Olwyn put her knife above Esma's heart. "Do you want her to die?"

Braedan stopped, blades drawn, stomach churning, heart racing. "Let her go. Take me. I'll help you find the Sidh, I swear, but this woman—"

Olwyn laughed, a low, silken sound that tickled Braedan's ears, even through the fear. "If you could have found the Sidh, love, you'd have given them to the one who bound you." She pressed the blade, and Esma whimpered. She struggled for breath under Olwyn's hand, her chest heaving, blood trickling down to her belly. "This one will lead me to them. Lower your weapons, and I'll spare her. Attack me, and I will kill you both and find another." She gestured toward the distant sounds of battle. "Once the tribe is subdued, the earth guardians will be easy to find."

Braedan's hands shook. "Your father won't win this."

She gave him a languid smile. "He will, *sire*." The title dripped with venom. "Did you think I would let him go into battle with only the soldiers from his estates?"

A chill passed through Braedan. *Assassins—like before, when she attacked Kiern. We have to help the tribes. But first, this one.* He set his jaw. "No," he said, and he swung the sword toward Olwyn.

She let go of Esma and reached up to snatch his sword arm in one hand. It felt like punching a stone wall. Braedan gasped and stumbled at the sudden stop. She stepped closer to him, her black eyes hungry. "Just one last kiss," she whispered.

If she touches my skin, he thought. He flinched back from her mouth, but her opposite hand took his head in hers. His breath left his body in a rush, and once again, his transgressions swirled around his vision. *Gods—the pain—*

Her lips were next to his ear. "You should read up on your country's history, love. Some myths are real."

No breath! He couldn't cry out. His sword toppled from his hand, and his knees turned to water. *I'm sorry, Igraine. I wanted to return to you.*

His left hand twitched. *The tribal blade.* A rush of warmth passed through the hilt, into his palm, up his arm. *I can move.* Some reason returned, and before Olwyn's lips could touch his neck, he drove the blade into her side. As flesh and muscle gave way, she drew back, her mouth gaping. He withdrew the blade. She clutched her side and stumbled backward, fell to her knees, and toppled over, still. A black cloud and a terrible keening howl rose from her body and disappeared into the mists above the forest.

Malcolm stepped toward Braedan, his sword dripping blood. Ewan lay on the forest floor. "One of them got him from behind," Malcolm said. He had a large welt on his forehead, and blood soaked one sleeve.

The murky stone on the hilt of the sacred blade glowed in Braedan's hand. He looked down at Olwyn's body. "What was she?"

"Alshada save us," he muttered, kneeling to draw a spiral in the dirt. "I don't know."

Braedan freed Esma and removed the gag from her mouth. He picked up Olwyn's cloak and covered her. "I'm sorry. You must believe, I did not order this. I did not—"

"I believe you."

He pulled the cloak tight around her and tied it closed. "We need to help the tribe. She's sent her own forces against Edgar, and he thinks there are only five hundred men to fight."

Esma nodded. "Go. Bring your men. I'll find Edgar."

"But you're wounded."

She gave him a strangely resigned smile. "I'll be well. I'm tribal." She waved him away. "Go!"

Braedan and his three remaining guards ran back the way they came, slashing through the thick brush with swords. The sounds of battle raged in the forest, screams and grunts mingling with the clash of steel on armor. When they reached the trees, Braedan snatched the reins of a riderless horse. He spurred the horse into a gallop and thundered along the length of the Taurin line, sword raised high over his head. "To arms!" he shouted. "To arms, all who call Taura home! Into the trees! Fight anyone who isn't tribal. Defend the tribes! Your king orders you to defend the tribes!"

Momentary confusion turned to obedience in a heartbeat, and Braedan led his men into the trees with his sword and dagger aloft as Malcolm shouted more orders to divide the men and fan out in the forest. The mists obscured Braedan's vision, but he saw enough to know he leapt over limbs and muddied his boots in blood and waste.

At last, the Taurin men burst through the trees into a tangle of men, swords, arrows, axes, clubs. Braedan roared and started slashing at anyone not dressed in Taurin livery or animal skins and furs. "For the tribes!" he shouted. "For Taura!"

The driving need for victory spurred him forward, and fear disappeared as battle lust rushed in. He hacked and slashed, stabbed and ducked. A hooded man in black jumped in front of him. Braedan leaned back just in time to hear the *whoosh* of a blade cut the air where his neck had been. The sacred blade warmed his hand, encouraging him, and he blocked the man's hand with one arm and stabbed with the other. The man howled and fell, and Braedan cut off his cries with a sword through the throat.

A body bumped him from behind, and he spun, ready to fight. "Edgar!"

The chieftain growled and gripped Braedan's undertunic at his throat. "Betrayer!" he shouted. "Liar! You swore—"

"We've come to help, I swear," Braedan shouted over the din. An arrow flew at Edgar's head, and Braedan pressed him down. The arrow landed in soft earth just beyond them. Braedan pointed. "I swear it! We're here to help you."

Edgar hesitated only a moment. He let go of Braedan. "Prove yourself, whelp."

Braedan nodded once, and then battle filled his senses again. Swing, thrust, parry, stab—he fought back-to-back with Edgar, slashing and stabbing. His feet sank into the waste and blood on the forest floor. He tried to gain purchase, but another assassin leapt from a tree and kicked him across the face. An explosion of lights blurred his vision. A blade shimmered, and he lifted his arm in instinct. The steel sliced into his skin. "Damn it!" He lowered his arm, and the steel shimmered again—

The man fell in a crumpled heap on top of Braedan, and Braedan grunted. He pushed the man off and took an offered arm. "My thanks."

Edgar grinned. "Now we're even," he said, turning to the next Mac Rian man.

The earth rumbled, and Braedan steadied himself with a hand on a tree. *What is this?* A dozen or more of Mac Rian's men held a small patch of earth ahead of him, and they lowered swords and daggers as the ground beneath them churned and swelled into a hill. Trees tilted and toppled and bushes tumbled. Panicked shouts echoed through the forest, and the men fell cursing and praying and begging as they ran from the rising hill.

Braedan looked at Edgar, expecting awe or panic, but the traitha only grinned. He gestured to the hill. "The Sidh," he said. "Do you still refuse to believe?"

By the gods. "No."

Edgar laughed. He climbed up the hill, hacking through the panicked soldiers to get to the top. "Wolves! This way!" He disappeared over the other side of the hill.

Braedan shook his head. *He's leading them deeper into the forest. I thought he wanted them out.* He followed Edgar.

But Edgar had stopped on the other side of the hill. He stood pointing at Sean Mac Rian. "That one is mine," he said.

His voice sent a shudder through Braedan. "Edgar—"

"Second thoughts, whelp? Turn away if you can't watch." He took several steps down the hill. "Mac Rian! Today, I avenge a good man with your blood!"

Braedan followed, slicing and stabbing and defending the traitha as he raced through the men to Sean Mac Rian's side.

Mac Rian gasped. "I know you. I've seen you—I've seen you watch my estate from the road." He parried Edgar's blow.

Edgar snarled. He drew his blade back, spun, swung again. Mac Rian's blade deflected his, but Edgar pushed forward, his short tribal sword brushing Mac Rian's shoulder. Mac Rian screamed. Edgar kicked him, and Mac Rian collapsed, clutching his belly and gasping for air.

Edgar stabbed again and again—an arm, a leg, a brush past the ribs—until Mac Rian bled from a dozen little cuts. *A cat toying with a mouse.* "Edgar, finish it!"

"He pays for what he did to Culain," Edgar shouted. He sliced Mac Rian's cheek, cut off an ear, pierced a shoulder.

Mac Rian lay on the ground weeping. "No—please spare . . . please . . . . Sire, help." His breath slowed, and his eyes turned glassy.

No, I won't let this continue. Braedan rushed to Edgar's side and pulled his arm back. "Finish it, now, or I will."

Edgar's chest heaved with rage, but when he met Braedan's eyes, he finally nodded. He knelt and leaned close to Mac Rian's face. "This is what you reap for killing my friend, you bastard." He drew his dagger slowly across Mac Rian's throat.

Braedan's stomach roiled as Mac Rian's screams echoed into the trees and faded.

Edgar straightened. "You're a bit green, boy." He trotted to meet the next opponent, Mac Rian's blood still draining out onto the soil.

Braedan swallowed bile and knelt next to the dead duke. *I can't be sorry that he's gone.* He closed Mac Rian's eyes, straightened, and followed Edgar into the melee.

The battle continued until late in the afternoon. Braedan fought at Edgar's side until his arms ached and his legs moved only by sheer force of will. Though his leathers were drenched with blood, mud, and sweat, Edgar still swung his blades with the same strength he had when Braedan first saw him, and his reflexes hadn't slowed. *The man is nearly twice my age,* Braedan thought, wiping sweat from his eyes once more as Edgar engaged one of the last Mac Rian men in the forest. *All I can think about is a very long sleep, and he's still looking for men to fight.*

The traitha ran his sword into the man's belly all the way to the hilt, kicked him off the blade, and turned to Braedan. "Any word from your other men?"

"Malcolm brought a contingent up from the south. Mac Rian's men are subdued, and the assassins seem to have fled." He paused. "What about Esma? Have you seen her? Did she make it back through the battle?"

Edgar sheathed his blade and put a hand on Braedan's shoulder. "Come into the village. We'll find her and toast our victory."

The village wasn't far from the site of the battle, but it took some time to step over all of the bodies and limbs and speak with the various leaders they met. Tribal losses were few, and from what Braedan could see, the Taurins hadn't lost many men, either.

They found Esma in the large community building in the center of the village, once more dressed in breeches and tunic. She straightened from the wounded tribesman she tended and wiped bloody hands on a rag. "It's over?"

Edgar nodded. "Mac Rian is dead."

She let out a long sigh and closed her eyes for a moment. "The sorceress is gone, too. For now."

"For now?" Braedan hated the faint squeak of fear in his voice. "What do you mean?"

"She was one of the Forbidden, sire. A being part human, part Syrafi," she explained when he shook his head in confusion. "Or she used to be."

"Used to be?"

Esma nodded. "They were born of human and Syrafi parents in the earliest days of the world. They called themselves the Blessed Ones and followed Namha, but the spells and magic they learned bound their souls to this world unless they are destroyed by the ravenmarked. You heard the keening when Olwyn died?"

Braedan nodded. "Some kind of cloud rose from her body, too."

"Her soul. A tainted soul." She shuddered. "I didn't realize what she was until she tried to kill me. Only one of the Forbidden could reveal a person's transgressions that way. She's not dead. She will take possession of another body, the way she did Olwyn's body, and she will not give you quarter if she sees you again."

"How did she get to you?"

"Her underlings killed your men." She rubbed her arms. "The Forbidden have much power, but many limits on it. They must often use humans to do their bidding. I believe the enchantments must have prevented her from coming into the great forest on her own. She could only do it once she had me."

Braedan suppressed a shudder of his own. *The dark man—that's what he's done with me. He used me because he was prevented from doing what he wished on his own. Gods, what a fool I've been.* He turned to Edgar. "I am sorry, traitha. I am sorry for my father's foolishness, and I'm sorry you had to endure Mac Rian and his daughter. I promise you, from this day on, Taurin forces will only enter the great forest at the discretion of the tribes."

Edgar crossed his arms. "And the estate? What will you do to make amends to Culain Mac Niall's family?"

"I will restore the Mac Niall name and estates and return them to Connor Mac Niall. As soon as I return to Torlach, I'll draw up papers legitimizing his name and giving him a seat on the Table."

Edgar nodded slowly. "You are not what I expected, princeling. You may yet make a good king." He held out an arm.

Braedan clasped it. "Is it all real? The Brae Sidh, the reliquary?"

"Yes."

"And are they safe now? With Mac Rian gone?"

"For the moment," Edgar said. He drew a dagger and offered it to Braedan, hilt first. "The wolf tribe will recognize your reign, your majesty."

Braedan drew the sacred blade and held it out, hilt first. "I thank you, traitha."

Edgar frowned down at the blade. "How long has that stone been glowing?"

"Since I killed Olwyn Mac Rian." Braedan stared down at it. "I don't know how, but this blade saved my life. She had me under control and would have killed me, but this blade just . . ." *It sounds impossible. But then, I saw a hill appear out of nowhere. How can I say what's impossible anymore?* "It came to life, and it guided my hand to stab her."

Edgar lowered the blade in his hand. "That is not mine to take. You shed blood with it. It's bonded to you now."

"What does that mean?"

"It means you belong to that blade," Esma said. She frowned. "It means you must go where the blade leads you."

Braedan shivered. "Or else what?"

"Or else you die," Edgar said.

Braedan's legs gave out finally, and he sank down to a mat in the common hut. Esma knelt next to him. "You need rest," she said. "Lie down. I'll bring you water, and you'll sleep, and we'll discuss the blade another day."

Braedan nodded, dazed, but in his mind he could only picture Igraine and wonder when he would see his princess again.

* * *

Maeve was standing outside the village as the sun set, waiting for news as the oremist swirled around her feet. The tingle of the magic comforted and soothed her, and the people in the village had a peace she hadn't felt in years. *It feels good to use the magic all together like this.*

She was so focused on holding the magic and weaving the braids of air, water, and stone that she didn't hear or see Edgar until he was next to her. She jumped. "Stop sneaking up on me!"

His wicked grin had a very satisfied undertone. "You're beautiful when you're flustered."

Her heart skipped. "Is he gone? Is the king out of the forest?"

"Mac Rian is dead. The Taurins are out of the forest."

The oremist dissipated in swirls and eddies around their feet. "Is Minerva all right?"

He nodded. "Braedan saved her life. Olwyn tried to take her, but he freed her and killed Olwyn. The Mac Rian forces are gone. Your magic worked." He grinned. "I liked that stone talent. Having hills just pop out of the ground like that confused Mac Rian's men and turned them around."

"And the king? Will he still seek the Sidh?"

"The king believes now. He understands his role. He promises to keep the Taurins out of the forest, and he'll be restoring the Mac Niall name to good standing," Edgar said.

Maeve's stomach lurched. "Restoring the Mac Niall name? You mean Connor—"

"I know that managing an estate and living the life his father led is not for him, but it should be his. He is the only one left of Culain's line. I suggested that the king find someone suitable to manage the estate in Connor's absence. You and I can make sure the estate is well-managed." He grinned, but the rakish edge in it was tempered by tenderness in his eyes. "Of course, that means we'll have to spend more time together."

She stepped closer to him. *Two can play at this.* "What do you have in mind?"

"Just an occasional meeting of two leaders who are protecting their villages and caring for an old friend's estate until his son returns." He folded his arms across his chest. She again noticed how well-muscled he was. "I suppose that might require an occasional cup of oiska together or a meal here and there."

"I suppose it might." She noticed the large, bloodstained tear in his leather breeches and gasped. "You're wounded."

"That? It's not bad. I'll dress it back in the village."

"No, you won't. Come into the Sidh village. I'll have a healer look at it."

He tilted his head. "A healer? You won't look at it yourself?"

She was grateful for the fading light. "I have no skill for healing. But I do have oiska. And food."

He mulled that over. "It's been almost thirty years since we shared a meal."

"No—has it?"

"After Connor was born I hardly saw you." He stepped closer to her. "But a meal without meat? It may be worth a try."

He was covered in sweat, blood, and bits of bone and leather and Taurin cloth, but she could only see the man she knew thirty years before. *Those eyes.* "You might find that it's more satisfying than you think." *I'm as bad as my son.*

The crooked grin widened. "I suppose I might."

"I'm not offering anything more than food, drink, and conversation."

"And a healer."

"Well, yes. And that." She wrinkled her nose. "You need a bath, Edgar."

"I suppose you can offer that as well?"

"There's a pool behind my hut. If you are interested."

He appraised her with a wolfish hunger. "I am."

I'm too old for this. Her heart was beating as it had the first time she'd seen Culain more than thirty years ago. She didn't need to say anything more. She offered him her hand to lead him through the Sidh boundary, and he fell in step next to her, seeming not to be in any discomfort from the wound on his leg. When they reached her hut, she dismissed Evie, shut the door, and forgot about calling for a healer.

CHAPTER TWENTY-NINE

The One Hand brings his will around, yes.
— Rhiannon, nursemaid to Connor Mac Niall

Minerva straightened at the well and drew up a bucket of water, pausing to draw a full, deep breath. The wolf village had returned to normal in the week since the battle. Tribal losses were low, and wounded men were healing quickly under Nedra and the other earth guardians' ministrations. Edgar had spent increasing amounts of time in the Sidh village and at the estate, discussing policy and plans with Queen Maeve and King Braedan alternately. *Or so he claims,* Minerva thought. Despite the impropriety of it, she had to smile. *He's not fooling anyone. He walks around the village like a newly wed warrior with that silly, besotted grin.*

She watched a warrior return from the forest with a young man about twelve or thirteen. *Not old enough for the initiation, but old enough to provide meat.* The younger man carried a brace of coneys, and the older man had a young deer slung over his shoulders. Elsewhere, a group of apprentices sat in a circle around a guardian, listening to her lessons with looks of deep concentration. Tribal children played a game in the village streets, and women went about the business of tending animals and harvesting gardens. Minerva leaned against the well. *This place is becoming home. I shouldn't let it. And yet . . .* Her palm itched, and she clenched her fist.

"Esma."

She turned. The bucket fell back into the well, and Minerva gasped and stared. "Traitha."

Alfrig stood before her, her mouth drawn into a tight frown and her arms folded across her chest. She jutted her chin. "So this is where you go? You risk my husband's wrath by living right under his nose?"

Minerva forced herself to swallow. "E-Edgar said I would be under his protection. F-forgive me, traitha, I—"

Alfrig held up a hand. "Nedra wrote me. She is, perhaps, more trusting than Edgar. Or more loyal. May we talk?"

Minerva nodded and led Alfrig to Nedra's hut. They sat down across the fire pit from each other, and Alfrig cast a glance around. "Nedra must keep a skin somewhere."

Minerva stood again and found the oiska and a cup for Alfrig. "Forgive me for staying in the forest," she said as she sat again. "Edgar offered me a place for the winter, and I accepted. I didn't want to risk seeing Hrogarth again. I swear to you, I'll be gone as soon as spring comes."

Alfrig poured oiska. "You should not have come into the forest at all."

"No one else could have found the tribes. None of the other sayas knew how to reach you."

"You should not have come."

Minerva's palm warmed inside her fist. "What would you have had me do, traitha? Let the pretender rule unchallenged? Leave the Brae Sidh to die?"

Alfrig's voice echoed with a cool, steely edge. "You still answer to me, guardian. Check yourself."

She is still my traitha. "Forgive me."

Alfrig unwrapped the fox sashes from her neck. "Nedra tells me you have trouble controlling your mark."

I don't know where to begin. "The earthspirit grows stronger. I need to be shed."

Alfrig drank her oiska. She poured another cup and let it sit. "The Morrag stirs. It grows harder to sate her every day."

I know. Minerva looked down. "I can't control it. I left—I didn't learn enough—I didn't expect the Morrag to awaken."

"None of us thought she would awaken. If we had thought she would demand so much blood, we would have taught you what you needed to know."

"If I performed the rites—" She bit off the words. *Alshada, forgive me.*

But Alfrig shook her head. "The simple rites you knew no longer sate her. She requires more."

"Can you teach me?"

"No. You would have to be part of the tribal web, and no tribe would take an oathbreaker."

That much was true. Even though Nedra let her serve as an apprentice, that was much different than taking the oaths and finishing her training. The tribe would never accept her as a full guardian. *Not that I would want the position. I only want to be rid of the power.*

"Nedra also tells me how you helped the tribes defeat the thief Mac Rian. For that, I will help you." Alfrig reached into a pouch at her side. She drew out a bone talisman that hung from a leather lashing. "Wear this. It will stifle the magic."

Minerva's blood ran cold. *The amasidh.* "Please, put it away."

"You must." She pushed it toward Minerva.

Minerva looked away. "Do you know what that is?" *Alshada, what child paid the price for that?* Her eyes watered, and she shut them against tears. "Please, I can't look at it."

Alfrig sat quiet for some time. "It is the only way to hold back your power. Wear it or refuse it, but it is all you have. Your blood will forgive you."

Minerva shook her head. "I thought they were all destroyed."

"There are a few left."

"Why would you have such a vile thing?"

Alfrig drank another cup of oiska. "If it were my blood, I might make the same decision." There was understanding in her voice. "I tell you only that it must be this way. I cannot shed you of the magic, and you cannot return to the tribes to embrace it. You are caught in the between place."

Minerva couldn't look at Alfrig, couldn't open her eyes. "If I don't wear it?"

"The Morrag will consume you when she becomes strong enough."

Minerva forced her eyes open and looked at the talisman again. It was thin, small—the bone of a rib or a forearm, a child's bone, carved with runes and dyed with blood. The Forbidden had sacrificed Sidh children to Namha before the children came into their power. *The blood of the unquickened. This was a child of my blood.*

She pushed the talisman away. "I will risk death. I will not wear that abomination."

Alfrig put the talisman back in the pouch at her side. She drank another shot of oiska, poured another shot, and pushed it over to Minerva. "Drink."

Minerva looked at the cup. *Nothing is as it used to be. Maybe nothing was ever what I thought it was.* She drank. The bite of the oiska traveled down to the pit of her stomach. *How many years? I can't remember the last time I drank it.*

Alfrig poured her another shot. "When you're ready."

"What will the tribes do?" she asked Alfrig. "And the earth guardians?"

Alfrig drank another cup of oiska. "That is not for you to know," she said. "You forfeited that right when you left."

Minerva nodded. Painful silence fell. "Traitha, I am sorry for leaving as I did," she said. She looked down. "I was lost when he died." Tears sprang up as the old pain reared its head. She still couldn't even think his name without crying.

Alfrig said nothing for a long time. "You would not be paying this price now if you had shed yourself of the earth wisdom. You pay the price of your choice, and now it is too late. You must learn to live with it."

Minerva nodded. She looked up. "Traitha, I ask a boon."

Alfrig didn't answer for a long time. If she said yes, she had to grant it, whatever the request. If she said no, she would appear dishonorable in the eyes of the tribes. "Ask," she said at last.

Minerva took a deep breath. "I ask your forgiveness. I am sorry. I should not have left as I did."

Alfrig's face softened. "I forgave you years ago. You were as a daughter to me, Esma. I thought, once, that you might take my place—that you might be traitha."

The words broke Minerva's heart. Tears spilled over. She looked down, ashamed. There was no room for tears in front of Alfrig. "I found peace with Alshada."

"Esma, he is in the tribes, too. He is everywhere. Did you never understand that?"

Minerva shook her head. "I couldn't stay. Everywhere I looked, there were reminders of my husband. It hurt too much. The earth wisdom couldn't save me."

"It wasn't supposed to," Alfrig said. "It was only a piece of you." She paused. "There is one other who might help you."

Hope rose in Minerva's chest. She raised her eyes. "Yes?"

"The wisdomkeeper."

She would have me go to the one who is closer to the earthspirit than anyone—the very keeper of it all? Alshada, I can't! But it was more hope than she'd had for weeks. *If anyone can shed me of this magic, this pain, it would be the wisdomkeeper.* The nameless crone lived in the far north, seen only by select earth guardians who sought her for knowledge of the deepest secrets of the earthspirit. "Have you met her?" she asked Alfrig.

The traitha's mouth tightened. "Once. Before I wed Hrogarth, I sought her for—" She bit off the words. "I will tell you another day."

"And you would take me there?"

Alfrig nodded. "If you wish. If you will agree to do what she says."

Minerva nodded, eager. "Yes. Of course, yes. Even to my death—just to be rid of this—"

A sad smile crossed Alfrig's mouth. "Youth promises what age regrets," she said, quiet. She stood. "We will set out tomorrow. I will discuss preparations with Edgar and Nedra." She left the hut.

Minerva stared at the cup of oiska in front of her and finally drank it. It went down easier the second time. She stood and followed Alfrig with the fire of the oiska burning in her chest as strong as the magic in her palm.

CHAPTER THIRTY

> *My heart is broken, for the one I rejoice in is no more.*
> *Alshada, I seek your presence. Fill my soul again.*
> — Songs of King Aiden, Book 25, Verse 1

The first days after Connor left Galbragh passed in a blur for Mairead. Elizabeth and Melik took her into the town, and Henry offered to pay for anything she wanted or needed, but nothing interested her. She found herself looking toward the leatherworking shops and blacksmithy with longing. When she found a peddler selling a well-made bow, she asked Melik for the money to buy it.

He frowned even as he handed over the coins. "Why? You have me for protection. You have no need for weapons."

She tested the weight and draw of the bow. "I'm good with a bow, and Connor took his when he left. I like to hunt." *And I won't sit around helpless, waiting for him to come back. I'll figure out my own path.*

Melik bought the bow and a quiver of arrows for her. He joined her when she went to the archery yard that night to practice. "Your aim is flawless," he said.

She fired again. "Connor taught me."

"Truly? I would have thought that you had been practicing your whole life."

"No. I just have a talent for it." She nocked, aimed, and fired another perfect shot.

Henry was an ideal host. The third night after Connor left, Mairead found Henry dining alone in his study. "Your highness? Where's Lady Elizabeth?"

"She had a party. Melik took her." He stood. "Please, join me."

She arranged the skirts of her linen dress and sat across from him. He poured wine and offered it to her. "Are you working?"

"Trying to." He smiled and held up his goblet. "You provide a pleasant distraction." She lifted her goblet, and they both drank. "How are you, Mairead?"

"I'm well. You've been a gracious host."

He let silence linger for a moment. "But?"

She twisted the goblet in her hands and considered what to say. "I miss him." Tears fell. Henry stood and moved around his desk to kneel before her. She took the kerchief he offered and closed her eyes. "What if he dies?"

He put his hands on hers. "My dear, Connor is at his best when he's on his own creating a bloody swath of destruction."

The next morning, she woke to knocking. She pulled a dressing gown over her shift and opened the door. Melik leaned against the side of the door with easy grace. His eyes drifted down her body. "I thought you might want to go hunting."

She blinked and rubbed her eyes. "Hunting? Now?"

"There are some good deer runs just outside of the city. It's property of the prince, so we shouldn't run into any slavers."

I need to do something, even if it's with him. Days of wandering the city and the palace in pretty dresses chafed her spirit. "Let me dress."

He inclined his head. "I'll have horses saddled and find some provisions for us."

"I'll meet you in the stable." She shut the door, pulled on her leathers and tunic, and braided her hair. She picked up the daggers Connor had given her, and a pang of loss went through her. *Stop being a foolish girl. He's gone. He says his path doesn't align with yours. Accept it.* She put the daggers in her boots.

Melik was waiting in the stable with her horse and his own. The big sorrel Connor had ridden was still in his stall, unhappy about the palomino leaving without him. He pranced and tossed his head. "He's not happy today," Melik said.

"He doesn't like being apart from her." Mairead went to the stall. "Shh, Thunder."

"Thunder?"

She closed her eyes and put her head against the horse's nose. "I named them. I never told Connor. I thought he'd find it silly."

"It's not silly." Melik stood close behind her. "The desert horse people in the southern part of the empire believe a horse's name is given by the gods. A horse isn't to be ridden until he's named."

She put her hands against the sorrel's neck. Thunder gave her a low whicker. "Saddle another horse. I don't want him separated from my horse for the whole day."

"Of course." Several minutes later, the sorrel and palomino were together in their stall once more, and Mairead had mounted a pretty dark brown mare with a spirited step.

They cantered away from the city and toward the low forest at the edge of the plain. Mairead's nose and fingers grew cold, and her breath formed white clouds in front of her. The snowfall of previous days lingered, but the sky was clear and bright with the promise of sun. She tried to make conversation when they slowed to a walk. "Do you miss Espara?"

Melik gave a low laugh. "No. Not really. I wasn't exactly welcome there."

"But Connor said your aunt—"

"Yes, well, if Connor asked Helene, I'm sure she would welcome me back with open arms. She would sell half her property to have him in her bed."

Is that where he'll go? Back to his foreign lady? She swallowed the lump in her throat. "Why weren't you welcome?"

He kept his eyes ahead for some time. "I owe money. A fair amount. I'm trying to earn enough to return and pay my debts, but even an assassin has expenses, and it takes time to kill a man the right way."

"You speak of it so coldly." She pulled her cloak tighter around her.

"It's not hard to kill a man."

"Do you kill people for Henry?"

He grinned. "No. Henry's not the type. I do other things—security things, freelancing, reconnaissance. I have no allegiance to anyone. I go where the money is."

So much like Connor. But he wasn't. Connor would never be a hired assassin, she was sure. *Would he? Isn't that what the Morrag wants?* "Did you warn Connor about Allyn?"

"Yes."

"Why?"

He adjusted his reins. The rising sun glinted off his earrings. "Who would I compete with if Connor were dead?"

She laughed at that.

They cantered toward the trees and found the trails. She dismounted and donned her bow and quiver. He walked next to her as they crept along the runs, listening and looking for deer. They searched for some time and then found a patch of dry ground under a fir tree.

Mairead sat, drank water, and snacked on apples. "Don't you want some?" she asked.

He shook his head and toyed with a knife. "I'm not hungry." He leaned against the tree and carved random shapes in the ground. "Connor told me you grew up poor."

I'm not going to lie anymore. "Not poor. Just not rich. I was raised in a sayada by the Order of Sai Atena."

"Then this life is new to you."

"This life is not for me."

"A woman with your beauty and grace? Educated? What life do you think you should have?"

She shrugged. "I don't know."

Melik leaned closer to her. He brushed loose hair back behind her ear. "You are a beautiful woman, Mairead. You deserve to be pampered and pleased."

She pushed his hand away. "Melik, stop. I've seen you with Elizabeth. I know—"

He laughed. "Elizabeth has no exclusive claim on my affections."

She stood. "We should go."

He stood as well. "Do you think Connor is pining for you? Regretting leaving your bed? Be assured, my lady. He's already found several willing tavern girls, and he hasn't shed a tear for you."

The self-assured tone angered her. She turned to him and straightened her shoulders. "You don't know—"

"I do know. I've seen him at his finest." He shot her a cocky grin. "I am him."

Her face grew hot. "He changed. He respected me. He protected my chastity and my honor."

Melik blinked in surprise. "Truly? I didn't know he had such discipline."

She couldn't help the smile that flickered across her lips. "He didn't know it either."

He inclined his head, and some of the arrogance melted away. "Forgive me, my lady. I should not have presumed—" He stopped. Hoof beats echoed in the distance, approaching at a steady canter. "Someone from the palace is probably looking for you." He brushed his clothes free of fir needles and dirt. "We can meet them."

Mairead fed her apple cores to the horses and put her waterskin away. They mounted and turned back toward the sound of the approaching horses, but as the other group came closer, Mairead's stomach tightened. "Melik, those men aren't from the palace."

"I know."

"Who are they?"

"I guess we'll find out." They reined in as the others did, and Melik addressed a tall man with pale green eyes and greasy, sandy-blond hair. "We've been looking for deer all morning. Have you had any luck?"

The man grinned. "No need for pretending." He nodded toward Mairead. "You weren't lying. She is a beauty."

They're here for me. Mairead wheeled her horse in the direction of the palace and kicked her into a gallop. The men shouted and charged after her, but she only leaned lower on the horse's back and gave the mare open rein to run as fast as she could across the fields. *Alshada, help me. Give this horse wings.* The thunder of hooves behind her—the gleaming palace in the distance—the men shouting, calling to each other. "Fly, girl. Fly!"

The horse reared with a sharp neigh of pain. Mairead clutched the saddle, but the horse was falling, going down on her side, and Mairead jumped free just in time to avoid her leg being crushed. The horse struggled against the arrow piercing her chest.

Mairead picked up her bow, nocked and aimed an arrow, and fired. One man fell. Nock, aim, fire—another man down, then a horse. The arrows were a blur, but the men weren't shooting back. *Why aren't they shooting at me?*

The six remaining men surrounded her. She prepared another arrow, but something hit her from behind. She fell into the snow. *My daggers—* She gasped for air, trying to reach her boot, but there was a knee in her back, and then two hands pulled her arms together and tied them at the wrists. The hands yanked her to her feet and turned her toward Melik. She choked, trying to breathe. "Melik?"

Melik still sat in his saddle. "I told you. I have debts."

She spit blood from a cut on her lip. "What have you done?"

The men all dismounted, Melik included, and he stood with calm self-assurance before the man with greasy hair. "Eight hundred gold pieces. No less."

The man scoffed. "Eight hundred? You told us six."

"She's a virgin. I just found out."

"Now how did you find that out? And how can I know she still is if you checked yourself?"

"She told me."

The man approached her. He ran a hand across her body with disquieting familiarity. He opened her cloak and lifted her tunic. Fear rose in her throat as she tried to catch her breath. He lifted her chin, opened her mouth, and looked inside. "She's pretty enough. A little muscular, but some men like that." He turned to Melik. "Unspoiled, you say? You're certain?"

"As certain as I can be. I suppose she could have lied, but she was raised in a sayada. I'm sure her chastity was well-guarded."

"She traveled with the one Allyn is after. How do you know he didn't spoil her?"

"He seems to have restrained himself. Unusual, but not impossible."

The man nodded. "I know you can fire an arrow," he said to Mairead. "What else can you do?"

She tried to calm her breathing. "Why does it matter if you're going to kill me?"

"Oh, lass, you're worth much more to me alive than dead. Can you read?"

She stared at him, resolute, and spit in his face. "Namha take you."

He pulled out his kerchief and wiped his face. "Give her the venom."

The man holding her pulled up the sleeve of her tunic, and another man approached with a writhing burlap bag. She struggled against the grip, but the hands were too strong. "Please don't do this—"

The man opened the bag and reached in with a gloved hand. Mairead saw the head of the snake just before she felt the sting and pain of the bite. She screamed. Her knees went weak with the sudden pain. Her head spun, and in moments, her body started to go numb. Colors and sounds and smells were disconnected; she struggled to breathe.

The sandy-haired man looked at Melik. "Seven hundred." He walked toward Melik with a purse.

"Done."

A flash of light. "I don't think that will be necessary," said another voice.

Through the haze of the venom, Mairead saw a cloaked man step toward Melik from the edge of the group. Without another word, his hand flicked out, and Melik crumpled to the ground. Sunlight shimmered off the pool of blood at his neck. The snow turned red. She blinked. The world grew hazy. She couldn't be certain of anything.

The sandy-haired man muttered a sharp curse. "What did you do that for?"

"He's the reason Mac Niall escaped. He overheard your master planning to kill Mac Niall and warned him to run. When Mac Niall didn't take the girl with him, this one decided to make some money." The cloaked man sheathed his dagger.

"More profit for me then, I suppose," the sandy-haired man said.

"Take her to your master. He can use her to find Mac Niall."

The man's face flickered disappointment. "He'll not pay me for her."

"You'll get something better—his gratitude."

"Fuck his gratitude."

The dark man sneered. "Trust me." He disappeared in another flash of light.

Mairead's head spun and she couldn't keep her eyes open. *The man—the Forbidden—flashes of light—gods, he found me.*

The sandy-haired man turned back to her. "Put her on a horse and take her to Allyn's house, but one of you fetch Phinneas. Allyn might let us take a cut if he can sell her to Phinneas."

It was the last thing she heard before she lost consciousness.

She woke without sense of time or place. The room she lay in was cold, windowless, and smelled of waste and death. *Alshada, give me strength.* She forced a deep breath. Vision cleared as she blinked and sat up. Her head reeled, and she leaned over to retch.

A woman was next to her with a chamber pot. Mairead heaved, but there was nothing in her stomach but water and bile. "Lass, 'tis the venom. Makes the strongest of us sick. 'Tis a fair small miracle ye've not been sicker."

Mairead's stomach roiled and she gasped for breath. "Why?"

"They dinna want to beat ye. 'Tis easier to keep ye quiet with the venom."

She closed her eyes. "Where am I?"

"In Master Allyn's house."

"Allyn. The slaver." Comprehension washed over her. *A slave—that's why the money, the exam. He wanted to know how much I was worth.*

"Aye. Ye've bin asleep two days, now. Ach, lass, dinna sit up too quickly."

Mairead pushed her hand away and struggled to sit up. She closed her eyes as her head reeled again, but she forced herself through the nausea. "I'm all right." They had put her on a cot with a thin mattress. She was alone but for the woman next to her. The dark room was furnished with the bed, a chamber pot, and a stool. She forced herself to focus on the woman's dark blue eyes. "Who are you?"

The woman smoothed her plain linen kirtle over her knees. Streaks of gray interrupted the smooth curtain of her coarse black hair. "Ula."

"Are you a slave?"

"Aye. I belong to Master Allyn."

"What do they plan to do with me?"

"I dinna know, lass. Master never brings slaves here unless he wants to bed them. He said he'd not bed ye yet—wants a man to look at ye, and wants ye for something else, too. I dinna know what." She shrugged. "'Tisn't so bad for a lass such as yourself. The man who's coming to see ye—Master Phinneas—he buys women for his lord. 'Tis a fair way, I've heard. They'll put ye in fine clothes and give ye all ye want."

Mairead's stomach lurched again, and bile rose in her throat. "Except my freedom," she said.

Ula's eyes flared with ferocity, and she lowered her voice. "I heard that ye killed two of the bastards."

Hope stirred. "I could kill more if you could get me a knife."

Ula shook her head, her ferocity replaced by fear once more. "Nae, lass. 'Tis best ye just let it be. Dinna try to escape." She stood. "I'll fetch ye a meal. When your stomach is ready, ye can eat." She left the room, locking the door behind her.

Mairead stood and walked around. *Melik, dead. Connor—who knows where. They brought me to Allyn's house. Will Henry try to find me? Risk his alliance with the slavers? Alshada, show me how to escape.*

Ula returned soon with a plate of bread and cheese and a goblet of water. She set it on the stool. "Eat, now. Master Allyn is coming to see ye soon."

Mairead nodded. Ula left and locked the door again, and Mairead sat on the cot and stared at the food and water. She had no intention of being drugged or poisoned again. Rather than eat or drink, she knelt next to her bed and bowed her head. *Alshada, help me. Give me wisdom. Help me confront evil with good. Help me serve you in all I do.*

As the hours passed, Mairead paced and searched for a weapon. She found nothing. Fighting moves Connor had taught her ran through her head. She practiced a few, but every move brought weakness and pain. Her stomach clenched from hunger and thirst. She didn't think she could fight anyone. *If I'm to get free of this place, it will be with my wits.*

At last, the lock turned. She stood in the center of the room and straightened her shoulders in a regal pose. A tall man with light red hair and a hard, weathered face entered the room. Two guards accompanied him, flanking him on either side. "Are you so afraid of me you need two guards?" she asked.

He folded his arms and appraised her. "Ye're a brave one for such a slip of a thing."

"Bravery is all I have at the moment."

"And beauty."

"I fear that's more a curse than a blessing."

He signaled to the two guards. They left the room, closing the door behind them. The man approached her. "So. Ye're Connor Mac Niall's whore."

The words stung. "No. Connor was my guard and escort only. You are Master Allyn?"

He inclined his head. "None other. I'm glad to see my reputation precedes me."

She lifted her chin. "You realize that you have captured a guest of Prince Henry, don't you? I'm in his care. If he finds out—"

"Henry is busy over at Mac Mahon's house. We gave him a few clues to lead him there. If I'm lucky, he and Mac Mahon will fight it out, and I'll be the one left standing."

"Then what do you plan to do with me?"

"I haven't decided." He stepped closer to her. "There's a man who buys ladies for his lord, the Emperor of Tal'Amun. Ye're the type he buys. I'd get a good price for ye. It would almost make up for the blood Mac Niall shed when he killed my son."

Mairead forced her fear back. "Revenge and profit. Is there anything else that drives you?"

"One thing. But I won't get as much for you if I take that." He appraised her body. "The man Melik—he said ye're a virgin. Is it true?"

"Yes."

"Your idea or Mac Niall's?"

"There was nothing between us. He didn't want me."

He put one hand on her neck. His hand spanned her throat and tightened in warning. It drifted down to her breasts. She refused to look away from his face. "Ye'd be a difficult woman to resist."

She picked up his hand and removed it from her body. "Try."

"I get enough ragged whores in the brothels and camps. Perhaps it's time to train a woman to my personal service." He gestured. "Take off your clothes. Let me see if ye're worth keeping."

The suggestion was so brazen that she laughed. "You think I fear you so much I'd obey an order like that without a fight?"

The back of his hand connected with her cheek. The blow knocked her to the ground. Light flashed around her head as blood filled her mouth. He pulled her up to her feet. Her head spun, but she saw the cold sneer that crossed his face. He stank of wine and sweat. "I was hoping ye'd fight."

She gathered the blood in her mouth and spit in his face. "Beat me, rape me, kill me—I don't care. Anything you want from me you'll have to take."

He grabbed her braid and twisted it around his hand, pulling her head back to expose her neck. She heard the whisper of steel from a sheath. Her pulse pounded against a blade on her skin. "One cut. 'Tis all it takes."

"Do it then. It's better than having you between my legs."

He hovered for a moment. The knife drifted down her body to her tunic. He sliced the tunic open down the middle and put his hand inside. She swallowed and fought the urge to scream as his hand kneaded her breast. He pushed up against her and put his mouth next to her ear. "Kirok bitches are all the same. Ye lift your chin and act the virgin, and all ye need is a good pounding between the legs."

"You think you can give me one? I doubt you're capable."

He spun her around. The knife sliced a shallow cut on her belly. Blood ran down to her breeches. He pushed her up against the wall and pulled both hands behind her back. One hand held her wrists tight, and he leaned against her with a shoulder while he untied his breeches. His breath quickened. He pressed up against her and grew hard. "Does that feel soft and weak?"

"You're no better . . . than your son . . . . He was . . . raping women . . ." Breath came only in gasps. Her belly stung against the wall. *Connor, help me! Please, help me!*

He pulled the tunic off her body and used it to tie her hands together behind her back. "Ye'll find out where he learned to treat women like ye." He spun her around again and dropped the knife. He put both hands on her breasts and pinched her until she screamed. "I don't care if I can't sell ye. I won't be talked to that way by a woman." He punched her in the stomach. The knife wound tore; she doubled over. He hit her on the other cheek, and she fell.

Connor, where are you? Help me! Trapped, hands behind her back, pain surging through her body, she couldn't fight Allyn's weight on her legs. He straddled her, untied her breeches, and pulled them down. She closed her eyes.

He slapped her again. "Open your eyes, bitch. Watch me fuck you."

She squeezed her eyes tighter. He slapped her again. "No. I won't." He forced her legs apart. She felt him hard against her. *Connor—help me!*

Someone pounded on the door. "Damn it." Allyn stopped. "I'm busy."

"It's Phinneas. He wants to see the girl."

Allyn hesitated. He leaned over and put his mouth close to Mairead's ear. "I suppose it's your lucky day. But if he doesn't promise me at least a thousand, I'll take ye the minute he's gone." He bit her ear until she whimpered. She felt more blood trickle down her neck. He stood and kicked her once in the ribs. He opened the door. "Did ye come to see how a real man fucks a woman, eunuch?"

A smooth tenor voice gave sharp contrast to Allyn's rough bass. "You've raped her? When you knew I was interested?"

"Ye caught me before I could finish. She's still a virgin."

Mairead closed her eyes and curled into a ball. Hope faded. Silence. The rustle of soft fabric tickled her ears. It made her think of the swish of her skirts when she'd tried to dance with Connor so many weeks before. A cool touch soothed her face. "You've beaten her badly."

"Fine. Leave her. I'll take what I can and put her in a brothel. She'll earn her keep."

"Do you know if she's educated?"

"Claims she was raised in a sayada. She acts noble."

Tense silence hovered as the man ran a hand over her head and back. "I will take her." The man stood, and she heard the jingle of coins in a bag. "One thousand. Our standard payment for a girl like this."

Allyn didn't move or speak for some time. Mairead prayed, silently begging him to take the money—*anything is better than this!*—but she didn't move or make a sound. She lay still, her eyes closed, rasping breaths struggling through her swollen, bloodied nose and mouth. *Connor, where are you?*

"One thousand. Your best offer?"

"You could buy ten youthful girls for a thousand gold pieces. For a girl with education, beauty, and virginity, a thousand is a fair price."

Allyn grunted. "All right. One thousand." The money changed hands.

"I want her cleaned up," the tenor voice said.

"She's your problem now. Take her as she is." Allyn walked away.

The rustle again. "Can you talk?" the tenor voice asked.

She forced herself to open her eyes and turn her head toward him. "Who are you?"

"You may call me Phinneas for now." He untied the tunic around her arms and helped her pull it over herself again. He helped her to her feet. She pulled up her breeches and tied them. Dim candlelight gave her a good view of his round, smooth face and dark brown, tilted eyes. He wore bright robes and a headpiece that trailed silk from the back. A large emerald sparkled in the center of the headpiece. "I'll attend your wounds when we're away. Can you walk?"

"I think so," she said. "Where are you taking me?"

"For now, to the camps. After I've treated your wounds and you can travel, to Tal'Amun." He tied her tunic closed. "Put on your boots."

She was too dazed to do anything but comply, and she could only think that she wanted to be gone from this house, whatever the cost. "So I'm to be a concubine for your emperor?"

"No. I have another plan for you. But I need to test you first." Phinneas reached into his robes and pulled out a dagger. He gave it to her hilt first. "Before we go, you must kill Allyn."

CHAPTER THIRTY-ONE

She calls her warriors with the bloodbond,
The ravenmarked ones with her heart,
And she brings peace to the land with no rule.
— Third Book of the Wisdomkeepers,
Year of Creation 5548 (approximate)

Connor, help me!

Connor stood with a start, his heart pounding. The Morrag struggled inside him, begging for release. He ached with the need to kill. Daggers in hand, he sniffed the air, listened, and was met by silent calm from every direction and every sense.

He'd left a bloody path for Allyn's men from the time he left Galbragh. In every town, he picked fights with slavers, trying to draw Allyn toward him and away from Mairead. The Morrag continued her constant, restless fluttering. He knew the men he chose to confront had committed injustice after injustice, and yet the Morrag had not been quelled or stilled since he left Mairead.

Is someone finally after me? But there were no sounds, no smells, no sense of tension that anyone was following him. The woods were still, calm, and peaceful except for the crackle of his fire and the Morrag raging inside of him.

Connor, help me!

Mairead. All warmth drained from his body as panic set in. He heard her voice in his head as clearly as if he were standing next to her. *Gods, I left her, and now—*

He had to get to her. He had to save her. *How?* He'd been riding for a week. There was no way—

You have a way.

His mother's voice came to him in memory from when he was a young man and she tried to teach him to travel with the air braids. He could never conjure strong enough braids to ride within the air like she could. He gave up.

What other choice do you have? You have to get to her. He stamped out his fire and stepped into the center of the clearing.

The Morrag still rose, begging for blood. He tried to quell it again, but it wouldn't obey. *I will not submit to you!* He tried to concentrate. He focused on drawing the air toward him, focused on weaving it into the thin, strong braids that would wind themselves around him. A small breeze came up, but only enough to draw his scent away.

The Morrag teased him. *You will be my first. My raven. Submit to me.*

No! Desperation distracted him, and he couldn't focus, couldn't hold the air long enough to make the braids. *Leave me alone!*

You will be my first.

He fell to his knees and put his face in his hands. *Gods, I can't. I can't.* "You *bitch.* I've fought you for so long—for years—and this is what you do? Steal my will? Hold Mairead hostage to get me?"

It is as it will be.

He closed his eyes. The Morrag beckoned him, as tempting and seductive as any woman he'd ever known, as tempting as Mairead's beauty and grace and charm. "And what will I become? You'll take me to her, and then what? I save her, but at the cost of my sanity? My will? I can't."

You will be my first. It is as it will be.

He took a deep breath. *If there is any hope for Taura and the west, I have to do this. I have to save her. She's the most important thing.* "If it will save her, I give in. Take me."

Loosed finally, given the freedom of his will, the Morrag swelled with the sweet taste of vengeance. He surrendered to it, merging with the touch of death, the longing for life and balance, and the need for justice. *If I had known—* He had thought he would lose his will, but his will was heightened, sharper than ever. Choices were clearer; decisions were focused. His path was carved for him. There was no more fear, hesitation, worry, or anxiety—only the assurance that he had purpose and strength and the ability to do what had to be done. *I understand, finally.* The Morrag was death, justice, vengeance, but not evil. She didn't desire death for death's sake. She wanted only to rid the earth of impurity. *Gods, now I see.*

Mairead—*Mairead. Take me to her. Take me on the air.*

All around him, the air braided itself. The Morrag wove it, and Connor was the conduit. He held out his arms. The braids of air lashed around his hands, grew up his arms, meshed with his tattoos. They twined up his legs, around his torso, covered his head—bright, flaming violet braids that he could see, feel, taste, smell, even hear. All the sounds and odors of the forest melded in the breeze, and it lifted him off the ground.

He lost himself to the magic. For the first time in his life, it wasn't a curse. *Alshada, please. If I get to her in time, I will never leave her again.*

The magic deposited him near the mountains outside of Galbragh. *At least it didn't drop me into a slaver's camp.* Braids of air slid down his arms, torso, and legs. He drew a dagger.

The Morrag's voice guided him. *She is in the house.*

In the distance, behind rows of slave tents and animal pens, a rambling structure rose over the camp as a dark overlord. Connor stared at it. *How do I get to it without someone seeing me? I don't know how to hide in the air like—*

Stone talent.

He suppressed a laugh. *Do you even know me? I only have air talent.*

You have all three.

No, only queens have all three.

You have all three. Summon it. The need is great enough. You will break the bonds that limit you.

He frowned. *This isn't possible.* He picked up a clump of soil. *If I have stone, then I should see the elements. I don't see them.*

You must try. You must focus. Break the bonds.

He wrinkled his forehead. *She was right about submitting to her.* He focused on the soil. *Elements. Look for the smallest pieces.* One by one, tiny sparking lights appeared in the soil, orange and red and yellow, and Connor shuddered. Warmth coursed through him, and elements surged through his veins in a rush, like water through a broken dam. He dropped the soil and shifted his focus to the ground. Orange braids crept up his body and enveloped him in the flavors and scents of earth. Metals and minerals and elements that formed the ground bound him and pulled him down into themselves, and he merged with the stones and focused on the house in the distance.

The braids and the Morrag let him go just outside the house. *Damn. Wooden.* Not even his mother could have managed to weave the stone, air, and water that made up wood.

Three guards stood at the door. In the distance, he heard the faint cries of slaves chained together in rows and huddled in pens. He sniffed the air again and wove faint braids that would bring scents to him. He tried to find Mairead, but there was no hint of her scent. *If she's dead . . . Or if they've taken her away already . . .*

For the first time, the Morrag's voice spoke with a soothing caress. *She is here. I would not have brought you if she weren't.*

I could kill the guards, but I'd still need to get through the house. He sheathed his daggers and tucked his pack into a shadow on the side of the house. When he stepped into the light, the three men straightened and put hands on swords. Connor held up his hands. "Did I startle you?"

The man in the center pointed with his chin. "Who're ye?"

"A friend sent me. Said you have a girl in there I might like."

The guard grunted. "There're a few in there. Some of 'em been used pretty badly. Ye'd not want a taste of them. Master brought in one, though—pretty thing, dressed in breeches. Think he's saving her for the eunuch."

The Morrag swelled. *It's Mairead.* "Saving her for a eunuch? Does your master know what a eunuch is?"

The men all laughed. "Nae, lad—saving her to sell to the eunuch. He takes 'em to Tal'Amun for his emperor. He's in there now." He gestured toward the door.

"Can you get me in to see her before they strike a bargain?"

The guard snorted. "Ye'd not have the money for a girl like that."

"You might be surprised."

The man evaluated him. Connor thought he might have to draw the three into a fight. With the ferocity of the magic swelling inside him, they'd be no match for him, but he didn't want to leave a bloody trail until he was on his way out.

At last the guard nodded. "All right. I'll take ye. Leave your weapons."

Connor unbelted his sword, and the guard removed his daggers. He opened the door and gestured Connor through.

The house assaulted Connor's heightened senses from every direction.

The Morrag soothed him and kept him from retching. *I'll give you strength.* Minimal candles cast small shadows over the sparse furnishings. Death and sweat, waste and fear permeated the house.

The guard led Connor through the house and up a long staircase. Footsteps approached, and Connor shifted his weight to be ready to fight. "Master Allyn," the guard said. "This one wants a look at the pretty girl. Did ye sell her yet?"

Three men stepped into the dim light, and Connor's hands balled into fists at his sides. He could smell Mairead on the big man. They were evenly matched in height, but the other was pale, ragged, weathered. *Allyn.* Connor frowned. *I see his transgressions.* The atrocities he had committed shrouded him as a cloak of evil and wove around him in dark, oily shadows, carrying lust and greed and abuse in every form. *How does a man live with all of that?*

Allyn crossed his arms. "Sold her. She's going to Tal'Amun. You wouldn't have wanted her, anyway. She can't keep her mouth shut."

Anger flared. He fought to keep it from his voice. "Whatever you sold her for, I can pay you more."

Allyn gave a rabid laugh. "Doubtful. He paid a thousand. But if ye can give me more, I'll let ye take her." He waved the guard away. "Ye can go. I'll take this one to see the girl."

The guard walked away, and Connor fell in step next to Allyn. Allyn's two guards walked behind him. "Where did you get this one?"

"One of the men who runs a camp brought her in. Her lover killed my son."

Focus on the task. Get Mairead, then you can kill him. "Why sell her? Why not use her to get the man you want?"

"Don't think he'd care. Seems he ran off." He scoffed. "Not surprising. The bitch can't keep her mouth shut."

Connor forced his hands to unclench. *I swear, when she's safe, I'll shove your heart up your ass.* "Why do you want her, then?"

Allyn's voice turned glacial. "She owes me a son."

The Morrag fluttered. *Destroy him, raven.*

Not yet. When Mairead is safe.

Her scent came to him, along with a heavily perfumed scent that he didn't recognize. Two figures emerged from the dark corridor. If it hadn't been for the braid and the scent, he wouldn't have recognized her. Her face was battered, cut, and bruised, and one eye was swelling shut. Her tunic was torn and bloodstained, and she walked with a shaking gait.

A man in multi-hued silks stood next to her. "What's this, Allyn?"

"This one wants to buy her. Says he can outbid you." He looked at Connor. "Well? She's bruised, but if ye can outbid a thousand, she's yours."

Her eyes finally fell on him and widened. *Please Mairead, don't say anything.* "Eleven hundred."

Something flickered across the face of the silk-covered Tal'Amuni—recognition? Connor couldn't tell. "You want this girl?" he asked.

A silken-covered mage, like the song. Could he be the one? He gestured to Mairead. "May I?"

Allyn nodded. "Go ahead."

Connor fought the urge to take her in his arms and win free of the place. *Keep a cool head. Get out with your wits, not your sword.* Her lip trembled. He touched her face. His hands drifted down her neck, shoulders, breasts—*I have to make this look good*—hips. He put a hand on her chin. "She seems healthy except for the beating you gave her. You swear to me no one has used her yet?"

"I can't be sure she's a virgin, but I'm the only man who's been in a room with her, and Phinneas here stopped me before I took her."

Connor turned back to the men. "I want her. Eleven hundred."

"No." The man named Phinneas took a step toward him. "Pay me. I'll sell her to you for a thousand. Don't pay him."

Allyn laughed. "You think you have some kind of authority here, eunuch?"

Phinneas turned a cool gaze on Allyn. "She's my property. I paid for her. You hold my coins in your hand right now. It's my choice what to do with her. I choose to sell her to this man for one thousand gold pieces. Until he pays me, she's still mine." He stepped closer to Allyn. "Do you wish to challenge me? Even you would not risk drawing the slavers of Tal'Amun into battle."

Allyn folded his arms, and a muscle twitched in his jaw as he weighed his options. "A thousand won't buy me a son." He grabbed Mairead's arm and yanked her away from the eunuch. "Two thousand. Which one of ye will pay it?"

Connor started to say he would, but Mairead's hand flicked out from her side with a flash of steel. She spun and thrust in one motion, driving the blade upward under Allyn's ribs, all the way to the hilt. His eyes widened in pain and surprise, and he gasped for air, but she pulled the blade out and stepped away from him. He fell forward. She kicked him onto his back, spit in his face, and shoved the dagger into his eye and twisted it. His legs twitched and jerked, then stilled.

The guards drew swords, but Connor blocked one swing and punched the man hard across the nose. The other guard dove at Connor from the side, but he ducked, twisted, lunged, and took the man by the throat with one hand. He pounded the man's head against the wall and twisted his head until he heard the satisfying crunch of bones breaking. The man slumped to the ground. Connor went to the other man and snapped his neck.

Phinneas was staring, awestruck, at Connor. "You have the Morrag in your eyes. You are her raven."

He can see it? Connor pulled Mairead into his arm. "Are you going to cause me any trouble?"

"No, I swear. I seek only to help you." He ushered them past the bodies. "Forgive me. I didn't know she was yours, raven. I would not have bought her—" He stopped. Comprehension dawned on his face. "Spirits, she is the ravenmaster."

"Ravenmaster?"

"Yes. The woman who will gather all of you. Don't you know of her?"

Connor shook his head. "I thought I was the only raven."

"No, there are others." He made an impatient gesture. "Why don't you know this? Have none of them found you?"

"How would they?"

"This girl calls them. You will have to work with her to defeat the Forbidden. It's written in the Second Book of the Wisdomkeepers."

The Second Book? "You don't know that. The second book has been missing for centuries."

"I've read it in our library in Tal'Amun." He took a long breath. "The Forbidden are rising again, and only the ravenmarked can kill them. We must meet somewhere—there is much to tell you."

If we go back to Henry, Mairead will be safe, and I can meet the eunuch in Galbragh. He's asking for nothing but conversation. The Tal'Amuni wouldn't do anything to anger Henry. He nodded. "We'll go to the palace. Can you go to the Golden Goose?"

"Yes, of course. It will take me a few days to win free of my camp, but I will come." He pushed them down the hall. "There are horses behind the house in a small stable. Take two and go to the palace."

They followed the corridor and went down the stairs to the front door.

"We worked out a bargain," Connor told the guards. He picked up his sword and daggers. "Thanks for your help."

He led Mairead around the side of the house. Phinneas followed. Connor put on his sword and pack. "Horses are over there," Phinneas said, gesturing. "The palace is about a three day's ride from here." He spared a concerned look for Mairead. "She's weak."

"I'll take care of her, don't worry."

Phinneas nodded. "The One Hand hold you both." He walked away, his bright silks melting into the darkness.

Connor led Mairead to the stable and went to the first pen with a horse big enough to hold two. "No time to saddle two. You can ride with me." He listened for sounds of pursuit as he saddled the horse and put bit and bridle on. When he was ready, he mounted, hung his pack from the saddle, and pulled her up behind him. Just as she settled in, he heard shouts from the direction of the house. "Someone found Allyn. Hang on."

He galloped from the stable as men scrambled to figure out how Allyn had died in his own house. As the horse ran, he cast braids of air down to the animal's hooves and wrapped them around the sound. They galloped out the back side of the camp until the sounds of pursuit faded.

Connor stopped in a copse of trees. Men shouted in the distance. Connor gathered the braids that held the sound of the hoof beats. He sent the braids to the west, past the camps and the house, and when they were close enough to the pursuers, he released the sound. The men changed direction, setting their horses in a westward path, and Connor breathed out a deep sigh.

He dismounted and pulled Mairead off the horse into his arms. "By the spirits, Mairead. I was so stupid. I almost lost you." He kissed her head, hair, and neck, and wrapped her in his arms. "I'm sorry—I'm so sorry. Please, Mairead, forgive me. I shouldn't have left. I thought you'd be safer without me."

She shed quiet tears against his chest, her arms folded in against her body, her shoulders shaking as he held her. She lifted her face to his, and he kissed her. She whimpered. "It hurts—everything hurts."

He tried to gentle his arms around her. "What happened?"

"It was him—the Forbidden. He had Melik try to sell me. Melik took me hunting one morning, and he had slavers set up to come buy me. They gave me snake venom. I saw the Forbidden come and go in flashes of light. He killed Melik, and then the slavers took me to Allyn. He beat me and almost—"

A sob caught in her throat. "How can a man do that? How can he treat a woman that way?"

He pulled her close. "I don't know. I would never treat you that way. I love you."

A choking laugh escaped. "This is what it takes for you to admit it? I have to nearly be raped and sold into slavery?"

He put his hand on her head and pulled her back to look at her. "I swear. I'm never leaving again."

Her eyes searched his. "You gave in to the Morrag."

The presence inside him ruffled and resettled its feathers, content and peaceful at last. "I did. I had to. I had to get to you. It was the only way."

"And now? What will she demand of you?"

"I don't know, but I know you're part of it." He kissed her forehead. "I was wrong. Our destinies—I thought they were separate, I didn't want to hurt you, but I was wrong. I'll serve you the rest of my days, however you'll have me."

She closed her eyes. "How did you know? How did you get here?"

"I heard you in my head. You called me. I knew you were in danger. The Morrag promised if I submitted I could get to you."

Her body started to relax in his arms. "I hurt so much. I thought I was going to end up across the world. That man told me he wouldn't make me a concubine. He said he had other plans for me, but the first test was to kill Allyn. He gave me the dagger. I don't know what he wanted. I didn't know if you'd get me out of there. I had to kill him. I had to pass his test. I couldn't be a concubine."

"Shh. It's all right. I'm here now. I won't lose you again. I won't leave you." He shut his eyes. "At least Allyn is dead. You gave him what he deserved."

"He got what we all deserve." She pulled away from him and wiped her eyes. "This is all such a hopeless place. Those people—they kidnap the least of the least, they sell their children, their wives, their enemies just for a few coins. And these traders have no consciences. Allyn was just one. Someone will rise up in his place. What if it's someone worse?" Raw emotions shook her voice. She turned back toward the camp. "This is why I'm here—to stop this. To bring order to this place."

"I believe you. You are meant to be here. You are meant to be their queen."

She turned back to him. "Remember how you told me some men can't be redeemed? I didn't believe you. But that man—Allyn—he was irredeemable."

"Perhaps I was wrong. Perhaps it's not up to me to decide who's irredeemable."

She lifted a hand to the leather lashing around his neck. "You're wearing the bear claw."

His hand went to it. "I put it on a new lashing as soon as I—" He stopped. *As soon as I left you.* He couldn't say it out loud. He took the leather lashing from his neck and put it over her head. "You should have it. I won't need it now. I'm not leaving again."

She fingered the claw. "I missed you."

"I missed you, too."

They mounted the horse and rode deep into the woods until he found a small grove where they would be safe. He pulled his blanket out of his pack and wrapped her in it, then built a fire. When the flames lit the clearing, he knelt in front of her. "Tell me where you're hurt."

She told him everything Allyn had done. "It's my belly that hurts the most. And my side where he kicked me."

He touched her face, and she flinched and hissed. "You're pale. I'm summoning my mother. She can send healers."

"Can you still do that now that the bond is broken?"

"I have an idea." He began to weave braids of air, stone, and water together.

Within moments, Maeve landed in the clearing, and the air dissipated around her. "I thought that might summon you," he said.

Her face was anguished and drawn. "You broke the bonds in your blood."

He straightened. "Why didn't you ever tell me?"

She let out a long breath. "I found you weaving the braids when you were only two. I feared you'd be uncontrollable, so I bound your talents—all but enough air talent to satisfy the people. I feared what would happen if the Sidh knew a man had all three talents."

"We'll talk about it later." He gestured to Mairead. "Right now, I need your help."

Maeve gasped. "What happened?"

"It's a long story. Can you summon healers?"

Her eyes turned glassy for a moment, and then multi-colored braids of the different talents trickled into the clearing. In moments, three Sidh women appeared. At Maeve's command, they knelt around Mairead, and braids of stone, water, and air wound around and through her. Mairead shuddered and sighed. When the bruises on her face had faded to little more than slight discoloration, the women stood. "You may be weak for a few days," one of them told her. "There were bruises inside. We've repaired them. We removed the venom in your blood, repaired the skin on your belly and ear, and drained the fluids from your bruises. You need to eat well. You are not Sidh, so you need meat—as soon as he can find some."

Connor helped Mairead to her feet and put an arm around her. She relaxed against his shoulder. "I'll be sure she eats well."

Maeve took a deep breath. "I have news. Do you want me to share it in front of her?"

"I have no more secrets from Mairead."

"Mac Rian is dead. Edgar killed him."

Anger Connor spent six years building tumbled like an unmortared wall. "What about Olwyn?"

"King Braedan killed her. There was a battle. Edgar drove Mac Rian's men out of the forest, and Braedan saved an earth guardian from Olwyn's sorcery." She put a hand on Connor's arm. "Braedan is going to give you the Mac Niall and Mac Rian holdings. He plans to abolish the laws of inheritance that kept you from them, and he will name you Culain's son."

Connor's mouth worked around words that wouldn't come. "I didn't want it," he finally said. "I don't want it."

"Perhaps not, but it is yours. Braedan promised Edgar that he would appoint a steward to care for the holdings. Edgar and I will be sure they are cared for until you return to Taura."

"Mother, I'm not going back to Taura. My place is with Mairead. Not there—not with you or the tribes or as lord of some property I barely know. Can't I give it up?"

"That's up to you, of course. Perhaps you'll have a son one day, though, and perhaps you'll want to pass your land down to him. Don't give up anything just yet. Think about it. You are the last Mac Niall. You have a responsibility to your father's name."

He nodded. "You're right. You are. I'll consider it."

Maeve blinked. "I'm right?"

"Leave it, Mother." His tone softened. "You were right about a lot of things. I forgive you for bonding me. Can you forgive me for being such an ass for the last six years?"

She smiled. "Of course. Yes." She pulled him into an embrace. "Come back and see Edgar. You need to forgive him."

He nodded. "I will. When I can."

She seemed to want to say more, but then shook her head. "Will you be able to get back to Galbragh safely?"

"We have a horse. I can catch some rabbits or fish. We'll be fine. Do you think you could go to the palace—tell Henry where we are? He can send someone north to meet us."

"Yes. I'll see to it." She paused. "You will need time to practice your talents. There may be Sidh who don't trust you."

"I have the Morrag inside me, and you're worried about the Sidh power? I think I can handle it." He bent and kissed her. "Goodbye, Mother."

Maeve nodded. "Be careful." She drew up the braids of air and disappeared.

When they were alone, Mairead gestured to her bloodied, torn clothes. "Do you have a fresh tunic?"

He gave her a fresh tunic and turned away to allow her privacy. When he turned around again, she was chattering with cold. He put the blanket around her and rubbed her back. "Better?"

"Yes." Occasional snowflakes sparkled in her hair. "I don't know how to feel," she said, quiet. "I want to believe that you're really here and you'll really stay, but—"

He tightened his arms around her. "I swear to you, I'm never leaving."

"You promised you would stay for the winter, and then you left. You told me you wouldn't break a promise, and you did."

He closed his eyes. "I wanted to protect you."

She sighed and rested her head against him. "I need time."

"You will have all the time you need. I will wait for you." He buried his face against her neck and tightened his arms. "I love you," he whispered.

She let him hold her for some time. "No promises. No swearing oaths."

"Mairead—"

She shook her head. "No. We aren't bound only to each other. There's still too much we have to learn."

He stroked her cheek. "Whatever happens, know that I don't ever want another woman."

She smiled and put her hand on his. She settled against his chest again. "Keep me warm? Like when we traveled before?"

"Always. For the rest of your life." He sat down near a tree and pulled her into his arms. They pulled a blanket over themselves, and the tree sheltered them as scattered snowflakes drifted into the clearing.

EPILOGUE

> *When royal blood leaves the land,*
> *When the Forbidden walks on holy ground,*
> *When the place of peace is bloodied,*
> *Then the hand of Alshada will be removed from Taura.*
> *— The Scrolls of Prophecy in the Syrafi Keep*

He'd lost track of time in the cave. He knew when it was morning and when it was night, but he had no idea how many days had passed. *Or is it weeks? Months?* His beard and hair were unkempt and matted. There was little water and less food. His clothes hung loose and ragged on his body.

He kicked bones that littered the cave floor. Human bones—skulls, femurs, ribs—mingled with animal bones. An ancient fire circle lay in the center of the cave. When the sun hit the walls just right, he could see the carvings and paintings of the people who used the cave for their rites. It smelled of death, blood, waste, but there were other sensations there—that the walls had watched couples copulating and birthing in repetition of an endless cycle.

The creature at the cave entrance screeched and stretched its wings. The dark man had promised him transportation away from Torlach when he swore to kill Igraine, but he hadn't mentioned he would be trapped in this cave for weeks. *If I'd killed her, would he have brought me here?* He didn't know. The only human contact he'd had since that night was the crone who brought the molding cheese, thin broth, and stale bread that kept him alive. He licked the walls of the cave when he thirsted. Sometimes, he found algae and counted himself blessed.

When the black beast deposited him here, he expected to die. He expected the dark man would kill him. He didn't realize it would be from slow starvation or madness.

The creature screeched again. The dark man stood at the cave entrance. Matthias laughed. The sound returned from the cave walls in an echo tinged with madness. "Have you finally come to kill me?"

The man stood emotionless, his black eyes bottomless in the thin light of the rising sun. "No. I've come to give you another chance."

Matthias grunted. "If it means you'll let me eat and swing a sword again, I'll do whatever you ask."

Matthias didn't need to see the man's face to know his lips had curled into a sneer. "Have you heard of the Nar Sidhe?"

"Of course. I grew up in Culidar. This is one of their caves. My mother used to say she'd leave me outside for their supper when I was bad."

"I need you to recruit them. The protections around the Brae Sidh village will soon be weak enough for the Nar Sidhe to come onto Taura and destroy it." The dead eyes stared, unflinching and unblinking. "It won't be hard to convince them. When they know that the magic is weakened, they will follow you."

Matthias shivered. *Follow me.* The idea of a group of savages following him made him almost giddy. "There would be great reward for someone who managed to destroy the Brae Sidh."

"Perhaps even the woman you desire. See that the Brae Sidh are destroyed, and I will see that you have her. I won't even require that you kill her."

The mere mention of Igraine made Matthias' groin tighten. "How do I find them?"

"The woman who brings you food is one of theirs. Follow her when she returns. You will know what to do. Continue to wear the talisman."

Matthias had forgotten about it. It was such a fixture on his body, along with the stone around his ankle, that he didn't think about it much. "When will you be back?"

But as usual, before he gave any answers, the man disappeared.

The screech of Bronwyn's owl and the flutter of wings outside her hut woke Maeve from a satisfied half-doze. "Maeve?" the Syrafi woman called. "Are you here?"

Maeve sighed. Edgar's arm was draped over her middle, and his heavy breath warmed her neck. "Edgar."

"Hmm?"

She picked up his arm and slid from under it. "I have to see someone."

"Not Connor again, is it?" Faint worry tinged his voice.

"No. Someone else."

He sighed and rolled over. "Hurry back."

She smiled and kissed his bare shoulder. "I will." She pulled a simple sidhsilk gown over bare skin and went to the window.

Bronwyn's emerald eyes were alight, and her flaming shock of red hair was tamed into a braid. "You've been out tonight. I sensed you outside of Galbragh."

Maeve nodded. "My son's blood broke through the blocks. He summoned me for help. The heir needed healers. Why?"

"There is forgiveness between you?"

Maeve nodded. "He said he couldn't be angry with the Forbidden in the world."

Bronwyn let out a long sigh. "Thanks be to Alshada. It was important that he forgive you." Edgar stirred in Maeve's bed. Bronwyn lifted an eyebrow. "Things have changed here, I see."

Maeve's face flamed. "He is an old friend."

"Just an old friend?"

Maeve sighed. "The wolf tribe has been guarding us. There is some new peace between the Sidh and the tribes."

"You didn't answer my question."

Bronwyn's penetrating gaze made Maeve shift her feet and fold her arms. "He is an old friend and a new companion."

"He's more than that."

Maeve bit her lip. "He wants more. I'm considering it." She stepped closer to Bronwyn and lowered her voice so that Edgar wouldn't hear. "These last weeks with him have been some of the happiest of my life. Edgar is much more than he appears."

Bronwyn smiled. "You look happy. Content. Have you told your son?"

"No. Not yet. It wasn't the right time. He is still angry with Edgar. And he loved his father. I need to find a way to tell him gently."

"The village is more protected than it was. Perhaps it is because of this new peace?"

Maeve shrugged. "Perhaps. I still feel the magic fading, but it's slower now. And Edgar comforts me. He does what he can to keep us safe. Will Alshada still remove his hand?"

"It is in the scrolls of our keep. Alshada does not undo what he has promised. It must happen. I'm sorry."

"Is there anything I can do to keep the reliquary or my people safe?"

"The reliquary must remain on the island. It is part of what stays Alshada's hand. But the one we fight has found a way to carry the reliquary, and he no longer needs the heir."

Maeve's blood chilled at that. "How? Only one of the Taurin heir's line can carry it."

"He believes he has found another of Brenna and Aiden's line."

Maeve's voice dropped to a whisper. "There are no others. We were so sure—"

"She believed her father dead, but he lived to marry again. They had a son together before the father died. The boy is a young man now."

So all of this—saving the Taurin heir, sending Connor to take her to Sveklant—it could all be in vain? "What should we do?"

"Continue to protect the reliquary. The tribes protect you. The heir is safe, or will be soon. All that remains is for—" She stopped, broke off, and tears came to her eyes. "There is one more thing that must happen, and then Alshada will remove his hand of protection."

"What is that?"

She hesitated, emotions raw across her face. "The Eiryan princess must learn to use her magic, and then she must be tested." Her voice broke.

Maeve had no magic to connect her to Bronwyn, but she could see the same maternal fear she had felt when Bronwyn asked Maeve to deliver Connor for his task. *Of course. The hair, the eyes, even their build—I see it now.* She put one hand on Bronwyn's arm. "She is your daughter, isn't she?"

Great silver tears rolled down Bronwyn's cheeks. "Quickly—catch them." She gestured to her face.

Maeve picked up a small earthenware jar and handed it to Bronwyn. Bronwyn let the tears fall into the jar. "The Syrafi do not cry often," Maeve said.

"No. There is nothing to cry about in the presence of Alshada." She gave Maeve a bittersweet smile. "We have much in common, Maeve."

Maeve put a hand on Bronwyn's arm. "We've both given much to this cause." *But I got to raise my son.*

A screech drifted from above the trees. "I must go. I don't know when I'll be able to return," Bronwyn said.

"Go with Alshada." Bronwyn stepped away from the window, shimmered into the owl form, and flew away.

Maeve turned back to Edgar. He had one arm behind his head, and one tattooed leg hung over the edge of the bed. She shivered. *How did I ever find tattoos repulsive?* "I'm sorry I woke you," she said, removing her gown and climbing back into bed with him.

He pulled the soft sidhsilk blankets over them both and kissed her. "Is everything all right?"

"For now."

"Good news." He nuzzled at her neck and nibbled her skin with wolfish hunger. "Since we're both awake, will you do that thing you do with the air?"

She laughed. "You like that?"

"Isn't it obvious?"

He loves my magic. How is it possible that a human loves my magic? "It gives me great comfort having you here."

He lifted onto one elbow and traced her face, shoulders, neck with one finger that trailed down her body as he spoke in his low, rumbling voice. "You know it's always been you, Maeve. Always. I loved you the moment I saw you. There's never been another."

"You can't tell me you've been celibate for thirty years waiting for me."

He laughed. "No. But I've never loved another." He kissed her, long, slow, and lingering. "You will remember—I offered thirty years ago. You turned me down."

"I did, but if I hadn't, I wouldn't have had Connor."

"True."

"Was it worth the wait?"

He smiled. "Yes."

She traced his tattoos and lines of muscle, raising gooseflesh across his torso. She untied the leather strip that held his braids back, twisted one braid around her hand, and put her face against his neck. The braids of air wound around them both, and he shivered with anticipation. "Show me."

He grinned. "As you wish, your majesty."

GLOSSARY

Aliom: The seat of the Great Kirok, Aliom is not a kingdom of its own, but a small city-state located on the edge of the Esparan Empire. It answers to no king or kingdom and is controlled by Prelate Johanan.

Alshada: Sometimes called the One Hand, sometimes called the Creator, Alshada is the main god of the kirok in Aliom. Some say he is the only god; others say he is one of many.

animstone: Pieces of gray, translucent stone from the Syrafi Keep that have the power to suppress blood magic when worn by Syrafi, Ferimin, Brae Sidh, or Nar Sidhe. The origin of this stone is unclear. Some say it may be a remainder of a world created before this one; others think it is matter from a distant star. The Brae Sidh queen wears one in her crown, and it appears she is the only exception to the rule of suppression. She is able to use the stone to augment her power.

Brae Sidh: Pronounced "bray shee," these are the "hidden folk" who live deep in the great forest on the Taurin Isle. They were created in the first days of the world as Alshada's workers. He gave them elemental magic; each Sidh is born with one of three talents—air, water, or stone. At his instruction, they formed the geography and weather patterns of the earth in the earliest days. They are ruled by a queen, and humans can come and go from their village, but only during sunset or sunrise when the veil between the village and the human world is thinnest. They now live hidden under enchantments and surrounded by the tribal people.

Cluith: A toast to good health and wellbeing.

codagha: The web of magic that binds the Brae Sidh queen to her people. She can sense where they are or if they are hurt. Through the *codagha,* she can bind the will of a Sidh to her own, but this is seen as abhorrent and only a last resort for someone who is a criminal or lost to madness. There is an unwritten agreement that the queens will respect the privacy of their people.

Ferimin: The dark counterparts of the Syrafi. They serve the sorcerer Namha; they split from the Syrafi after being seduced by the sorcerer with promises of great pleasure and power. When they left the service of Alshada, they were tainted and tarnished, and now they can only shapeshift into giant crows. They are still immortal, but can be banished to the sorcerer's prison by tribesmen with the warriormark. If they are not banished, they can take over a human body and possess it, but they lose the ability to shapeshift. They can still create illusions, however, and they are still persuasive and able to tempt humans into great folly.

Forbidden: Creatures born from the union of Syrafi with humans. The humanity taints the Syrafi magic, but the creatures are still immortal. They have human desires and needs, but can never be sated. They can steal souls and are strengthened by the sins of humans. They can travel between the elements, appearing all around the world in a blink. They are able to turn a man's sins back on himself to use as torture, and they are able to use human blood to augment their power. When their human bodies die, they find new bodies to inhabit. They can only be completely destroyed by one of the ravenmarked. Limits: When a human is protected by Alshada, the Forbidden cannot act on that person directly—he or she must send something else. They cannot act against Brae Sidh magic, and they are bound by the rules of the earth wisdom. Those who know how to use the earth wisdom can weave spells that keep the Forbidden away.

Great Kirok: The main religious power in the western world, seated in Aliom and dedicated to the service of Alshada. It is governed currently by Prelate Johanan, who has served for twenty years.

kirok: The name for any of the smaller individual groups of worshippers of Alshada throughout the known world. Run by men known as kirons.

kiron: A priest bound to the Great Kirok in Aliom. They belong to one of several different orders, among them the Order of Sai Johan (itinerant preachers) and the Order of Sai Cyphus (permanent kirons).

The Morrag: The personification of the avenging spirit of the earth. The Morrag uses ravens to take the shape of a woman. She marks men for her service by branding them with a raven tattoo on the thigh. When she calls them to kill, they are driven to exact justice in her name.

Nar Sidhe: Formerly part of the Brae Sidh, the Nar Sidhe followed Namha in the earliest days of the world and split apart from the Brae Sidh to take up residence in Culidar. They live in the southern forest of the country on the border between Culidar and the Esparan Empire. They are ruthless about attacking merchants and nobles who pass through their territory. Their presence at the southern edge of Culidar is one of the reasons for the poverty in the country. Only a handful of very capable freelances are able to escort merchants through Nar Sidhe territory. Unlike the Brae Sidh, who have remained fairly insular and still have dark features, the Nar Sidhe have spent a thousand years capturing women and men to breed with, and they have diluted their blood enough that they look very much like most of the people in Culidar.

The Rending: The separation of the Sidh into Brae Sidh and Nar Sidhe. When those who followed Namha left the Sidh, the damage to the *codagha* was so extensive that it killed the Sidh queen.

sayada: The home of the sisters of the Order of Sai Atena. There are few sayadas left; the largest, the one on the Taurin Isle, was destroyed when King Braedan overthrew the regency.

sayana/saya: Sisters of the Order of Sai Atena. They are sworn to uphold wisdom, devotion, and service to Alshada mainly through study of the ancient scriptures and service to the poor. The sayanas are leaders of the sayas.

Syrafi: Beings created to serve Alshada as warriors. They are immortal and able to shapeshift into the form of giant white owls. In human form, they are unique and distinct in appearance. They can also cast very realistic and elaborate illusions, and they have unusually persuasive speech.

Syrafi Keep: The earthly home of the Syrafi in the most northern mountains of the world, before the great ice seas and beyond the edge of Sveklant. The keep is surrounded by magic and impossible for humans to see. Sidh can go into the keep, but once accepted, they can never return to the human world.

talents: The magic of the Brae Sidh and Nar Sidhe. There are three talents—air, water, and stone. The Sidh speak of braiding elements; to others with Sidh blood, the magic will look like colored braids. Air appears as shades of violet; water appears as shades of blue and green; stone appears as orange and brown and other earth tones. Only those with Sidh blood can see the braids.

ABOUT THE AUTHOR

Amy is a freelance commercial copywriter and editor. In her spare time, she reads, knits, herds children, and writes fiction as a hobby. Amy and her family love to hike, camp, and spend time in the great outdoors of the Pacific Northwest.

Ravenmarked is Amy's first novel. She is currently working on Bloodbonded, book two of The Taurin Chronicles. She has also published several novellas and short stories; her work is available in all major e-book stores.

Connect with Amy online:
Twitter: http://www.twitter.com/amyrosedavis
Facebook: http://www.facebook.com/amyrosedaviswriter
Website: http://www.amyrosedavis.com

EXCERPT: SILVER THAW

Summer

Niko stood with goblet in hand examining the illuminated script of an ancient book on Lord Darrick's desk. He swirled the water. *A lord who reads ancient scripture but puts men to work in his mines and gives them whores for entertainment . . . A dichotomy indeed.* He pulled his purple church robes tighter around him. Even the summers were cold to his southern blood. *The sooner I solve this, the sooner I can be rid of it.*

The door opened and Niko turned. Lord Darrick entered with a polite nod. "You must be Niko."

"Bishop Niko, yes," Niko said. He would not have people assuming he was still a lowly brother, worthy only of being called by his first name, now that he'd been raised to the purple. He set down his goblet, folded his hands, and bowed. "Lord Darrick. My superiors say you have some trouble they believe I might be able to help you with."

"I do." He gestured to a seat and then sat down behind his own desk. He poured wine from a carafe and leaned back in his chair. "What do you know of the legend of the Syree?"

Niko frowned as he sat down across from Darrick. "I know they are supposed to be daughters of pagan gods of sky and sea—that the Shigani say they resulted when the sky and sea mated. They live on the seas and lure men to the depths with their haunting songs." He shrugged. "A foolish legend of a pagan people."

Darrick nodded, slow. His hazel eyes examined Niko with a cautious edge. "A foolish legend. Hmm."

Niko covered his frown with his goblet and sipped. Darrick was a friend of the king—a close friend, one who had helped the king's cause twenty years before and who then had earned great wealth for the crown and himself by mining silver and farming the vale. Easily the most powerful lord in the realm, Darrick was still, even in his late forties, unmarried and without an heir. Niko wondered if he planned to live forever. *As wily as this one is, he might manage it.* "Do you have reason to believe it isn't a legend, Lord Darrick?"

Darrick stood. "Come with me."

Niko rose and followed Darrick from the room. The tall, slender lord of the north walked with the confidence of a man who knew his skill with a blade. *They call this one the Scourge of the North,* Niko reminded himself. Darrick's conquest of the vale and the mountain was the stuff of legend. After the king vanquished his own enemies, he gifted Darrick with the lands of the north, and Darrick took all men who swore fealty to him away from the king's court and cut a swath of destruction northward. He conquered minor lords and made them choose between the gallows or fealty to him. He gained the allegiance of peasants who killed their overlords in his name. Darrick soon had a firm grip on everything from the western taiga to the eastern border of the country, from the mountains in the north to the edge of the king's forest in the south, and the vast holdings had made him richer than even the king.

Darrick led Niko across the estate to a stone prison keep where a guard stepped aside for them and another guard escorted them down steps into a dungeon. "Have I offended you, Lord Darrick?" Niko asked, only half joking.

Darrick grinned, his teeth flashing in dim torchlight. "No, of course not, bishop. I want you to meet someone."

"A criminal?"

"Once. Now just one of my men. Or he was before the madness overtook him. We keep him here because . . . Well, you'll see."

They at last stopped at a thick oak door, and the guard opened it for Darrick and Niko. Niko followed Darrick in and blinked to let his eyes adjust to the even dimmer light of the cell. A ragged, crusty shell of a man looked up from beneath a shaggy head of white hair. "Job, it's Darrick. I brought someone who needs to talk to you."

Job blinked pale blue eyes from where he sat against the far wall of the cell. His knees were pulled up tight against his chest. The cell was as clean as could be expected, with fresh rushes on the floor, but Niko still held a kerchief up to his nose. The chamber pot hadn't been emptied yet for the day, and Job's clothes were tattered and soiled.

Job snorted a laugh. "Talk. Talking won't solve anything. The music is coming down the mountain whether you want it or not. She's coming. She'll take you all and make you hers." Job put his face down on his arms. "She'll take you all. She wants your praises." His voice rasped. "She'll be a god."

Niko's blood chilled. He crouched low. "There are no gods but the One God of the church."

"God, demon—call her what you will. She'll take you."

"Who?"

Job looked up again. For a moment, sanity returned to his eyes. "The Syree."

Niko shook his head. "The Syree is a myth."

"No, truth. She glows. Golden, with fire. Men reach for her and scream when she takes them." A smile edged in ecstasy crawled across his mouth. "They die smiling. Bleeding and shrieking and crunching and smiling."

Niko straightened. "Yet you lived."

Darrick tapped Niko's shoulder, and they backed toward the door. "This man is the only one left from a contingent I sent up the mountain in the early spring. I sent my captain of the guard, Yeshu, a Shigani, and two dozen of my best soldiers with wagons and supplies to restock the mining settlement on the mountain. No one came back. When this one wandered back down the mountain babbling this story, I sent another man up to the base camp. He went just a bit beyond and found Yeshu's body, and he said he heard strange voices in the wind. He came back down at a full run. Killed the horse he was riding."

Niko nodded. Job had begun a slow, self-comforting sway against the wall of the cell. "This man . . . He was with the group that went up in the spring?" Niko asked.

"Yes. There was an avalanche. It buried the whole mining settlement. When Job is lucid, he talks about how the sound of the avalanche cut off the sound of the Syree. He ran to escape. When he's not lucid, he screams and rants and begs her to free him." Darrick paused. "We caught him on a good day."

Niko frowned. "Your Shigani escaped the avalanche? How?"

"We don't know. It looked like he was trying to get down the mountain when he died. Stabbed himself, we think." He paused. "He had a woman here—a serving girl named Lara. She's expecting his child any day now. She wants to know why he would have killed himself when he was so looking forward to their child's birth."

Niko held the kerchief back up to his nose. "Not his wife?"

"The Shigani don't marry. Yeshu told me that when he first asked for her. She knew he wouldn't marry her, and she consented to be his concubine."

Pagans. Beastly practices. Niko sniffed. "I would speak with the one who found Yeshu."

Made in the USA
Middletown, DE
05 February 2025